Y0-BEO-878

DENALI

Story By
AC ALGER

This is a work of fiction. Names, characters, places, and incidents are the products of the author's imagination or are used fictitiously. Any resemblance to actual persons, living or dead, is entirely coincidental.

Copyright © 2020 AC Alger

All rights reserved.

Cover Design: Nathan Ray Dantoin
Cover Model: Eric E Allen
Cover Model: Luke VD

2nd Edition

ACKNOWLEDGMENTS

I would like to thank my parents Jim and Laurie Alger for not selling me to the circus and putting up with me all these years. You have been my biggest supporters since day one even though I still secretly think you favor the elder child. I would not have been able to get where I am today without Nathan Ray Dantoin and Taylor Hilgart, for they are much smarter than me and know how words work. Then the impastanator, Jake Wallner, thank you for dealing with my many hours of brainstorming.

3   AC ALGER

For Melvin Albers
Wild Blue Yonder

5   AC ALGER

CHAPTER ONE

Shock, a curious thing, a defense mechanism casting a veil over the body hiding the true impact of trauma. A young man ran his hand through his dark hair, feeling matted blood on his scalp. He pulled his hand away and stared at it intently memorizing every detail of the blood staining his skin. He slumped in a cold metal chair facing a mirrored glass window. The man reflected was distant and foreign. He studied his face, a bruise showed on his cheek bone, blood flowed from a deep gash on his forehead. He set his hands down and folded them neatly on the cold steel surfaced table. He fought the urge to pick the dry blood that coated his rough knuckles. His confinement in the small dark room was made a shade lighter by a solitary bare light bulb hanging above him. He sat still, thinking about the events which had unfolded that night.

The door opened and a professional looking woman walked in. Her blonde hair was pulled back tight into a neat bun. MI6 Agent Bennent took a seat across from the young man. A look of dismay crossed her face. She stared at him. The particular situation that the young man found himself in was tragic and she sympathized with him. The thought of benefiting at the cost of someone else's pain did not sit well with Bennet, but the information the young man provided to her partner may be the break they needed.

"Here's what we can do for you, James," Bennent proposed. "Due to the magnitude of the case the local authorities are no longer investigating the incident. That being said, you won't have criminal charges."

"I suppose that's some good news," James said plainly as he turned his hands and studied the lines on his palms.

"We have decided that it's too dangerous for you to stay here in London," Bennent said.

"Well, that's obvious isn't it," James replied with a touch too much attitude for the agent's liking.

"James, this is serious," Bennent stated and planted her elbows on the table leaning forward.

"I do realize that. I'm not incompetent," James said.

"Then you understand that we're doing our best to come up with a plan to keep you safe."

James didn't reply. He nodded in agreement.

"We have decided that the best action to take in this instance was to contact the Americans. Garrick has been on their radar for awhile now with his international crimes and his history in New York. We've all decided the best option for you is to go into witness protection," Bennent explained.

"Wait, you're sending me away?" James inquired with an intense aggression in his voice.

"James you have to understand— this is the best option for all of us. You're an American citizen anyway. The best thing for you right now is to get you out of the country. Where Shaun Garrick can't find you."

"But I'm also a British citizen, I live here. Why should I run? I should stay here and help you guys fight that bloody wanker." James stated, almost shouting.

"James, that isn't going to happen. If we want to put Shaun Garrick away, we need you to stay alive to testify against him," Bennent informed.

"But you can't do this to me," James pleaded.

"Frankly, I don't really care what you think. You're on a plane tomorrow morning to Illinois," Bennent stated.

"Illinois— What? Where?" James asked.

"Exactly," Bennent replied. "Where, indeed."

The shock wore off and the gravity of the situation sunk in. James dropped his face into his hands. He felt the rough texture of the dried blood on his face. He couldn't get the horrifying images out of his mind, the screams, the gun shots, and the cruel murder of his mother. Emotion engulfed him, he wanted to jump from his chair and smash something, anything to rid the hatred that possessed him so deeply. His throat tightened and his shoulders shook.

"I can't believe this is happening," James muttered as a tear cascaded down his dirty cheeks. "I should have done something. This is all my fault."

Bennent stared into James's eyes with the utmost sincerity and said, "This is a lot for a seventeen year old, for anyone one really– James, don't blame yourself for your mother's death. There was absolutely nothing you could have done to prevent it. If you would have intervened, Shaun Garrick would have killed you too."

James knew she was right, but he didn't want to believe it. He wished he could have done something to prevent his mother's death, but in all reality if he would have, his fate would have been the same as hers. Deep sadness gripped James to the point of overwhelming grief. He lifted his head and stared at Bennent's kind face with fear in his deep blue eyes.

She smiled softly, it was the only thing that she could do in hopes to reassure James that everything was going to be alright. Although she could not promise anything. A difficult time laid ahead until Shaun Garrick would be arrested, but until then James was still in grave danger anywhere he went.

"Don't worry, James. You're going to be well protected," Bennent stated. "There will be a team of the best U.S. Marshals that will be in charge of your case over there. We have already made living arrangements with one of them and you've been enrolled into Cambridge Preparatory Academy," Bennent finished explaining.

"You serious?" James asked.

"I am not in the business of lying?" Bennent replied.

"All right. What else do I need to know about my new mysterious identity?" James asked.

"Not much has changed, but I'll be sending you on the plane with a file of everything you'll need to know. You just need to be careful and not divulge any information that can link you to Garrick. Should they discover your identity then the risk of Garrick finding you will increase dramatically. Just stick to the file," Bennent explained and rose. "As soon as we find Garrick, we'll contact the Americans and you'll be free."

He stared at Bennent perplexed.

"Don't worry, James, or I should say Jude. You're going to be fine," Bennent assured and stepped to the door.

James flipped open the file. "Jude?"

"Good luck," Bennent smiled and departed the room.

CHAPTER TWO

Some are apt to shut their eyes to the evils of the world. Others have answered their nation's calls and taken the role of protectors, warriors for the country. They are proud of their nation's noble heritage. They are men of honor. Those deemed heroes follow a legacy of valor. These men protect the flag and with their lives in the name of freedom. They believe in service before self. Their path is guided by one light and that is the light of liberty and justice.

The summer sun was scorching as it beat down upon the earth. Bradley slouched in the seat of a beater car watching a detail shop down the street that they believed was linked to the Cartel. The shop had a close link to a fugitive they were hunting. The dash was hot as he drummed his fingers with the intensifying boredom.

He had been sitting there for days, watching, waiting, for their target. A flash of light drew his attention to the cup holder where his phone sat. It was a message from his supervisor, Ethan Pyke, *10-19 immediately.* That was code for get your ass back to headquarters.

Bradley wondered what wrath he would be enduring when he arrived at the U.S. Marshal headquarters. It must have been something serious for him to be pulled from surveillance but he could not recall violating any policies as of late. The drive was not terribly long and Bradley was soon walking into the briefing room. He was surprised to see the rest of his team present, impatiently waiting for Pyke to inform them what they had done wrong or what shitsandwitch they would be served.

Bradley sat next to Clayton, his close friend, whom he had served alongside in Ramadi in their younger years. When they had turned elite in their respective branches they were stationed together in JBAD, Jalalabad, doing a joint op here and there.

"Do you know what this is about?" Bradley asked.

"No, Bradley, I do not," Clayton replied in a smooth Virginian accent and scratched his dark blonde beard.

"I'm assuming we did something wrong... Why else would we be taken off of an assignment," MacTavish said as he swiveled in the chair and adjusted his backwards ball cap.

"Why always so negative?" Nicks, their team leader asked and touched his beard covered jawline. "It could be a multitude of things."

"Well if you don't know what's going on, then we are surely fucked," MacTavish said, crossing his arms.

Pyke hurried into the room frazzled. He took the open seat next to Nicks and adjusted his tie. The fluorescent lights reflecting off of his bald head.

"You're sitting?" Bradley asked knowing that if Pyke wasn't leading the brief something was definitely up.

Pyke glared at Bradley. "I know as much as you do... nothing–"

"Oh! Fantastic... we're getting canned aren't we? I swear I thought the incident with Mazzanti was behind us."

"It is, MacTavish," Pyke said firmly.

An older well cut man walked with purpose into the briefing room. Willemsen, the Executive Director of Special Operations of the US Marshals, held files in his hands that he immediately passed around the table. The file skidded towards Bradley and he placed his hand on it to stop it. He read the file name in bold, *Denali.*

"You're being pulled from your current assignment," Willemsen said and placed his palms on the table.

Bradley flipped the file open and saw a booking photo of a teeanger and scanned the documents inside.

"You need special operations to find a kid?" Nicks asked.

"No, I am utilizing you as a witness protection team."

Pyke tilted his head puzzled. "Sir... We aren't babysitters, and quite frankly, these glue stick sniffers are not suited for such work. That one loses his gun on a regular basis, and writes his reports in crayons." Pyke pointed to MacTavish.

"Colored pencils."

"Whatever."

"Listen, I am aware that this seems unorthodox—"

"Sir, with all due respect... There's an entire division dedicated to this very task... We're good at kicking in doors and blowing shit up."

Willemsen nodded slowly. "Yes, Pyke, I am aware of your team's special skill set, seeing as I hired a couple of them... This case needs a team of that caliber."

"A Special Operations team? To watch a kid?" Nicks asked.

"Yes, Nicks... This kid has wrapped himself up into quite the shitstorm. There are multiple agencies working on this case and your job is to simply keep this kid alive. He has a powerful man seeking to kill him for what he knows. Shaun Garrick is not one to be underestimated and has nearly endless resources. He has been a high valued target for the CIA and MI6 for quite some time."

Bradley flipped a page and studied Garrick's bulletin. *Manufacturing and distribution of weapons.* He was a high profile arms dealer.

"By the looks of this kid's sheet, he should probably be in prison for what he's been involved in," Clayton said.

"People who are in prison don't generally help the feds with investigations." Willemsen straightened. "They need information from him to catch Garrick. And– since they are focused on catching him, the CIA has tasked us with investigating possible Stateside contacts of Garrick. Inside you will find a list of names of possible threats towards this kid's safety... Good luck, he'll be here in..." Willemsen looked at his watch. "About twenty two hours or so. Any questions you can direct them to Pyke."

Willemsen nodded to Pyke and exited the room. Pyke closed his file and folded his hands neatly on top. "Well, MacTavish, you can be the permanent house nanny."

"Oh come on! The house nanny? Fuck me..."

"I'll get you a froofroo apron."

The house nanny, the term used to describe the unfortunate soul that's job is to maintain the secondary safe house. A job in itself not viewed as glorious but needed nonetheless.

Nicks snickered and MacTavish glared at him.

"Nicks, as team leader you will be the innkeeper."

Nicks nodded accepting his role as the sole guardian of the kid. "The addresses of the primary inn and secondary house are in the files. Memorize them now because they do not leave this room," Pyke said and pointed to Bradley and Clayton. "Evans, Bradshaw, you will be the watchmen. Now– conveniently there are four pages of names, you each get one."

MacTavish flipped his hand in the air. "So we just forget about the Cartel and Garza-Estrada then? We've spent months tracking this asshat down."

Pyke closed the file. "That's exactly what you're going to do..." He studied his teams' unhappy faces. "Look, I'm not happy about it either. I rather enjoy our time together breaking down doors, but we don't have a choice in the matter..." Pyke stood and mumbled, "This better not interfere with my vacation to Bermuda, so help me God you'll find me living in a box if I can't take my wife there."

"A judge wouldn't convict her."

"You can always live with me, sir. I haven't wet the bed in months," MacTavish offered.

"I'll pass, thanks..." Pyke left the room.

"This is going to be a nightmare... Witness protection? Are you kidding me? This is not what we do," Bradley argued.

"You took an oath to serve and protect. This is part of that," Nicks replied.

"It might not be as bad as you think." Clayton shrugged.

"He's a juvenile delinquent, good luck," MacTavish said. "Maybe I should be happy I was appointed house nanny."

"It may be a challenge, yes. But Willemsen picked us for a reason, so lets not let him down," Nicks said.

—

The worst betrayal comes from those that are trusted. Betrayal, a treachery of the utmost when it comes from those held in a high regard. Trust no one and you cannot be betrayed. The file contained Jame's new identity and backstory. He studied the file during the long flight from London to Chicago. He stared at the name. *Jude Hendricks, could they not come up with anything better?* His stomach twisted with the thought of the man he betrayed. Shaun Garrick, a powerful man, thirsty for his blood. He was a man with nearly endless resources and was not afraid to get his hands dirty. One thing that Garrick underestimated was James's drive for revenge. To put the man responsible for his mother's death behind bars forever or if the opportunity would present itself, take his life.

James stood in a bare room, his luggage next to a small bed. The accommodations certainly did not rival that of his home, a home he would probably never see again. The dying summer sunshine filtered into the window casting a dusty beam to his feet. Reality set in and it hit him hard. His mom was dead, a high-level weapons facilitator wanted his head, and everything he knew was gone.

"I know you're probably jetlagged, but I want you to meet the guys," Nicks said and scratched the back of his peppered head.

He motioned for James to follow. He had met Marshal Rauri Nicks at the airport. To the outside world this man was now James's uncle.

"Jude, this is Marshal Bradley Evans and Marshal Clayton Bradshaw," Nicks introduced.

"Hi," Jude said and crossed his arms.

"There are some ground rules to address," Nicks said and handed Jude a cell phone. "One, this phone is to stay with you at all times. It has our numbers programmed as various names along with the Marshal's Office. It also provides us a way to track you."

"Talk about a nanny service."

Clayton stifled a laugh and Nicks shot him an unamused look. Jude chuckled, taking a liking to Clayton.

"We want you to have some normalcy. So as long as we know where you are, you have some freedom."

Jude made eye contact with Nicks. "Nothing about this is normal. I don't belong here."

"It is a big adjustment, Jude. But–"

"It's a bloody nightmare."

"We will take it one day at a time. We're all in this together," Nicks replied.

"Right…"

"Listen kid, you've landed yourself in a shitstorm. Now, it's up to us to protect you. To keep you alive, so you can put that prick, Garrick, away," Clayton said.

"See, I like him." Jude pointed to Clayton.

"At least someone does…" Bradley interjected.

Jude chuckled and Nicks closed his eyes slowly with a sigh.

"Jude, why don't you get some rest. We have a long couple days to get you ready for the new school year," Nicks said.

"Oh, joy. I am just bursting with excitement to go to a school filled with entitled yanks."

Clayton covered his mouth and laughed.

"You are not helping…" Nicks said.

Jude stepped to the hall. "At least I'm not the only one that thinks that school is a joke."

"Charming kid…" Bradley said.

Clayton sat down. "Do you blame him? The shit he's already been through, certainly not a cake walk."

"He's arrogant."

"And you're not?"

"I'm confident, there's a difference."

Clayton spat out a laugh. "Yes, Bradley, you are correct."

Sleep did not come easy for Jude. He tossed and turned until he drifted into a light sleep.

James sprinted down the street to his home, fear gripping him. His legs could not move fast enough. His mother was in grave danger as Garrick had learned of her betrayal. The wooden gate swung open with ease. James entered the back of the garden. His heart sank as he saw Garrick confronting his mother. Their butler, an old man, Cecil, tried to reason with Garrick. A flash erupted from the muzzle accompanied by a loud bang. Blood projected in a thick stream from the back of Jennifer's head and splattered on the glass of the large window. Her body collapsed, her lifeless hand falling. James covered his mouth holding in a scream. Cecil dropped to his knees next to Jennifer overwhelmed with grief. James was in disbelief that Garrick killed his mother. He gasped for air trying to catch his breath. James felt weak trying to stay upright. He tripped over his own feet navigating the garden.

James was lifted from his feet as he was embraced from behind. "Where do you think you're off to?" Payne whispered in James's ear.

The cold steel of a blade pressed against James's neck. He knew that Payne was going to deliver him to Garrick. After all he had learned of his mother's betrayal to Garrick and instead informing him, James planned to help his mother flee. He could not allow Payne to serve him to Garrick, he would be killed. James whipped his head back and Payne's nose crunched against his skull. Payne stepped back holding a hand to his nose. James hit the knife out of his hand and it fell into the grass. The wind was knocked out of James as Payne tackled him to the ground. Blood dripped from Payne's nose onto James's face and he hit James in the cheek with a fist. James hit back and struggled to get out from under him. He thrusted his foot into Payne's stomach allowing enough time to reach above and grab the knife. Payne recovered and went for James, outstretching his hands to grab his neck. James stabbed the blade into the windpipe of Payne. His eyes went wide as blood spilled out of the wound and onto James.

James scrambled away from the dead man. His eyes darted to Wallace, one of Garrick's men who rounded the hedge. They stared at each other for a moment. Wallace's face went soft and he nodded for James to leave. He found his footing and darted out of the garden. He ran down the quiet sidewalk. The images of Garrick killing his mother replayed in his mind over and over. The gun shot, the blood, her lifeless body.

Jude sat bolt upright in his bed. His heart was racing and his breath was quick. His skin was clammy and a bead of sweat rolled down his forehead.

"Hey, kid. You all right?" Nicks asked from the door.

Jude snapped his attention to Nicks as his eyes adjusted. "What?"

"You were yelling in your sleep. I thought someone was attacking you."

Jude stared at his hands relieved they were not covered in blood. "Oh– I, uh. Sorry for waking you."

"Don't apologize–"

"Right, yeah– thanks for checking in."

Nicks took a step back. "If you ever want to talk about anything–"

"I'm good– but yeah, thanks."

"Try and get some sleep."

Nicks closed Jude's door quietly. Jude laid back down and stared at the ceiling.

The next few days were strenuous. On top of learning a whole different life, Jude was inundated with protocols and procedures. He learned the layout of the school, basic routes through the city, the location of the other safehouse, phone numbers, codes, and what one might do in various scenarios. It was a lot of information to take in. Jude quickly gained an appreciation for the three Marshals based on their in-depth knowledge and dedication.

Jude stood in the living room adjusting his emerald and silver striped tie.

"Ready?" Nicks asked and put his Boston Red Sox baseball hat on.

"Can I say no?"

Nicks chuckled. "It won't be that bad."

"I haven't been around people my age for sometime… I can't even imagine the pathetic drama I will be subjected to."

"Keep a low profile and no one will notice you're there," Nicks said and motioned for the door.

"Have you actually looked at me? I mean, really looked?" Jude asked, pointing at himself. "Then there's the fact that I have a British accent."

Nicks rolled his eyes and held the door open for Jude. "Besides being ugly, modesty is not a strength of yours."

"I am just stating a fact, Yankee Doodle Grisly. There is absolutely no way these yanks will leave me alone."

"Get in the car…"

The ride to school was only a few minutes and Nicks pulled up to the curb where students were dropped off. Jude stared out the window with a strong disdain for being thrusted into a preppy American soap opera.

"This is bollocks," Jude said.

"If you need anything, we will be around. Remember to try to keep a low profile."

"I will try my best…" Jude opened the door and slung his backpack.

He walked up the steps to the main entrance of the school. Students eyed and gawked at Jude. The halls were narrow and old with lockers lining one side. The head-turns and stares continued. Girls turned to each other and whispered about the new guy. The classroom for his first hour was empty, except for the teacher, a small older man. Jude found a seat in the back and settled in. Mr.

Jennings looked up from his desk peering down through his horn rimmed glasses.

"Good morning."

"Good morning, sir," Jude said.

Mr. Jennings lifted a brow, surprised by the accent. "You must be Mr. Hendricks. Welcome."

Jude nodded. "Thank you."

A slim blonde female walked in. She flipped her hair and sat in the seat next to Jude.

"Vanessa, meet Jude. He is a new student from England."

Vanessa smiled and held out her slender hand. "It's nice to meet you."

Jude shook her hand but did not say a word.

"I would be delighted to show you around in between periods," Vanessa said and crossed her legs shifting her weight to pose.

"I can manage."

Students filed into the room, taking their seats. Jude turned his attention forward and sank into his chair. The bell rang signaling the start of the day and the new school year.

"Welcome class. It is good to see all your bright faces. Let's take a moment and enjoy the slim window of time where we all want to be here before the year drags on as long as the exams in Mrs. Littman's History class," Mr. Jennings said.

Some of the students chuckled at the poor attempt of a joke.

"Most of you all know each other, however we do have a new student. Someone joining us all the way across the pond." Mr. Jennings motioned to Jude. "Mr. Jude Hendricks– Jude would you like to tell us a little something about yourself?"

Jude touched his face hating the attention. "There's nothing really to tell."

Jude let out a long breath, having noticed the blank stares and agape mouths after he spoke. It was like they didn't believe Mr. Jennings or they were too thick to understand what across the pond was.

"How about," Mr. Jennings pressed. "What brings you to Chicago?"

"Family," Jude said shortly.

"Okay… Well we are glad to have you." Mr. Jennings picked up on the hint that Jude did not want to divulge any more information about his life.

Much of the day progressed in the same manner. Jude navigated the lunch room and settled on eating an apple and having tea. He wasn't looking forward to the American tea but it was better than anything else the school served. He found a table that was mostly empty and hoped he would be able to have some time to himself. A girl at a table across the aisle turned and stared at him. Jude narrowed his brows. She turned around offended and immediately complained to her girlfriends. A tall, fit boy approached Jude with two wingmen on each side. He sat down across from Jude, his face stern.

"Can I help you with something?" Jude asked sarcastically.

The boy, Asher, picked up Jude's bottle of tea and mimicked a poor attempt at a British accent. "Look at this laddies, he es drink'n tea. Innit 'umourous?"

Jude raised a brow. "Who are you? Dick Van Dyke?"

"What did you just call me?" Asher asked, scrunching his face.

"Actually I called you two things. Dick– you know, nevermind. Obviously you're a bit thick for good British wit." Jude took a bite of his apple.

Asher slapped the piece of fruit from Jude's hand and it tumbled onto the floor. Jude stared at the rolling apple.

"I was eating that…"

"How's your wit now?" Asher taunted and screwed the cap off of his tea. He hocked a loogie and spit into the bottle.

"Now you're just being rude." An image of slamming Asher's face into the table crossed Jude's mind.

"Go fuck yourself." Asher turned and walked away, his cronies following like pups.

Jude leaned over and picked up the apple from the floor. He took a couple calming breaths eradicating the violent thoughts of harming Asher. He pulled his phone out of his pocket. He took a bite from the apple.

Jude 12:07PM
Is it against the rules to
break someone's nose?

Nicks 12:07PM
Making friends already...

Jude 12:08PM
What kind of arse spits
in someone's tea?

Nicks 12:08PM
Please don't do anything stupid...
It's your first day.

The bell rang and Jude tossed his apple and tea into the bin. The last few hours dragged on until the end of the day came. Jude threw his books in his locker and headed for the door. He was oddly surprised to be relieved when he saw Nicks parked in the lot waiting for him. Jude hopped in and loosened his tie.

"Ah, see. Not so bad... You survived," Nicks laughed.

Jude glared at him. "Have you met those people? Christ, what a bunch of wankers– Honestly I do not know how you expect me to survive that place."

"You've survived worse."

"Yes– Thanks for that reminder."

"Sorry– I didn't mean…"

"It's all right, I get it. I'm just frustrated."

Nicks patted Jude on the shoulder. "You're a strong kid, look at it as another challenge to get to the goal. Bide your time until Garrick is caught."

"That day can't come fast enough."

The following days of school were replays of each other. Jude did not wish to get to know anyone, but he felt more alone than ever. The gawking continued but his callous demeanor kept the other students away. Jude picked up his fork and pushed the baked beans on his plate. He stared absentmindedly at his food.

"Sorry… I'm not much of a chef– We can order take out if you want," Nicks said.

"Huh? Oh– No, I appreciate you making dinner. I have a lot on my mind," Jude set his fork down.

"Do you want to talk about it?"

Jude scratched his head trying to find the words. He wasn't accustomed to expressing his thoughts and feelings. He certainly did not want to come off as weak.

"I was just thinking about my mum… " Jude smiled. "She was an awful cook as well. I dare say worse than you, sir."

Nicks chuckled. "That is saying a lot about your mother. I have a hard time believing someone is worse than me. The beans are from a can and that marinara is expired ketchup."

Jude stared at him, setting down his fork.

"I'm kidding."

"Well, she would burn everything, but she tried. Most of the time Cecil, our butler, cooked, or takeout was our option when he wasn't there to save the day. She kept at it though, wanted our family to be normal..."

"Your mom sounds like a wonderful person."

"She was..." Jude took a moment reflecting on memories and smiled. "For my sixteenth birthday we were in the countryside and she surprised me with a motorcycle. The only condition was that she got to ride it first. She never rode a bike before... She pulled back on the throttle and sent the bike in the air. The look on her face..." Jude shook his head. "I miss that bike. Even more so I miss days like that... Now look, I'm hiding in the States eating dinner with a Marshal that thinks toast with garlic salt is gourmet."

"Certainly is a turn of events. And the toast is buttered too."

"I do appreciate what you're doing for me, Marshal Nicks."

"That's what I'm here for, Jude... And you can call me Rauri. You're always so formal."

"Sorry, old habits die hard."

The next morning Jude was sluggish getting ready for school. He had been awake most of the night with his mind racing.

"Come on, Jude. Pitter patter," Nicks called down the hall and walked to the door of the garage.

"You don't need to yell, I'm coming."

"I'm not yelling."

"What happened to your face?" Jude asked and pointed at Nicks's bare face.

Nicks touched his face in panic. "What?"

"You shaved–"

"Oh– Yeah, trying to look younger."

"It's not helping–"

"Well aren't you just a ray of sunshine... I like it."

Jude lifted a brow and followed Nicks into the garage. Jude stopped mid stride his eyes landing on a matte black BMW sports bike.

"Surprise!" Nicks said.

"What is that?" Jude asked, stepping to the bike and running his hands over the handlebars.

"It's my bike– I'm letting you borrow it. To have a little bit of normal in your world right now."

Jude choked back tears. He could not have expected such a kind gesture from a man he barely knew. Jude set his backpack down and gave Nicks a hug.

"Thank you."

"Don't mention it kid," Nicks said, patting him on the back.

He lifted a helmet from the shelf behind him. "You'll be needing this."

Jude smiled accepting the helmet and put it on.

"This way you don't have to be embarrassed with your 'lame uncle' driving you to school everyday. Gives you a bit more freedom too," Nicks said and tapped the top of the helmet.

Jude did not realize how much he missed the feeling of riding a bike. Nicks was right, it was exactly the bit of normal he needed. Something he enjoyed from his past to ground him, to give him a small amount of joy in the midst of chaos. It gave him a sense of freedom in a situation he had little control over.

CHAPTER THREE

An explosion sounded and the pieces of a door flew inward. Heavy steps of boots pounded on the dirt covered floor into the dilapidated building. Strobes of light filled the dark room making it difficult to see. Heavy metal music blared disrupting any concentration one may have. Marcus meetered a door spotting a hostile crouched in the corner. The muzzle of Marcus's rifle flashed sending three rounds into the man. The team of operators continued deeper into the building clearing room by room quickly and systematically. They were nearly finished when a man emerged from an open door spraying rounds. Bonnet, who was next to Marcus fell to the ground.

"Fuck!" Bonnet yelled and his teammates returned fire, dropping the shooter.

The strobe lights desisted and the overheads turned on. The metal music turned off although the pounding continued in Marcus's ears. Major Maxfield of the United States Army Delta Force descended the steel steps from the catwalk of the tactical training house.

"I was going to congratulate you for the record time, however, seems you lost a man..." He glared at Bonnet whose uniform was speckled with pink paint.

"Sorry, sir." Bonnet dropped his gaze to his boots.

"Don't apologize to me for dying," he pointed to the team. "They're the ones that have to carry your ass and deal with your family."

"Yes, sir," Bonnet said.

Other ranking officers descended the catwalk along with a young man in cammies. Marcus raised a brow wondering who the guy was that was obviously out of place.

Maxfield clasped his hands behind his back. "I know I have been pushing you all pretty hard, but I assure you it's not because I think you're dainty girls. On the contrary I have boasted about your hard work and it seems that your dedication has paid off." Maxfield paused.

The team straightened up as they clearly saw the rank on the officers' uniforms when they neared. It wasn't just the usual Captains and Majors from other squadrons. It was a couple Colonels and a Brigadier General.

"This past week was your test to see if you'd be picked for a special assignment and it seems that you have passed. With that being said, we're adding a position to make your team an even ten since Dugast is out on injury."

Dugast had missed a step and fell down a flight of stairs a few days prior fracturing his collar bone. The team all turned their attention to the young man who held his hat confidently in his hands.

"This is Staff Sergeant Shae Kinney," Major Maxfield introduced. "I'll leave you to it to get acquainted." He stepped away and turned back to the team. "Also, enjoy your leave. Don't do anything stupid and please don't get hurt. And for fuck sakes, no more fights."

The team stifled their chuckles.

Captain Adam 'Hatch' Karn stepped forward and shook Kinney's hand. "Welcome to the girl scout squad."

—

Never take for granted the simplicity of life, for a single moment can change the course of events. Kari sat in her last hour history class tormented with boredom. She propped her head up with her hand and stared blankly at the white board in front of her. She wanted the day to end so she could see her family. She would be having dinner with her brothers, whom she hadn't seen for sometime. Dread swept over her thinking about saying goodbye to one of them, possibly for the last time. Kari's thoughts were suddenly interrupted by an outburst of some loud disagreement by the classmate seated next to her. The surprise of the boy's voice banging down the door of her musings, nearly made Kari fall out of her seat.

"Brett Farve is a God," Matt said coolly and slouched back in the blue plastic chair crossing his arms over his chest.

"Matt, please. Try and stay focused. We're discussing World War One, not Brett Farve," Mrs. Cummberson said in a calm tone. She walked over to the white board her thin figure resembling that of a stick.

Kari could not help but agree with her teacher. She did not care about football at all, let alone some quarterback. But her classmate was obsessed with football, especially the Green Bay Packers, their State's professional football team. Kari really just wanted to shove a sock in the kid's mouth.

"Well, that's just not the point. Brett Farve is the greatest," Matt argued.

"Matt, we're not talking about Brett Farve, would you please stay on topic," Mrs. Cummberson stated, getting frustrated. "Where was I? Oh! Yes. The second reason, of twenty four, why trench warfare shaped the French countryside…"

Kari soon became bored from the conversation and drifted back into her thoughts from before. She tuned out the useless conversation in a heartbeat. She gazed non-responsively at the white board transfixed. She was in deep thought about her brother, Marcus, and his upcoming deployment. The news reports of the war in the

Middle East filled her thoughts, not making the situation any easier. Gunfire, explosions, innocent people suffering. The images would not leave her. Marucs had only been home for a week and they were having a family dinner, their last before his fifth deployment. Saying goodbye never got easier.

The loud sound of the bell echoed in the classroom. The students did not hesitate to leave. They filed out of the rooms and filled the narrow hallways of the old high school eager for the weekend and break to start. Kari walked down the long hallway dodging countless students, including two boys fighting over a backpack, three girls gossiping in the middle of the hall, and a long line waiting for the only drinking fountain. She just wanted to get on with her day. Not only was she excited for dinner but she was eager to be leaving for a whole weekend in Chicago with her brother, Bradley and his wife, Jessica.

Beth, Kari's friend, fell instep next to her. They chatted and retrieved Kari's belongings and switched out books for homework from her locker. They walked down the hallway back towards the commons. The halls thinned as eager students left for the long weekend. A trickle of soccer players walked through in their practice gear towards the front doors. Kari slowed her pace seeing her ex, Ryan, she let out a heavy sigh when he looked at her. She wanted nothing to do with him. But of course, he marched up to Kari quickly.

"Do you have a minute?" Ryan asked.

"No," Kari said and stepped around him.

He grabbed her arm. "Please?"

"Get your hand off of me." Kari barred her teeth and pulled away. Beth stepped between the two staring Ryan down.

One of Kari's friends, Diego, also on the varsity soccer team, walked over to Kari's side.

"Is there something wrong here?" Diego questioned protectively.

"I don't think there is and even if there was it wouldn't concern you," Ryan replied more annoyed.

Diego shot Ryan a death stare. "Looks like the diva has spoken," Diego said and threw up a hand.

"Stay out of this, fairy," Ryan shot back with as much force.

"We're going with fairy, original–" Diego said under his breath.

"He's simple minded, Diego, not even worth anymore words. Let's go," Kari said and walked past Ryan.

Diego and Beth followed. Diego turned and posed with a hand on his hip, knee raised, and blew Ryan a parting kiss. Ryan hissed and narrowed his eyes as they exited the school. Kari unlocked her car throwing her bag in the back.

"Do you need anything hun? Before you leave? We're here for you," Diego asked.

"No, I'm okay."

Diego kissed Kari on the cheek. "Well you have fun my dear."

"Of course."

"Bye, chicka," Beth said and with a smile Kari closed the door.

Kari sped down the freeway excited to see her brothers. They didn't get together as often as they should. But considering Marcus being in the Army and Bradley being a Marshal it was difficult to schedule. Although since Bradley got out of the Army a couple years ago Kari thought she would have seen him more often. Turns out being a Marshal was just as time consuming.

The Evans family had a rich history of serving their country. Her father, Matthew had served as an Officer in the Army and had fought in the gulf war towards the end of his twenty year career. Their grandfather served in the Vietnam war in a Special Forces unit. Her grandfather no doubt was the reason her brothers both went Special Forces, even after their father had attempted, and failed to persuade them not to. When Bradley joined it nearly killed their mother. It was September 11, 2001, a date that would forever live in infamy. Al-Qeada was found responsible for the terror attacks. Bradley quit school in his last semester of college and joined immediately. Kari was only five years old and didn't fully grasp what was going on. She just remembered her parents being glued to the TV and sobbing.

The years continued and at times her parents were zombies. There were reports of Ramadi, of U.S. military being killed. It's all her parents talked about *Ramadi* this, *Ramadi* that. In 2007, Marucs joined right out of high school. It devastated Kari's mother. To make matters worse for any mother, after a few years Marcus and Bradley were both Delta Force Operators, Tier 1, elite, serving in different teams of course. It was bad enough to have your sons both in the Army but even worse to have both of them in Delta, lord only knew what they were tasked with. Every knock at the door would send Kate into panic, expecting there to be men dressed in pressed uniforms there to deliver the worst news a mother could hear. Needless to say when Bradley came home for good, Kate was less of a nervous wreck, key word less, she was still a mess with Marcus.

Kari killed the engine to her little blue car when she arrived at Mavelle's, a well-known supper club in the upper northeast Wisconsin. She scanned the bar looking for familiar faces when she spotted Bradley shaking his head chuckling. He was probably laughing at one of her Dad's lame jokes. Kari's father, a well-defined man, with the strangest sense of humor.

Kari walked excitedly over to her family to join them. She said her hellos to her parents and barely had a moment to say hello to Jessica before being embraced into a bear hug. One that felt like her ribs were going to snap from Bradley squeezing so tight.

"Are you trying to kill me?" Kari asked as Bradley released her.

"I have to super size my hugs because I never see you," Bradley explained.

"And who's fault is that–" Kari said and stepped back. "So, where's Marcus? Stuck in traffic?"

"Well, you know how Marcus is. He's late for everything," Bradley stated.

He pulled out the bar stool next to Kari and took a seat. He raised his hand slightly to get the bartender's attention and ordered a beer.

"So kid, what have you been up to lately?"

"Nothing since the last time you saw me. I'm still the same clumsy Kari you know and love."

"How's that boy you're seeing? What's his name, Rodger, Robert, Ray– Oh, Ryan."

Kari twirled the straw in her glass. "Actually, we broke up a few weeks ago."

"I'm sorry to hear that."

"Don't be– He was an ass."

"Well… I wasn't going to say it," Bradley stated.

Kari froze and smiled seeing Marcus walk through the door.

"It's about time you decided to show up for your own going away dinner," Bradley joked.

"Well, you know how it is. I enjoy being the center of attention, making people wait." Marcus leaned over and kissed their mother on the cheek. "Mom."

"You're late," Kate said.

"I know, I am sorry."

They started towards the dining room and took their seats. Marcus picked up a menu.

"Headed to Pope Air Force Base a week early?" Bradley asked Marcus. "Want a jump on your pre-deployment process?"

"Yes, because I enjoy getting poked and prodded before I get shipped to Bagram."

"I can say, I do not miss that place."

"Don't miss playing in the sand, melting and then freezing?"

"No–"

"I'm sure Major Maxfield would take you back in a heartbeat," Marcus said.

"Tell him I say hi. And let him know that my left ass cheek still twinges now and again from saving his hide from that IED. Nothing like a shard of metal sticking out of you."

"Do you boys ever talk about anything else?" their father Matthew asked.

"I'm sure you could tell a story or two about Desert Storm," Marcus prodded.

"It's not appropriate dinner talk," Matthew said and turned his attention to Kari. "Kari has decided on a college. Why don't you tell them where you're applying."

"The University of Madison, maybe looking at getting into Law."

"That's great, Kar. Madison is a good school. You'll do well there," Marcus said.

"What? No West Point?" Bradley asked. "You were Dad's last hope of going to his alma mater."

"She's the only one smart enough to get in, out of you three," Matthew chuckled.

"You could always change your mind," Bradley said.

"Nope, definitely not going that route. I would rather not get shot or blown up."

"You know, they're always looking for Jag Officers," Bradley said.

"Don't want to come play in the sandbox?" Marcus asked.

"Not particularly," Kari chuckled.

"Oh come on now, you'd be an Officer and have it made," Bradley said.

"I'm not military material."

"You'd be surprised." Marcus said and pointed at Bradley "I mean this idiot did well."

Kari chuckled.

After light conversation and dinner it was time to say goodbye. They stood in the parking lot near their vehicles. Kari's mother began to cry and hugged Marcus. A possible last goodbye. Kate touched Marcus's cheeks for one last close look at her son.

"You stay safe, Marcus. You hear me?" She sobbed.

"Ma, don't worry. I've done this before," Marcus said as comfortingly as he could.

Kari felt the pressure in her eyes and her throat tighten. She looked up to see that she was not the only emotional one. Kari's father put his arm around her and held her as a steady stream of tears cascaded down her rosy cheeks. Kari waited her turn to say goodbye to her brother. After Marcus hugged his father he turned to Kari. He smiled at her and she felt her heart warm. He reached out and wiped away her tears.

"This is goodbye, for now at least. When I get back I'll be visiting you at West Point." Marcus hugged Kari.

Kari buried her face into Marcus's shoulder and began to cry even harder. She thought that it could be the last time she would ever get to hug her brother. When Marcus let go, Kari locked eyes with him, giving him a serious look.

"Don't get yourself blown up," Kari ordered.

Marcus put his hand on her shoulder and sincerely replied, "I will do my best."

Marcus looked to his family and waved goodbye as he got into his rental car to head back to Milwaukee for his flight in the morning. It was never easy to say goodbye to his family. They had been his final thoughts on a couple occasions, but they were always a driving force to continue to fight and to win.

After the final goodbyes, Kari was on her way with Bradley and Jessica. Chicago was four hours away, and it was another half hour south of Chicago to Tinley Park, where they lived. Kari, drained from a long day at school, felt the heaviness of sleep overtake her and she soon drifted into a soundless sleep.

—

The sound of baseball filled the background. Nicks sat at the kitchen table, documents strewn about the surface. He glanced at his phone and watched Jude's dot get closer to the house. He flipped through the newest After Action report from the British SAS op.

The dark sky opened up and raindrops fell fiercely on the team of operators as the back doors to the vans opened. Jedi turned on his night vision and followed behind Loch descending down an alley with the team. When they neared the thin three story flat, two operators broke off to cover the front of the building. Hawkeye stood off to the side of the door. He pressed his ear to the wood for a moment. He shook his head, no sound. The team leader, Griffin, nodded and Hawkeye swung the ram into the door just below the knob. The door swung in with ease and he dropped the ram.

Loch led the team as they dynamically cleared the first level. The home was clean and neat. It didn't look to be that anyone was staying there. Red lasers bounced off of the walls in different directions that only the team could see through their night vision, it was invisible to the naked eye. Loch's attention trained on the steps that opened to an open second story. Jedi was a step behind him going up backwards. The muzzle of his rifle sweeping the open space waiting for a combatant to emerge. Loch reached the landing and covered long watching the doors down the hall.

They cleared the rooms. The beds were made, the sink was dry. Nothing was out of place or touched. The steps creaked to the third floor and opened to an office space. The desk and cabinet were left open. Any intelligence they may have found had been taken. Garrick was nowhere to be found.

"Bandit 1 to House, location is clean," Griffin radioed.

———

The door for the garage opened and Jude set his backpack down on the counter.

"Sorry I'm late, I just needed some time to clear my head. That school is awful."

"Hey, I'm just glad you let me know you went for a ride." Nicks lifted his phone. "Plus I knew where you were."

"Right... I'm not used to being tracked." Jude strolled into the kitchen and grabbed a glass of water.

"There's left over chinese take out, if you're hungry."

"Maybe later." Jude sat down at the table. "Looks like you've been busy. Any leads?"

Nicks picked up the file he finished reading. "Looks like SAS hit Garrick's flat in Victoria."

"That was a waste of time, he's probably not even in England."

"They have to start somewhere kid."

"I gave MI6 a list of places, have they looked into those yet?"

"I think they were going off of the ones close to home that they know about first."

Jude leaned back in the chair. "Why do I have a feeling they're never going to find him?"

"It's going to take time, Jude. You need to be patient."

Jude cocked a brow. "Have you been to that school? Have you dealt with those people? When you have, then tell me to be patient."

Nicks chuckled. "How's your bully?"

"Oh he's a git, pushed me into a locker and threw my bag down the hall. A real charming lad." Jude tipped the bottle of water towards Nicks. "I would enjoy tossing him down the stairs."

"Please, don't. That's a headache I don't need."

Jude returned to the kitchen to put his glass in the dishwasher. Clean dishes filled the space, yet again. Jude set his glass down on the counter.

"I am beginning to wonder if you are capable of living on your own."

"I was going to put them away in a bit."

"Yeah– I've heard that before, who's the adult here?"

"You nag more than my ex wife," Nicks said and walked to the kitchen.

Jude cocked a brow and lifted the silverware tray out of the dishwasher. Nicks froze and stared at him in disbelief, his mouth slightly agape.

"What– Oh come on! Seriously? You didn't know the tray came out?"

Nicks stared at the dishwasher. "That is some witchcraft."

"And you're in charge of protecting me? Christ–"

"Don't judge– I've spent a good portion of my life perfecting my craft as a warrior. I missed the lesson on being Martha Stewart."

"It shows…"

CHAPTER FOUR

Kari was woken by a sharp bark from Jack. Her eyes flashed open in terror. For a moment she didn't know where she was. The room was strange and unfamiliar. She looked around the neat bedroom remembering that she was in Tinley Park. Her head was spinning from being pulled from sleep. She focused on the brown American Bulldog standing at the foot of the bed looking dumbfounded up at Kari.

Kari threw off the covers and noticed she was still fully dressed in the clothes she had been wearing yesterday. She rolled out of bed and walked downstairs to the kitchen. Bradley finished pouring a cup of coffee and made his way to the other side of the counter. He took a seat on the black steel stool, his eyes darting to the disheveled zombie.

"You look like shit, " Bradley greeted and took a sip of his fresh brew.

"Good morning to you, too," Kari replied with a sarcastic grin.

"There's a fresh pot of coffee, if you'd like any," Jessica said, her eyes were hidden behind thick-rimmed square glasses as she studied her laptop.

"Perfect," Kari crossed the kitchen and helped herself.

Bradley returned his gaze to the newspaper. Kari sat down, took out her phone and scrolled through various social media sites to see what she missed while she slept.

"So Kar, what do you want to do today?" Bradley asked as he turned a page of the newspaper, his eyes never leaving the page.

"Uh– I don't know, perhaps something low key. Maybe just hang at the park?" Kari suggested. "You know I haven't seen Clayton and Amelia in awhile, think they're busy?"

"It's Clayton, I'm sure he's not doing anything," Bradley smirked. "I can text him."

"Cool–" Kari's focus was on her phone when a text from Marcus popped up. She opened the text to see a picture of a rather stout bearded man sitting in the uncomfortable airport seats. *It's the fat version of Bradley. Tell him to lay off the sweets or this is his future. I saw those love handles.* Kari giggled and showed Bradley the text.

Bradley shook his head. "I do not have love handles."

Kari put her phone down and the sadness hit her. She missed Marcus already. She leaned back in the stool staring at the earth toned back splash behind the stove top.

"You okay?" Bradley asked seeing the sudden shift in mood.

Kari avoided eye contact at all costs, not wanting to talk. It was the same every time Marcus deployed. It never got easier, in fact it got worse. She feared one of these times he wouldn't come back at all.

"Marcus... I just have this bad feeling."

"It's okay to be worried about Marcus. I would be lying to you if I told you he will be fine, but he's prepared for what he will be facing. I mean he's already walked away from a helo crash and then there's that one time–"

"You're not helping." Kari wiped the tears from her eyes. "I just want him to be safe and come home."

"I know... Come here," Bradley opened his arms and Kari hugged him.

Bradley's phone dinged and he looked at the text. "Ah, see, Clayton wasn't doing anything. They'll meet us at the park. Even better, he'll cook for us too."

"It's not going to be anything weird is it? Last time he made some odd tomato and bean monstrosity."

"I can't promise anything."

"Great..." Kari replied and hopped off the stool. "I think I might go for a run before we head out."

"Want me to come with?" Bradley asked.

"No, I can't keep up with you."

Bradley smiled. "Learn to run faster."

Kari stuck out her tongue and scampered out of the kitchen.

———

Jude tossed and turned, a cold sweat matting his brow. The London street he walked down was dark and rain cascaded from the sky. A heavy fog blanketed the ground around him. Footfalls echoed behind him and Jude whirled around his eyes desperately scanning for movement in the fog. Sharp talons grasped his collar and forced him to the ground. Fear swept over Jude as he tried to fight Garrick off of him. His ice blue eyes pierced through the darkness. Tightness gripped Jude's throat as Garrick wrapped his hands around his neck.

"I'm coming for you, James," Garrick snarled and released one of his hands to draw his pistol.

Gunshots rang and a searing hot pain erupted in Jude's abdomen. He felt hands on his shoulders and Garrick disappeared.

"Kid, wake up," Nicks said and shook Jude.

His eyes sprang open scanning the room quickly and resting on Nicks's concerned face.

"You good?" Nicks asked.

Jude's mind raced to catch up to reality. "Yeah…"

"Do you want to talk about it?"

"It was just a nightmare, I'm fine." Jude threw the covers off and got out of bed.

"You haven't slept since you got here... It's not just nightmares," Nicks pressed.

Jude tossed the drenched shirt and threw on another. "I'm fine, really."

"You're not fine."

Jude walked to the door. "I don't want to talk about it, okay–"

"Jude..."

He paused in the doorway and stared at Nicks. "You can't help me with this... I'm going to go for a ride."

"Okay... I'm here if you want to talk."

Jude nodded and disappeared down the hall. The motorcycle roared to life and Jude sped down the road. His mind was a garbled mess of thoughts that he tried to sort through. The one thing he knew for certain that the freedom of the open road was refreshing. He took to the roads south going into unexplored suburbs of Chicgo. He approached an intersection with the cross traffic having a stop sign. He watched for cars regardless, people had a tendency to not see motorcycles.

Kari concentrated on the rhythm of her breath and her footfalls on the pavement. Heavy rock blared in her ears. She stepped off of the sidewalk to cross the road. Jude slammed on the breaks causing his back wheel to rise off the road. He stopped inches from striking Kari.

Her head whipped and her eyes widened from the near collision. Her fear stricken face reflected off of Jude's tinted visor of his helmet. Once Jude landed, he planted his feet on the ground and raised his hands in the air.

"I am so sorry," Kari said, turning red from embarrassment. She turned and looked to where the stop sign was on the corner but there was none. She immediately realized her error and had assumed it was a four-way stop.

Jude shook his head annoyed by the lack of awareness Kari possessed. She awkwardly ran out of the road and caught her breath on the sidewalk. Jude took one last glance at the girl he nearly hit. Frustrated he accelerated. His bad mood only intensified and he decided to cut his ride short and return home.

"That was a short ride," Nicks said as Jude set his helmet on the counter.

"I almost crashed–"

"Uh– What? You didn't hurt Siobhan did you?"

"No– Wait... did you name your bike Siobhan?"

"Don't judge me, child."

Jude laughed.

"So what happened, chuckles?"

"Some stupid girl ran out in front of me. Do people not pay attention to where they are going?"

"Welcome to Chicago. I'm glad you didn't get hurt."

"Or are you just glad I didn't wreck your bike."

Nicks placed a hand on Jude's shoulder. "I would never value a bike over a human life."

Nicks picked up his coffee and walked into the living room.

"That is a bunch of bullocks."

"But over your life…"

"See, I fu—"

"What? I can't hear you– The Sox are on."

"No they're not–"

Nicks took a sip of his coffee and picked up a file and glanced at the TV. Jude rolled his eyes.

"You watch old matches?"

"It's the 2004 World Series." Nicks shrugged. "I like the ambient background noise. The Sox got me through some dark times."

Jude sat on the couch. "Really?"

"Uh– yeah. Well it started with my childhood, not the greatest."

"You and me both."

"Ha, yeah– I suppose..."

"What happened?"

"You really want to listen to my story?" Nicks was surprised.

"I do."

"Okay– story time it is… I grew up in a shittastic city called Pittsfield, it's in western Massachusetts. My parents were drunks. I'm actually surprised we weren't homeless with how much they drank away my father's paycheck. I'm also surprised he even held a job at all, but that's what happens when you work a union job. We lived in a small house, that could have been alright if it was kept up. I remember many nights I'd gone without food and it was a good month if we had electricity."

"Christ—"

"It gets worse kid… My parents fought when they were drinking, which was everyday. I was four when I witnessed my dad grab my mom so hard he snapped her arm like a twig. I will never forget the sound it made and the awful cry of my mother. After that night I never saw her again. She went to the hospital and never came home. I used to hate her for leaving me with that monster, but in reality she was no better than he was. The only problem was now that she was gone, my father turned his aggression to me. There would be nights he would hit me with his belt until my ass looked like hamburger meat, yeah try and sit with that."

Jude cringed. "That's awful."

"My saving grace was our next door neighbor. He was a tough leathered geezer, Howard. He was a frogman in WWII."

"What's a frogman?"

"They were the first Navy SEALs."

"Oh—"

"Yeah— I was terrified of him at first but he had taken a liking to me. Perhaps he knew what my father was doing to me and felt sorry. Regardless, as I got older I spent the majority of my time over at his house, working on cars, motorcycles, and most of all listening to the Red Sox... He brought me to my first game at Fenway. Best day of my life, besides maybe getting my trident."

"Your what?"

"We'll get to that part."

"Anyway, my dad continued to beat my ass. One time he hit me so hard he knocked me out. I woke up on the livingroom floor with no recollection of what happened. Fuck, I hated that man. Although, I can probably thank him for preparing me for my career in the military."

"What exactly did you do in the military?"

"We're getting there."

"As I got into my early teens I stayed away from the house as much as possible. But then my father got sick, real sick. He went into liver failure... I know shocker. He passed away not too long after. So there I was, thirteen with absolutely no family and I was going to be put into foster care. Howard stepped in and made sure social services didn't haul me away. He adopted me a few months later. I would never again have to carry the name Thayer again and was then a Nicks. Because of Howard, I became a SEAL. I earned my trident after the hell of BUD/S."

"I thought you were in the Army?"

"We'll get there when we get there."

"Okay, what's *Buds*?"

"It's SEAL training– Don't ever become a SEAL. You know what, don't ever do any kind of Special Forces, it all sucks. Better yet don't join the military, you're too smart anyway."

"Was it really that bad?"

Nicks cocked a brow. "Those are stories for another day. To this day I refuse to eat sugar cookies."

"What does that have to do with anything?"

Nicks spoke in a deep drill sergeant voice. "Get wet and sandy!" Nicks took a sip of coffee. "As punishment we would have to dive into the surf, getting nice and wet. Then roll in the sand and do whatever other punishment they had in store for us. We looked like giant sugar cookies but believe me, doing anything with that sand chafing you everywhere was not pleasant."

Jude let out a chuckle.

"Anyway when I was nearing my limit in BUD/S guys were dropping out left and right. I was fearful I was next. I would remember how Howard and the Sox had saved me from my father. If I could push out the pain as a kid, I could do it during BUD/S. I passed and sure shit a few years later I thought it was a good idea to go to the Marine Sniper school. It was awful but I passed, surprisingly…"

"I didn't know you were a sniper."

"I'd like to think a pretty good one. Good enough anyway to have recommendations to try out for DEVGRU."

"DEV what?"

"Super secret squirrel ops."

Jude cracked a smile.

"That training was– How do I put this– I think I'd rather be married to my ex wife again. Anywho, after I got back to Virginia Beach from Green Team. I was notified that Howard was in the hospital and had a massive heart attack. I was granted leave to see him and he died a couple days later."

"I'm sorry." Jude was beginning to realize that there were people who had it worse off than he, Nicks being one of them.

"Don't be, he went out like the stubborn old man he was. After that the Sox meant more to me. A way to remember him by. And to remember what I was able to get through."

"He sounds amazing."

"He was–"

"I didn't think that baseball could mean so much."

"Yeah about that– Another story!" Nicks took another sip of coffee.

"You're enjoying this aren't you?"

Nicks nodded. "I was stationed in Mogadishu with a Delta unit– That's the Army version of the SEALS, but less cool. They were in need of a sniper so I was voluntold to attach to their unit. I would listen to the Sox games whenever I could. Brought a little piece of home with me to that shithole.

"During an Op we were ambushed. We lost nineteen brave men, and seventy three wounded. I was one of those seventy three. I was shot three times. Once in the arm, and twice in the leg. When I was in Bethesda healing, feeling sorry for myself I was able to listen to the Sox. Brought me back to reality that I could get through whatever was in front of me.

"After Mogadishu I was offered a lateral transfer into the Army Special Forces. I had been deployed with them more often than my own team. We had been through hell and back. I took them up on that offer and left the Navy. The Sox eventually got me through more deployments and a divorce."

Jude glanced at the TV listening to the fans roar. He gained a new appreciation for baseball. "I admire your strength. I wish I was more like you."

"You're stronger than you know."

"Thanks," Jude paused. "You know— It's still boring as fuck."

Nicks laughed louder than Jude had ever heard.

—

The early September breeze was still hot from the dying summer days. The park was a sprawling open area with a line of trees on the far side of the soccer field. Kari dropped the tattered soccer ball to the grass. She laughed while Jack jumped impatiently around Kari's feet, wanting so desperately for her to kick the ball. She booted the ball across the vacant field. The dog tore off in a flash to hunt the ball down. As he approached the ball, he pounced at full force, knocking the ball a few feet in front of him. He bit at it, trying to get hold of the ball. It spun away from him, causing Kari to laugh at him again. After Jack figured out he could not fit his slobbery mouth around it, he gave up and punched the ball back to Kari with his face. She dribbled the ball with Jack running around her feet.

Bradley watched Kari laugh and smile. He wondered when she had grown up. He had been gone most of Kari's life. He'd never really thought about it before. He had taken an oath to serve and protect the country. Delta had become his family more than his own. His family had come to visit him more at Fort Bragg than he ever went back to Wisconsin.

Clayton elbowed Bradley and smirked, nodding towards Kari. Bradley chuckled and they ran up behind Kari. Bradley grabbed ahold of Kari by her waist and tossed her onto his shoulder. Distracted, Clayton stole the ball and dribbled the best he could down the short distance to the goal, Jack prancing next to him. Clayton stopped and hesitantly kicked the ball at the net. It mercilessly went in.

"G-O-A-L!" Clayton cheered.

Kari laughed watching Clayton run in a circle with his hands held high. Bradley returned Kari to her feet and she shoved him playfully.

"Cheaters…"

Kari shook her head and joined Jessica and Amelia on the jungle gym.

"Giving up that easy I see," Bradley called after her and went to retrieve the ball.

"You two are more than capable of entertaining yourselves."

The afternoon dwindled and they headed to Clayton's for the evening. The drive from Tinley Park to Matteson, where Clayton lived, was only a fifteen minute drive. The neighborhood was older, but distinct with the rows of wealthier castle-looking homes. Old trees lined the sides of the street giving character to the neighborhood. Clayton's house was a small old Victorian manor. It had the classic rounded bump out in the front. It was stunning with the dark maroon paint and black trim. Clayton and his late wife Isabella had moved there after Clayton gave up his career in the Navy. The home was Isabella's grandparents and Clayton couldn't part with it, even though it was extravagant for him and Amelia.

Fate had a strange way of intertwining lives together. The first time Clayton and Bradley fought alongside each other they had been pinned down by enemy fire in Ramadi. On the buttpucker meter it was a seven out of ten. They had been separated from the rest of their team from a series of IEDs. With their team scattered and taking heavy fire they were worried it would only be a matter of time before they were picked off one by one. They had to hold out until the Quick Response Force,

QRF, came to rescue their asses. Bullets whizzed past their heads eating the crumbling stone of a building they were using as cover.

Jokingly Bradley said. "I'm supposed to be getting married in a few months. I can't die here, she'll be pissed and kill my ass again."

"Someone was dumb enough to want to marry you? Does she have any friends?"

"For you, if we make it out of here... I'll make sure you have a chance with one of Jess's best looking friends."

"Ha, deal!"

After they were rescued and safe at base. Bradley kept to his word and had convinced Jessica to have her longtime friend, Isabella, write to Clayton. It was history after that. When she was diagnosed with cancer, Clayton left the Navy first chance he could. It was difficult at first with Amelia being only a year old, he leaned on Isabella's mother for support. Isabella was a fighter and had gone into remission for two years but the cancer came back with a vengeance. It nearly killed Clayton losing her and not being able to do anything. He was supposed to protect her but he was helpless against the war that had raged inside her own body.

Clayton picked up Amelia as they filed into the spacious living room. "Let's get you some dinner, how does chicken and peas sound?" Clayton brushed his beard on Amelia's forehead and kissed her as she giggled.

Bradley followed and helped himself to the beer. Kari plunked down on the couch and scratched Jack behind the ear. Bradley returned to the living room. Jessica was standing by the small table set beneath the wide window. Resting atop it was a picture of Clayton and Isabella at a Cubs game, happiness illuminating their features. Jessica missed Isabella tremendously and the warm spirit she had.

Bradley handed Jessica the beer. "You okay?"

Jessica smiled. "Of course." Jessica sat next to Kari and engaged in small talk about college.

Bradley wandered back into the kitchen Jack following behind.

"Be a gent and let Branch out of the crate," Clayton said and prepared Amelia her dinner.

Bradley took a gulp of beer and set the bottle on the counter. He opened the door to the laundry room and Branch looked up at him with his big blue eyes. He wagged his tail and let out a whine. The crate clanked open and the black and white husky pup pounced out, scurrying into the kitchen. Bradley was steps behind the puppy and reached out for his beer. Branch chomped at Jack's tail. There was a deep bark and growl. Scared, Jack jumped and flew at Bradley. The eighty pounds of bulldog plowed into Bradley and took him clean off his feet, sending him into the wall headfirst.

"Jack!" Bradley yelled.

Jack flew into the living room like a big chicken and leapt onto Jessica trying to hide.

"You big baby," Jessica said. "Are you afraid of Branch?"

Bradley rose touching the back of his head feeling the blood.

"Did you bleed on my wall?" Clayton asked and threw a washcloth at him.

"I'm okay thanks for asking, dickwad."

The small black and white fluff ball came running, hopping, into the living room. The tiny husky puppy barked. Jack, scared of the puppy, dug his boxy head into Jessica's stomach. Kari lit up at the sight of the puppy. She climbed off the couch and played with Branch.

"You didn't tell me Clayton got a new dog," Kari said and Branch tried to chew on her hand.

Bradley and Clayton entered the room. Both of them had guilty faces. Bradley held his hand behind his head.

"What was that huge bang?" Jessica questioned.

Bradley shifted on his feet. "That would have been my head smashing into the wall." He explained, removing the bloodstained washcloth from the back of his head.

"Oh my God! What the hell?" Jessica yelled and leaped off the couch, Jack flopping to the ground. She hurried over to Bradley to see how bad the damage was.

"Your dog is a coward that's what happened. He took Bradley clean off his feet. Ehem... you can see the damage for yourself," Clayton explained as Jessica looked at the gash.

"Hun, I'm pretty sure you're going to need some stitches. I'll take him in. Kari why don't you stay here and help Clayton with dinner. This shouldn't take too long."

"I've had worse– a lot worse... It's fine."

Jessica glared at him. "It's not fine."

Jessica reached into Bradley's pocket and slid out the keys.

"We'll be back," Jessica said as she and Bradley went out the door.

"So..." Kari trailed off, breaking the awkward silence not knowing what else to say.

Jack laid on the floor, his big sad eyes staring hopelessly up at Kari as Branch played with his tail. Amelia fell asleep, exhausted from all the commotion. Kari glanced up at the circular clock on the wall. Only five past six o'clock. Clayton entered the living room with a deck of cards.

"Rummy? I think they're going to be at the hospital longer than they think."

———

Hatch raised his hand and shouted at the bartender. "Pauly! Another couple of pitchers on the FNG!"

Pauly smiled and a look of dismay spread over Kinney's face. FNG, a term of endearment, because hazing was forbidden. What does it mean? Fucking new guy. With Kinney being the newest member of the girl scout squad, or Golf team as they were officially named, he needed to prove himself worthy. The goal was to get the team and especially Kinney shitfaced on his dime. The team had been going strong for a few hours already and it showed. The more alcohol that flowed the louder they became.

The door opened and a rowdy group of country boys staggered into the bar. They were three sheets to the wind and dare say, even more rambunctious than the girl scout squad. Pauly motioned that the pitchers were ready. Marcus elbowed Kinney in the shoulder. Kinney stepped away from the hightop table and stumbled over his own feet. He wasn't what a typical person would picture as a spec ops operator. Kinney was lean and on the shorter side. He had a neat and styled haircut and was clean shaving. Definitely a contrast to the team's beards and various stages of shaggy hair.

Kinney successfully made it to the bar without falling over. He grasped the pitchers firmly and turned around. One of the stocky brickhouse country boys stood behind Kinney impatiently trying to get at the crowded bar. Kinney's ability to maneuver was hindered significantly due to the amount of alcohol he had consumed. He bumped into the country bumpkin and sloshed the beer onto his short sleeve flannel shirt.

"I didn't see you there, man," Kinney said and took a step back to go around the guy.

The hillbilly stared at his shirt and back at Kinney. He hit the pitcher out of Kinney's hand. The plastic clattered onto the tile floor and the beer splashed everywhere. Kinney walloped the country boy upside the head with the other pitcher. The beer drenching both of them. His friends instantly descended onto Kinney.

"Oh, fuck!" Hatch yelled and hopped off his stool.

The team lept into action to back their brother. Marcus indexed one of the fat hillbilly's wrist and wretched it behind his back while simultaneously punching the guy in the side of the face. The country boys did not stand a chance against Delta Force operators, even if they were seeing double.

"Badger, knife!" Hatch yelled seeing that the fat hillbilly with a missing tooth Marcus was fighting with pulled a blade.

Fatty swung his massive paw at Marcus the knife clenched tight. Marcus released the man's wrist and caught his other hand before Chunks could stab Marcus. Swiftly Marcus manuved and put the country bumpkin into an arm bar. The hillbilly yelped when Marcus applied pressure at the elbow and the knife clattered to the ground. BANG! The bar went silent and everyone froze from the shotgun blast. Pauly held the 12ga, the barrel pointed to the ceiling.

"Get your hands off of my boys, you redneck cunts," Pauly seethed.

Marcus smiled as the country boys scurried out of the bar.

Pauly set the shotgun behind the bar. "I'd ask if you boys were all right, but I know better than that."

"Thanks, Pauly," Hatch said and offered a hand to Kinney, assisting him back to his feet.

Kinney wiped blood from his nose.

"The rest of the night is on me, fellas. Those shit for brains hicks don't know what real heroes look like if it shot them in the ass."

Marcus picked up the knife and set it on the bar. "We owe you one."

"Just keep kicking ass out there."

———

Kari sat pretzel legged on the floor and tapped the coffee table waiting for Clayton to play his turn. He eyed Kari and made his move. Amelia was sleeping on the couch next to Clayton. His phone lit up with a text from Bradley.

"Looks like they're going to be leaving soon. Shall we make dinner?"

"What are we making for dinner?" Kari asked, standing up. She walked to the spacious kitchen.

"Sushi and..." Kari made a face. "Or not."

"Got any pasta?"

"I do..."

Kari smiled. Clayton opened the pantry and tossed a box of pasta on the counter and slid a jar of marinara sauce.

"Will you eat that?"

"Yes…"

Clayton pulled a pot from the cabinet to start dinner. Kari plunked down on the stool. A pencil sat next to a pad of paper. She looked from Clayton to the paper. She picked up the pencil and ran the graphite across it.

"What are you doing? You're supposed to be helping."

"I'm drawing you."

"What?"

"Just keep doing what you're doing." Kari waved at him.

Bradley opened the door to the passenger side and got in a dull throbbing on his head. Jessica started the car and drove down the busy street. The strobing lights from Bradley's phone sitting in the cupholder caught his attention.

"Evans."

"Hey, it's Nicks."

"What's up?"

"Pyke wants us to brief next Thursday at 1500 hours on any leads," Nicks said and shuffled his files on the kitchen table.

"What does he expect us to have in a week and a half?" Bradley replied.

"I don't make the rules. Just make sure you have something."

"Yeah, I'm working on it. So far the contacts I've run with are in prison."

"Well... That's something at least."

A billow of smoke emerged from the oven and the fire alarm sounded. "Honestly, do you not know what a timer is?" Jude asked.

"What's going on?" Bradley asked, pulling the phone from his ear.

"Uh– nothing, the kid is trying to burn the house down... Gotta go," Nicks hung up the phone and hurried into the kitchen. "Ah damn it."

"So... order pizza instead?" Jude asked, holding the charcoal chicken.

"You can't say I didn't try."

"Valiant effort, sir."

Jessica glanced at Bradley and back to the road. She knew the phone call was work related and by the look on his face she wasn't going to be happy.

"Was that work?"

"It was, Pyke wants us to meet next Thursday at three."

"Bradley, no. You promised–"

"I know, but I have to."

"We are supposed to have dinner with my parents. We have already had to reschedule because of Pyke!"

"Jess–"

"You said after you got out we would be able to spend more time together and all that has happened is you cancelling plans because of work. I feel like you're gone more than ever now!"

"Jess that's not fair…"

"No, what's not fair is you finally being home for good and I still don't get to see you."

"Come on!"

"No! You know it's probably a good thing we can't have kids, because you would just end up missing everything anyway."

"Are you being serious right now? It's dinner with your parents."

"It's all the time!"

Bradley shook his head staring straight ahead fuming. "You are unbelievable."

"We shouldn't even be talking about this right now—"

"No, we shouldn't."

Kari poured the noodles in a serving dish when the front door opened and closed. Bradley looked pissed off and Jessica looked as if she was about to start crying. Clayton knew they had gotten into another argument.

"How many stitches did you get?" Clayton asked, trying to get them distracted.

"None… glued it instead."

"Well aren't you lucky… Put yourself to use and grab the plates."

Bradley picked up the plates and followed Kari into the dinning room.

"Wow, guys this looks really good," Jessica commented in her fake enthusiastic voice and took a seat.

"It's spaghetti..." Clayton replied.

"I love spaghetti," Bradley chimed in and took a big spoonful.

Kari looked from Jessica to Bradley on edge from the tension. Bradley's phone rang and he dug it out of his pocket.

"Can't you at least turn your stupid phone off while we're eating?" Jessica snarled.

"No. I can't because it could be work," Bradley spat through clenched teeth.

"They just called you, what could they possibly want now?"

Bradley glared at her for a moment with a clenched jaw before answering. "Evans."

After a few seconds, his annoyed expression faded into a grim worried gaze. Kari froze knowing something had happened. She wondered who he was talking to and what was going on. Her first thought was Marcus, but he hadn't even left the States yet.

"Joan, Joan... Calm down. I can't understand you," Bradley said.

Kari dropped her fork and it clattered against the plate below. She stared frozen at Bradley, her blood running cold.

"Why is Aunt Joan calling you? Bradley what happened?" Kari asked. Bradley looked at Kari but did not answer her.

"Joan, don't worry we're leaving right now. We'll be there as soon as we can," Bradley stated.

Bradley sat silently for a moment trying to grasp what he had been told. Kari could not handle the silence anymore.

"Bradley!" Kari shouted in distress. "What happened? What did aunt Joan say?"

Bradley was unresponsive; he stared straight ahead. Jessica got up from her seat to stand next to Bradley. She placed her hand on his shoulders in a comforting manner and asked. "Bradley, hun. What happened?"

"There was an accident.... Mom and Dad, didn't make it," Bradley said softly, almost in a whisper.

Kari was overwhelmed with grief and emotions. "This is a joke, right?"

Bradley shook his head. Tears cascaded down her cheeks. "How could this be happening? They can't really be gone!"

Clayton stood and brought Kari into a hug and held her tight. Kari did not protest and she tucked her face into Clayton's shoulder. Tears streamed down her cheeks and onto Clayton's tee shirt.

"I'll drive you guys," Clayton said calmly. "Kar... lets go."

Kari stood and her knees buckled. Clayton's strong arms scooped her and she buried her face back into his shoulder. She prayed it wasn't real.

Bradley and Jessica followed, comforting each other like their argument never happened. Jessica had Amelia hoisted in one arm. Clayton set Kari gently in the front passenger seat and buckled her in. Hot tears flowed as she gazed ahead in a daze. Clayton climbed into the driver's seat. He pulled out of the garage and sped down the street.

Kari's whole world was shattered. She felt like a part of her died with her parents. Kari could not picture her life without them. She thought about their smiles and she felt alone and lost in a world now unfamiliar to her.

"I have to call Marcus," Bradley muttered to Jessica.

"Is he going to be able to come?" Jessica asked.

"He doesn't leave for another five days. We will just have to have the service soon." Bradley tapped Marcus's contact and held his phone to his ear listening to it ring.

Hatch walked to the table with a pitcher of beer in his hand. Kinney had folded his arms on the table with his head down.

"Enjoy it while you can," He said and poured the beer in Marcus's awaiting glass.

Marcus slapped Kinney on the back of the head. "Wake up!"

"Ugh," Kinney mumbled.

Marcus felt the vibration of his phone in his pant pocket and set the beer down. He stood and said, "I have to take this."

Hatch cocked a brow seeing a flash of worry spread across Marcus's features. Marcus stepped out of the bar onto the warm streets of Fayetteville.

"Hey, what's up?"

Bradley was silent for a moment. "Uh…"

"Bradley, are you okay?"

"No– Mom and Dad… They were killed in a crash–"

"What!"

"When can you get here?"

Marcus pinched his forehead. "I– Uh– It's late and I'm drunk– I won't be able to catch a flight until the morning."

"Just get here when you can."

"Bradley… Do you know what happened?"

"No, Aunt Joan called and had limited information."

"How's Kari?"

Bradley glanced up seeing Kari pressed against the window crying. "Not good."

"I'll be there as soon as I can." Marcus hung up.

He walked into the pub in a daze.

"Badger?" Hatch asked.

Marcus shook his head placing his palms on the table. "My parents were killed."

"Oh fuck– Uh… Sorry man, what do you need?" Hatch asked.

"I have to get home," Marcus said.

Hatch snapped his fingers at Moose and dug into Marcus's pant pocket. "Go to his place and pack him a bag. He'll need his Class A's for sure." Hatch tossed the keys to Moose.

Moose was the only one in the team that didn't drink. Came in handy for rides and usually a level clear head kept them out of trouble.

Marcus was about to protest but Hatch ushered him towards the door. "Let's go find you a pilot. We'll get you home."

———

Clayton turned onto the interstate accelerating to a high rate of speed. The car was silent except for Clayton talking to Nicks about picking up the dogs.

Kari sat in the front passenger seat staring out the window, watching cars as they zoomed past them. The cars looked like statues from another world. Tears trickled down her cheeks like the rain outside. Memories of her parents flooding into her thoughts tormenting her at what she lost forever.

Nicks set his phone down with a grim face.

"What's wrong?" Jude asked fearing it had something to do with Garrick.

"Marshal Evans's parents were killed in a crash."

Jude dropped his gaze. "That's awful."

"Yeah… It is…" Nicks looked blankly at the empty pizza box on the counter. "We have to run over to Bradshaw's place and pick up the dogs."

"Okay–"

"Yeah… where are my keys?" Nicks asked, searching the counter.

"Wow, old and blind…" Jude said picking up the keys that were on the table.

Nicks snatched them out of his hand. "If I was allowed to, I would slap you."

Jude smiled. "I'd be worried you'd dislocate an elbow with how frail you are."

Nicks shook his head and closed the door behind him.

The front door was left unlocked and Nicks waltzed into Clayton's house. "This is why he can't have nice things."

The dogs bounded to the front door to greet their visitors with wagging tails. Nicks picked up the puppy and opened the storm door for Jack.

"Can you go into the kitchen and find some dog food? I'll load these guys in the truck."

Jude wandered through the house, impressed that Bradshaw lived there. He walked into the kitchen and looked around. The sketch of Clayton sat at the edge of the counter and caught Jude's eye. He gazed at the great attention detail and was amazed by the talent of the artist. In the corner of the paper a *KE* was scribbled. He tore his attention back to matters at hand. He needed to find the food. The pantry was ajar and he could see the green bag of dog food. He hoisted the once fifty pound bag into his arms and hauled it out to the truck meeting Nicks on the walkway.

"You didn't need to take the whole bag."

"I wasn't about to go snooping through Marshal Bradshaw's kitchen looking for tupperware."

"Fine... let's go," Nicks said and shut the door behind him walking back to the truck.

"Did you lock his door?" Jude asked and placed the food in the truck.

Nicks pointed a finger at Jude. "You are so smart."

Nicks jogged up the walkway and secured the door. He hopped into the truck where Jude was already seated.

"How do you live alone?"

"Sometimes I do get scared at night and have to leave the lights on."

Jude chuckled. "Christ..."

———

Clayton pulled into the dark driveway.

"Kari," Clayton said, gently shaking Kari to wake her.

Kari's eyes sleepily rolled open. She noticed the car was no longer moving. She looked around in a haze and her eyes locked on the window. She saw the comfort of home surrounding her. She turned her head and focused on Clayton's kind face. Kari opened the car door and slid out. She stood in the driveway sorrow filling her knowing that when she walked through the door her parents would not be there.

CHAPTER FIVE

Two days after Kari's parent's deaths she found herself dressed in black, standing in the cathedral. Her brothers, donned in their class A uniforms, stood on each side of Kari. She was in a daze with a surreal scene in front of her. She followed the procession outside. The loud bang of the twenty one gun salute signaled for the sorrow filled bugle to sound the notes of Taps. She glanced at her brothers who did not waver in their stance but tears filled their eyes. The breeze was cool against her skin. Her gaze fixed on a single blade of grass next to the caskets. It danced in the gentle wind. Kari heard the distant cries of her aunt Joan beside her. Kari could not cry anymore. There was nothing left. Everything had been ripped out and now she was broken-hearted and empty. Nothing would matter to her from that day on, she was sure of that. The words from the priest were silent to Kari.

She was too tired to focus on his voice. Kari stood with an empty pain because a drunk driver took her parents away from her. Nothing would ever make up for what was taken. Nothing could replace what she lost. The happy spirit she had was gone and left with a black hole.

Kari went through the day like a zombie. She was there but her mind was elsewhere. It was as if she stopped and the whole world was put into fast forward and everything was swirling around her without her needing to be there. Offered condolences were lost on Kari, they fell soundless onto deaf ears.

Beth and Diego sat next to Kari underneath an oak tree in Kari's back yard. They seemed unsure how to handle the situation. They were afraid that if they tried to comfort Kari, they might say something wrong and make everything worse.

"I'm really going to miss you." Beth choked back the tears.

"I don't want to go. I'd rather stay here," Kari replied as she played with a blade of grass.

"We'll come visit you in Chicago. As much as I can," Diego replied. "We'll stay in touch."

"Guys, I leave in two days."

"I don't know what to say, Kari," Diego said.

"I don't want to go."

"I know. But Bradley will take good care of you," Beth said.

"Yeah..."

Diego hugged Kari. "We love you."

In the distance Kari could see Marcus walking towards them. He looked out of place wearing his class A's with a scruffy beard. It was against normal Army regulation, but with being SF that goes out the door for them.

"Looks like Marcus found us," Beth informed.

"Eh, it was bound to happen," Kari replied with little hope in her voice.

"He looks scrumptious as always," Diego added.

Kari giggled. "Deigo…"

"I got you to laugh didn't I?" Diego kissed Kari on the cheek. "We will give you some privacy."

Diego and Beth walked away giving Marcus a short wave and smile.

"Hey, Kari can I talk to you for a moment?" Marcus asked.

Marcus sat beside Kari. "I– Don't even know what to say–"

Kari gazed off into the distance, listening to Marcus.

"Life… isn't fair at times. You have been robbed of many coming milestones with Mom and Dad."

"You don't need to remind me," Kari wiped the tears from her eyes. "My whole world is upside down right now. I don't know which way is up."

Marcus wrapped his arm around Kari's shoulders.

"In time, it will get easier. Plus you'll have Bradley and Jess."

"I don't want to leave home. All my friends..."

"It's going to be rough for awhile but you will get through this."

"I wish you didn't have to leave." Kari hugged her brother.

"I'll call when I can." Marcus kissed his sister on the top of her head.

Kari soon found herself on her way to Chicago, leaving memory laden places and everything else she loved behind. A new life awaited and she didn't think she was ready for it. Four days flew past in a single blink of an eye. Marcus left days ago and she missed him already. She remained in shock that her parents were gone.

Bradley glanced over at Kari as they sped down the interstate. "So... I enrolled you, or I should say Jessica enrolled you into school."

"Okay... And?"

"You're not going to be happy."

Kari turned her head and stared blankly at him. "Why? It's not an all girls Catholic school is it?"

"No, not at all, but it is a private academy... Cambridge Preparatory Academy."

"You're sending me to a private school? Why would you do that? Are you trying to make this situation worse than it is?"

"I'm trying to make sure you don't get shanked at school."

"Shanked? Really?"

"Look at it as a stepping stone to look good on your college applications."

Kari set her head back on the headrest. "I don't even want to go to college anymore."

"Don't say that–"

Tears flowed from her eyes thinking about her mom and dad.

Bradley reached over and grabbed her hand. "It's going to be okay, we will get through this… Together."

When Kari arrived at Bradley and Jessica's home she grabbed her giant suitcases, a box full of her belongings and headed for her new room upstairs. The room was empty and bare which resembled her soul as of late. She set the box on her bed. She scanned the room and looked over the near empty closet. The school had uniforms and they were hung inside. She gagged. A dark green plaid skirt that had no hope of covering her knees. On a separate hanger was a white long sleeved button up dress shirt with the school crest embroidered on it. Beside the clothes was a dresser on which was placed three pairs of long white stockings and a short green and silver tie. Kari sighed, less than enthused to be every school boy's perverted wet dream. *Why a skirt?* She thought. She had always been more of a pants type of girl.

Kari drew her attention to her belongings and opened the box on the bed. Inside were her beloved posters of classic rock bands. Kari spent most of the day unpacking and filling her room, trying to find a semblance of normalcy.

"Kari... Dinner is ready," Jessica said smoothly and entered the room.

Kari had been avoiding speaking with either of them. Both her and Bradley had attempted to comfort her with pointedly placed cliches and bits of advice on mourning. All of which did not fill the void where her parents once were. She did not have anything to say in return.

Kari followed Jessica to the dining room. She didn't even notice what was on her plate as she moved the food from one end to the other.

"Kari, I'll bring you to school tomorrow," Bradley stated, breaking the silence.

"K," Kari replied.

"You can take the bus home though, because I have to work tomorrow. The people in the office will tell you which bus is yours," Jessica informed between bites.

"Okay, I got it." Kari set her fork down not eating a bite. "May I be excused?"

"You may," Bradley replied.

Kari pushed from the table and went to her room and called Beth. She did not know what else to do.

Bradley looked to Jessica for help.

"What am I supposed to do?" He asked.

Jessica shrugged her shoulders. "Give her time?"

Bradley put his face in his hand. "I don't know if I can do this, Jess."

"It's going to be tough but we can handle this. She just needs time."

Bradley stood and grabbed his plate. "She should have gone to Joan."

"Bradley…"

"It doesn't matter. I have to get to Nicks for work."

"Of course you do…"

"Please, don't do this now. With everything going on—"

"I'm not doing anything. Go– Work."

Bradley huffed and climbed the stairs. He stood outside Kari's door for a moment before knocking.

"Come in," Kari said.

Bradley opened the door. "Hey, I have some work stuff to attend to. Jessica will be here if you need anything… But uh– did you want to talk now?"

"No– I'm okay."

"All right, I'm here if you need anything though."

"I know."

Bradley sat at Nicks's kitchen table with his arm propped up and his head resting in his palm. He was exhausted and emotionally drained.

"I'm sorry about your parents, Marshal Evans," Jude said.

"Thanks, Jude."

"I know you still don't think you made the right decision," Clayton said. "Taking Kari in is a big step, but that's what your parents wanted."

"She should be in Marinette with our aunt. I don't know how to raise a teenager," Bradley admitted.

"You and me both," Nicks piped up glancing at Jude. "You'll be fine, and I think having her go to Cambridge Academy is a good move."

"Which brings me to my next concern…" Bradley stared at Jude. "Please stay away from my sister. The last thing I need is for her to get mixed up with you. No offense or anything, but you understand."

"I'm not offended, sir," Jude said.

"Don't talk to her– You know what, don't even look at her."

Clayton laughed.

"What's so funny?" Bradley asked.

"You are being dramatic. It's a big school, I don't think you have to worry," Clayton said.

Bradley focused back on Jude. "I'm not joking around, keep your distance."

"He gets it," Nicks said. "Can we get to work now?"

Bradley continued to stare at Jude who looked from him to Nicks nervously.

Nicks tossed a file in front of Bradley. "Evans."

Bradley broke his gaze and flipped open the file.

"There's a person of interest I'd like to follow up on," Nicks said. "He doesn't frequent Chicago often but it looks like he has an associate here."

"Who is it?" Jude asked. Nicks spun the file around and slid it in front of Jude. "Makar Rosakov? That's a mistake. He hates Garrick."

"Isn't this guy the one–" Clayton said.

"It is–" Jude said shortly.

"Regardless... I did some digging and Rosakov and Garrick had been associates at one point in time," Nicks explained

"That was until Garrick screwed him over and started doing business with Rosakov's enemy in Azov. Trust me, there is a lot of bad blood between them. There is absolutely no way Rosakov would help Garrick. If anything Rosakov would hide me away out of spite."

"I still want to look into it. So far it has been the only link to Chicago I can find."

"But that's a good thing. Means the kid is safe," Clayton said.

"We need to be prepared," Bradley interjected. "Nicks is right, we might as well run with it."

"So who's the associate here?" Clayton asked.

"Demitri Fedorvo. Owns a fish company," Nicks replied.

"I'm sure he does..." Bradley said.

"I can work on a warrant for phone records to see if they've even been in contact," Clayton said.

"Did you want surveillance or wait?" Bradley asked Nicks.

"Let's hold off for now," Nicks said.

"Would you mind if I took a look at the contacts? I may be able to help," Jude asked.

Nicks handed Jude the folder of names. "Knock yourself out."

Jude scanned the documents in search of familiar names. He picked up a highlighter on the table and ran the ink acrossed a couple names.

"Here," Jude said and handed Nicks the document back. "These are the guys I know for sure are still doing business with Garrick. But they are predominantly on the East Coast and one of them I believe is in France."

Nicks removed the three highlighted pages and distributed them. "Well, lets make these our top priority for now. And this way we now have something to show Pyke that there's some progress."

"I'm sure he'll still yell at us for something," Clayton muttered.

"Maybe if you'd suck less and do better, that wouldn't happen," Nicks joked.

"May I remind you we are a team, so that means we all suck."

CHAPTER SIX

The morning sun peeked through the window as Kari snuggled in her blankets. The first time in days she had finally had a restful sleep. Bradley knocked on the door and pressed his ear to the plank. There was no sound. He couldn't remember if he had told her what time they needed to leave and time was dwindling. He opened the door slightly.

"Kari?" There was no answer and her room was still dark.

The door swung wide and he entered. He gently shook Kari and she turned over with a groan, burying her face into her pillow. Bradley looked at his watch and grabbed her blankets, yanking them from the bed. Kari's eyes flew open from the sudden temperature change.

"Jerk!" Kari shouted sitting up.

"Good morning to you too," Bradley replied cheerily. "You know, if you didn't talk to Beth till two in the morning— You would have been awake by now."

Kari's eyes focused on Bradley. He was donned in muted green tac pants and a simple black tee.

"What time is it?" Kari asked, wiping the sleep from her eyes.

She walked to the closet. Kari held the uniform out and sighed heavily.

"Quarter to five."

"What? Are you serious? Why did you wake me up so early? School doesn't start till eight."

"Well, I have to be at work at six. And since I'm the only one that can bring you to school..."

"You never told me that you have to be at work at six." She groaned.

"I thought I did... But I may not have, sorry."

"What am I supposed to do while you guys work?"

"You're coming with us."

"Do you know what the people at school will think when I come to school in the back of a squad car?"

"It's unmarked and barely looks like a squad car. You'll be fine,"

Kari groaned as she tossed the uniform on her bed and pushed Bradley out of her room. She shut the door in his grinning face.

"Be ready in twenty," Bradley announced, walking down the hall to the kitchen.

Twenty minutes cut it a little close. Kari got ready at her quickest 5 a.m. speed, which was not fast at all it turned out. She threw the atrocious uniform on. It was torture beyond words. How could Jessica suggest a snooty private school? She ran a brush hastily through her long, wavy, ebony hair and topped it in a messy bun. Strands of hair fell out of place at every chance. She quickly applied a touch of makeup to shade her pallid cheeks. To complete the hot-mess look, she finished with thick rimmed eyeliner. She grabbed her backpack and swung it over her slender shoulders. She walked down the hall. Bradley stood at the end of the hall drinking his coffee, waiting for Kari. She walked past him and took the thermos from his hand.

"I need it more than you," Kari stated before Bradley could protest.

"Fair enough," Bradley replied.

Kari slipped on her black Chuck Taylor's that were sitting next to the garage door. Outside, Kari saw Clayton parked on the side of the road in the unmarked Tahoe. The black paint was dull with dirt and grime. While it was unmarked, Kari thought it screamed, *law enforcement.* Kari opened the door and climbed in the back. She crossed her arms in protest to the morning's events.

"What's wrong with you?" Clayton asked, looking at Kari through the rearview mirror.

"I'm tired," Kari stated firmly.

Bradley got into the front seat.

"You sister doesn't seem to be in a chipper mood."

"She isn't a morning person," Bradley answered.

"Yeah, the dark eyes and the medusa bun gave her away."

"You wouldn't be in a good mood either if you were me," Kari spoke up.

"Oh the struggles of teenage life," Clayton laughed.

Kari shoved earbuds in and cranked her music. She stared out the window sulking. The time seemed to go by quickly with the distraction of music. Clayton's eyes darted to the mirror every once in a while, checking in.

"We have to stop at HQ first so I can get the warrant," Clayton said.

"Is Baker going to be in this early to sign it?" Bradley asked.

"Yes, I called ahead."

Kari pulled up her news app and scrolled through the headlines. Her thumb lingered over the bold red text *Seven American Soldiers killed in Afghanistan.* Kari's heart sank. She hadn't heard from Marcus since he deployed. Anxiety and uncertainty filled her being. She hoped he was safe. The worst part was she didn't even know where he was being deployed, their unit bounced around where ever need be.

—

"He's fucking running!" Marcus yelled and chased his target out of a residential building in a Beirut slum.

"Sierra Leader to Nest, HVT Minto is Oscar Mike. Viper 6-5 engaging," Hatch radioed.

"Copy that Sierra Leader– We heard loud and clear the first time," the tactical operations center, they called Nest, replied.

The six team members followed after Marcus in their civilian clothing and body armor. The man in Chinos and a white button shirt rounded a corner and continued through a thin alley. The high valued target turned sharply at the end of the alley onto a street. The buildings were unfinished with blankets and tattered materials covering doors and windows. The streets were littered with rubbish and debris. Marcus dodged people and each step he gained on the man. Minto ducked into the entrance of a five story complex. He continued out of the building into a small concrete and dirt covered courtyard, the building surrounding it in a square.

The target yelled in Arabic and continued to run towards a tunnel in the building. Marcus hated it when people yelled in Arabic, shooting usually followed shortly after. Muzzle flashes erupted from scattered locations in the complex. The sound of rapid fire echoed from the concrete and bullets pecked away at the ground Marcus was running on. Marcus growled praying he wasn't going to get pegged off. *Fuckers.* Hatch and the others positioned behind cement pillars in the open ground level of the complex. They fired at the hostiles in the windows. Marcus ducked and continued his pursuit.

"Badger! We're pinned down. You're on your own," Hatch said and shot a Hezbollah insurgent in the chest causing him to topple over the banister of the balcony.

"Copy," Marcus said quickly, his breath heavy.

"We'll get to you when we can."

"Nest to Sierra Leader, we are tracking Badger South from your location."

The HVT skidded from turning the corner out of the tunnel too quickly. He regained his balance and climbed the stairs to the building next to the complex. The gunfire continued from the courtyard. Marcus reached the landing of the steps. Minto jumped over a two foot wall onto the next rooftop. Marcus followed closing the distance. The target ran to a door and pulled on the handle. The door did not move. He turned to flee but Marcus leapt through the air and tackled him. The force of their bodies broke the door inward and they landed with a hard thud on the concrete dust covered floor.

Minto grabbed Marcus by the shemagh and punched him in the face. Marcus reached up and put the HVT into a headlock. Minto slid a knife from his back waistband and sliced Marcus in the arm. With a groan he loosened his grip.

"Badger!" Hatch called hearing the muffled sounds of a fight.

Marcus manipulated Minto's arm joint and pried the knife away. Marcus slashed at Minto, the blade cutting his left cheek. Minto headbutted Marcus, blood smeared on both of their faces. Marcus was disoriented for a moment giving the target enough time to knock the blade out of his hand. The knife was kicked away as they struggled against each other attempting to gain control.

"Nest to Sierra Leader, Badger is two buildings to the west of your location. Second story inside a residence."

Marcus kicked Minto in the chest causing him to fall onto his back. Marcus rolled on top of him pinning him to the ground. He removed his pistol from his drop holster and pointed it at Minto. He narrowed his brow and raised his hands in surrender.

"I got him," Marcus said out of breath.

Hatch bound through the doorway while the other team members provided cover.

"Nice job, Badger," Hatch said and hit the target with the butt of his rifle.

Marcus holstered his sidearm and flipped the HVT onto his stomach. He grabbed his wrists and secured him into flex cuffs.

"Sierra Leader to Nest, HVT Minto secured."

"Copy that Sierra Leader, good work."

"Sierra Leader to Viper 6-4 for EVAC."

"Viper 6-4 enroute ETA five mikes. Lima point two clicks to you, south in the alley," Bonnet, the team leader of Viper 6-4, confirmed.

A woman stormed out of a back room and shouted in Aribic as she swung a frying pan.

"Kin–" Hatch tried to warn but was too late.

The pan struck Kinney hard in the back of the head. His eyes rolled back and he fell to the ground like a board. Marcus and Minto both looked at Kinney who was out cold. Hatch wrestled the pan away from the woman and shouted at her. The woman disappeared back into the depths of her poverty ridden house. Hatch tossed the pan into the corner and crouched next to Kinney.

He tapped him on the cheek. "Hey, you broken?"

Kinney groaned and blinked his eyes open. He pushed himself to all fours and touched the back of his head that had a small trickle of blood.

"My ex has done worse. I'm good," Kinney rose with a sway.

"Excellent to hear. I do believe you have a new name."

"Please not pan–"

"Even better... Plank."

"Christ..."

"You know– Cause you–" Hatch pantomimed his fall.

"Yeah... I get it."

"Okay, girl scouts, we have a date. Don't want to be rude."

Hatch placed a hood over the target's head and escorted him into the alley. A small blue panel van pulled up. The back door swung open.

"Afternoon gents," Bonnet said.

Hatch pushed Minto into the van head first, his body thudded against the metal floor. Marcus climbed in behind the captive along with Hatch and Moose. The door closed hard and Plank slapped the back door. The remaining three operators piled into the second van.

"There's blood on your face," Hatch said.

"When is there not?" Marcus lifted his arm and examined the steady stream of blood. "Think that will scar?"

Hatch laughed.

———

Another morning and another day. Jude groggily walked into the kitchen welcomed by the smell of something burning.

"What are you trying to cook now?" Jude asked.

Nicks turned from the stove pointing the spatula at Jude. "I only burnt the first few."

Jude perched on a stool at the counter and Nicks slid a plate of flapjacks to him. "Dig in champ."

Jude picked up his fork and took a bite. His eyes went wide and he spat the piece back out. Nicks stared at him offended.

"They can't be that bad– I followed Martha Stewart's recipe!"

Jude took a drink of tea. "Was it for spicy cakes, because then it would be spot on."

"What?" Nicks took a bite of a pancake and spit it into the sink. "Good god."

"I applaud the effort, sir."

Nicks picked up the spice container. "I thought this was cinnamon, it clearly says cayenne."

"Is it time for you to get glasses?"

Nicks took a powerbar from the cabinet. "I have the eyes of an eagle– Eat this and get out of my house."

Jude chuckled. "And grouchy."

"Kid…"

Jude stood holding his bar. "I'm– I'm gonna go before you do Garrick a favor and put a bullet in me yourself… If you can even see me that is."

Nicks quickly stepped around the counter and Jude bolted out the door with a chuckle. Nicks grinned and picked up the plate of pancakes. With a huff he tossed them into the garbage.

"It really can't be this difficult."

———

The SUV pulled up to the curb in front of Kari's new school. The campus was spacious compared to her old school, but the walkways were as crowded as anywhere she had seen. The building was beautiful with its aged brick and contrasting landscape. The campus was vast with tall trees sprouting up in various places. Curious people stared at the tahoe. She knew they were wondering why there was an unmarked squad car on their campus.

"What are you doing?" Kari asked frantically.

"I'm dropping you off. What does it look like?" Clayton questioned back.

"Can't you park in the parking lot like a normal person? Plus it clearly says no parking."

"You see that's the beauty of being a Marshal. You can park wherever you want."

"It's not parking," said Bradley. "We aren't staying, for long anyway." He winked over the headrest.

"Come on," Kari said, crossing her arms and glaring at him.

"Let me get the door for you," Bradley smiled.

Surrounding kids started to gather. Bradley walked to Kari's door and opened it. Kari slowly exited. Her cheeks flushed and her pulse quickened. She clutched onto her backpack strap. A preppy blonde girl, Venessa, was standing by the steps that led to the main entrance. A group of girls surrounded her.

"Oh look another juvy girl with rich parents," Vanessa said when Kari was in earshot.

Bradley and Clayton walked alongside Kari towards the stone steps to the school. Heads turned, watching plain clothed officers escorting the new girl.

"You don't have to walk me in," Kari said barely moving her lips.

"I have to speak with the headmaster. Few things to sort out for your enrollment."

"Jessica should be doing that."

"I agree but she isn't here."

Kari's stomach turned, filling with anxiety. Everyone was staring, wide-eyed with comically confused looks on their faces. After the bell rang, the halls emptied into the classrooms. Kari stood next to Bradley fidgeting with her fingers, waiting. The headmaster's office was attached to a more open room like a teacher's lounge. Clayton stood posted outside having not felt the need to join in the meeting. A beautiful woman entered the room. Her black dress pants hugged her hips revealing her curves. Her shoulder length hair dangled in front of her strong angled face. When she bent to pick up a piece of paper that she had dropped upon entering, Clayton folded his arms across his chest and titled his head to get a good look at her. The women straightened and glanced at Clayton. He quickly looked away pretending to hide the fact he stared at her. She turned her attention back to the copy machine, placing the piece of paper on the surface and punched in a code on the keypad. She turned her eyes to Clayton and smiled. He nodded to her. His shirt was tucked in slightly displaying his star and gun. The woman approached him.

"Hello, Officer," She greeted politely. "If I may be so bold as to ask. What brings you to Cambridge Academy?"

"Well... It's actually Marshal... And if you must know... We believe a prison escapee is masquerading your quiet campuses as beautiful a professor. We have to question everyone," Clayton said.

"Am I a suspect, Marshal?" She asked with an emphasis on 'Marshal.'

"Of course. But the local police station is having all their interrogation rooms professionally cleaned, as it were, leaving little options for interviews. We would need a quiet place, perhaps Venicci's, and I have a slot open for seven," Clayton said.

"Wow. Just getting right to it then?"

"Too much?"

"A bit. I would have started with an introduction," she smiled.

"Clayton Bradshaw," he offered his hand.

"Andi Taylor." She replied as she shook Clayton's hand. "Do police departments have their cells tossed by Merry Maids as well?"

Clayton cleared his throat. "I may have stretched the— You know— Nevermind that." Clayton paused as he stared into Andi's aqua eyes. "Where would *you* like to go?"

"Hmm…" she mused. "Relentless."

"A guy can try."

The copy machine beeped and shuddered, signalling the copies were done. Andi glanced at the machine and back to Clayton.

"Well, Marshal…"

Clayton mouthed his name.

"… Bradshaw. My copies are finished. I should probably get back. My students will think I've been captured by a vile prison escapee." Andi gathered the stack of worksheets.

"Goodbye, Andi."

"Goodbye, Clayton," Andi replied and walked out of the office.

Clayton leaned against the wall with a love struck face.

The door leading into the headmaster's office swung open. Bradley, Kari and Preston Black, the headmaster, exited the room. The headmaster wore an expensive, expertly tailored, black suit. The sharp suit and equally sharp features allowed him to carry himself in an authoritative manner. His face was serious and showed no emotion. The light from overhead shone off of his bald head. Kari thought he looked like a walking version of Professor X.

"It was nice to meet you, Mr. Evans,." Headmaster Black said, shaking Bradley's hand. "I'll keep an eye on

Kari to make sure she doesn't get into trouble." He winked at Kari.

Kari smiled back. Headmaster Black might appear formidable and threatening but he had a lighthearted and jovial voice.

"Well Kar, I'll see you at home. Don't forget to take the bus home," Bradley said .

"Yeah, yeah, I know. You can stop reminding me. I won't forget to take the bus home. Obviously," Kari acknowledged.

"Alright."

"Bye, guys."

"See you later, Kari," Clayton replied.

Kari watched her security detail leave the room.

"So, are you ready to take on the day?" Headmaster. Black asked.

"Um, not really. But I guess I'll have to eventually," Kari replied with a shrug.

"Don't worry. It won't be that bad. I have someone coming to help you out today so you won't be completely lost."

Kari cringed. "Oh, that sounds great."

A girl walked into the room, her long black hair pulled into French braided pigtails. Her big blue eyes were shielded behind thick-framed glasses. Kari could see her spunky up-beat attitude radiating off her.

"You sent for me, Headmaster Black?" she asked.

"Ah yes. Kari Evans, meet Marley O'Dwyer," he introduced. "Marley, I would like you to show Kari around today. You guys have similar schedules."

Headmaster Black returned to his office and shut the door behind him.

"Can I see your schedule?" Marley asked, skipping over the greeting, gesturing to the paper in Kari's hand.

"Sure." Kari handed it to Marley without hesitation.

"This is good. We have all the same classes except for two; calculus and economics."

Kari was confused over her schedule. Mainly because of the whole "Day One/Day Two" ordeal. At her old school they had seven hours every day and switched classes at semester. Her new schedule had twelve hours spread out over two days, lasting the entire year. One good thing about her new school is that they had open campus lunch for an hour. Not that she had any idea where to go.

"Well, let's get to first hour. You'll enjoy this class. Mr. Jennings is really funny."

They walked through the narrow, clean hallways. Dark green lockers lined one side of the hall.

"Kari, may I ask you a somewhat personal question?"

"Sure, go for it."

"Why were you escorted by two cops this morning? What did you do?"

Kari laughed.

"What's so funny?" Marley questioned nervously.

"The Marshals are my brother and his partner," Kari explained.

"Oh, okay. That explains a lot. You didn't really look like the criminal type anyway, but the rest of the school doesn't need to know," Marley said. "You could work the mysterious and dangerous angle."

"Thanks?"

"Which one was your brother?"

"The dark haired one. The blond was Clayton."

"How old is Clayton?"

Kari laughed. " Too old for you."

"Well he's hot."

Marley slowed her pace until she was standing outside the classroom door.

"Here we are, physics," Marley said and opened the heavy door.

Marley entered the room first. Kari followed her, cautiously. Mr. Jennings was a scrawny man who looked older than he was. He wore an ancient sweater and Kari would not have been surprised to see elbow pads on his old corduroy blazer. The man reminded her of one of her math teachers back at her old school. The short man stepped out from behind his podium.

"Class." He paused and motioned Kari to come stand by him. Her stomach sank and her cheeks flushed. "This is Kari Evans. She'll be joining us for the rest of the year," Mr. Jennings announced. "You can sit in that open desk."

He motioned to a desk that was behind Jude. Kari thought he was handsome with his dark hair tousled. He glanced at Kari and back to his desk. He recognized her instantly. She was the idiot that ran into the road on his bike ride last week. He shook his head and went back to copying the notes from the board. Jude looked down and saw he started writing the same line twice. *God damn it.*

Kari walked down the row of desks. Her stomach turned. Everyone watched as she settled into the desk behind the gorgeous boy. She was not graceful and stumbled into her seat. The desk lurched forward hitting Jude's chair. Marley turned around and gave Kari a confident smile from the desk a row over and up one. Jude thought it was comical on how clumsy Bradley's sister was.

Jude turned around. Kari melted when her eyes locked onto his deep blue eyes. Jude was stunned by how beautiful she was, but Bradley's words rang through his mind. Kari did not get the response she expected. Jude narrowed his eyes and stared at her with a stone face. Kari recoiled into her seat. She could not understand why he would be that agitated by a little bump to his seat. Or did she do something else wrong? Did she smell bad? *No, impossible.* She distinctly remembered to put deodorant on. Did she do something wrong to upset this guy so much to deserve that look? Jude turned back around and hung his head placing his hand in his hair.

"Okay class, you have an assignment on the board. Get to work."

Mr. Jennings walked over to Kari and set down a textbook on her desk.

"Here is your book. If you have any questions at all, don't hesitate to ask." Mr. Jennings walked back to his desk.

When the bell rang fifty minutes later, Jude sprang to his feet and bolted out the door. *Christ, why did she have to be pretty?* Jude thought. Kari sat for a moment, stunned by his harsh attitude towards her. Marley walked over to Kari looking concerned.

"He's certainly rude," Kari said and collected her bag.

Marley followed Kari's gaze. "Oh, yeah, Jude... He's new here too and has kept his distance from everyone."

"Well, I'm glad he hates everyone and it wasn't just me."

Marley giggled. "Let's get to English."

They navigated the halls engaged in small talk about where she was from. A boy, Karsten, joined them, one of Marley's friends, and exchanged pleasantries. Jude rounded the corner and fell in step a few paces behind her.

He watched Kari laugh, getting to know those beside her, a hint of jealousy on how easy it was for her to fit in. A small book fell unnoticed from her hands. She kept walking. Jude picked up the old leather bound journal. Kari felt a tap on her shoulder and she stopped.

"Pardon. You dropped this," Jude said.

He handed Kari the journal her father had given her. It must have slipped off of her physics book. Karsten and Marley stopped a few steps ahead of Kari noticing she was not with them.

"Thanks," Kari said surprised by the British accent.

Jude nodded politely and stepped past her. Marley shrugged and they entered the classroom just as the bell rang. The white haired women gave them a curious look and pointed to the empty seats. Jude sat in the back row, Kari was two rows up. She glanced back at Jude and smiled. He dropped his pencil on the floor and he hurried to retrieve it, smacking his head on the desk in the process. Kari let out a small giggle and turned around. Jude rubbed his forehead, *smooth, real smooth you git.*

The day progressed in a daze until the lunch hour rolled around. Marley and Karsten took Kari to a restaurant just off campus with what they claimed was the best Gyros around. As they descended the steps, a group of students thinned and there was a clear line of vision to where she could see Jude. He sat casually on the stone wall. His head turned slowly as if he knew Kari was there and their eyes connected for a moment. Kari looked away quickly and continued to walk. Jude realized that staying away from Kari may be more difficult than he imagined. She was everywhere. Asher and his goons walked in front of Jude obscuring his view of Kari.

"Did you see the new girl?" One of them asked.

Asher's eyes were tracking Kari like prey. "I have– I will get me a piece of that. The things I'd like to do to her."

"Hey, git, she's a person not a piece of meat," Jude said sickened.

Asher narrowed his eyes squaring up to Jude. "I don't think I asked for your opinion."

"And I didn't care to hear yours in the first place. But here we are."

Asher pushed Jude's bag from the wall. Jude watched it hit the ground and the contents splay out.

"Was your father too busy fucking whores to teach you how to be a decent human being?"

Asher clenched his fist.

"What lost the plot?" Jude taunted.

Asher took a step towards Jude.

"Oh, struck a nerve have I?" Jude asked.

One of Asher's friends elbowed him. "Hey."

Asher spotted the Headmaster standing at the entrance of the school.

"You'll get what's coming to you," Asher threatened.

"I'm bursting with anticipation to see you throwing a wobbly later." .

Asher snarled and walked away with his cronies. Jude shook his head and dropped down from the steps to retrieve his belongings. His phone vibrated in his pocket.

Nicks 12:03
You good?

                              Jude 12:03
                              Never better...

Nicks 12:04
That kid really doesn't like you...
I can't imagine why.

                              Jude 12:04
                              Bugger off!

Nicks 12:04
Is that English for fuck off?

                              Jude 12:05
                              Absolutely not, sir

Nicks 12:05
That's what I thought

Jude finished collecting his books and glanced across the parking lot down the street to see Nicks lounging in his car stuffing his face. Jude crossed the campus and plunked under a tree to eat the lunch he packed not trusting Nicks's judgment on food.

—

Jude walked into the house and threw his backpack down on the kitchen table. Nicks walked in behind him.

"How was school?"

"Another successful day of Garrick not showing up and killing me."

"That's good. Means I earned my pay today."

"Honestly– It was awful."

"Why's that?"

Jude sat down on the couch. "Have you seen Marshal Evans's sister?"

"No–"

"She's beautiful... and she's everywhere I go."

Nicks chuckled. "Don't let Bradley hear you say that."

Jude pulled his shoes off. "How pissed do you think he'll be if I talk to her."

"Do you really want to find out?"

"No, but I'd rather have the wrath of Evans than the thought of that git Asher get anywhere near her."

"Is that what your tiff with him was about?"

"I'm surprised that you can't lip read when you watch me through your binoculars."

"Well, when you say it like that–"

"But to answer your question, yes, he had made a snide comment about her."

"Please... I am asking you not to get involved."

"I won't make any promises."

"Ahhh, you're going to make life difficult aren't you?"

"And I haven't done that already?"

Nicks shook his head. "I see what you did there."

CHAPTER SEVEN

Lavish lights illuminated the robust atrium of the elegant building in the heart of Bucharest. Agent Bennet ascended the smooth stone steps donned in a sleek black gown. Elite members of society made their entrances into the Gala.

"Maisie, may I say you are looking exquisite tonight," Agent Conner said through their hidden coms as he adjusted his bowtie at the bottom of the steps.

"I'm going to miss these compliments when you're off in the States."

"Please, don't remind me. I am deeply saddened by our parting."

"I'm sure you are Seth."

Debussy echoed off the grand pillars at the entrance. Maisie stepped towards the social secretary.

"Name, madame?"

"Octavia Veres," Maisie responded.

The man turned the page and nodded. "Enjoy the evening."

Maisie smiled and entered the grand entrance of the historic building. Seth climbed the stairs.

"How are you gents coming along?" Seth asked over the coms.

Loch worked on prying a grate off in the sewer to enter the depths of the building where the Gala was held. A rat scurried over Jedi's foot and he let out a small child-like scream.

"Christ, Ay hate rats," Jedi seethed.

Loch glared at Jedi and pulled the grate down. "Are you sure you're a Scot?"

"We are making entry into the basement now. We will need five minutes before we're ready," Griffin replied to Seth.

Maisie mingled but kept watch not paying much attention to what her company had to say.

"There he is… On your two, near that charming ficus," Seth said and leaned casually against the bar.

A dashing woman smiled at Seth. "Well, hello there."

Maisie tilted her head and looked around a stout bald man. A clear view of a well cut man. Grey speckled through his well groomed beard.

"If you would excuse me," Maisie said to the couple she was engaged with.

The tail of her dress flowed when she maneuvered around guests. She took two flutes of champagne from a server's tray. Garrick was turned away from Maisie as she approached.

"Here you are, darling," Maisie said and offered the flute.

Garrick turned, his icey eyes naturally wandered to Maisie's low cut dress.

"Oh, you are not my date... Although, perhaps you should be. You are more handsome and possibly less boring." Maisie handed Garrick the champagne.

He gazed at the crowd and smiled. "Mistaken me for your date you say? Perhaps you needed a reason to speak to me."

Maisie smirked. "That obvious?"

"I am delighted for the company regardless," Garrick took her hand and kissed it. "Shaun Garrick."

"Octavia Veres."

"Hungarian, but a Brummie accent... I feel as if I am at home."

Maisie smiled. "I was going to say the same thing."

Seth rolled his eyes at the small talk. "Ah yes, all very lovely... Are you gents in position?"

"We are ready," Griffin radioed.

"So tell me Miss Veres, what brings you to Romania?"

Maisie stepped close to Garrick leaning inches from his cheek. "The same reason you are, I expect. I have too much money to know what to do with and am looking for a good time."

A small discoloration in Maisie's ear caught Garrick's attention. He looked closer to see it was an earpiece, expertly concealed and nearly unnoticeable. Garrick kissed Maisie's cheek and slid the tips of his fingers down her arm.

"You are beautiful."

Garrick pulled away and tucked a strand of blonde hair behind Maisie's ear.

She smiled. "Charming."

Seth crossed the room weaving through people. He turned his back to Garrick and pretended to scan the crowd looking for someone. With a quick turn he bumped into Garrick and purposely spilled the contents of his glass down Garrick's arm.

"My apologies," Seth said and turned to find a server.

Garrick glared at Seth. "An unfortunate accident indeed." He drew his attention back to Maisie. "If you would excuse me."

"Of course," she said and Garrick headed towards the restroom.

Seth tracked him through the crowd and watched Garrick disappear down the hall near the restrooms. Garrick retrieved his phone when out of sight.

"Meet me on the roof. MI6 is here." Garrick turned to the stairs.

"Showtime," Seth said through the com. "Anchorage is headed to the loo."

Seth casually approached the hall. He adjusted the cufflink on his arm and opened the heavy door to the men's restroom. He had anticipated Garrick to be inside by the sinks. But there was no one. A quick looked under the row of stalls confirmed Garrick was gone.

"He's not here."

"What do you mean?" Maisie questioned quickening her pace to the hall.

"You heard me the first time. He's gone."

Maisie looked down the hall and saw a door to the left of the restrooms, stairs.

"He took the stairs," Maisie announced.

"Approaching stairwells now. If he's going down, we'll head him off," Griffin replied.

Maisie pushed the heavy oak door open. Garrick looked down from the open stairs several flights above. He took off up the flights multiple steps at a time. Maisie's heels flew off and she bound up the stairs after him. The concrete was cool against her skin.

"He's going to the roof," she said quickly over the coms.

Seth bolted out of the restroom and collided into a gaggle of women talking, obstructing the entire width of the hall and moving ever so slowly preventing Seth from effectively getting to his destination. *Move out of the way you cows.* Jedi and Loch heard the heavy footfalls above them. They quickened their pace, gaining on Maisie's pursuit. The metal roof access door swung open and clashed against the stone building. The thump of helicopter rotors echoed down the stairwell. Maisie pushed hard in a desperate attempt to apprehend her target.

Her hands hit the bar of the door and pushed it open. The concrete behind her chipped away in a spray of bullets. She dove to her right behind a half wall. Muzzle flashes erupted from the entryway and Jedi and Loch returned fire at the assailant aboard the helicopter. The small bird lifted from the rooftop.

Garrick waved to Maisie. "Sorry I've got to cut short our evening," shouted Garrick. "Business, you know."

The bird turned sharply away. The access door again flung open. Seth huffed seeing the bird in the distance. He bent forward placing his hands on his knees. "Damn it."

"Bandit 1, HVT has escaped," Loch said over the coms.

———

"Sorry I'm late," Nicks said and took a seat in the briefing room.

Pyke slid a file to Nicks. "Did your knitting club go long?"

"No, sir, my visit with your wife took longer than I planned."

Pyke shook his head. "I hate you."

"Can we start now? I have an episode of *The Young and the Restless* to get back to," MacTavish said.

Pyke stared blankly at MacTavish for a moment. "I have given you the latest After Action Report from MI6. They had a failed op where they attempted to apprehend Garrick at a Gala in Romania. If Garrick wasn't being careful before we can guarantee that he will be even more difficult to find. The HVT, Preece, captured by Delta in Lebanon is a dead end, in more ways than one. However, a piece of intel they were able to pull from Preece was from his cell phone, leading MI6 to Romania. SAS and MI6 have hit multiple targets that were provided by Jude and everything had been cleaned out."

"What does the CIA have?" Bradley asked.

"They have been surveilling the Middle East. Garrick isn't going to close up shop so they're certain they'll come up with something," Pyke explained. "Where are you guys at with the domestic contacts?"

"We were looking at Makar Rosakov, but Jude is certain that he would not help Garrick. Clayton was granted the warrant for phone records from the contact in Chicago," Nicks said.

"And…?" Pyke asked.

"There doesn't seem to be any contact from Rosakov that I can find. I don't think there needs to be any more effort put into that lead," Clayton said.

"There are three leads that Jude narrowed down for us that he knows still work with Garrick. I put an alert on their passports and security cams at the major airports," Nicks stated.

"Good, good. Um… who are they?" Pyke took a drink from his coffee mug.

"Pierre Daquin, Kristoph Maas, and Daniel Muller." Nicks handed Pyke the POI, person of interest, sheet.

"Excellent work, keep it up." Pyke drumed the table with his hands. "That's all I had. Let me know the progress on the three POIs. Oh, I also scheduled Jude's interview with the CIA. I will email you with the details when I get back to my office."

"He's going to be thrilled about that…" Nicks muttered.

"It's a necessary evil, just make sure he's ready." Pyke stood. "And Nicks the jokes on you, you can have my wife. She nags too much."

Nicks chuckled and shuffled his papers together.

"How is living with the delinquent?" MacTavish asked.

"He's not a delinquent. If you'd take a moment to get to know him… Oh wait, that's right– House Nanny."

"Ha, I am rolling in laughter."

"No, he's really a good kid."

"Right... What do you actually think his body count is up to?"

"What's yours?" Bradley chimed in.

"I don't work for an arms dealer though."

"Like he had a choice... What's your deal today MacTavish?"

"Didn't you hear him earlier? He's missing *The Young and the Restless*," Clayton said.

Nicks stood holding his files. "Well if you'd excuse me, I have a Sox game to watch soon, with the assassin."

"I'm surprised he hasn't turned you into a soccer fan yet," Bradley laughed.

Nicks paused at the door and pretended to be trying to recall something. "Oh, I forgot to tell you... Jude thinks your sister is hot and plans on asking her out tomorrow."

Bradley turned a ghostly white. "What?" MacTavish and Clayton bursted into laughter.

"Good night," Nicks said and disappeared.

———

"Did you see that?" Jude asked, pointing to the Sox game on the TV. "The– what do you call that guy again? The wicket-keeper, you know the one with the mask at the first base that catches for the bowler?"

Nicks looked up from his computer thoroughly confused. "What did you just say?"

"The wicket-keeper…"

"Do you mean the catcher?"

"Whatever! Did you see that we scored because the… Catcher missed the pitch from the bowler."

Nicks pressed his temple. "You're going to give me a stroke… The pitcher. I swear you are doing this to me on purpose."

"Yeah, that's what I meant, the bowler." Jude smirked.

Nicks shook his head and glanced back at his laptop in dismay. He had been reading through records and scouring databases digging up anything he could on Kristoph Maas.

"Are you okay? You're not even watching the match," Jude asked.

Nicks slowly shut the laptop.

"What's wrong…? You didn't even correct me."

"We need to chat–"

"Oh?"

"MI6 had located Garrick in Bucharest."

Jude felt like he was thrown into ice.

"That's a good thing isn't it? They can go get him."

"They tried, and he got away."

Jude stared at the floor. "Of course he did… They're never going to catch him. I'm going to be hiding the rest of my life."

"It's going to take time–"

"You keep saying that..." Jude stood. "Are you sure I can't have a pint?"

Nicks took a breath and set the laptop down on the coffee table. "Sit down, Jude."

Jude gazed at the ceiling and reluctantly sat. His leg bounced from the anxiety coursing through his body. The image of Garrick killing his mother played through his memory. He balled his fist on his knee fighting the urge for blood, for revenge.

"I can't do this–" Jude said nearly a whisper.

"Can't? Are you serious? *Can't* is an excuse. *Can't* is what you say when you don't have the drive or the motivation to conquer the task at hand."

Jude stared at Nicks, a darkness in his eye. "I'm sick of hiding. I want him to find me. I want this to end. I can't look over my shoulder anymore. I can't hold back the rage I have. I can't get the images of him killing my mother out of my head."

"Revenge is not a road you want to go down. It will only end with your death."

"Then so be it. I have nothing left anyway."

"What a load of horseshit. You have your whole life ahead of you. This– this whole thing will end one day. This does not need to define you. This can make you stronger. This can give you the motivation to make something of yourself, but that is up to you. The pity party needs to end. I know you've been through hell and back and have a long way to go but you need to get your shit together. Do you think your mother would want you to throw your life away? I doubt it. She'd want you to move on, to put this past you. But what do I know? If you are hellbent on throwing your life away... There's the door." Nicks motioned to the front door. "Go find Garrick. I'm sure he'll be eager to see you."

Tears formed and Jude desperately held them in. He turned his attention back to the TV. "Your favorite batsman is up."

Nicks stared at Jude, a young man with a heavy weight on his shoulders. "It's batter." Nicks wished Jude would open up so he could help him.

———

The dark living room flickered with lights from the TV. Kari was curled into a ball snuggled in a blank at the opposite end of the couch from Bradley. The lamp next to her illuminated the pages of the book she was reading for school. Nicks's comment continued to ring through Bradley's ears.

"How's school?"

"It's school. I met some nice people that I think I'll be friends with," Kari said, not tearing her gaze away from the pages.

"That's good..." There was a long pause. "Any of them boys?"

"Uh– Yeah, a couple."

"Any of them might turn into being more than friends?"

Kari picked her head up. "What?"

"Do you think any of them will ask you out?"

"Um, I doubt it. Not exactly something I'm looking for right now."

"Right... Smart."

"Why are you being so weird?" Kari asked.

"I just want to make sure you're doing okay... With everything that's going on. I didn't want something like that to make things more complicated. Just trying to look out for you."

Kari wiped the forming tears away. "You sound like dad–" The tears flowed more and she didn't bother to rid them as her shoulders trembled. "I miss them so much."

Bradley scooted over to Kari and hugged her. "Me too."

Kari wiped the tears and sat up. "So... I've been putting a lot of thought into this and I'm going to apply to West Point."

"You what?" Bradley was utterly surprised.

"I think it would have made dad proud."

"Dad would have been proud of you with whatever you do."

"I know but, it's a way to keep his memory alive for me. It's something I feel I have to do. Like you said, the Army always needs JAG Officers."

"I'm not sure I like the idea of you out ranking me–"

Kari punched Bradley in the arm. "You'll have to call me Lieutenant."

Bradley chuckled. "That will be the day."

CHAPTER EIGHT

A week went by and Kari was everywhere. Jude would take alternate routes around school to avoid her. The board in Physics outlined questions needed to be answered in groups. Jude and Kari's desks faced each other as they had been paired up. Her eyes a dark hazel that Jude couldn't help but stare at. *I'm dead, Marshal Evans is going to kill me.*

"What did you get for the second one?" Kari asked, flipping through her text book.

"Uh..." Jude was so focused on Kari that he hadn't read the question. "A clear object can be transparent and seen at the same time because of refraction."

"Right... duh. The object is still translucent but we're seeing the distorted waves through the object."

"Exactly," Jude said transfixed by her.

Kari cocked a brow. "Why do you keep staring at me?"

"I'm not." Jude dropped his head reading his textbook.

Kari set her pencil down. "If you would like you could come with us to lunch today. I think we're going to that little taco stand down the block."

Jude didn't lift his head. "I have plans for lunch."

"Like sitting by yourself?" Kari didn't mean to come across as snippy but there it was.

Jude lifted his eyes slowly. "I don't need any more friends."

"I was trying to be nice."

"Well, don't be."

"Noted... So let's just get these questions answered and be done with it." Kari turned the page of her textbook.

"What do you think I've been trying to do?" Jude said scribbling down an equation. "For number five, use the equation for kinetic energy."

"I know."

Kari flipped her notebook over having filled her current page. An intricate sketch of Jude sitting by the wall outside took up most of the paper. Kari's cheeks turned red and she tried to quickly turn the page hoping Jude didn't notice. Jude stopped her with a touch.

"You drew this?"

"Uh– yeah."

"You're talented." It dawned on Jude that the drawing at Marshal Bradshaw's home was from Kari.

"Thanks... I uh, hope you don't mind that I drew you."

In the picture Jude sat on top of the wall looking down the street with a stern and worried look. She had captured a moment that Jude so often had; thinking about Garrick.

"No– It's good. I'm astonished by how detailed it is. You have a real gift."

"Thank you." Kari turned the page. "We should finish this."

"Yes."

Kari dropped her head to scan her text book. Jude glanced at Kari amazed by her.

The bell rang signally the end of Jude's torture. He wanted nothing more than to get to know the beautiful and talented person in front of him.

"Remember class, take a permission slip before you leave. I would hate for any of you to be left behind while the rest of us get to experience the kinetic thrill of roller coasters," Mr. Jennings said, pointing to the stack of papers on his desk.

Jude turned his desk back around, grabbed his permission slip and left the room without another glance.

When the final bell rang for the day, Kari walked out of the classroom, her math book clenched in her hands. She turned the corner and ran into Jude. Her book fell to the ground. She tucked her hair behind her ear as she bent down to retrieve her book.

"I'm sorry." She felt like an idiot for not watching where she was going.

Jude picked up the book before she could.

"It's okay," Jude said. He stood and smirked reading the title, *The Canterbury Tales*. "Chaucer, my father would read this to me when I was a child."

"It's for my Brit lit class–"

"If you need help with it, uh– I would be happy to assist… I know it can be difficult to decipher."

"Yeah– thanks, I'll keep that in mind."

Kari walked away and turned around after a couple steps. Jude smiled at her and turned the corner. The halls were crowded with everyone leaving for the end of the day. Marley offered Kari a ride home and was told to meet at the oak tree in front of campus. She was thankful that she had made at least one friend. It made the transition to a new school easier.

Jude walked out of the main entrance, his attention drawn to Kari. She was literally everywhere, all the time. Asher shoulder-checked Jude from behind causing him to lurch forward.

"Oye look! Et's Harry Potter," Asher taunted in his sad attempt at a British accent. "You going to ride away on a broomstick?"

This wanker, I swear. Jude had enough of him. He was not one to let someone push him around and he had reached the final straw.

"Touch me again wankstick—"

"A wankstick?" Asher tapped his chin. "You know, I never did get to finish our encounter from last week. I forgot what set you off... Oh that's right, the things I'd like to do to the new girl. Have you seen that ass?"

"Stay away from her," Jude warned.

"Is that a threat? Do you know what I do to people like you?"

Jude laughed. "You think I am afraid of some git like you?" *If you only knew.*

"What are you looking at?" Kari asked, following Marley's gaze.

Ahser shoved Jude. Jude took a breath, staring him down. Asher rolled up the sleeves of his dress shirt.

"Come on then, Brit," Asher egged Jude on.

There was a group of people noticing the dispute between the two. The surrounding students started cheering on Asher. Kari guessed that *Mr. Popular* was high and mighty up on the totem pole. Asher was tall and strong, his short dark cropped hair made him look rugged and handsome. She wondered what could have happened for a physical fight to arise. Nicks sat across the school on a side street reading the newspaper. He glanced up seeing a group of students accumulated at the bottom of the steps looking over each other's shoulders. He didn't think anything of it and went back to reading the paper waiting for Jude to leave school.

Marley walked over to the commotion, wanting to see whatever might develop. Kari reached out and grabbed her arm to restrain her.

"What are you doing?" Kari asked, surprised Marley would want to watch something like that.

"I'm going to watch this. It'll be a good fight." Marley pulled away with Kari hesitantly following.

Jude watched Asher intently as Asher pranced around in a boxer's stance. There was no fear in Jude's eyes, just anger. Asher stepped forward and threw the first punch with immense force. Kari held her breath. At the last second Jude shifted his weight to his left deflecting the punch. Asher's fist whizzed past his head. At the same time he threw his left fist into Asher's face. The blow was too fast for Asher to see coming. Asher staggered back shaking his head, stunned by the blow.

Kari looked around for the teachers but none came. Asher wiped blood from a split lip and held his fists up shaking out the pain. Asher spat blood in Jude's face and threw another punch. Jude narrowed his eyes and side-stepped to Asher's right, grabbing a hold of his arm. Jude used Asher's own momentum and directed him to the ground. Asher fell hard with a thud. Jude wound Asher's arm behind his back and drove his knee into the middle of his shoulder blades keeping Asher planted. Kari looked up again searching for the teachers that should be running out of the school doors to stop the fight. Nothing. No one came. Not one person. She helplessly turned her gaze back to the brawl to see something she had not expected. While she looked for the teachers the tables had turned on Jude.

A well-built boy grabbed Jude from behind, restraining him. Asher smiled, rose and stood in front of Jude smiling. He punched Jude in the face. Jude took the blow and struggled to free himself from the massive arms that trapped him there.

"I'll enjoy this," Asher sneered and took a step back. With all his strength he threw a low punch into Jude's abdomen.

Jude winced in pain as the second strike came. The wind was knocked out of Jude. His anger rose and he wanted to inflict great harm on his attackers. He stomped on the guy's foot and whipped his head back striking the kid in the nose. The grip was loosened and Jude dodged a wide fist from Asher's other croany. Asher took a step back and launched his fist into Jude's jaw when he wasn't looking. Jude's head went with the motion of Asher's follow through. Kari closed her eyes tight, wishing it would end. The cheers of the crowd grew louder. Jude bent his head forward, blood ran down the side of his face. Kari couldn't take it anymore. She had to do something.

"Stop it!" Kari shouted with every ounce of breath she could muster.

The cheering stopped abruptly and everyone froze. They stared at the new girl who dared speak out against Asher. Kari felt her cheeks burn bright red with embarrassment. She could not believe she shouted. Kari tried to compose herself so she wouldn't look like a frightened deer. Asher approached to give her a piece of his mind.

"So, you don't like it when people take out the trash?" He asked with a matter of fact tone.

"I... I..." Kari stammared.

"What is it? Can't talk now?"

"I can speak," Kari said, irritated.

"Then what's your problem? Or do you just like being a pain in the ass?"

"I don't like it when people gang up on innocent people and beat them to a pulp," Kari stated more bravely than she felt.

Kari gazed at Jude who was on his hands and knees staring back at her with soft confused eyes, blood dripping from the gash on his brow. He was thankful for her intervening but he worried what Asher was going to do. The guy who had held him, kicked him in the face. Jude collapsed to the ground unconscious.

"That bag of shit behind me is not innocent. He made the mistake of mouthing off to me." Asher defended his actions with a bright smile.

The gathered students were frozen, waiting to see what would happen. Marley fled the scene to get help.

"That doesn't give you the right to inflict physical harm on someone," Kari snapped back.

"You're new here, right?" Asher asked. "You're quite beautiful. I would hate to see anything happen to you."

Asher brushed her cheek with the back side of his hand. She swatted his hand away. He snarled and grasped her wrist tightly.

"Do you know what I do to people who talk back to me?" He asked, his anger rising.

Kari's blood froze and she stared at him, anxiety brewing.

"I teach them lessons. Like the one you saw with that piece of shit. But sometimes I'm not as nice. Sometimes I get carried away." Asher grabbed her bicep with his other hand.

"Don't touch me!" Kari spat baring her teeth.

Kari took a step back and another, but Asher stepped with her, his grip tight. Her heart raced and her breath quickened. Kari took another step back. She glanced down at Jude, who was motionless. She pulled from his grip and sprinted through the crowd and continued as fast as she could down the sidewalk. She could hear the footfalls behind her. She had no idea where she was going but she cut down an alley a block from the school. Asher grabbed her by the waist and picked her up from the ground. He pinned her against the wall, brick scratching the back of her head.

Jude opened his eyes, his head throbbed. He looked up and saw that Kari and Asher were both gone. He scrambled to his feet. The herd of students were dispersing. One of Asher's goons was still there. Jude grabbed him by the collar and shoved him against the wall.

"Where did they go?"

The boy was caught off guard and pointed down the sidewalk. Jude took off in a sprint ignoring the pain from his beating and weaved through the students.

"Where do you think you're going?" Asher snarled and pinned her wrists above her head.

"Let me go!" Kari yelled and looked to see if anyone had followed. Her heart sank and fear gripped her when she saw no one.

"I don't think so."

"Get your hands off of me!"

"Don't worry it won't take long."

Kari tried to struggle free but he was too strong. Kari screamed in fear, hoping someone would hear her. Asher wrapped his thick hands around her thin neck. He applied pressure to her throat. Tears rolled down Kari's cheeks and she gasped for air.

"Don't scream again," Asher warned.

Kari grabbed Asher's forearm trying to pry it off of her. She dug her nails into his skin. Jude rounded the corner and his stomach sank seeing Asher attacking Kari. He wrapped his arm around Asher's neck and pulled him from Kari. Blackness crept into her field of vision and she collapsed to her knees. A violent cough escaped her lips. She peered up from the ground to see Jude on top of Asher throwing punches. Rage flowed through Jude. He would not tolerate someone putting hands on a woman let alone Bradley's sister.

Footfalls echoed down the alley. Kari's eyes darted to see Headmaster Black and another teacher running towards them.

"Jude. Jude!" Kari said, trying to get his attention, "Black is coming." She worried that Jude would get in trouble.

Jude ignored her. Asher managed to throw a fist and nailed Jude below his eye. Jude pushed Asher back to the ground and grabbed the collar of his shirt lifting him slightly from the pavement. Jude brought his fist back ready to finish Asher off. But before he could strike him, Black wrapped an arm around Jude's chest and with little effort pulled him off of Asher. The other male teacher went to Asher's aid. His head lobbed as he gripped onto consciousness. Jude did not resist Black's restraint.

"That is enough!" Black stated, fuming and released Jude. "The hell! My Office now!"

Jude stepped to Kari before Black could.

"Are you alright?" He asked.

"Uh... I will be, yes." Kari grabbed Jude's hand and he lifted her to her feet.

Kari had gotten up too fast and felt faint. She staggered for a moment and fell into Jude's chest. Jude placed his hands on her shoulders stabilizing her and pushed her gently away from his body putting space between them.

"Thanks," Kari said weakly.

"Don't worry about it."

Jude gently held onto Kari as she steadied on her feet. Her eyes lingered on him feeling drawn to him.

Headmaster Black put a firm hand on Jude's shoulder. "Let's keep it moving." Black gave Kari a concerned look.

They walked back to the school silently. Marley sat in one of the chairs in the office, her leg bounced with anxiety. Marley got to her feet when Kari entered the room, a wash of relief came over her.

"Kari, I came here as fast as I could. You good?" Marley asked.

"Of course," Kari lied. She wasn't fine. She wanted to curl up in a ball and cry. She was overwhelmed to the point she felt sick to her stomach.

"Are you sure? Because I know what Asher has done to people and I'm just worried I may have been too late." Marley glared at Asher and touched Kari's face turning it every which way.

"Marley, I'm okay," Kari stated and grabbed Marley's wrists, removing her hands from her face. Kari glanced at Jude and back at Marley. "Besides, Jude was there to help."

Marley turned her gaze at Jude with an odd sort of look of disbelief.

"You know it was your fault to begin with," Marley said pointing a finger at Jude.

Jude furrowed his brow and cast his gaze to the floor. *How was this my fault?*

"All of you sit, and no talking," Black commanded, pointing to the open seats before he disappeared into his office.

Kari stared up at the clock watching it tick. Time was moving slowly and her anxiety built with each passing second. Jude glared at Asher, hate brewing. He cast his gaze back to the floor when it hit him. He just got into a substantial fight, they were probably going to call the Police. Nicks was going to be furious. Jude was anticipating Nicks to storm in any second. *He had to see what happened right?* Jude was surprised Nicks hadn't intervened earlier.

"All right," Black said, shutting the door behind him. "Your guardians were notified. Seems none of them wish to involve the Police at this time. But that still is yet to be determined, until we can figure out what had occured."

Jude felt guilty that the reason Asher wasn't going to be getting into real trouble was because of him. The Marshals no doubt were saving Jude's ass. Asher sat in a chair across from Kari, an ice pack laying across his eye. He glared at her for a moment before returning his attention back to the headmaster. Jude put his head in his hands.

"What happened?" Black questioned.

No one answered.

"This is serious and I better get some answers," Black said, increasing the intensity of his voice.

Kari didn't know what to do. If she told him what happened would Asher come back for her? She started picking at her nails avoiding Black's eyes.

"Fine, if this is how it's going to be, I'll ask all of you questions individually. Kari you're first," Black informed and opened the door to his office.

Kari got up. She hesitated, not knowing what she was going to do. She glanced at Jude and saw that he was looking up at her with a concerned gaze. She proceeded to Black's office. He sat at his desk waiting for Kari to sit down.

"Kari, I have a pretty good idea about what happened. Just start from the beginning..."

Kari divulged the events to the headmaster.

Nicks walked into the office seeing Jude holding a bloodied washcloth. Jude looked up at him anxiety coursing through his body. Nicks motioned for Jude to stand and looked him over placing his hands on his shoulders.

"Are you okay?" Nicks asked, touching Jude's face getting a closer look at the damage.

"I've had worse," Jude replied. "Where were you?"

Nicks pushed Jude in the back. "Let's have a chat outside for a moment," Nicks said looking at Asher and Marley.

Nicks closed the office door behind them. "I didn't see what happened. Christ kid, what were you thinking? Why didn't you walk away? And then Evans's sister– Jude."

Jude wiped his face. "I don't know, I just snapped. I couldn't take getting pushed around. And then–" Jude gestured to the office. "Bradley's sister is not very smart! She interjected herself... I couldn't just leave her to fend for herself with that prat."

"This is not what we needed..." Nicks grumbled and turned his head hearing the front doors open and close down the hall.

Bradley stormed down the hall, Clayton trailed a step behind him.

"Uh– He doesn't look happy..." Jude muttered.

The door opened again and an older business man walked in. "Good luck with him..." Nicks motioned to Bradley with a thumb. "I'm assuming that is Asher's father. If you would excuse me.."

Jude stepped back bracing himself from the wrath of Marshal Evans.

"Explain yourself!" Bradley demanded.

"I–"

"A fight! Look at your face." Bradley peered into the office and saw the damage done to Asher. "Christ!"

"If you–"

"What happened to keeping a low profile? And my sister! How did she get wrapped up in your mess? You're supposed to be staying clear of her."

Jude threw his hands up in the air. "It's not like I planned for any of this to happen!"

"I am sorry this happened to you," Black said to Kari. He stood and made for the door.

Kari followed and exited his office only to be surprised to see that Jude was no longer there. She looked at Marley and followed her gaze. Kari saw Bradley ripping into Jude in the hallway. Jude was equally animated and it shocked Kari that they would be yelling at each other in such a manner.

"I don't know why she felt the need to step in. But if I hadn't found her, sir, I don't want to know what Asher was going to do to her. I wasn't about to let anything happen to her."

Bradley took a calming breath and touched Jude on the shoulder. "Thank you, Jude. But this doesn't mean you're off the hook for fighting." Bradley glanced up and saw Kari staring at them.

Bradley pushed the door open and hugged his sister.

"Kari, did he hurt you?" Bradley asked. He looked Kari over for any sign of harm.

"No... I'm okay. I just want to go home."

"Are you sure?" Bradley asked, seeing the trauma in her eyes.

She shook her head ever so slightly no. "Can we just go home?"

Kari's eyes wandered back to Jude. He was engaged in a conversation with Clayton.

"Yeah, we can go." Bradley said.

"Way to piss off Evans, do you know how much work it is to calm him down?" Clayton said.

"Sir, I–"

"You don't have to defend yourself to me, I get it... But from now you are going to try a whole hell of a lot harder to stay clear of Kari. We can't have him like this all the time, it's bad for everyone."

"Message received, sir."

Bradley picked up Kari's backpack that Marley had brought in.

Kari looked at Marley. "See you tomorrow"

"Bye," Marley replied quietly and scooted out the door.

Bradley held the door for Kari.

"You're lucky kid," Clayton said sternly out of context pointing his finger in Jude's face.

Jude dropped his gaze when Kari passed and Clayton fell into step behind them. Nicks and Asher's father walked to the office. Nicks pointed to the door for Jude to go back inside for his interview.

The black SUV awaited, and Kari climbed in the back. The ride was unusually quiet. Kari was surprised that they weren't lecturing or drilling her with questions. Her stomach turned with the growing silence.

"Kari, you really need to be careful," Bradley said. "Getting involved in a fight... Christ, to think what could have happened."

"I know, I'm sorry.."

"Kari, that boy Jude, you're not friends with him are you?"

"No–"

"Please keep it that way."

"It won't be a problem." Kari leaned her head against the window.

Anxiety filled her stomach as she wondered what Asher would have done to her if Jude didn't show up.

Nicks sat back in a chair with his arms crossed. Asher and his father, Aldrich, sat across from him. He eyed Nicks in his jeans and Red Sox t-shirt, probably wondering how someone like him could afford tuition at Cambridge.

"What is it that you do exactly?" Aldrich asked.

"I'm an importer/ exporter."

"What is it that you import and export."

"Nylon mostley."

"Nylon?"

The office door opened and Jude stepped out looking defeated. Nicks draped his arm over Jude's shoulders and they walked out.

"What's the damage?" Nicks asked.

"Detention once a week and a write up."

"Not so bad... Could have been much worse."

"Yeah, I know."

"Let's go home, and put this behind us."

The sight of Jude's new home was welcomed. He dismounted his bike and walked in, Nicks a couple paces behind him. Jude pulled his gloves off and saw the dried blood on his knuckles. He stared at it, the room spun and he felt a heaviness in his body. Panic set in the longer he stared at the blood. Images of killing Payne flooded his mind. The sound of a gunshot pierced his ears, his mother falling to the floor. Jude's breath quickened and he gasped for air. His mind shifted to Asadabad, something he had not thought of in quite some time. It was all too much. The blood on his hands would not leave him.

"Payment has been secured," Wallace said in a Scottish accent.

Jon turned to his client and spoke in Aribic. "The weapons are yours."

The leader, Qasim Asaad, nodded and turned to his men ordering them in Aribic. The soldiers lifted the heavy crates of RPGs and disappeared out of the small house in a village outside of Asadabad. They loaded them into a truck and threw blankets and wooden vegetable crates over their cargo, as they had done many times before. Asaad was one of Garrick's prominent customers at the time. Dust flew as they drove down the sand packed road.

"Well gents, shall we?" Collin said slinging his rifle and stepped to the door.

"Yes, I hate this shithole," Wallace said.

They exited the building to their two pickup trucks. Gunfire erupted from behind them. Four military trucks sped towards them filled with Afghan soldiers.

Jon returned fire. "Get to the truck, James!"

Jude sprinted to the truck. Wallace stood behind the engine block shooting the soldiers that climbed out of the back of their trucks. Collin hopped into the driver's seat and started the truck. Jon yelled out in pain and fell to the ground holding his abdomen.

"Go!" Jon ordered waving at Jude to leave him.

Jude shook his head and hurried to his brother.

"Shite!" Wallace ran to help Jude.

Jude lifted Jon, his arm wrapping over Jude's shoulders. Jon lifted his rifle and continued to shoot. Wallace stepped in front of Jude providing cover with suppression fire. Collin put the truck in reverse, stopping steps behind them. Wallace jumped in back and lifted Jon onto the bed of the truck. Rage ignited within Jude and he stared down his sights. He aimed at the closest soldier and fired two shots hitting him, blood splattered from his head. Jude pivoted looking past his sights and aligning them quickly squeezing the trigger of his rifle. Another soldier fell.

Wallace fired from the bed of the truck. "Get in!"

Jude lowered his rifle and climbed into the truck. Wallace continued to fire and mule kicked the cab signalling Collin to move out. The truck lurched forward and accelerated quickly. Jude sat down using the tailgate as cover and fired at the Afghan military. They loaded their trucks and followed. Collin drove evasively through the small town and hit the open road towards Jalalabad losing the squad of soldiers.

Jude slung his rifle behind him and lifted Jon into his lap.

"Jon, hang in there," Jude said looking at the blood flowing out of his wound.

Jon reached up and Jude grasped his blood covered hand. Jude choked back the tears as his brother stared at him, the light slowly leaving his eyes.

Tears streamed down Jude's cheeks. His body trembled. He stared at his hands, all he could see was his hands dripping with his brother's blood, and the blood of people he killed.

"Jude!" Nicks called out stepping in front of him.

He placed both his hands on the side of his face. "Jude, look at me!"

Jude shifted his eyes from the blood to Nicks, terror gripping him. Nicks grabbed a chair from the table and slid it behind Jude.

"Sit down." Jude collapsed in the chair. "Breath, slow your breathing."

Jude tried to concentrate on his breathing but the images of death and gunfire would not fade.

"Deep breaths... slow your breathing..."

Jude shut his eyes tight and focused on Nicks's voice. He could feel a slight calm taking hold as his breathing returned to normal.

"That's it kid."

Jude opened his eyes seeing Nicks crouched in front of him. Panic, terror, sorrow, plagued Jude's features. Nicks wrapped his arms around Jude and pulled him in for a hug. Tears cascaded and he shuttered from the emotions he was experiencing.

"You're okay... Let it out," Nicks coached.

After a moment Jude sat back wiping the tears away. "I'm sorry, I don't know what just happened."

Nicks pulled a chair and sat in front of Jude placing a hand on his knee. "That was an anxiety attack."

Jude took a breath. "But I don't have anxiety."

Nicks took a napkin from the table and wiped the blood from Jude's hands. "You have experienced a lot of trauma."

"My brother– It wasn't a hunting accident... "

Nicks glanced up at Jude. "I know–"

"We were in Asadabad, I... I... Couldn't save my brother. I watched him die in my arms and there was nothing I could do. I killed them, I killed those soldiers that attacked us. I can still hear the gunfire and feel the recoil of the rifle."

Jude's breathing quickened, his eyes fixated on the floor.

"Jude–"

"I haven't told anyone—" Jude shook his head. "I can't... I can't get the look in his eyes out of my head. The blood on my hands." Emotion flowed through Jude.

Nicks wrapped his arms around Jude and held him.

"I don't want to do this anymore," Jude cried.

"We'll get through it," Nicks reassured.

CHAPTER NINE

"Alright girl scouts, we have three hours to rest before the last leg of our godforsaken trek through this shit side of the mountain. Viper 6-4 you're on guard duty for the first half, lucky you– 6-5 night night," Hatch said, his breath could be seen from the cold. Light flurries danced in the dark sky. "I suggest buddying up for warmth."

The six men from Viper 6-4 fanned out taking tactical positions for any unwelcome guest. Marcus watched his comrades disappear into the dark. It was Marcus's turn for a much needed break. Marcus picked up his MRE from the dirt with a heavy sigh. He tried to brush the sand from the top of the MRE. He took a couple bites and packaged the rest disappointed by the ruined taste, if that was possible. His cammies had accumulated a supply of sand that chafed his skin. They still had a full day of hiking through the Zagros Mountains to get to the target location, a weapons compound. Their objective, to secure data before the Air Force bombed it into tiny pieces.

"Badger." Hatch patted the ground behind where he was laying. "You can be the big spoon– I swear to God, if I feel anything poking me in the back I will stab you."

"Do you want to be warm or not?" Marcus asked and wrapped his arms around Hatch.

Marcus tucked his face close to Hatch and sniffed. "What shampoo do you use? Is that Axe?–"

"Dude."

"Suave? No– definitely old spice."

"For the love of God–"

Marcus pinched and rolled Hatch's jacket between his fingers. "Soft. Do you use fabric softener? I'm a fan of bounce."

"Badger– I regret asking you to be the big spoon…"

"No you dont."

"Oh– It's Mountain Mist."

The next day the team trekked through the rugged terrain. The sun set over the desert mountains. Hatch signaled to his teams to halt on the ridge above the compound. There were two long storage units to the north, a small central building, a square metal building to the west of the central building, and a long warehouse to the south.

"Pear to Hatch, I have numerous tangos posted on the rooftops, a technical north of the compound, and a second technical on the east side near the central building." Pear looked down the scope of his sniper rifle.

"Well this is not going to work…"

"Hatch, there was that truck on the road about a click back–" Bonnet said.

"Blow that bitch to kingdom come–" Hatch turned to two of the Viper 6-4 men. "Wyatt, Pope, go set the charges."

"Yes, sir," Pope and Wyatt responded, running off.

"Now we wait…"

Several minutes later went by and the team posted on the top of the ridge watching the compound below.

"Charges set, on our way back," Wyatt said.

"Can you hurry back? Tight schedule," Hatch replied.

Wyatt and Pope returned out of breath.

"Go time," Hatch said and Pope pushed the detonator.

The earth rumbled with a loud explosion and plume of black smoke.

"Jesus, how much did you use?"

Wyatt and Pope looked at each other. "Three…"

"Five…"

The north technical, a black pick-up truck with a mounted machine gun, left their position along with over half of the foot hostiles. Pear started picking off the roof tangos.

"Engage," Hatch ordered.

Viper 6-5 descended down the face of the ridge, the cover of darkness on their side. Viper 6-4 remained on the ridge to provide cover for their withdrawal. The landscape was lit in a hue of green from their night vision. They posted on the east side. Marcus quickly peaked into the building.

"Two tangos inside," Marcus informed.

"We can sneak by, stay low," Hatch said.

They crouched beneath the windows and continued to the central building. The operator of the technical turned his head and did a double take. He moved his hand to the trigger. His head exploded in a spray of blood. The glass cracked and blood painted the interior of the truck cab. Pear took a deep breath, *That was close.* Marcus ran behind Hatch and posted by the main entrance of the small central building. Marcus peaked into the window. There was a fighter sitting at the computer station, another one staring out the window with the view of the main road into the compound, and last leaning back in a chair with his feet up next to the computer.

"Three tangos," Marcus said. "One, west window. One at the computer, and one next to him."

"We can't storm in there, it will give away our position," Phantom said.

"Follow my lead…" Hatch said and stood pressed against the wall next to the door.

Hatch slung his rifle and drew his pistol. He removed a suppressor from a pouch and screwed it onto the barrel. He pressed his knuckles on the door and knocked.

"Window tango, approaching," Marcus said.

The door opened and the man saw no one. He poked his head further out and Hatch grabbed him firmly pulling him out. He pressed the barrel to his chin and squeezed the trigger. The body fell to the ground. Hatch quickly moved past the threshold of the door. The shots were quick and struck the two men in the head. The team filed in behind.

"Get that DSM going now," Hatch ordered.

Moose withdrew the data storage module and hooked it up to the computer.

"Seven minutes," Moose said.

Marcus posted near a window keeping eyes on the compound, the other operators taking up their positions.

"All right girl scouts, keep your eyes peeled. They'll be back soon," Hatch said.

The worst part was waiting. Marcus counted down the minutes, watching for movement from his perch.

"Viper 6-5 inbound hostiles from the north." Pear said.

Yeti peaked out of the door and saw a man. He pressed his back to the wall.

"Think he saw me?"

Bullets pelted the side of the building and shredded the wooden door frame.

"He saw me."

Viper 6-4 opened fire on the hostiles converging on the central building. Moose removed the DSM and tucked it in his pack.

"DSM is good," Moose said and moved to a window to return fire.

"Nest to Sierra Leader, inbound air strike. Five mikes."

"Sierra Leader to Nest we are pinned down, hold off."

"That will be a big negative, Sierra Leader. Predator drone has been engaged. Evacuate site."

Marcus fired from his post hitting a hostile in the chest.

"Move out!" Hatch yelled.

"Viper 6-5 we'll try and clear a path," Bonnet said.

They filed out of the building and sprinted. Death was imminent for the team. The possibility of being able to flee to safety was slim. Bullets whizzed past Marcus's head. He pushed his legs as fast as they could carry him. He reached the base of the ridge and climbed, the sand and pebbles slipped beneath his boots. There was a small trail in the ridge that he followed. Large rocks and holes littered the path. Hatch followed close behind Marcus the rest of the team in front of Marcus.

The hum of the Predator sounded overhead followed by the whistle of the hellfire missiles. The explosion was deafening and the percussion wave passed through Marcus accompanied by an intense heat. The light of the inferno blinded Marcus with his night vision activated. Marcus missteped and plummeted to the ground. The momentum from his stride sent him into a skid down the face of the ridge. Secondary explosions blasted into the night sky.

"Badger!" Hatch yelled watching his friend fall.

CHAPTER TEN

Jude tossed and turned. A gunshot sounded and he violently woke. His chest heaved and his heart pounded. The reflection in the mirror showed a broken soul with bruises to match. His eye was still black and blue but his forehead had scabbed over. After he readied himself for another day, he walked into the kitchen. Nicks sipped his coffee and read the paper.

"You were yelling again," Nicks said looking over the top of the paper.

Jude pulled the orange juice from the refrigerator. "I'm sorry if I woke you."

"Jude, what can I do to help you?"

"I don't know... It's the same variation of the same dream. I can't get it out of my head. It's always revolving around my–"

"Mother." Nicks set the paper down. "Her death is not your fault. You know this right?"

Jude took a breath. "If I would have gotten there sooner–"

"Then you would be dead too. You know Garrick would have pulled that trigger for not coming to him about your mother's betrayal. For helping her plan her escape."

Jude dropped his head. "I just– I wish I could have done something, anything."

"I know, kid."

Jude looked at his hands.

"Her blood is not on your hands."

Jude stared at Nicks. "But isn't it? If I could have saved Jon this wouldn't have happened. If he was still alive, she wouldn't have done any of this."

"You don't know that for certain. Listen carefully, people die. Everyday. You will try your best to prevent it but in the end people die. It's not fair at times but that's just the way it is. But blaming yourself and hanging onto the hate and the sorrow will eat you alive. That is no way to honor the ones you've lost. You cannot continue to live this way. You need to come to terms with what happened and move on. Do not let those tragedies hold you back. You need to be stronger than that. You did not kill your brother and you did not kill your mother. You did what you could, the best that you could. Do you understand?"

"I do…"

"Jude, I do care about you. You are not in this alone."

Jude grabbed his backpack leaving his orange juice untouched. "I have to get to school."

Nicks handed Jude his permission slip for his physics field trip to the amusement park. "I'll be going as a chaperon."

"Naturally..."

"It'll be fun. I love roller coasters. Except for the tea cups. Damn those things spin fast."

Jude chuckled. "Then that will be the first thing we go on."

"Get to school."

The bustle of the beginning of the school day surrounded Jude. He reviewed his notes from the day prior but he was more interested in the conversation behind him. Marley and Kari chatted. But what was so distracting was Kari's intoxicating laugh. He enjoyed hearing her sharp wit and humor. Marley took a seat.

Kari leaned forward, her face inches from Jude's ear. "I saw you smile. It suits you. Maybe you should lighten up more often."

"If I did that then people would think I'm likeable," Jude said.

"Would that be such a bad thing?"

"It could be. I've worked really hard to be an arse."

"Well, you're not working hard enough." Kari relaxed back into her seat.

Jude sank into his chair and ran his hand through his hair. Class started and the physics lecture went onto deaf ears. Jude stared at the powerpoint. He tried to focus but his mind was elsewhere in scattered thoughts.

—

The morning sun was a welcome warmth from the cooling nights. Jude slumped against the bus window as Nicks drummed his hands on his knees. Other students and parents filed onto the bus and picked their seats. Kari walked past flashing Jude a small smile and continued down the aisle. Bradley followed close behind and shot Jude a stern look.

Nicks smirked. "I guess you weren't kidding about her being cute."

Jude groaned. "Ugh."

Nicks playfully slapped Jude on the cheek. "Why aren't you more excited about this field trip? This is going to be a blast."

"Because I'm stuck with you... and the one person I'd like to be with, I can't say anything to."

"Wow– that hurts a little."

"You don't have feelings."

"I have 'a' feeling."

"Still... Kari–" Jude raised his hand weighing the options. "Or you..."

"I see– I see. I forgive you and will still be your butt buddy."

Jude stared at Nicks terribly confused and slightly concerned. "What?"

"Butt buddy– It's what you call your friend that you ride on the roller coasters with. What do you think it means?" Nicks said as innocently as possible.

"Sir, my advice… You shouldn't say that again–"

It wasn't a long drive to Gurnee, Illinois. About an hour. The park was bustling with families and schools despite the early hour. Nicks speed-walked to the entrance Jude following a few paces behind.

"Come on, kid. No time to waste." Nicks seemed more excited than most of the students.

Jude cracked a smile at his enthusiasm. "So, teacups first?"

"God no! What's wrong with you? *Superman* needs to be first!"

The lines were not terribly long. They stood on the platform while they were strapped into the hanging seat on *Superman*. Nicks drummed his hands on the harness as they were hoisted into a prone position. Nicks shot his hands out in front of him and let out a *woo!* Jude shook his head. The rollercoaster catapulted them at a high rate of speed, twisting, turning, plummeting, climbing, hanging upside down in loops. Thrill and excitement coursed through Jude and he joined Nicks with his arms splayed out in front of him. The ride ran its course and halted back where it started. Jude unbuckled himself and he swayed for a moment, finding his legs.

Nicks hit him on the back. "See, told you it would be fun."

"What's next?"

"Is *Iron Wolf* still here?"

Jude shrugged. "How should I know?"

"Right– Uh well *Batman* if it's not."

The day continued with rollercoaster after rollercoaster. Jude could not remember a time he had that much fun. While they prepared for their ride on *Viper,* Jude glanced at Nicks, the man charged to protect him. He had slowly turned into much more than a guard. A friend, a mentor. More of a father figure than he ever had.

"Why are you staring at me, kid?" Nicks asked.

"I'm having a good time. Thank you for coming."

Nicks smiled. "I wouldn't have missed this for anything."

After lunch they wandered towards Nicks's favorite roller coaster, *Raging Bull.* Jude looked up at the drop and heard the screams from the descending train of cars. They navigated the zigzag of the line until reaching the end. The spot wasn't far from the split where you can wait longer to ride in the front car.

"We're riding front row," Nicks announced.

"I didn't expect anything less."

Jude leaned against the fence and stared at the coaster. He had never been on one before today and he was loving the thrill.

Nicks turned his head and saw Bradley trailing behind the gaggle of teenage girls. He looked miserable and a tortured pain flashed across his face seeing Jude. Nicks chuckled to himself waiting for the entertainment to start.

"Oh hey, fancy seeing you here," Kari said in a sad attempt at a British accent and smiled wide at Jude.

Jude chuckled. "Are you mocking me?"

"I would never–"

"You are also a bad liar."

Kari laughed. "I try my best." She stepped close to Jude and fixed his hair. "Wind has not been kind to you, good sir."

Nicks let his eyes wander to Bradley who was turning a shade of red he'd never seen before. Nicks covered his smile with a fist trying desperately not to laugh.

"I appreciate it." Jude was loving the attention from Kari and there was nothing Bradley could do unless he wanted to blow his cover. "You have some dirt on your face." Jude gently brushed the speck from her cheek.

Kari leaned in close. "See, you're not a complete arse."

"Don't tell anyone."

Bradley stepped between them and waved his arm. "Come on we're going with the peasants. No need to wait just to ride in front."

Kari smiled sweetly at Jude. "I'll see you later."

"Yeah," Jude said and Kari followed Bradley into the other line.

Nicks let out a laugh. "He hates you right now."

"That's fine, it was worth it."

Jude could see why *Raging Bull* was Nicks's favorite ride. It started with a towering drop followed by fast turns.

After the ride came to a stop, Jude followed Nicks out of the exit line, his adrenaline coursing from the excitement.

"Miss, would you mind taking a picture of us?" Nicks asked a young woman that Jude recognized as a student from his class.

"Sure thing," she said and accepted Nicks's phone.

Nicks stepped behind Jude putting his face next to Jude's with a goofy look. His arms stretched wide and his hands in the shape of bull horns. Jude laughed and his classmate captured the moment. Nicks looked at the photo.

"Well at least one of us looks good in this picture."

Jude pointed to the picture. "I'm surprised your shirt hasn't ripped from your biceps. Do you buy your shirts in the boys section?"

Nicks shoved the phone in his pocket and flexed his arm. "Raw power."

"You are ridiculous."

"Ridiculously awesome."

"Let's see how your 'raw power' does on the tea cups."

"Nope, not a chance." Nicks shook his head. "And we just ate lunch."

"Sounds like excuses…" Jude stepped towards the nonexistent line. "I mean, I thought you were this tough warrior. Not afraid of anything… Capable of doing the impossible."

"I am."

"So, tea cups," Jude said pointing at the twirling giant cups. "I see an eight year old girl smiling in that one. Look. Is she tougher than you?"

"If I puke on you, it's your own damn fault."

Jude clicked the door shut. Nicks sat up straight holding tightly to the wheel in the center.

"What's wrong with you?"

"I told you, I don't like this ride."

The cup started spinning slowly picking up pace as it went around the floor. The faster they swirled the greener Nicks turned.

"Uggggggghhhhh…" Nicks groaned.

Jude laughed at Nicks's pain.

"I need to get off of his thing," Nicks said, his stomach churning.

Jude raised his hands and he slid into Nicks amused. The ride ended and the giant cup eventually came to a halt. Nicks opened the door and nearly fell out of the cup. He gathered himself and walked sideways to the exit gate. He struggled to the garbage can and leaned against the building with his hand over his stomach.

"Blimey, you weren't joking."

Nicks looked at Jude sternly.

"Well, let it out so we can continue on with our day."

"Old people don't spin well. Give me a minute." Nicks looked into the garbage can.

A moment later there was a heave followed by a grumble and the sound of semiliquid falling into the garbage can.

"Gross," Jude said looking away. "Bet the chipped cup in *Beauty and the Beast* terrifies you."

Nicks pulled a water bottle from his pocket and swirled it around his mouth and spat it into the bin. He screwed that cap on and returned the bottle to his pocket.

"You good now?" Jude asked.

"I fucking hate you." Nicks pointed. "Walk."

"Yes, sir," Jude giggled.

After a fun-filled day they were headed home on the bus. Jude leaned against Nicks's shoulder fast asleep from the long day of excitement and lack of restful sleep from the night prior. Nicks looked down at his phone with a smile staring at the photo of him and Jude.

—

The next day dragged on in a haze after the day of fun at the amusement park. Jude walked to the front of the school and realized he forgot a textbook. After retrieving it from his locker he spotted Kari briskly walking down the hallway to the main entrance. She appeared to be flustered and he wondered what had happened. He followed her out the door a few passes behind her. The busses pulled away from the curb and merged into the busy streets of Chicago. Her heart sank and she wanted to scream as her streak of bad luck continued.

Kari ran down the stairs muttering, "No, no, no! Damn it all to Hell! What am I supposed to do now?"

"I could take you home," Jude offered, stopping next to her. He knew the consequences but he was also beginning to tire of having a forty something maybe fifty something year old man as his only friend. And what better way than to be a gentleman and assist Marshal Evan's sister safely home. Also gave him an excuse to talk to her.

"Jude?" Kari was taken by surprise. "No, you don't have to. I'll walk."

"I would strongly discourage you trying to navigate Chicago on your own," Jude said.

"I don't want to burden you with my own problem. I can call for a ride if I have to. Really it is okay." Kari pulled out her phone and saw that it was already dead.

Jude smiled. "Don't worry you won't be a bother.

Jude pulled out his phone seeing Kari's was dead. He knew Bradley would have a fit if he answered and Kari was on the other end. "Or, you can borrow my mobile."

Kari took his phone ready to dial Bradley's number. He and Jessica were both working late. She would be an issue they didn't need and that was the last thing she wanted.

She handed the phone back to Jude. "I suppose I could take you up on your offer."

"You will not be disappointed."

Kari raised a brow. "I don't know what you are expecting, mister. It's just a ride."

"I am not expecting anything. I will enjoy the company is all."

Kari smiled. "The 'arse' is really a gentleman."

"Don't tell anyone."

Kari winked and bumped into Jude. "Your secret's safe with me."

Jude led her across the street to the student parking lot. Kari was still not used to the sight of the vast array of luxury and sports vehicles. She was used to seeing beaters and trucks. Jude walked to a white Lexus. Kari went to open the door.

"No, this one," Jude said and put on a matte black motorcycle helmet.

Kari walked past the car and saw Jude mount a black BMW sports bike.

"Actually, your head is more important than mine," Jude stated and removed the helmet.

Kari pulled her hair tie out and let her hair cascaded down her shoulders. Jude locked eyes with Kari, holding her gaze for a moment and gently placed the helmet on her head. He adjusted the strap under Kari's chin.

"Does it make me look goofy?" Kari asked and made a funny face.

"Not at all," Jude laughed and snapped the visor down.

"Actually– Marley invited me to the beach. I wasn't going to go with having to catch the bus... but now... Do you want to go?" Kari asked.

"I would rather enjoy that." Jude was excited at the prospects of spending more time with Kari.

"I don't remember the name of the beach though."

"I have an idea of where they go." Jude often heard students talking about going to the beach after class. He never had a reason to go before.

Kari climbed onto the back of the motorcycle. Jude's phone vibrated in his pocket. He pulled it out to see a message from Nicks, *Where are you going with Bradley's sister?* Jude couldn't help but grin, *The beach, I'll be home in a few hours.* Nicks replied, *I hope the wrath will be worth it. See you when you get home. Have fun kid.*

"Who are you texting?" Kari asked, knowing it really wasn't any of her business.

"Uh, my uncle. Just letting him know where I'll be."

"Your uncle?"

"Yeah, I live with him… It's a long story. He was with me yesterday,"Jude said

"Oh, I just assumed he was your dad."

"Uh– yeah no." Jude started the engine ending the conversation and backed out of the space.

Kari wrapped her arms around Jude's waist in fear of falling off. He liked the feeling of Kari's arms around him. Jude weaved through traffic. Tall buildings zoomed past them and the bustle of the city was not but a blur. The engine of the bike purred as they hit the freeway. Kari clung to Jude tighter. The lake came into view. The vast open blue lay as far as the eye could see. Kari's gaze was drawn to the mixing dark blue of the water and the light blues of the sky as Jude exited the highway. Jude pulled into a small parking lot and slowed to a stop. Kari unwrapped her arms from Jude and slid off the bike. The sound of waves lapping to the shore and seagulls cawing filled her ears.

"Where are we?" Kari asked as Jude took the helmet off of Kari's head.

"The 12th Street beach," Jude said and slung the helmet on the handlebars.

Jude removed his tie and shoved it in his backpack. He unbuttoned his shirt and rolled up the sleeves. He removed his dress shoes and argyle socks leaving them next to the bike. Kari followed suit. They trekked down the path to the beach. Marley and her friends were easy to spot from their energetic banter.

"Glad you could make it!" Marley announced with a friendly smile.

The others looked Jude over with questionable looks.

"Hey Kari, you play soccer right?" Karston asked and twirled the ball in his hands.

Kari thought about Ryan for the first time since they broke up. "I'm not too bad."

"We're not the best but we enjoy it just the same," Karston stated and dropped the ball.

"Uh… Jude. You can be on Karston and I's team. We'll play the girls," Rob said.

The group took their positions on the beach.

Kari turned to Jude. "They don't seem too happy that I brought you along… I…"

"It's okay. I have not made it a point to make friends here."

"Jude!" Karston waved him over to start the game.

Kari dropped her gaze. She wasn't sure what to say.

"Maybe that is changing," Jude said with a wink and jogged towards Karston who had the ball.

Karston passed the ball to Jude and the game started. The goals were close together and small making the game fast paced and fun. Kari sprinted at Jude and slide-tackled him. Sand flew into the air. Kari made contact with the ball, sending it sailing down the beach towards Prue. Jude toppled onto Kari with a groan as he tried to brace himself. Kari propped herself on an elbow. The heat from his exhale touched her skin. Their eyes locked and Kari felt her pulse quicken. He wanted to kiss her but fought the urge. Jude stood, grasped Kari's hand and lifted her to her feet.

"I can say, I wasn't expecting a tackle," Jude smiled.

"I play rough." Kari smirked and jogged to join the game.

They played for an hour until their uniforms were covered in sand and sweat.

Marley nudged Kari. "We're going to head for some ice cream before going home..." She looked at Jude. "You're both welcome to join."

Jude stared at Kari, waiting for an answer. Kari's eyes shifted and glazed over as she stared at the water of Lake Michigan. She started to think about her mom and dad and how they would love to see this beautiful landscape of beach and water.

"Um… I think I will pass. But thank you for the invite."

"No worries. You guys will have to come out again. It was fun."

Kari smiled and Jude said, "I hope me coming uninvited was alright."

"It was. You're welcome anytime," Marley said and waved goodbye.

Kari's new friends trekked back to the parking lot. She shifted her gaze back to the never ending water. She took a deep breath holding back the tears.

Jude saw that Kari was in deep thought and was unsure if he should disturb her. "Did you want me to take you home?" Jude asked.

Kari didn't answer because she was in a trance. "Kari?"

"What?" Kari focused and shifted her eyes back to Jude.

A tear rolled down her cheek. Jude stared at her concerned and he gently wiped away her tears with his thumb. He's seen this pain before, experienced the same pain.

"There's something wrong," he said. "You can talk to me."

Jude could see the conflict in her eyes on whether or not she wanted to open up. He didn't blame her, it had taken him a long time to open up to Nicks, and he wasn't sure he was comfortable doing that with anyone. Kari swallowed hard, choking back the grief. The pain she was in, mirrored that of his own. He pulled his brows together gazing at her with deep concern. Tears fell and she wiped them away with a heavy sigh.

"Have you ever lost anyone you loved?"

Jude did not respond right away. "Yes, I have."

"Really?" Kari questioned as her shoulders trembled trying not to cry.

"My mum. She died a few months back from cancer," Jude said with a wince as the sounds of her screams filled his memory followed by a loud bang.

"I'm sorry."

"Kari, it's okay."

"This is the last thing you're going to want to listen to…" Kari tried to stand.

Jude grabbed her arm and pulled her back to the soft sand. "I don't mind. This is important."

Kari avoided Jude's concerned gaze and stared out at the setting horizon. "My mom and dad were killed by a drunk driver a few weeks ago." Her throat tightened and she fought the tears. "I moved here to live with my brother. Or more like, forced here… I know he means well and is trying but… It's been hard. I miss my parents, every day, every second. The last thing I wanted was to be uprooted from everything I knew…" The tears fell from her eyes. "I don't think I am strong enough to survive this…"

Jude wrapped his arm around Kari's shoulders and pulled her close to his body. She buried her face into his shoulder.

"I'm sorry you are going through this... I'm here for you."

Kari pulled away and wiped the tears. "We should probably go, it's getting late."

"If you want to talk more–"

"No, but thank you for letting me talk. It was... relieving to get some of that out."

"I'm here if you need anything, really. I can empathize with what you're going through."

"Thanks, that means a lot."

Jude assisted Kari to her feet and they walked back to the parking lot. The cold air whipped past Kari as they sped down the road causing her to shiver.

"Thanks for the ride... and everything else," Kari said and handed Jude his helmet while he was parked in the driveway of her house.

"I'm just glad I was able to help," Jude said.

"I'll see you tomorrow then."

Jude smiled. "Tomorrow."

The single tail light from Jude's bike disappeared down the dark street. Kari walked up the driveway to the house, the warm lights flooded through the windows into the darkness of the night. Kari stood in front of the dark green door wondering what was going to happen next. It was after nine, she had lost track of time. She took a deep breath and opened the door. Jessica was sitting on the stairs, her face in her hands. Kari felt terrible for putting her through agony. Jessica heard the door and looked up to see Kari, unharmed. Jessica jumped to her feet tears forming in the corners of her eyes. She hurried to Kari and embraced her.

"I was worried sick," Jessica cried and stroked Kari's hair. Jessica released Kari and backed away a couple steps. "Where were you? You should have called! What the hell were you thinking?" Jessica snapped at Kari.

"I'm sorry. I missed the bus and I hung out with some new friends and then Jude gave me a ride home," Kari explained. "My phone was dead and I lost track of time."

"Kari, it's nine thirty. How can you lose track?"

"I'm sorry."

"You can't just do what you want."

"I… I..."

"Where were you anyway?"

"The beach."

"What can you possibly do at the beach this late at night where you wouldn't notice it getting dark?"

"I did notice. Jess, I'm sorry."

"Well sorry doesn't cut it."

"It won't happen again… I promise."

"You bet it won't. You are grounded. School and straight home," Jessica said with her hands on her hips.

"This was the first time I've actually had fun with friends since my life was uprooted and you're punishing me?"

"You were being irresponsible, Kari. This is the consequence."

"Unbelievable… You know, I hate it here. I hate it so much that some days I wish I could just disappear."

"It hasn't been easy for us either! Do you not think our lives have changed too!"

Tears streamed down Kari's face and she dashed up the steps and slammed her door. Jessica sank to the floor, furious. She had never spoken to Kari in that manner before. It was foreign to her. She was not a parent, she had no idea how to be one. She picked up her phone and texted Bradley that Kari had returned home.

Jessica was milling about in the kitchen when the backdoor opened. Bradley set his keys down on the counter and placed his palms on the surface. He hung his head exhausted from his search. Jessica wrapped her arms around his waist and kissed him on the cheek.

"You missed the drama," Jessica said.

"It is probably for the best…" Bradley turned around. "I am just glad she's safe… There will definitely be a lecture tomorrow."

"Don't be too hard on her… I think I may have been a bit harsh."

"Jess, she really messed up. She deserved it… I was driving around losing my mind, she doesn't know this city. I didn't have the slightest idea where to even look."

"I don't know how we're going to survive raising a teeager."

"I don't know how my parents survived with Marcus and I."

Bradley turned around and embraced his wife.

"At least she's making friends. Some boy, Jude, brought her home."

Bradley's body went rigid with anger.

"What's wrong?"

"That's the boy from the fight– I told Kari to stay clear of him."

"Well–"

"How am I supposed to trust her if she can't adhere to my rules?"

"Give her a break Bradley."

Bradley groaned. "Not on this one…"

———

Jude set his keys on the counter and dropped his backpack on the table. Nicks lounged on the couch watching whatever was on ESPN.

"Sorry I'm past curfew…"

"Not by much. Besides, I was tracking you," Nicks said and shook his phone in the air.

"Right– I forgot you do that."

"So, how was your night?"

Jude plunked down on the recliner.

"I had a good time… Kari, she's fun and beautiful."

"Slow your roll there, kid."

"I don't see why we can't be friends. She's going through a lot. Death of her parents, new school. She needs someone."

"And that someone shouldn't be you. Bradley was very clear."

"Yeah, yeah. I know…"

"Do you? Seems like you may be a bit hard of hearing."

"No, I get it."

Nicks sat up and placed his elbows on his knees. "Good, because we don't need any more drama. Now, changing gears… Your interview–"

Jude dropped his head and rubbed his face. "Don't remind me–" Anxiety flooded Jude. "I was trying to forget about it– had forgotten about it."

"It's going to be a long intense few days."

"I just want this to be over. I just want to forget everything…"

"I know, kid… I can be in there if you want."

"I would appreciate that…"

Nicks stood and patted Jude on the shoulder. "Get some sleep, we have a long flight tomorrow."

Nicks's phone rang and he picked it up from the table. "Oh boy–"

"What?"

Nicks showed Jude the caller ID. "I think he knows…"

Jude's face drained. "Should I be concerned?"

Nicks chuckled and answered the phone. "Hey, Evans."

"Did you know?"

"Know what?"

"That Jude was with my sister all night doing God knows what," Bradley said, trying not to raise his voice.

"Uh–"

"Rauri!"

"Hey– Hey– Don't raise your voice to me kid."

Bradley took a breath. He was not about to get into an argument with Nicks no matter how mad he was. Nicks wasn't only his team leader for the Marshals but his team leader when Braley was a green Delta operator. He owed his successful career as a SF operator because of Nicks's leadership. "Can I speak with him?"

Nicks stared at Jude. "I don't think that's a good idea right now."

"Rauri, will you please talk to him then… He cannot be involved with her."

"I will–"

Bradley pinched his forehead. "He's not going to listen is he?"

"Um– I will talk to him."

Bradley grumbled. "I'm going to strangle him."

"Don't do that, I like you just a little and would hate to visit you in the clink."

"That's not funny."

"Try not to have a stroke. I'll handle this."

"Okay, okay…"

"Sleep tight, Bradley."

"Fuck off."

Nicks hung up the phone and lifted a brow at Jude.

"He's mad isn't he?" Jude asked.

"You think? I told you it was going to be bad. If you want to keep your kneecaps, stay away from Evans's sister."

"I will try…"

"Do or do not, there is no try."

"Did you just quote Yoda?"

"Go to bed you will," Nicks said in his best Yoda voice with a hand wave.

Jude laughed. "I can see why you're single."

"Kneecaps–"

"Right– I'll see you in the morning."

CHAPTER ELEVEN

The next morning Bradley waited for Kari in the kitchen. She walked in avoiding eye contact with him. She did not want to deal with another lecture.

"Don't even say anything... I already know."

"We have to talk about this, Kar."

"Bradley, I know I screwed up. You don't have to drill me about what happened."

"I don't? But you seem not to understand the situation at hand."

"I do, and I'm sorry... Okay."

"Kari, do you know what happens to girls like you in a city like this? This isn't Marinette."

"Don't you think I know that?" Kari raised her voice.

"Kari, please. This is serious. I know you were with friends, but at the time we didn't know that. For all we knew you were in dire trouble."

Kari dropped her gaze. "I really am sorry."

"I know you are... Still doesn't change the fact that Jess grounded you and I agree with her. You are going to have to earn our trust back. This was reckless and frankly I do not trust your ability to make good decisions at the moment."

Kari's emotions were high. She already felt like the world was against her. She couldn't hold it in anymore. Her depression was growing and It was clear that she was a strain on Jessica and Bradley. Anger and sorrow boiled over. "You want to talk about decisions! How about the decision to make me move here!" Kari raised her voice. "But sure, let's blame Kari for trying to make the best of a situation and make new friends."

"I'm not the enemy here," Bradley said firmly.

"You're the one that made me move here! If anyone is to blame it's you!" Tears started to form. "Maybe you should just stop caring. If I am such a burden then just let me be and perhaps I will just disappear!"

"Kari–"

Kari grabbed her bag and bolted out the door. Bradley grumbled irritated and too old for high school drama. Kari walked down the sidewalk not exactly knowing where she was going. She wanted to get away. Nothing was going the way it should have. She felt like her emotions were taking over every inch of her body. She pulled out her phone and texted Jude. *Nothing is going right... Had a fight with my brother.* It did not take long for her screen to light up. Jude replied *I'm sorry to hear that. We can talk later, I have some stuff I have to do.* Bradley pulled up next to her.

"Kari, what are you doing?" Bradley asked through the open passenger window.

"I'm going to school. What does it look like?" Kari stared ahead.

"You plan on walking there? That's a long walk."

"Does it really matter?" Kari questioned and turned to face Bradley, fresh tears rolling down her cheeks

"Get in." Bradley said plainly

"Why?" Kari asked as she started to cry.

"This is not going to be an argument."

Kari did not say a word and opened the front passenger door. The car ride was silent. Bradley pulled up to the curb in front of the school. Kari did not say a word and got out.

"Make sure you come home tonight," Bradley called after her.

"Oh, don't worry I will," Kari replied.

Students hurried to class after the first bell rang. After last night, Kari looked forward to seeing Jude in their first class. She stepped through the threshold of the classroom and her stomach sank. His desk was empty. Kari sat down and stared at the clock. Time was counting down, and he hadn't shown up. The bell rang and Kari glanced at Marley, disappointment filling Kari's face. Kari pulled her phone out hiding it under her desk. *Where are you?* She stared at her phone but no response came. She feared something had happened.

———

Jude sat between Nicks and Clayton on a commercial jet. Jude stared absentmindedly at the seat in front of him. Clayton elbowed Jude.

"Licorice?" He asked and waved the candy whip in his field of vision.

Jude laughed. "Nah, I'm good."

"No– Look they're the good ones, the pull and peel." Clayton pulled strips of the candy and laid them on Jude's face.

"What are you doing?" Jude took the strands and ate one.

"Getting you to lighten up." Clayton pulled another piece out and poked him in the face. "Weedoo."

"You are strange…" Jude pulled the licorice from his hand.

"I'll take one," Nicks said and reached over Jude taking the candy.

"Get out of here! I did not offer it to you," Clayton said and swatted Nicks's loot loaded hand away.

"I appreciate you sharing," Nicks laughed.

"I wasn't…"

"Say– Aren't you from the DC area? You can show us around," Nicks said and bit the candy.

"That I am not... I am from Charlottesville."

"North Carolina?" Jude asked.

Clayton waved his hand. "Thomas Jefferson is rolling in his grave. No dear boy, Virginia– Charlottesville, Virginia... And that's Charlotte North Carolina."

"Isn't the south pretty much all the same?"

"No, Jude, it is not."

"He's– A real 'southern boy.' He's gotta go wrangle some cattle and eat grits," Nicks said with air quotes.

Clayton raised a brow. "That is not accurate in the slightest."

Once they landed in Washington D.C. they settled into their hotel, a larger suit with two beds and a pullout couch. Jude sat at the small kitchen table staring at the text message from Kari asking where he was. He wasn't sure how to respond. All his focus was on his upcoming interview tomorrow and was not in the mood to respond.

"Put your phone away..." Nicks said, taking a seat next to Jude setting down a Yuengling. Nicks flipped open a file. "We need to make sure you're prepared tomorrow."

Clayton settled in across from Jude.

"They're going to ask you difficult questions, questions that are going to make you feel like you're on trial. Jude, you've been a part of some serious crimes and they're going to make you answer for it."

Jude bowed his head and pulled at his fingertips.

"They're going to make you relive the worst moments of your life. You need to think about how you're going to answer those questions without falling apart."

"I don't know if I can do this..." Jude admitted.

"You got this, kid, but I would be lying to you if I'd tell you it would be easy."

After his long conversation with the Marshals Jude stared up at the ceiling waiting for sleep. His mind raced thinking about what tomorrow would bring. He turned over wishing his life was different. That none of this happened. He envied the kids his age and their simple, normal lives.

The next morning Jude was escorted to CIA headquarters in Langley. Each step to the building brought with it more anxiety. He soon found himself in a small conference style room. Two agents sat across from Jude. The lead female agent had her blonde hair pulled back into a neat tight bun. Her features were sharp and her eyes ice. The man next to her was just as stern, his eyes dark as they analyzed Jude. Nicks sat next to him in a fine pressed suit.

"What knowledge do you have regarding Shaun Garrick's business?" Agent Bartlow asked in a low booming voice and rested his elbows on the table.

Jude was surprised by such a broad question. "I have a great deal of knowledge, obviously. He supplies many terror groups weapons."

Agent Bartlow folded his hands on the table. "Have you ever seen him conduct business exchanges with clients before?"

"Yes, many times."

"Would you be able to identify them?" Agent Bartlow handed Jude several photos of terrorist leaders.

Jude was able to name a few pointing to the men he recognized. Agent Bartlow tapped the pages on the table to collect them and placed them back into the folder.

"Have you ever participated in the business yourself?"

"You know I have…"

"To what extent?"

Jude took a breath. "I have accompanied Garrick and others in meetings. I've done exchanges with our suppliers and our clients."

"Where does Garrick get most of his weapons?"

"Russia, Mexico, the US."

"Do you know names?"

"No, I was never present during those meetings."

"If I showed you photos, would you recognize any?" Agent Bartlow opened another folder.

"I don't know… The exchanges were usually with low level hands."

Agent Bartlow handed Jude the photos and he skimmed through them.

"No, I'm sorry... I don't know who these people are," Jude said and handed the photos back.

"What about locations of storage compounds, places of operation, and safe houses?"

"Do you have a map and a piece of paper? I don't have many exact addresses but I can at least give you a general location. All of which I had provided MI6 with already."

Agent Conway handed Jude a tablet and a notepad ignoring his comment about MI6. "Just tap the location on the screen and it will drop a pin."

Jude took a few minutes recalling locations he had been to, or known of. He tapped the screen and wrote down what the location was. He handed Agent Conway the tablet back and the notepad. Her eyes lit up by the intel Jude provided.

"Now, James– There are a few specific incidents I'm going to ask you about," Agent Conway said.

She adjusted her glasses and slid multiple photos in front of Jude. His eyes jumped from one photo to the other. Carnage laid before him, metro cars burst open and charred from explosives. Blood and lifeless bodies on the ground. The last photo was of an ISIS leader, who he had met.

"April 27, 2011, there was a terror attack in Paris. ISIS bombed four trains... There were 193 killed and

2,050 injured." She pointed to each train as she said the names of the stations. "Gare du Nord, Gare de l'Est, Gare de Bercy, Gare d'Austerlitz." She pointed to the picture of the man. "Ibrahim Aslam Rashid… You know this man. Was Shaun Garrick supplying Rashid for this attack?"

Jude looked up from the photos, he remembered seeing the news headlines of that day on the teley. "Yes, I was present during the initial meeting with Rashid and Garrick."

"Tell me about it."

"We were in Al-Qa'im the month prior. I was asked to accompany Garrick. He wanted me to start observing meetings. This was the first time I had met Rashid. Garrick had done business with Rashid in the past."

"Was there discussion on what the explosives were going to be used for?"

"No, there is never talk about what the munitions are used for. It's best that way."

Agent Conway removed a piece of paper from the file.

"The list of products and prices here… Does it match what you can remember being discussed from that meeting?"

Jude looked over the invoice. "How could I possibly remember? I don't know, maybe."

She gathered all of the paperwork back into the file and pulled out a second one. These photos contained a picture of damaged and destroyed vehicles from a U.S. Army convoy and American flag draped caskets in an air hanger. The final picture was of a Taliban leader.

"February 12, 2012, a U.S. convoy was traveling in the Northern Balkh Province in Afghanistan. They were ambushed by a cell of Taliban insurgents at a checkpoint. There were seven American soldiers and ten Afghan soldiers killed and five American and eight Afghan injured. Shehzad Akhund Razaq was responsible for this attack. Was Garrick involved with Razaq?"

"No... Garrick wasn't involved directly with this transaction that I know of. My brother Jon was in contact with this client."

"Are you certain?" Conway asked.

Jude stared at the American flags, the lives lost. "Yes, I was with Jon during both the initial meeting and the exchange."

"This was at Garrick's order though?"

"Well, yeah... Everything needed to be approved by him first."

Agent Conway pushed the invoice to Jude. "Does this accurately account for the weapons and currency exchange."

Jude looked at the numbers. "I suppose so... I was not paying close enough attention to know specifics."

Agent Conway pushed the photos to Agent Bartlow to collect. She opened another folder splaying out the photos. It was Piccadilly Circus, Jude was there that day. He looked away from the remnants of an exploded van and death. He pushed the photos away and closed his eyes. Nicks placed a hand on his shoulder.

The cool spring air whirled and whipped through the streets of London. Jude pulled at the collar of his jacket. His mother flung her scarf, adding a fold to her neck.

"Just a couple more stores. I want to find your father a gift for his birthday."

"You end up getting him the same thing every year; a bottle of scotch and a new watch. Why change now?"

"I just figured since we were here already… We have time before the show starts, anway."

Jude shook his head and accompanied his mother towards the shops on Regent Street. Her gaze was drawn to the illuminated signs as they entered the heart of Piccadilly Circus. A crack and roar of an explosion pierced Jude's ears and the wave of the blast hit his body. He was propelled to the concrete, an intense heat washed over him. Glass and debris rained down on him. Car horns blared and screams filled the air. Smoke billowed veiling the street. Jude turned his head seeing still bodies laying next to a flaming car. Gentle hands grasped his shoulders.

"James! James!" His mother called, pulling him.

His eyes focused seeing her soot covered face. "Mum."

He staggered to his feet. A mother clung to her lifeless child screaming.

"Darling! Darling," she readjusted her tone. "We need to leave." His mother pulled on Jude's arm, he was transfixed on the terror and chaos.

Agent Conway pressed on giving little care to Jude's emotional state. "April 13, 2012, London. You should be very familiar with this incident, it was right in your own backyard. ISIS used a car bomb to kill eighteen innocent people and injured fifty."

"You don't need to remind me. I was there." Jude dug his fingers into his hair.

Agent Conway continued. "Garrick has a history of supplying Ibrahim Aslam Rashid, was he responsible for this attack too?"

"Yes…"

"How do you know?"

"I was with Garrick in London the month prior to meeting with Rashid."

"What was discussed?"

"Prices. Weapons."

"Nothing about the attack?" Agent Conway pressed.

"No— I already told you there was never discussion on what the weapons would be used for."

Agent Conway shuffled the papers over to Agent Bartlow again. She removed the last file. The photos contained a brutal scene of a war riddled city of Kubal, innocent people dead.

"May 25, 2012, the Taliban had orchestrated to have insurgents and suicide bomers launched multiple attacks throughout Afghanistan. This included a siege on Kubal with their primary focus on embassies. The attack took one hundred and thirty-four lives, injuring many more. The leader of the attack was Qasim Asaad."

Jude leaned forward planting his elbow on the table and putting his face into his hand. He did not want to travel down this road. Agent Conway sat up seeing the change in Jude's behavior, she was intrigued to know what information he had about Qasim Asaad.

"You know him, Asaad? He's one of Garrick's clinents?"

"Yes, he did extensive business with him."

"When and where was the most recent?"

"April– In Asadabad"

"Was Garrick part of it?" Agent Conway asked leaning forward.

"Initially he was, Garrick always handled the first couple meetings. But after we had done business with Asaad many times, Jon took over the account."

"So Garrick wasn't there for the exchanges?"

Jude dropped his head scratching his head. Soldiers yelling in Arabic, gunfire, and his brother getting shot all ran through his mind.

"No, he wasn't... He rarely does exchanges. That's what he had us for." Jude fought to keep it together.

Agent Conway could see there was more. "Your brother— Jon, died in May... It wasn't a hunting accident was it?"

Jude looked up at Agent Conway tormented.

"What happened during the last exchange, James?"

Jude trembled and his heart raced. Nicks tightened his grip on Jude's shoulder.

"Jon was shot..." Jude's eyes were glued to the table, the scene replaying in his head. Jon's eyes faded staring up at Jude.

"Shot by who? Did you retaliate?" Agent Conway was on a hunt.

Nicks stood abruptly. "That's enough. Do you have any more questions about Garrick? Otherwise I think we are finished here."

Agent Conway eyed Nicks carefully. "We can be done for today." She stood. "We will pick up tomorrow."

"Come on, Jude, let's go," Nicks said and assisted Jude to his feet.

They were escorted through the maze of the building to the lobby by an agent. Clayton sat in a chair, also in a pressed suit, his gun and badge on his belt. He was talking on the phone when they approached.

"I have to go sweetheart, I will be home soon… Be kind to Uncle Pyke now," Clayton said and hung up the phone.

Jude looked awful. "Went that well?" Clayton asked.

Nicks opened the door holding it open for Jude. "They grilled him pretty hard."

"I am not the least bit surprised…" Clayton muttered.

They made it to the car and Jude slumped in the back letting his head fall back on the headrest. He stared out the window watching the cars pass by.

"How are you doing back there?" Clayton asked looking in the rearview mirror.

"Fantastic– Just peachy," Jude snapped.

"I feel your words are not matching how you really feel…"

"Great investigator you are."

"I resemble that remark."

Jude rolled his eyes and shook his head.

"Let him be…" Nicks said.

Jude pulled at his fingers. "Thank you, by the way."

"For what?" Nicks asked, turning in his seat.

"For stopping the interview… I…"

"It's all right, kid. I didn't want you to relive that again."

There was an awkward silence. Clayton drummed his fingers on the steering wheel and sang. "I'm a sky-bo. That's a new kind of hobo... for planes."

"Please– Please don't start," Nicks said.

Clayton pointed in the mirror excitedly. "I have something in mind to cheer you up."

"What's that?" Jude asked.

"A fantastic Irish pub in D.C."

"Oh! I think I know which one, The Dubliner," Nicks interjected. "Jude you like Irish right?"

"Potatoes and beer... yeah."

"Well, no beer for you..." Nicks replied.

"Best shepherd's pie," Clayton kissed the tips of his fingers.

"I will have to disagree as you obviously have never been... To Dublin," Jude said.

"Cheeky bastard... best shepherd's pie stateside– Happy?"

Jude chuckled. "Even that's a big claim."

Clayton shook his head. "I can't win."

It had taken a few minutes to find parking and Clayton finally settled on paying an arm and a leg for parking in a ramp nearby. They walked down the sidewalk, Union Station in it's grand alure was down the block. Jude lifted a brow as they walked past a bar. He pointed to the Police squad car doors that were mounted on the rod iron fence and walls.

"What's going on here?" Jude asked.

Nicks chuckled. "That's Kelly's... A staple around here."

"Looks like a junkyard."

"Safest damn junkyard in the country probably. That is the nation's cop bar."

Nicks held the door open for the others and they walked into the Irish Pub. Jude was thankful for the light banter during dinner. Listening to the Marshals' stories was a good distraction to keep his mind from the interrogation.

"There I was standing with a towel around my waist holding onto a bucket of ice outside our hotel room in Venice. My ex-wife passed out in the room... I had to go down to the lobby in this towel to get a new room key. I may have been slightly inebriated and well... The towel came loose. There I was... hanging out, in front the clerk. So what do I say you ask? 'Yeah, that's really how big it is.' Not one of my finest moments..." Nicks said and took a swig of Yuengling. "Couldn't even blame the cold."

Clayton stared at him dumbfounded. "I'm not sure what I'm supposed to do with that information."

"Always double tuck your towel." Nicks winked at him. "So yeah. Advice. Do what you will with it."

Jude stared at Nicks horrified.

"Say– speaking of relationships aren't you dating a teacher now?" Nicks asked.

"I am," Clayton responded.

"How's that going?"

"Very well, thank you."

"Some more advice… Make sure you always have a room key."

Clayton shook his head. "An' a bigger dick."

The night of fun came to an end. Jude stared up at the ceiling wishing for sleep. His mind raced from the interview and anxiety flooded his body with anticipation for the next day. He had a strong desire to flee but he knew he needed to push on. He wanted Garrick to rot in a prison cell till the end of time or put a knife through his heart.

The next day repeated much like the last. Jude rested his folded hands on the table avoiding direct eye contact with Agents Bartlow and Conway. Nicks sat next to him, helping with his anxiety. Agent Conway slid a picture to Jude. He recognized the man immediately.

"I would think you would recognize this man… After all you did plant explosives in his storehouse in New York."

"Makar Rosakov…" Jude replied.

"What do you know about him?"

"He was Garrick's ally years ago and now competition."

Agent Conway narrowed her eyes. "Are you sure?"

Jude was confused. "Positive."

"You are unaware of any meetings between Garrick and Rosakov?" Agent Conway pressed. Nicks's stomach sank, they had discounted Rosakov as a threat to Jude. The CIA must know something that the Marshals didn't.

"I am... They hate each other, I don't know why they would be meeting," Jude said.

A flash of disappointment flashed across her features. "Does Garrick have any other contacts in Russia?"

"He has a supplier in Azov and Dalnegorsk, but I do not know their names, nor have I ever met them."

"That's alright, the information you have already provided us will be a tremendous help. Now there is something I want to revisit from yesterday." Agent Conway pulled out a photo of the dead Afghan soldiers.

She slid it to Jude. "Take a good look at these men."

Jude placed his head into his propped hands staring at the soldiers he had killed. He focused on the blood around their bodies.

"What is this agent?" Nicks asked anger flowing from the witch hunt.

"The Afghan's want to know who's responsible for killing their men. I know what happened, I just want James to say it."

"For what reason? He has immunity, it doesn't matter."

Agent Conway focused back on Jude. "You killed them didn't you? Who else was with you?"

Jude continued to stare at the photo.

"This is enough," Nicks interjected and stood.

"You took their lives didn't you? Out of cold blood." Agent Conway raised her voice. "Answer the question!"

"Agent Conway–" Nicks stated.

"Fine! I killed them! Are you happy?" Jude glared at her.

A smile crossed her face and disappeared as quickly it had appeared. "Who else was with you?"

"Wallace and Collins." The pounding of his heart was making it difficult to think clearly. He was unraveling. "Can we be finished?" Jude looked pleadingly at Nicks.

"Agent, if you don't have any further questions about Garrick, we're leaving," Nicks stated.

Agent Conway gathered her papers and tapped the ends on the table to collect them. "No this should conclude the interview."

The days of being grilled over Garrick and his sordid past took its toll on Jude. He was mentally and physically taxed. Jude tried to keep his eyes open on the plane to focus on homework. The tray in front of him was down and on top of it was his world history textbook. His head lobbed and his eyes were heavy. He fell into Nicks asleep. It was unexpected and Nicks looked down at the sleeping boy. He gently propped Jude up for a moment to lift the armrest and readjusted in his seat letting Jude fall into him with his arm draped over Jude's shoulders.

Clayton set his book down. "You've grown fond of the boy."

"He's a good kid."

"This may complicate things... He is an asset, Rauri, do not let emotions get the better of you."

"I didn't think I would ever receive a lecture from you–"

"I am speaking as a friend... Things could get messy– complicated... Are you prepared for that?"

Nicks looked down at Jude and hesitated. "Yes."

It was a long flight and Jude was glad to be home, or the closest thing he had to a home anyway. He threw his bag next to the closet and sat down on the end of his bed. Kari's messages remained unanswered. Guilt plagued him but he felt empty and did not possess words. He had his own demons to face. Nicks popped into the doorway.

"I was going to order pizza– Any preference?" Nicks asked and his happy demeanor quickly faded. He sat down next to Jude. "What's up kid?"

Jude set his phone down. "I can't stop thinking about the interview, about Garrick..."

"We will have a debrief tomorrow at the Marshals office, that should help..."

"And then what? Go back to playing house?"

"Jude–"

"Then if Garrick is caught–"

"When…"

"After all of that, what am I supposed to do? Go back to England, and try to move on? I have no family left, no friends. I have no one… Maybe it would have been better if Garrick would have killed me that night."

"Jude– Don't say things like that. There are people that care about you. You are not alone in this," Nicks said and placed a firm hand on Jude's shoulder.

"What? You and the other Marshals? It's your job to protect me… And when that's over, I'm on my own."

"You don't have to be, I mean– You could stay here," Nicks hadn't planned on saying that but the words fell out.

Jude opened his mouth to speak but no words came.

"I– Could, uh– Adopt you–" Nicks fumbled.

"What?– You can do that?"

"Why not? I may have to buy a bigger house, the condo I have now is small for two," Nicks thought out loud.

"You're serious then?"

"I am. You deserve a fresh start, hopefully after this is all done I can give you that."

"I… I don't know what to say." Jude stared at Nicks in disbelief.

Nicks hugged him. "We will have to convert you into a baseball fan."

Jude laughed. "That will never happen."

The next day Jude sat in a small conference room at the Marshals Office. Pyke waited impatiently to start the debrief. Clayton hurried into the room in a distracted state.

"Nice of you to finally join us," Pyke said, tossing a file down the table to where Clayton took a seat.

"My apologies, sir. Amelia had a fit going to daycare. Apparently she was upset that she's not allowed to play Mortal Kombat there…"

Pyke smirk. "Atta girl."

"I may have to reevaluate my decision to allow you to watch my child."

Pyke chuckled and readjusted in his seat. "Now, to business. Garrick is still off of the radar according to the CIA. However, there was a successful op where Delta Force operators were able to deploy a DSM and gather much needed intel. Seems their captive from Beirut wasn't a complete wash and they were able to decipher more intel off of his phone."

"Who did they capture in Beirut?" Jude asked.

"Not important…"

"Actually, it could be important. Jude could know the man and have some insight on how to get him to crack if need be– It was Preece," MacTavish said.

"Oh, you won't get him to crack," Jude replied.

"Remember when I told you fucks he was a dead end? I literally meant it, the man hung himself," Pyke stated.

"See…" Jude muttered.

"Now… How did the CIA interview go?" Pyke asked.

Nicks glanced at Jude. "Jude was able to provide them with a lot of valuable information."

"Were they dicks?" Pyke asked blatantly.

"They're the CIA."

"So, Yeah?"

"Yeah."

Jude was taken aback from the remark. Pyke sighed seeing he needed to explain himself. "I have some mistrust with the CIA. In the 90's they were premature on sending my unit on an op. Needles to say we got blown up. I lost a lot of men, and I had a nice vacation in a few hospitals."

"Pyke, doesn't play well with others," Bradley said.

"So… were they extra dick-y?" Pyke asked again.

"Well, I certainly don't want to have tea with them," Jude responded.

"They were pretty aggressive and harsh," Nicks added.

Pyke sat back in his chair. "See– This is why they should have sent agents here… They would have never gotten away with that under my roof."

"At least it's over with," Clayton said.

"Well– They may need him back–" Pyke saw the look of terror spread across Jude's features. "Not anytime soon, but it is a possibility as we proceed forward. I will also do my best to have them come here next time."

After the meeting Nicks walked Jude to the lobby.

"I think I'm going to take a walk before heading home... To clear my head," Jude said.

"Okay... just keep your phone on you, and be safe. I'll see you later tonight," Nicks replied.

Jude exited the building and looked up at the sun that peeked through the towering skyscrapers. He took a deep breath and headed towards Millennium Park for some much needed time to himself.

Nicks returned to the briefing room and sat down. "I think the CIA has more dirt on Rosakov and we need to seriously take a closer look at him."

"Actually– I may have something," Bradley said and pulled out a sheet of paper. "While you guys were on your vacation I was doing some digging. Looks like Pierre Daquin had assisted Rosakov with a deal a year ago in Turkey."

"Okay we need to focus more on Rosakov and Daquin. If Garrick and Rosakov have aligned and have a mutual associate we need to be concerned," Pyke said.

Seth entered the room adjusting his tie. "Sorry for my tardiness, I was helping Delenger with a GPS track," he said in the best American accent he had.

"Actually, it was good timing," Pyke said. "This is our newest member, Riley Halifax, the tech guru and analyst." Pyke pointed at each of them. "Bradley Evans,

Clayton Bradshaw, Rauri Nicks, and that crayon eater is Zachary MacTavish."

"Hi," Seth said with a wave.

"Welcome," Nicks said.

"Just in time we may need some facial pings set up," Clayton smiled.

"Groovy," Seth said and took a seat.

CHAPTER TWELVE

No matter how many times Kari checked her phone, the text messages she sent Jude remained unanswered. She hoped he was all right, yet there was a pang of regret for letting him in. It was far-fetched but it was still in the back of her mind that he could be avoiding her. Kari was dragged along to go shopping with the girls. She was at least grateful for the distraction, even though she loathed shopping malls.

"Kari, what do you think of these pants?" Marley asked and held up a tight pair of black jeans.

"They look good."

Marley smiled, turned and headed for the small dressing booth. Kari sat in a chair in front of the booth waiting for Marley to try the pants on. She tried to keep her mind from wandering to Jude, but it was difficult, she wanted to know where he was. Marley exited the room with a new pair on and picked up on the vibes from Kari and she sat down next to her.

"Jude?" She asked.

"That obvious?" Kari asked plainly as she looked down at her classic black Chuck Taylor's.

"You can roam around... Doesn't seem like this store is your cup of tea anyway."

"Are you sure?" Kari asked unsure about leaving her friends behind.

"Don't worry. Just go. I'll text you when we leave here."

"Thanks... I may head down to Millenium park," Kari said and stood from the pleather chair.

Kari took one last glance at Marley and walked out of the posh store. Michigan Avenue was certainly a sight to be seen. The hustle and bustle was overwhelming with the tall buildings and endless stores and restaurants. Kari wanted to retreat to a peaceful bliss. The call of the forest pulled at her heart. She missed the smell of pine and the dampness of the forest floor. She missed the canopy of trees, the light filtering through the lush leaves. She would not be finding any of that in a concrete jungle. The best she could do was settle for any form of green space.

Kari walked past the famed giant mirror bean. Families and friends smiled taking pictures in front of the structure. Grief rushed through her. The memories of the first time she explored Millennium Park was with her entire family. Her dad asked where the falcon was and if Jack had misplaced his bean. She wiped the liquid from her eyes. She wandered deeper into the park. She found the Lurie Garden. Beautiful flowers bloomed and bees buzzed around. Kari saw a bench and sat down taking in the plant life. She laid down on the bench and stared up at the blue sky. The clouds were nothing but whisps and the sun was warm on her face. She shielded her eyes from the sun and quickly drifted off into a light sleep.

Kari was jerked awake leaving her pleasant dreams behind. Her eyes flickered open and panic set in. Once reality came back to her she sprang to an upright position and looked around. Her eyes fell upon Jude, who stood over her, arms crossed, and a look of disapproval.

"What do you think you're doing?" Jude asked firmly in astonishment by Kari's choice to nap in the middle of the park.

Kari looked up at him. "What?"

"What are you doing?"

"Enjoying my day… What are you doing here?"

When Jude left the Marshals Office he did not expect to find Kari. It was pure coincidence he found her. "I was here with my uncle." *Not a total lie.*

"Where is he now?"

"Working. You shouldn't be wandering the city alone."

"Why do you care what I do?"

"What?– I do care," Jude said.

Kari stood up, anger brewing. "Well you sure have a strange way of showing it. Where were you the past week? You didn't even have the decency of returning my texts."

"Kari—" Jude wasn't even sure what he was going to tell her. With the stress of everything he forgot what the cover story was but he needed to explain. It tore at him seeing how much he had hurt her and it would only get worse. It pained him, but he needed to distance himself from her, for her own protection. If he learned anything from his interview with the CIA was that he wasn't good company to have.

"No, Jude–" Kari attempted to step around Jude but he blocked her.

"Just listen for a moment."

"Get out of my way," Kari tried to maneuver around Jude but he grasped her by the arm.

"Kari, I am sorry. I was out of town for the past few days. I should have told you."

"You were purposely ignoring me, why?"

Jude ran a hand through his hair and dropped his eyes. "I wasn't ignoring you, I was busy–"

"That is a poor excuse."

"It doesn't matter, I'm not good for you Kari. I'm just going to end up hurting you, and that is the last thing I want to do. Perhaps we shouldn't see each other anymore. We shouldn't be friends and certainly nothing more than friends... Even though– We can't– I can't–"

Kari fought back the anger that would bring with it tears. She had feelings for Jude and it killed her that he also did but was pushing her away. She took a calming breath and closed her eyes for a moment. "So, that's it then?"

"It's not that I– It has to be this way."

"See this is why I don't get close to people. I wish I never opened up to you."

Kari was not making this easy for Jude. "Kari… Please, it has nothing to do with you. I'm sorry this is hurting you but it's for the best. I have a past I'm not proud of… I just–"

"Don't push me away then! I'm not fragile, and I don't scare easily." Kari touched Jude's cheek.

Jude grasped Kari's hand and smiled. *I'm in deep shit.* "I– I– You made me forget what I was saying."

"You were saying that just because you had a past doesn't mean you can't have a fresh beginning."

"Is that what it was? I feel you are putting words in my mouth."

Kari intertwined her hand into Jude's. Her phone sounded in her pocket.

"Sorry– It's probably Marley." Kari stared at the text message from Marley telling her they were finished at the store and where to meet.

"Time to go?" Jude asked a hint of disappointment in his voice.

"Why don't you come with," Kari said and quickly texted Marley she was on her way with Jude.

"Are you sure? I do not want to intrude?"

"You won't be intruding. I want you to come." Kari smiled.

They walked down the street to the pizzaria. Jude texted Nicks to let him know he was going to be out longer. Marley, Alice and Prue waited outside the restaurant. Marley smirked at the sight of Kari and Jude together.

"Hey, Jude, glad you could join us," Marley said.

"I hope I am not intruding."

"Oh, not at all." Marley reassured.

"Well, I mean– It was supposed to be a girl's outing…" Prue piped up with a bite.

Alice grabbed Prue's arm. "Shhh, let them be."

The group entered the restaurants and Kari shrugged at Jude. Prue's behavior was a bit harsh.

After dinner they stepped outside.

Marley turned to Kari. "Are you going to to ride back with us on the L, or—"

"I can bring you home. I rode my bike into the city," Jude offered. "If you want to– that is–"

Marley smirked. "Of course she does."

Kari smiled. "Um… yeah… of course."

"See you later, Kari," Alice giggled.

"Bye, guys," Kari waved.

Kari watched her friends disappear into the crowded sidewalk.

"So, what do you want to do?" Kari asked shyly and turned back to Jude. "My curfew isn't till ten."

Jude held out his hand. "I have an idea."

"What is it?"

"Just trust me."

Kari took his hand and he led her to his motorcycle that was parked down the block from the US Marshal building. The sun was setting as they drove down the freeway. Kari held on tight to Jude. She was not a fan of the motorcycle on the freeway. They pulled into a small dimly lit parking lot. The asphalt was crumbling and riddled with potholes.

"Where are we?" Kari asked and set the helmet on the cycle.

"Palmisano park."

"It's so secluded for being in the city." Kari looked down the path to the tree lined quarry. "But it looks like it's closed."

"It is but... I know how much you miss home and the woods." Jude grasped Kari's hand remembering a conversation he overheard between her and Marley in Physics class.

"Eavesdropping much?"

"You were standing next to my desk."

Kari smiled. "Jude... this is great."

Kari sauntered down the path spinning every few steps swinging her arms wide. Jude smiled and followed Kari to the fishing pond. The surface of the high quarry walls reached up to meet the trees that grew upon them. The dark water mirrored the flames of the late evening sun. She lowered herself on the edge of the planked platform that reached out over the water. Jude sat down next to Kari letting his legs dangle from the side.

"See Jude, you're not a bad guy," Kari said and nudged Jude.

"But we've still only just met," Jude smirked.

Kari gave him a sideways glance. Jude interlaced his hand with Kari's. He raised her hand to his lips and gently kissed the back of her hand. He didn't know what it was about her but she made him crazy. Being with her made everything else go away, the pain, fear, and chaos.

"There is much you do not know."

"Then tell me," Kari said.

"You don't want to hear about me... "

"That is not true... Tell me how you ended up here."

"Kari..."

"Jude..."

Jude sighed. "It's complicated."

"But it's not."

Jude glanced at Kari and back over the water. He rehearsed the lines but it felt wrong to say them out loud, to her. "Well, when my mum died... I didn't have anyone else. So my uncle took me in. I hadn't even met him before."

"That must have been hard for you."

"Losing my mum was hard, but leaving London behind was not. I don't miss that place."

"But is Chicago any better? This place..."

"Is interesting... That much is for sure."

"There is one thing that's true... This city does have its fair share of danger." Kari stood with a smirk.

Jude tilted his head. "What are you about to do?"

Kari tossed her shoes off and stripped down to her underwear. Jude stared at her nearly nude body. Her dark hair cascaded down her pale skin. *Marshal Evans is going to kill me.*

"Kari..."

"Oh, Jude," Kari said and took off at a light jog down the path and hopped over the railing.

The earth was sharp beneath her feet but it reminded her of home when she would run through the woods barefoot.

"Kari!" Jude called after her.

Kari stopped when she made it to the cliff's edge of the quarry. The sun had been replaced by the night sky. She looked down at the black glass below. It was calling to her. Kari took a step forward ready to fall into the dark unknown. Jude grasped Kari's arm tightly and pulled her back.

"What are you doing?"

"Living life on the edge. You should try it," Kari said and plunged forward.

Jude hung on tight to Kari in an attempt to thwart her jump but her momentum was too great and he plummeted in after her. The cold water came fast and hard. The wind was expelled from her lungs and wrapped its cool talons around her. Kari enjoyed the ice against her skin, it made her feel at peace. A calm came over her and she wanted to drift into the dark unknown. All of the pain could be washed away. An arm wrapped around Kari and Jude pulled her to the surface. She took in a sharp inhale of fresh air. Jude swam for the both of them to shore.

"Why would you do that?" Jude said, hoisting Kari onto the platform.

Kari helped Jude out of the water. "I wanted to feel again."

Kari lowered herself onto the planks and pulled Jude with her. The weight of his body pinned her to the dock. He gently brushed her wet matted hair out of her face. Kari stared into Jude's worried eyes. Kari reached up and cradled Jude's face in her hand. She felt his breath on her skin. Her heart was racing with each passing moment. Kari lifted her head, her lips connecting with Jude's. His strong hands ran through Kari's hair as he pressed his body up against hers. Kari moved her hands along Jude's torso. She grasped the bottom of his shirt and pulled it from his body. She lifted the drenched tee shirt over his head. She pulled him back to her kissing him passionately and ran her hand down the side of his bare chest taking in every inch of his body. The heat from his body warmed her. Jude pulled away, his breath heavy. Jude lifted himself from Kari and rolled back on his heels to a sitting position by her feet.

"I'm sorry. I can't," Jude whispered. *You, woman, are going to be the end of me.* He gazed at her curved body wanting her.

Kari was confused, she assumed he would want to. She quickly stood and retrieved her clothing, holding it in front of her.

She found it impossible to look at Jude. "I'm sorry... I thought..."

"Kari... It's not that I don't–"

Kari held up her hand. "It's fine."

"What I mean is–"

"It's fine, I said. Really..."

Jude picked up his shirt and stood. Kari dressed herself holding back the tears.

"Can you just listen for a second?" Jude said.

Kari's eyes were glued to the planks, staring at the gouges in the wood. If she stared through the silence any longer, she might scorch right through the dock.

"Kari, I–"

"Can we go?" Kari asked, breaking her concentration on the rickety dock and walked back toward the path. Jude would have been her first and she was mortified by the rejection.

Jude watched her go and sighed. "Yeah, I guess we'll go." He said to no one in particular and pulled his shirt over his head.

Kari clasped the strap to the helmet and waited for Jude. She was upset with herself and embarrassed.

"I'm sorry tonight didn't go the way you hoped." Jude picked up his leather jacket.

"You know what–? Forget it. It's alright– Honestly, Jude."

Jude handed Kari his jacket. "It's not alright... We should talk about this."

Kari avoided eye contact and put the coat on. "Don't worry about it. I just thought you wanted to... I put you in an awkward position. I'm sorry."

Jude grabbed Kari's hips and kissed her neck. "There's nothing to be sorry about. I want to, just not tonight. A gentleman does not partake in such activities until the lady has been properly courted."

Kari smiled. "You are too proper, Jude."

The twenty minute ride back to Tinley Park was cold. Kari hung onto Jude tightly. She was freezing with a jacket, she couldn't imagine how cold he was.

"I'd have you walk me to my door, but I don't think that would be a good idea," Kari informed and handed Jude his helmet.

"A gentleman always walks a lady to her door," Jude said and set his helmet down even though he feared the reaction from Bradley.

Kari smiled. "Well if you insist."

Kari and Jude walked up the sidewalk together. They stopped on the porch. Jude turned to Kari looking deep into her eyes.

"I did enjoy our day together," Jude said and grabbed Kari's hand. "You are beautiful."

Kari stepped close to Jude. He didn't move and Kari kissed him. Jude touched the side of Kari's face wanting more. He pulled away keeping his hand where it was.

"I should go," Jude whispered.

"I–"

The front door flew open, the light from the house blinded Jude.

Kari felt the color drain from her face. "Bradley… we… were just…"

"Go inside, I would like to have a word with this young man," Bradley said.

Kari was nervous for how calm her brother was. "Bradley…"

"Don't worry, it's just a quick chat."

Kari shot Jude an apologetic glance and retreated into the house. Bradley closed the door and motioned for Jude to walk. They strolled down the sidewalk a few steps to make sure they would not be overheard. Bradley paused crossing an arm over his chest and his chin in his hand.

"Marshal Evans, I can explain," Jude defended.

"Please do… Please explain to me why you were kissing my sister after I told you to stay away from her."

"I…"

"Jude, I am here to protect you. But the hell if I will allow my sister to get involved with you and put her in harm's way."

"Sir, with all due respect, Kari needs someone right now… I haven't know her long–"

"No, you haven't."

"But something tells me that she wasn't always so reckless…"

"What do you mean?" Bradley shifted his weight.

"Ah well… for starters, I found her napping in Millennium Park. She just walked off from her friends."

Bradley turned his gaze to the sky upset by the lack of self security Kari seemed to display.

"Where did you two go then?"

"Uh– We snuck into Palmisano Park–"

"You did what? If the local cops–"

"I know, I know, run my fingerprints."

"Do you? Do you know? I feel as if we just had this conversation after you got into a substantial fight at school. Did the CIA scramble that small brain of yours?" Bradley poked Jude in the forehead.

Jude swatted Bradley's hand away. "I got in that fight to protect Kari."

"And I appreciate that, more than you know but it does not give you the right to—"

"I am sorry Marshal…"

"You have also said that before– Why did you go there anyway?"

"I was trying to be nice and take her somewhere that reminded her of home."

Bradley sighed heavily and ran his hand over his face. "Jude– You are making my life difficult." He placed a hand on Jude's shoulder. "Wait why are you wet?"

"About that sir– Kari–" Bradley stared Jude down. "She thought jumping from the cliff of the quarry was a good idea."

"Jesus–" Bradley closed his eyes for a moment. "Anything else happen tonight that I should know about while we're at it?"

Jude remained quiet.

"Christ, what other stupid choices have you two made tonight?"

Jude swallowed hard. "Nothing, that's it, sir."

"I wasn't born yesterday… What, else?"

"Well…" Jude shifted uncomfortably. "We kissed… and…"

Bradley held out a hand trying to contain his anger. "I am trying very hard–"

Jude spoke quickly. "Nothing happened! I swear to you, Marshal Evans. I stopped!"

Bradley squeezed his forehead. "You need to end things with her, Jude. You cannot be in a relationship with her."

"Sir– I don't know if I can," Jude admitted, disappointed about his weakness.

Bradley looked up to the dark sky and returned his gaze to Jude with a heavy sigh. "Stay away from her, Jude. You're not going to like what happens if you don't."

"She needs someone though..."

"Let me worry about it."

"Uh, Marshal Evans. Are you going to tell Marshal Nicks about this?"

"Yes, and you can be assured that some of your privileges will be revoked."

Bradley turned away and returned to the house. He opened the door and Kari was sitting on the steps.

"What did you say to him?" Kari asked a snap to her voice.

"Kari, you cannot see him."

"You can't stop me," Kari bit.

"You are living under my roof and will do as you are told."

"You're not Dad!"

Bradley took a breath and stepped into his office to the right of the foyer. He picked up a manila folder from the desk and handed it to Kari. He had set it aside in anticipation Jude wouldn't listen. She looked at the folder in disbelief and then back at Bradley.

"You did a background check on him?"

"He's not who you think he is."

Kari opened the file and saw Jude's mugshot and an aggravated battery charge, burglary, and possession of a concealed weapon. Her heart sank. She could not believe what she was reading.

"This was when he was sixteen! Why are you bringing this up?"

"That's correct, last year if my math is accurate... I am protecting you."

"You ruin everything! You know that?" Kari tried to wipe the tears from her eyes and stood quickly. "I wish I would have been with mom and dad the night of the accident, then none of this would even be happening."

"Kari–"

"Leave me alone!" Kari ran upstairs and slammed her door.

Bradley stared at the top of the landing where Kari was. He was not cut out to be a parent. He rubbed his hand on his face with a long exhale. He retreated to his office and called Nicks.

Jude opened the door and gently shut it behind him. He hoped that Nicks was already in for the night but of course no such luck.

"Glad you're finally home…"

"Hey–"

"Come sit, we need to have a chat." Nicks pointed to the couch.

Jude sat. "I'm sorry."

"What are you exactly sorry about? Your poor decision making or the fact that you got caught?"

"I'm sorry, I wasn't thinking." Jude leaned back on the couch.

"I know you have been through a lot this week, but you need to be careful. We cannot afford to have a slip up that will land Garrick on our doorstep," Nicks lectured. "And with Bradley's sister? Come on, kid."

"I know–"

"I did not enjoy getting an earful about that from Bradley… Again– Your privileges are suspended for now. School and home, nothing else."

"You're grounding me? Can you do that?"

"I guess I am grounding you– hmph," Nicks smiled.

"I'm glad one of us is amused."

Nicks stood and in a serious tone stated, "I am not amused."

Jude shook his head not sure whether or not Nicks was trying to be cheeky or not.

—

Bradley sat in his office and flipped open a file. His phone rang assuming it was Nicks. He saw it was an international number and cocked a brow.

"Evans."

"Do you always answer the phone like that?" Marcus asked.

"Ha, no– It's been a long day, I thought this was my work phone. How the hell are you?"

"There's a perpetual amount of sand in my ass and I have now spooned with another man to stay warm more than once. I have no idea what day it is or where I am the majority of the time."

Bradley chuckled. "Just get back from an op then I assume?"

"More like back to civilization… They had us hunkered down at an outpost for a few days after an op. Now we're just waiting to get the green light to go kick some more ass."

"Did you guys run into some issues on the last op?"

"Kind of, I mean we had no casualties. I may have taken a tumble down the side of a mountain during our EVAC in the middle of the night but that's minor. But from the delayed EVAC trying to find my unconscious ass, we lost our window to beat feat from the area and got stuck at that outpost for a few. Apparently the Air Force was busy or something."

"Forget how night vision works?"

"There may have been an explosion blinding me momentarily."

"Well, I'm glad you're still in one peice."

Marcus paused. "How are things?"

"Difficult–"

"That bad huh?"

"Marcus, I don't have the slightest idea how to handle her. I am at a loss. She is rebelling and I don't know what to do. "

"What's she doing?"

"Staying out late, going places she shouldn't, all with a boy she's not supposed to be with."

Marcus chuckled. "Sounds like nothing compared to what you used to do."

"Marcus–"

"Want me to talk to her?"

"She would love to hear from you. Let me get her."

Bradley walked up the steps and knocked on Kari's door.

"I don't want to talk to you!" she yelled.

"Marcus is on the phone– Did you at least want to talk to him?"

Kari opened the door. "Give it."

"Here." Bradley handed her the phone.

"Hey! How are you?" Kari asked.

"In one peice. You?"

"Not great, to be honest. Bradley is a tyrant."

"That seems extreme."

"No… There's a guy I've been seeing and he did a background check on him and forbade me to see him."

Marcus took a breath. "Well– I'm sure he had a good reason to. Bradley just wants to keep you safe."

"I know but it's really hard. I miss mom and dad, everything reminds me of them and for once I found someone that makes me forget for just a little bit."

"Kar–"

"Marcus! Time to mount up!" Hatch yelled.

"Sorry Kar– I gotta go." Marcus hung up without a proper goodbye.

"Wait!" Kari said into the phone, the dial tone sounding in her ear.

Marcus joined his team at the Marine humvee escort.

"HVT Kodiak is Oscar Mike to target location," Hatch said and the unit loaded into two humvees. "Viper 6-5 ten mikes to drop point. Remember girl scouts, we are on our own for this one."

Marcus adjusted his thigh rig over his grey tac pants. Hatch rolled his shoulders under his black body armor. The team was not wearing their standard uniforms but a hodgepodge of civilian tactical clothing and gear. The humvee rolled to a stop.

"Here's our stop, boys," Hatch said. "Say goodbye to the Marines."

Marcus waved. "Bye Marines."

"Good luck, Viper," Marcus's driver said.

Hatch leaned into the open passenger window. "I left a box of crayons under the seat. I hope you don't mine but I took a bite out of the red one."

The Marine laughed.

The six man team left the humvee escort and proceeded down the street.

"Target location: two point seven klicks to the south east," Hatch advised.

The team maneuvered through the narrow streets of Mosul converging onto the target location.

"Viper 6-5, one klick to HVT location. Engage," Hatch reported posted in a doorway.

Hatch stepped out aiming his rifle scanning the windows of the buildings covering long with Marcus covering left. A masked tango popped out of an alley and threw a grenade down the street.

"Grenade!" Marcus yelled and fired rounds at the enemy, hitting him in the chest and head.

The team dispersed, finding any cover they could. Marcus flattened to the ground alongside a car and covered his head. The explosive wave passed through Marcus and the debris rained down on the car. A burst of rifle shots sounded. Marcus could not see where they were coming from due to the smoke. They tinged against the metal of the car he was under.

"Hostiles to the east; red car!" Moose yelled returning fire.

"Hostiles to the north; third story!" Plank shouted.

"They're everywhere!" Yeti advised and moved to Marcus's forward position.

Hatch hit a window in the building directly next to him with the stock of his rifle.

"Viper 6-5, pull back, building to the west," Hatch ordered.

Marcus stood and provided cover for Yeti's retreat. They pushed into the building clearing for primary security.

"Sierra Leader to Nest. We need immediate QRF to our location or an EVAC. Abort HVT Kodiak."

"Sierra Leader, negative on EVAC to current location. We've sighted numerous tangos proceeding to your lima. Head to the roof. Searching for EVAC site. Stand by for QRF."

"Copy, Viper 6-5 Oscer Mike," Hatch said and motioned to the roof.

"QRF ETA fourty... We'll get you that EVAC."

"Copy that Nest." Hatch muttered under his breath. "So much for the quick part... fucksticks."

The team climbed the stairs through the building. Hatch led the team to the rooftop. Bullets flew at them from smashed windows and rubble piles.

"Move!" Hatch ordered and provided suppression fire at the ISIS rebel on the rooftops across the street.

Phantom led the way across the first roof, the others falling in formation behind him. Marcus posted behind a tin structure and shot at the insurgent providing cover for Hatch. Their footsteps were heavy on the makeshift platforms and war riddled roofs. Bullets whizzed past the men as they fled for their lives.

"Nest to Viper 6-5, EVAC site half a klick north. The building with the green roof."

"Viper 6-5, copy," Hatch managed to yell through heavy breath.

The team turned north on the roof and jumped down a story to get to the next building. Marcus landed hard and the unsteady sand caused him to slide. Immense pressure erupted in Marcus's chest, the force knocking him to the ground. His plate prevented the round from killing him. An insurgent ran out from behind the shadow of the building, pointing his rifle in Marcus's face. He shouted in Arabic and pulled the trigger. Marcus feared his life was at an end, the rifle clicked, a malfunction. Marcus firmly grabbed the barrel of the rifle, pulling the combatant towards him. The man tore the gun from Marcus's grip and struck him hard with the butt. The man's eyes went blank and blood pooled out of his forehead. Marcus turned his gaze behind him to see Moose lowering his rifle. He pulled Marcus to his feet.

They trailed behind the rest of the team, trying to catch up. The green roof was in sight, along with the welcoming site of the chopper. A loud whooshing sound approached, followed by a deafening explosion. The ground crumbled away and the building consumed Moose and Marcus. Dust and debris fell upon them. Marcus staggered to his feet coughing dust from his lungs. He gazed up at the ruined two story freefall. The falling debris made it difficult to see.

"Badger! Moose!" Hatch yelled over their coms.

"RPG, we're good. Oscar Mike to EVAC," Marcus responded.

"Let's go!" Moose yelled and led the way through a hole in the ruble.

They ran into the open alley into a building. They darted through the tunnels carved out in the walls to easily move from location to location. Bullets sprayed through the windows as they ran. Marcus paused at the open door. They needed to find a way back to the rooftops. Moose exited his cover and fire erupted. Blood splattered and Moose fell to the ground. His eyes still and locked onto Marcus.

"Moose!" Marcus shouted and returned fire killing the insurgent. "Eagle down!"

Marcus bent down and pulled his tags from his friend. Marcus stepped over his dead friend and exited the building, a continued rapid fire sounded around him.

"Can you get him to cover?" Hatch asked.

"He's dead! Moose is dead!"

Marcus ran through another building trying to evade the ISIS militants.

"Badger, you need to get to the roofs. The hostiles are surrounding you," Nest informed.

The adrenaline coursed through Marcus. He slung his rifle. In a mad dash he maneuvered through the maze of tunneled buildings. He tried not to panic while running for his life. At any moment he could be killed or worse captured. He desperately searched for stairs as the tangos enclosed on him. He climbed rubble and wrecks, finally reaching the stairs to the roof. He jumped over walls and slid down platforms, angry yells in Aribic behind him.

"Badger, we see you," Hatch said.

Hope ignited within when his eyes laid upon the sight of the chopper. He jumped down from a roof to the next building. The chopper steadied at the end of the building. Rounds sprayed at Marcus, hitting the concrete. Marcus inhaled sharply and launched himself from the roof. His hands reach out for the swinging rope ladder. The rope burned his hands and arms as he slid down from the impact. He wrapped his leg into the rungs securing himself. The chopper lifted with an evasive tilt away from the hot zone. Once the helo leveled out Marucs climbed the ladder. Hatch grabbed a hold of him and hoisted him into the chopper.

"Sierra Leader to Nest. Viper 6-5 secured on EVAC. One KIA," Hatch reported.

Marcus stared out the open side of the chopper at Mosul below.

"They knew we were coming," Phantom said.

"And we lost Moose because of it," Marcus turned to his team, their faces covered in dirt and soot.

Hatch unstrapped his gloves. "We all know what we signed up for."

CHAPTER THIRTEEN

The ride to school Monday morning was quiet. Kari had her ear buds in and refused to acknowledge Bradley's existence. Braldey parked the car and Kari opened the door. She swung a leg out and Bradley grabbed her arm. Kari pulled her earbud out and looked at her brother.

"It's Dad's birthday today–"

Kari casted her gaze to the sidewalk. "I know."

"I miss him– Kari, I know I'm not Dad, but I am trying. I just want you to be safe."

Kari choked back the sorrow. "I don't know if I can do this anymore."

"What does that mean?"

"I'm sick of feeling this way and I feel alone."

"You're not alone, Kari, I'm right here."

"Yeah, you keep saying that but you're always gone."

Kari shut the door and walked away. Bradley stared after his sister feeling defeated. She was hurting and he didn't know how to fix it. Kari walked to where Jude usually sat near the main steps leading to the entrance of the school. He was nowhere to be found. Her heart sank and she pulled out her phone. She texted Jude *Where are you?* There was a delay in the response and she held her breath. *I'm running late. But, your brother made it clear he didn't want me around. Maybe we should keep our distance for the time being.* She typed, *I need to talk to you, it's important. Today sucks… I can't even… I can't keep it together. It's my dad's birthday… I feel alone and… Please…* Kari wiped the tears with the back of her hand thinking about her dad. She was furious with Bradley for ripping open the fragile tape that was holding her together. Nothing was going right, it was one thing after another and she couldn't take much more.

Jude stared the text message. *Ah the hell with Bradley.* Jude texted her back, *I will see you in first period. We'll talk. It'll be okay.* Jude walked towards their first class after stopping at his locker. He looked down at his phone and there was no response from Kari.

Kari lurched forward from the impact of someone shoulder checking her. Her phone dropped to the ground and Vanessa kicked her phone and it skidded a few feet in front of Kari.

Vanessa stepped on it, the screen cracking. "Oops," she said holding her hand to her mouth. The girls with her giggled. "I hadn't seen you there, I don't usually pay attention to trash."

"Fuck off!" Kari yelled.

Vanessa was not phased and took the leather bound journal from the crook of Kari's arm.

"Give that back!" Kari demanded and swiped at Vanessa but she just stepped back and another girl shoved Kari.

Vanessa opened the cover and saw a personalized letter from Kari's father that he wrote to her before giving her the journal.

"What is this? Looks important," Vanessa took the page and ripped it out.

"No!" Kari cried and lurched forward at Vanessa.

The same girl pushed her harder, sending Kari to the ground. Vanessa pulled out a lighter from her pocket and held the parchment page to the flame. It turned brown and black shriveling to ash. Vanessa let the chard remnants float to the ground.

"Oops," she said and turned on her heel.

The group of girls walked away. The tears streamed down Kari's cheeks as she stared at the last words of her father. There was nothing left and a hole was ripped in her heart. She looked over and picked up her phone. The screen was shattered. An emotional whirlwind engulfed Kari. Her hands shook as she shoved her phone in her backpack. The sorrow was too great, she couldn't handle it. She wanted it to end, to not feel the pain anymore. Kari stared up at the entrance of the school and could not bring herself to walk through the doors. She looked around in one last hope to see Jude but his face was not amongst those around her. She turned and walked away from the school.

Jude waited outside their first class. There was still no message from her. With each passing moment his heart sank and stomach twisted. Marley walked to the door. Jude reached out to her.

"Have you seen Kari this morning?"

"I haven't... She was supposed to meet us this morning but she never came. I even sent her a text and she didn't respond... I assumed she was with you."

Jude ran his hand through his hair. "I have to go." Something was wrong.

"Jude!" Marley called after him.

Kari cut down an alley a block behind the school. She wiped the tears from her eyes and took a deep breath. Her world was upside down. She was drowning and couldn't surface. She missed home, her parents, her friends. The nightmare was never ending and she needed a break from reality.

"Hey, princess. Your school is that way," an older boy said, sitting on the trunk of a car in a small parking lot off of the alley.

"And?"

"You don't want to be wandering around neighborhoods you don't belong in," another male said, stepping around the car.

"Well unless... You do belong and you're looking for something..." The boy stood and pulled a baggie from his backpack.

Kari looked from the baggie to the boy. "What is it?"

"Narcs and benzos– Gateway to pure bliss of emotionlessness."

"What do they do?"

"Make you numb to the world, great way to escape."

Kari swallowed. "How much?"

"How much do you have?"

Kari dug into her backpack. "A hundred."

The boy stepped to her. "That will do."

They made the exchange and she continued down the alley towards the park. Kari stared at the small baggie filled with a plethora of different pills. She had never done drugs before, but what did she have to lose? She just wanted to be numb from the pain. She looked around the small empty park. She wasn't sure who she expected to see, certainly no one that gave a shit about her. She opened up the bag and grabbed a few of the twenty pills in the bag. Tears formed and slid down her cool cheeks. She missed her parents and could not bear the pain. She swallowed them and leaned up against the thick tree. She stared up at the sky waiting to not feel, she had no idea how long it was supposed to take or how many to take.

Jude walked out of the main entrance of the school in a hurry. His phone vibrated in his pocket. He was not the least bit surprised. Jude pulled the phone out and answered the call.

"Where are you going?" Nicks asked.

There were a few straggling students walking near Jude. "Oh hey– Uncle Rauri, yes I'll remember to feed the dog when I get home–" Jude watched as the student went past. "Kari is missing… I'm going to look for her."

"You will do no such thing. Go back to class. I will let Evans and Bradshaw know," Nicks stated.

"Sir, I cannot do that," Jude said and hung up the phone.

Nicks inhaled sharply. "Damn that boy." Nicks picked up his radio. "Evans."

"Yeah?" Bradley sat on a bench reading a newspaper. His hat was drawn over his eyes.

"It appears that Jude is going awol from school to look for your truant sister."

Bradley took a long breath. "That girl is going to be the death of me. Keep a visual on Jude, I will start looking for my sister."

Clayton pulled up next to Bradley in a dark Chrysler 200. He opened the passenger door and got in.

"Roger," Nicks responded and exited his vehicle tailing Jude at a distance.

Jude crossed the street, the light changing behind him allowed the heavy flow of traffic to proceed. Nicks sighed, watching Jude get farther away. Jude turned the corner down the street to check the park. He saw someone dressed in a school uniform in the far corner of the park sitting up against a thick tree. He crossed the grass and saw it was Kari, her eyes closed. His stomach lurched, something wasn't right.

"Kari?" Jude called her name and crouched in front of her.

He cradled her face and she opened her eyes. "Huh?"

The sky was overcast and bleak, yet her pupils were pin point. A baggie full of pills sat next to her. He picked it up and saw the array of medications.

"What did you take?" Jude asked and shoved the baggie in his back pocket.

"Does it matter? Go away."

"Bloody hell–" Jude grasped her arm. "I need to take you to a hospital."

"Get off of me!" Kari yelled.

"Kari, stop," Jude said calmly and pulled her arm to try and get her to stand.

"Let me go!" Kari screamed and unshouldered her backpack and swung at Jude hitting him. Her backpack flew out of her hand scattering some of the contents on the grass.

"Kari!"

Kari kicked Jude in the thigh and he stumbled backwards. Jude reached out to grab Kari but a strong arm wrapped around his chest. His feet left the ground and he plummeted to the earth with a thud. Jude tried to get up from his blindsided tackle.

"Stop resisting, shitbag!" The officer growled and pinned Jude to the ground with a knee to the back.

"Are you all right, miss?" the other officer asked Kari.

Jude's arms were wrenched behind his back and the cold steel ratchetted in place around his wrists.

"Think you're tough, huh? Going after a girl–" The officer hissed and lifted Jude to his feet.

"That's not what's happening–" Jude said as the officer patted him down. "If you would just let me explain–"

The officer stopped over the pocket that Jude had placed the drugs in. The officer dug into Jude's pocket and pulled out the baggie.

"Well, what do we have here?" the officer asked and turned to his partner looking at the pills. "Looks like some benzos and oxy. What else you got?"

His partner looked at him and gestured to Kari. "This one is strung out."

The officer grabbed Kari tightly and spun her around. She tried to pull away and the officer twisted her arm up her back. Kari let out a small cry.

"Don't do that," the officer warned and placed Kari into handcuffs.

"Let's go," the officer ordered.

The police escorted Kari and Jude out of the park towards their squad car. The cops leaned both of them up against the car and did a thorough search of both of them.

"Let go of me," Kari seethed and tried to pull away.

The officer rolled his eyes and stabilized her against the car. "Stop."

Nicks rounded the corner of the block and shook his head irritated.

"We have a problem," Nicks radioed to Bradley and Clayton. "Jude found your sister at the park and the locals are dealing with them... Where are you guys at?"

"Just down the street. Hang tight." Bradley said.

"What's your name?" the officer asked Jude.

Jude knew that he was in serious trouble being in possession of the drugs. Either way he knew he could be arrested.

"I refuse to answer that."

"Look, you're already in a lot of trouble... Do you really want to make matters worse?"

Jude remained quiet.

"When you get booked in they're going to run your prints anyway."

Jude's blood ran hot, his mind whirling. He needed to get out of there. He could not have his prints run through the system. Jude's eyes darted, scanning the area. He was confident he could out run both of them but he couldn't leave Kari behind. A wash of relief spread when his eyes landed on Bradley and Clayton. His eyes spotted Nicks in the corner of the park staring him down. Jude was not looking forward to the lecture Nicks had in store for him.

Kari spotted them as well. "Oh! Just wonderful."

The officers turned to see the approaching parties. The thinner of the two officers stepped towards them.

"Can I help you with something?" The officer asked.

"U.S. Marshals," Bradley announced.

The officer looked at Bradley and Clayton skeptical. "Uh… What?"

Bradley lifted his sweatshirt to expose his gun and badge. "I'm Marshal Evans and this is Marshal Bradshaw. We are going to need those two in your custody to be released to us."

"Excuse me?" The officer was baffled and did not believe that the two random people dressed in street clothes were Marshals. "Anyone can buy a badge online and this would not be the first time I've dealt with impersonators before. Now we may have an issue with you carrying a concealed weapon." The officer gripped his gun.

Clayton unzipped his jacket. "Like my partner said we are US Marshal's." He reached into an inside pocket to produce his credentials. His hand crossed over his green tactical vest that read US Marshal. The officer looked Clayton up and down as he handed the officer his credentials.

The officer let go of his gun and studied the ID for a moment. "Look, you have to understand where I'm coming from here. We roll up seeing this disturbance— And they are not the most cooperative. The boy had oxy and benzos on him and the girl is high as a kite. So you can see my hesitation to just hand them over to you. I mean they're high school kids. What would the Marshals want with them anyway?"

Bradley smiled. "That information is confidential, officer."

"Right... Well I'm going to have to call my supervisor on this one."

Bradley opened his palms. "Do what you need to."

The officer pulled out his phone and dialed.

Jude and Kari were seated on the curb while the other officer had his head turned watching his partner. He had given up asking questions with Kari's snarky responses. Kari's head lobbed and she fell sideways. Jude's heart sank watching her body go limp.

"Marshal!" Jude screamed.

Bradley looked past the officer standing in front of him to see Kari unresponsive and the other officer crouched next to her, speaking into his radio. The cold feeling of fear gripped Bradley as he darted past the officer to get to his sister. Kari's breaths were shallow.

She was in a place of peace, there was no more pain. The officer stood and hurried to the trunk of his squad. Bradley knelt down next to Kari and removed the handcuffs and laid her flat on her back. The officer returned with narcan, the reversal for an opiod overdose. The narcan was administered through Kari's nose. Her breaths remained shallow. The officer grabbed a hold of Kari's arms and picked up his handcuffs.

"What are you doing?" Bradley asked.

"Junkies have been known to fight when the narcan works."

"She's not a junkie." Bradley stared at Kari wondering if he knew her at all.

"Right…"

Kari's eyes fluttered and she stirred. Anger engulfed her. Her peace and tranquility were taken from her. The pain of the world crashed down on her. She let out a scream and swung a fist at the shape hovering above her. Bradely moved his face out of the way of Kari's wrath and caught her wrist.

"Kari! Stop!" Bradley ordered.

Kari screamed and tried to pull her wrist away. Her screams turned to sobs and her fight faded. Sirens blared in the background and the ambulance sped down the street approaching the scene. The paramedics stopped next to the squad car and exited the ambulance with their blue medical bag.

"Excuse me," the female paramedic said to Bradley.

He let Kari go and rose. The paramedic knelt next to Kari. She examined Kari the best she could.

"What did you take?" She asked Kari.

"Leave... me... alone!" Kari yelled.

Kari could not control her emotions. Anger, sorrow, dread and anxiety coursed through her body. Her mind was in a whirlwind unable to catch up to reality. She swung her arm at no one in particular but the paramedic stood and jumped back quickly in fear of getting hit. Bradley grasped Kari's wrist and forced her arms behind her back. He pulled a pair of handcuffs from his back pocket. The cold steel pressed against Kari's wrists and ratcheted into place. Bradley's heart sank, but it needed to be done.

"Take these off!" Kari screamed.

Bradley took a deep breath and said to the medics. "I can escort her to your bus and ride in with you."

"That would be best," the male medic answered.

Clayton released Jude from his cuffs. Jude stepped forward to help Kari but Clayton grabbed his shoulder.

"No, stay out of this," Clayton ordered.

"But–"

"You will do as you're told."

Bradley picked Kari up from the ground by her arm and she pulled away.

"I hate you!" she screamed.

Bradley adjusted his grip and Clayton grasped Kari's other arm. Jude picked up Kari's discarded backpack. He collected the loose paper and books putting them back inside. He paused seeing a file with the top of a sheet sticking out with his cover name on it. He opened up the file to see his booking photo from New York. He was angry and hurt knowing that Bradley was trying to prevent Kari from seeing him. He couldn't blame him though. He tucked the file safely in her backpack.

"Walk," Bradley ordered.

Kari dropped her weight. Bradley growled and together he and Clayton lifted Kari off her feet and carried her the short distance to the ambulance. Bradley set Kari down on the cot and she was restrained to it.

"I'll follow you," Clayton said and shut the doors to the back of the ambulance.

Clayton looked to Nicks who waved for them to go.

"Come on, Jude," Clayton said motioning to the car.

Kari screamed and fought the majority of the way until her fight was gone. She drifted into a deep slumber, her body fighting to normalize.

Bradley stood outside Kari's hospital room, his arms across his chest watching the nurses tend to Kari, who continued to sleep. Kari's wrists were shackled to the bed to ensure she would not become violent again. Jude and Clayton walked around the large nurses station to get to Bradley.

Bradley glanced at Jude. "Thank you for finding her."

"I do care about her…"

"I know–" Bradley replied his attention was still on Kari.

Jude set the backpack down and pulled out the file. "Um– Marshal?"

Bradley turned and saw the file in Jude's hand. "I had to, Jude."

Clayton took the file and scanned it quickly. "Don't you think this was a bit risky? I mean– This is his actual criminal record from New York, you just changed his name."

"I was trying to scare Kari into staying away from him," Bradley said. "But I can see that it may have made matters worse."

"I realize that, but in the unlikely event this fell into the wrong hands…"

"I know, Clayton–"

Clayton exhaled slowly. "I'm taking this."

There was a moment of silence and Bradley spoke. "Can you take Jude back to school."

"I would like to stay," Jude said.

"Come on kid, they're going to need some time," Clayton motioned for Jude to walk.

Jude walked away taking one last look at Kari.

Jude stared out the window not wanting to speak with Clayton as he drove him back to school.

"Christ… Did you know about the drugs?" Clayton asked.

"No, I couldn't believe she took them when I got to her," Jude said.

"This isn't Kari. I've known her for a long time… What has gotten into her— You don't think– She wasn't trying to commit suicide was she?"

Jude swallowed hard. "I hope not…"

Jude was more distant than usual at school. He had ignored Marley's pleas to know what happened but Jude walked passed her. He was a zombie in class. Another stress added to the pile. He wished he would have met Kari before school like they planned, then none of this would have happened.

Bradley sat on the wheeled stool, his forearms resting on the rails of the bed. Kari stirred with a moan and fluttered her eyes open. She tried to move her arms but the steel of the handcuffs tethered her to the bed clinking against the metal rail. The bright light blinded her before her eyes could adjust. Her mind raced trying to decipher what had occured. She had little recollection of what happened. Anxiety coursed through her body when she noticed the handcuffs on her wrists.

"Hey…" Bradley touched her shoulder.

Tears fell from her eyes and she stared at Bradley. "What happened? Why am I handcuffed?"

"You overdosed on pills and were out of control."

Kari dropped her head, her hair fell in front of her eyes. Bradley uncuffed both of Kari's hands and sat back down. Kari massaged her wrists and examined the red indent on her flesh from the steel.

"Kari, where did you get the drugs?"

"I don't know, some guys down the street from school."

"Some guys– And you thought it was a good idea to take what they gave you?"

Kari shrugged. "I didn't want to feel anymore."

Bradley crossed his arms. "I cannot even begin to explain how upset I am with you– You do know you could have died, right?"

"I'm sorry."

Bradley hung his head. "I have to ask you a difficult question and you need to tell me the truth– Were you trying to kill yourself?"

The tears came. "No–"

"Are you sure? We can get you help."

"I didn't want to die, I just wanted to get high and not have to deal with everything."

Jessica frantically walked into the room and embraced Kari in a hug.

"I was so worried. I'm sorry it took me so long to get here." She stepped back beside Bradley. "What did the doctor say? Is she going to be okay?"

"She's lucky Jude found her, otherwise it would be a different story– We're just waiting for the drugs to leave her system then we can go."

"Kari–"

Kari shook her head, her throat tightening and tears formed in her eyes.

"What were you thinking?" Jessica asked.

"I just needed a break, I can't handle everything right now. That school is awful and I miss mom and dad so much."

Jessica climbed into the bed and held Kari tight as she cried. Jessica looked up at Bradley who was barely keeping it together.

The hours passed from the mandatory observation and Kari was discharged from the hospital. She locked herself in her room and buried her face in a pillow and cried herself to sleep.

Jessica sipped a glass of wine on the couch. "I think she needs to go spend a weekend at Joan and Tony's? Being with her aunt and uncle may help."

"You want to reward her behavior?"

"No, but I think she needs it. She needs to see her friends and regain some happiness. I fear if she continues down her current path, we will lose her."

"Jess–"

"And Jude, doesn't seem so bad. I don't understand why you have been so hell bent on keeping them apart."

"No, he's not a bad kid…"

"I want to have him over for dinner, to thank him properly for saving Kari."

"I don't know if that is a good idea."

"You won't say no to me," Jessica said and slid her bare foot up Bradley's leg.

—

Jude sat at the kitchen table doing homework. Nicks sat eerily quiet all evening setting Jude on edge. Nicks pulled out a chair and sat.

"Do you have a minute?" Nicks asked.

Jude didn't look up from his work. "Are you going to yell?"

"I don't yell…"

Jude set his pencil down and stared at Nicks who didn't look mad at all but worried.

"You scared the hell out of me today, kid."

"I didn't mean to, I just–"

"I know… You were concerned about Kari."

"Sir… Never would I have thought that was going to happen. I– I– almost panicked. If Marshal Evans and Bradshaw didn't intervene I don't know what I would have done."

"Jude– You're not going to like what I have to say, but you cannot be associated with Kari anymore. If this is the way she's going to act, you cannot have any part of it. You need to think real long and hard about what is at stake here if you continue to see her."

"Sir– Please…"

"It has to be this way, your life is too valuable to compromise."

"I think I may be falling for her, sir."

Nicks groaned. "Christ, you're seventeen, you don't know shit and you certainly don't know what love is. And a girl certainly is not worth your life, ever."

"Sir–"

"Seriously, please don't see her anymore."

"Yes, sir…"

CHAPTER FOURTEEN

The next day Kari and Marley walked out of school towards the oak tree. It was a long day and Kari was glad it was done. The news of her incident had gotten out. The looks she received from other students only made her feel worse. They had already thought she was a deviant and her actions the other day only solidified their suspicions.

"It'll get better. Someone else will be the focus of gossip and they'll forget about you," Marley said. "I'm glad you're okay."

"I just want it to all be over with. I'm sick of the gawking."

Jude stood under the tree near the main entrance of the school waiting for Kari. His eyes lit up when he saw her and her heart fluttered. After the horrible long day she was glad to see him. Jude hugged Kari and she hadn't realized how much she needed it.

"Jude, we need to talk," Kari said and slowly pulled away from him.

"Of course," Jude replied, having much to say as well but was dreading it.

"I'll see you guys later," Marley said and walked away with a wave.

Jude touched Kari's face. "How are you feeling?"

"Everyone keeps asking me that."

"You scared me–"

"I know... I'm sorry... Look, I wanted to talk to you about something," Kari said and opened her backpack shuffling through her books not seeing the file.

"It's not in there– I found the file when I picked up your backpack."

Kari slung her bag over her shoulder. "Was that what you were keeping from me?"

Jude was glad he had come across the file and was not blindsided. It gave him time to think. "It was... I didn't want you to judge me."

"I'm confused. I would have never guessed you were capable of something like that–"

"It wasn't something I'm proud of– I was a different person then. A lot has changed."

"Can you tell me what happened?"

Jude ran a hand through his hair. "I had associated myself with the wrong people. In an attempt to prove myself, I was tasked with– Well, it doesn't matter. Things did not go according to plan and I ended up– I ended up nearly killing someone."

The memory flooded into Jude's mind. The night Garrick sent Jude on his first assignment with two other men, his brother Jon and Wallace.

"I am uncertain with my decision to let you partake in this op," Garrick said and placed both hands on Jude's shoulders.

"It's the only way I can prove to you that I can be a capable member of this team," Jude replied.

Garrick looked Jude over and adjusted the collar of his jacket. "You will listen to Jon and Wallace."

Jude stared into Garrick's cold blue eyes seeing the worry. "You said it yourself, this is an easy in and out job. Even Jelly could do it." Jude motioned to the plump older man that was the designated driver.

Garrick stepped back. "Right you are. Well off you go then. Good luck, gentlemen."

They loaded into the black Land Rover and drove to one of many ports along the shores of Brooklyn. New York was one of many port cities that Garrick operated from with smuggling and distributing weapons globally. Their objective was to steal files from Garrick's competitor, Makar Rosakov, who had made the mistake of encroaching on Garrick's clientele. What the files contained, Jude was not privy to that information.

"Are you ready for this?" Jon asked, holding onto the door handle of the black SUV. "Once you become a part of this world, there is no going back."

"I know. Let's do this," Jude nodded.

"Rusakov's office is on the second floor," Wallace said. "Remember we have twelve minutes, in and out. Then–" Wallace tapped an explosive on his vest. "It go boom."

They exited the SUV. "Goodluck my friends," Jelly said and drove down the alley to wait for them at the pick up location.

Jude stood next to the back door of the shipping office. Jon shoved the breaching tool into the door jam and bypassed the lock. The door popped open and the alarm sounded. They filed into the office and climbed the stairs. Jon turned on his shoulder light and rummaged through the computers while Wallace posted on the door.

"Nine minutes," Wallace stated.

"Downloading now," Jon said. "Will take three minutes."

Jude stared at an open folder written in Russian and a blueprint of some sort.

"Hey, Wallace– What do you think this is?"

Wallace stepped towards Jude and craned his neck. "Who cares."

"Alright, I got it– Let's go," Jon said and stood unplugging his device from the computer.

"Jelly, be ready we are on our way," Wallace said over his com.

"I'll be here."

They descended the stairs. Wallace turned to Jude holding the explosive. "Care to do the honors?"

Jude smiled. "Bloody hell I would."

"Make it quick. We will meet you at the pick up. You have three minutes before we leave your arse," Wallace said handing him the charge.

Wallace and Jon exited the building through the same door they had entered. Jude turned and planted the charge at the base of the wall under the steps. Jude walked to the door.

"Charge is planted. I'm on my way," Jude said in his com.

Jude stepped out of the doorway into the alley. A crack sounded and his vision went dark. A man struck Jude with the grip of his pistol. Jude fell to the ground on his hands and knees disoriented. The man kicked Jude in the abdomen and he went rigid. The man crawled on top of Jude and flipped him over.

"Who are you working for?" The man questioned in a thick Russian accent.

Jude could not reach his sidearm as the man's thick legs were pressing against his drop holster. He reached out hoping to find anything he could use as a weapon. The cool rough texture brushed against his hand. He picked it up and swung the rock, hitting the man in the side of his head. He toppled over to the ground, his gun skidding away.

"Jude, we're out of time, where are you?"

"Held up," Jude gritted his teeth and swung again.

Blood splattered from the man's face and a tooth flew in a stream of blood.

"Hands! Let me see your hands!" a deep voice yelled.

Jude raised his hands in surrender.

"Abort detonation. Police have me," Jude said.

A team of officers moved up on Jude their flashlights blinding him. An officer pushed Jude to the ground with his foot and the other handcuffed him.

Jude shook his head, clearing his mind of the memory. Kari took a step back.

"He wasn't entirely innocent. That man led a life of crime."

"I am not sure if that makes it better–"

"Kari–"

Kari drew her brows together. "Why were you in New York anyway?"

"My mum, she was from New York, we spent a lot of time there."

"Your mom was American?"

"Yeah…"

"I guess that explains why your uncle lives here."

Jude took Kari's hand. "Does this change the way you see me?"

Kari shook her head. "No, Jude, it doesn't. I am happy you told me the truth though."

Jude felt a pang of guilt for lying again and squeezed Kari's hand. New York was just the beginning of Jude's criminal career. He had since proved himself to Garrick and was assigned ops in the Middle East.

"Yeah... Me too," Jude said and released Kari's hand. "Do you need a ride home?"

Jude couldn't start the conversation to tell Kari he couldn't see her. Not yet, not then. He needed more time, he wanted more time with her. Maybe Nicks was wrong and Kari's incident was isolated.

"No... My brother is picking me up," Kari replied and her eyes caught Bradley's car. "Speaking of which..."

"Let me walk you," Jude said and motioned for Kari to lead the way.

Bradley exited the car and met them.

"Jude," Bradley greeted.

"Sir– I will see you later, Kari," Jude stepped to leave.

"Uh– Jude, I actually wanted to invite you to dinner. Tonight, if you'd like," Bradley said.

Jude raised his eyebrow. "Really?"

"Jessica and I wanted to thank you for finding Kari."

"It's really not necessary, but I accept your invitation." Jude eyed Bradley skeptical and Bradley nodded.

"Good. Six should be fine…" Bradley stepped away and turned back to Jude. "Do not be late. I don't want the wrath of my wife to come back at me."

Jude chuckled. "Yes, sir."

Kari smiled and kissed Jude on the cheek. His eyes darted to Bradley and he sighed. Kari hopped into the car beaming. Bradley pulled down the street.

"Thank you," Kari piped up.

"I had nothing to do with this, it was Jessica. If it were up to me you'd be locked in your room," Bradley said.

Kari sat quietly watching the outside world go by.

"I don't know how many times I have to tell you, I'm sorry."

"Kari, you're my baby sister. You need to make better choices. I don't know what I would do if I lost you too."

"I made a mistake. It won't happen again."

"I want to believe you Kar– I really do. But you're going to have to regain that trust."

"I understand…"

The rest of the car ride was silent. Bradley pulled into the driveway. Kari stepped out of the car without a second look and walked up the small path to the door. She stepped inside leaving the door open for Bradley. The home was quiet when Kari set her backpack down. There was a loud blast of drums and music. It made Kari jump. She caught her breath holding her hand to her heart and glanced back at Bradley. He shrugged with a chuckle and disappeared into his office. Kari ventured into the kitchen. Jessica was singing and dancing to *Queen*, "Fat Bottom Girls," to be exact. Jessica picked up a wooden spoon, signing the chorus to Kari. She shook her head with a chuckle and hit the power button to the speaker. The music cut out and Jessica pouted.

"What are you doing? The whole neighborhood could probably hear that."

"Just having a little fun," Jessica said with a shimmy of her shoulders.

"You are so weird," Kari laughed and backed away from her.

Jess smiled wide. "Weird is the new cool."

"Yeah, okay." Kari rolled her eyes.

"Before you scamper off, there is something you will want to hear..."

Kari set her hands on the counter. "I'm all ears. But I should tell you, I already had my lecture of the day from Bradley."

"Don't worry, no lecture– I spoke with your aunt Joan and we think it would be best if you spent the weekend up there."

Kari was filled with a joyful sadness. She missed her friends, her old life. She walked around the counter and hugged Jessica.

"Thank you."

"And... one more thing. I haven't broken the news to Bradley yet, but Jude is welcome there as well."

Kari pulled away. "Really?"

"You deserve happiness."

"I don't know what to say."

"Just promise me that you will stay out of trouble–"

"I will."

"Good, now hop to it and get some homework done before dinner."

Kari was excited and bounced to her room. Kari flung herself on her bed and grabbed the phone off the small table next to her bed, seeing how she hadn't gotten her cell phone replaced yet. Kari was grinning ear to ear and dialed Beth's number to tell her the exciting news. As chance had it Beth told Kari Diego was having a team party, good opportunity for Jude to meet her friends.

———

Nicks opened the fridge door. "What do you want for dinner?"

"About that sir–"

Nicks turned. "Come on... I'm getting better."

"No, doubt you are.. But– Marshal Evans invited me for dinner."

"Did he now? So much for heeding my words to stay clear of Kari."

"I– Uh, couldn't say no."

"I suspect you couldn't... I'll be having a chat with fuckstick Magee." Nicks shut the fridge. "I guess I'll just eat by myself."

"I'll make it up to you..."

"Yeah, I'm sure you will... Hey, since I have you here. Your birthday is next month..."

"Sir– I'd much rather forget about my birthday."

"Nonsense, it's the big one-eight. How would you like to go to a Chicago Fire game?"

Jude cocked a brow. "I mean it's better than baseball, but it will be nothing compared to a proper match."

Nicks chuckled. "Get out of here, I'm sick of seeing your mug."

Jude smiled and disappeared down the hall to get ready.

—

Kari opened up her books and started on her homework, trying to get a portion of her English paper done. The doorbell rang and Kari's head snapped to the clock. She hadn't realized the time. She shut her book and hopped off the bed. Jessica set a plate on the table. She walked from the dining room to the foyer. She glanced in Bradley's office to see him nose deep in a case. He had a concerned look.

"Did you not hear the doorbell?" Jessica asked.

Bradley lifted his head. "Huh?"

"The door–"

"I am sorry, hun. I was just—"

"Working. I know," Jessica smiled. "Don't frown too much, it'll leave lines."

Bradley smirked and went back to analyzing the document.

Jessica opened the door and smiled. "You must be Jude."

"I am. It's nice to meet you, Mrs. Evans," Jude greeted politely.

"Please, call me Jessica," she stated.

"Yes, ma'am."

"Jude, how are you?" Jessica asked and motioned for Jude to enter.

"Great, thank you. And yourself?" Jude asked.

"I am good. Thanks for asking." Jessica paused by the stairs. "Dinner is nearly ready. Kari is upstairs." Jessica heard Bradley's phone ring and she glanced at him.

Jude smiled and went to take his shoes off. "Oh— Don't worry about that."

"It's fine," Jude replied.

Jessica smiled and walked away. Jude finished untying his shoes and stepped to the staircase.

"Pyke, I don't think that is a good idea at the moment," Bradley said. "Yes— I understand— But— Sir—" Jude knew they were probably talking about him. Bradley looked up from his desk and made eye contact with Jude.

"Jude," Kari called to him, standing at the top

landing of the stairs.

Bradley waved Jude away and he drew his attention to Kari. She descended the stairs with a smile on her face. Kari interlaced her hand with Jude's and kissed him on the cheek. Bradley massaged his temples, witnessing the innocent act before him. His attempts of keeping her away from Jude had failed. Nicks was not happy with him for inviting Jude over for dinner and voiced his adamant disapproval. But they agreed that after, they would keep them separated, to the point of enrolling Kari into a different school if need be.

Kari led Jude into the living room and plopped on the couch. "Are you busy this weekend?"

"I am not. What did you have in mind?"

"How would you like to come with me to Marinette?"

"I'm not sure my uncle will allow it–"

Kari leaned closer to Jude. He could feel her breath on his lips. "Then maybe you can sneak off with me."

"I will ask. But I make no promises..." Jude whispered and closed the distance, kissing Kari.

Kari grasped the nap of Jude's neck and pulled him close.

Jessica cleared her throat and they looked at her standing in the arch way to the dining room. "Dinner is ready."

Jude avoided eye contact, embarrassed. Heat

ignited in Kari's cheeks and Jessica smirked. Bradley walked past the two. They stood and filed in behind him.

Everyone took their seats around the table. Jessica and Bradley both sat at the heads of the table. Bradley took a sip from his beer, not thrilled with Jessica's decision to allow Jude into their home. It was no fault of her's. She did not know Jude's history, or that Bradley was charged with protecting him.

"So Jude, when did you and your parents move to Chicago?" Jessica asked

Jude paused for a minute and gave Bradley a nervous look. He finished chewing the piece of chicken. "I moved here shortly after summer and I live with my uncle."

"Oh– I'm–"

"It's okay. I don't mind. My mum died from cancer and my father had never been in the picture much," Jude explained.

"I'm so sorry, Jude. That must have been hard."

"It's all right, really," Jude said. "I have to believe that everything happens for a reason."

"That is a wonderful outlook, Jude," Jessica said. "I'd love to hear more about England though."

"Jess– Let the poor boy enjoy his dinner."

"I apologize again– I hope you are enjoying your meal."

"I am, thank you."

Jessica set her fork down. "I told Kari the news

already."

"And what news would that be?" Bradley took another drink of his beer.

"I arranged with Joan to have Kari and Jude stay there for the weekend."

Bradley nearly choked on his beer. He set it down, spilling some of the contents. "Excuse me, what?"

"Kari needs to be around friends–"

"I'm sorry, but, Jude... You will not be going with her."

"Yes, sir," Jude said.

"Seriously?" Kari said disappointed.

"Kari, it's all right. Your brother and I will be discussing this later," Jessica said.

Bradley sighed heavily, staring at his wife. To her, Bradley's attitude towards Jude was unwarranted. He could not tell her his reservations of allowing Kari to associate with him. Bradley dug in his pocket and pulled out a new cell phone. He slid it down the table at Kari.

"Please be more careful with this one," Bradley said.

Kari picked up the new iPhone excited by the gift. "Thank you."

The evening wound down and Kari walked Jude out to his bike. He pulled her close to his body and kissed her.

"I would like to pick you up tomorrow, if that's okay."

"I would enjoy that."

"Good, I will see you tomorrow then."

Kari stepped from Jude. "And think over my proposition... Live on the wild side."

Jude chuckled and put his helmet on. "I will think about it."

Kari scampered up the walk and opened the front door. Her spirits were elated with the prospects of spending a weekend with Jude in her hometown.

"I don't understand what the big deal is?" Jessica raised her voice.

Kari froze and immediately felt guilty that they were arguing because of her.

"Can you trust me for once?"

"Just let her have this. Everything else has been taken from her."

"I am not going to argue with you. He's not going with her and that is final."

"Oh, final? Really?"

Bradley left the kitchen pinching his forehead together with a hand. He rounded the corner and made eye contact with Kari. She stepped down from the first step. She debated on telling Jessica about Jude's record. It tore at her that she was being an advocate for her and they were fighting. Bradley did have a valid reason to be leery about Jude. Kari didn't understand why Bradley hadn't told her, or maybe he had and she was willing to look past it, like Kari had. Bradley took a long breath staring at his sister, it had been a long evening.

"I am trying– This hasn't been easy for me either," Bradley said. "I don't want you to think I am the enemy. I'm trying to keep you safe."

Kari bowed her head and stared at the hardwood floor. She had been caught up in her own drama. She never stopped to think about how Bradley had been affected. "I haven't been fair to you. I will do better, I promise."

"We'll get through this."

Bradley's phone rang and he saw it was Pyke, again.

"Evans," he answered and Kari shook her head irritated that yet again, his work was getting in the way.

Bradley watched as Kari bound up the steps.

"We have a hit on Pierre Daquin," Pyke said.

"What?"

"He just landed at O'Hare. Riley is doing his best to track him through street cams. You need to get here now."

"Yes, sir."

Bradley hung up the phone and walked into the living room where Jessica sipped on a glass of wine.

"I have to go into work… I don't know when I'll be home."

Jessica clucked her tongue. "Of course," she said with an attitude.

Bradley picked up his keys from the small table in

the hall. "You need to stop."

"And you need to be present in our lives. But go, you're good at that."

"You are *frustrating*." Bradley opened the door and left.

———

Nicks drank a beer watching the Sox's game.

"Enjoy your dinner?"

"I did… It was nice of Marshal Evans to have me over," Jude said with a smile.

"I hate to crush your happiness… But Jude, this was the last night you are seeing Kari."

"Sir– I think you are overreacting…"

"Evans and I are taking a hard stance on this kid. If you can't do as you're told, Bradley will be transferring Kari to a different school."

"Why am I being punished for something I didn't do?" Jude asked.

"It's not forever, Jude…" Nicks hated seeing the sorrow on Jude's face. "Are you going to do as you're told?"

"I was supposed to pick Kari up for school tomorrow… Can I still do that?"

Nicks took a long breath, trying to decide how to answer that. "It will be the last time, then I mean it Jude… Please don't make this more difficult."

"Understood, sir."

Nicks's phone rang. "Nicks."

"It's Pyke, we have a hit at O'Hare for Pierre Daquin, get here now… Bring the kid, he'll stay at the office while we work."

"Understood." Nicks hung up and looked at Jude. "Grab your bag, we're going to the office. It's going to be a long night."

"What did they say?" Jude asked and grabbed his backpack.

"Pierre Daquin is in Chicago."

Jude's blood ran cold. "Do you really think he's here for me?"

"That's what we're going to find out."

CHAPTER FIFTEEN

The briefing room had a chill in the air. Jude watched as the Marshals geared up and were briefed on the newest intel.

"The last known location was just outside of LaSalle Street Station on W. Ida B. Wells. He possibly entered a building in the four hundred block of S. Financial Pl. I didn't see him reappear on Van Buren," Seth stated.

"Start checking security cameras to verify where he went," Pyke ordered.

Seth turned to the computer counsel. "I am already working on it." He hacked into networks and let the facial recognition program do its magic. "Grand Ballon, French restaurant on the 38th floor of 423 Financial."

"Alright let's hop to it and get this done," Pyke said and pointed to Jude. "Halifax you're in charge of the kid."

Seth and Jude stared at each other. "Okay..." Seth replied.

The Marshal strike team loaded into two vans in the garage. MacTavish drove and Pyke sat shotgun. Bradley adjusted his gloves and Clayton bopped his head to a song he was humming.

"Can you not?" Nicks asked charging his rifle before getting in the back after Clayton.

Bradley shut the sliding door. "He won't."

Clayton smiled and took a spot on the floor. The van had no seats as it was used as a troop hauler for ops. They parked down the street from the target location while the other van parked on the opposite side.

Pyke pushed his thumb in his ear. "This damn thing never stays put." The ear piece fell out and Pyke growled. "Fuck it!" He unplugged his radio.

MacTavish turned in his seat. "It's because your ears are so big."

"One of these days I'm going to shove crayons in your fucking ears, then we'll see who has big ears you damn bleech sniffer."

"Command to 905 Robert," Seth radioed, keeping his eyes on the screens.

"Go ahead," Pyke answered.

"The target finished with his bill and is now headed to the lift."

Jude's ears perked and he cocked a brow at the blatant British term coming from Seth.

"Copy that," Pyke acknowledged.

Pyke tilted his head to the opening between the seats. "Get ready to move."

The elevator door dinged and Daquin stepped onto the polished marble floor of the main lobby.

"He's making his way to the west entrance."

The breeze tousled Daquin's thick wavy hair. He placed his hand in the pocket of his fine light grey three piece suit. He glanced down the sidewalk and proceeded north. The street was narrow with parked cars and little to no pedestrian traffic. MacTavish put the van in gear and pulled from their parking spot and slowly crept down the street.

"905 Robert we have eyes on him. Engaging now."

Clayton rolled the side door open. They stepped out of the slow moving van and crushed the target. Bradley firmly grabbed Daquin's arms, sliding flex cuffs over his wrists and Clayton threw a bag over his head. Daquin tensed his arm and tried to pull away. Nicks nudged the barrel of his rifle into Daquin's back.

"Don't be foolish," Nicks said.

Clayton grasped Daquin's other arm and they threw him into the van. Nicks climbed in last and closed the door. MacTavish sped away.

"Target apprehended bringing him to the barn," Pyke said over the radio.

Jude sat back in his chair. "It looked like they just kidnapped that guy."

Seth chuckled. "And they didn't even have to lure him with wine and cheese."

Jude pulled his brows together and Seth explained, "I see you're confused... It's funny because he's French."

"Right..."

MacTavish pulled the van into the underground garage of the Marshal Office and stopped in front of the elevator. Bradley and Clayton pulled Daquin out of the van.

"Whoever you are, I have powerful allies and they will make sure you never draw a breath. I hope you are prepared," Daquin threatened.

Clayton leaned in close to Daquin's ear. "I welcome the challenge. It has been a great while since I have had a good fight. Wait until you hear my war cry."

Pyke raised his hands at Clayton and mouthed. "What are you doing?"

Clayton shrugged and smiled.

"Get him inside," Pyke said motioning for the elevator.

The elevator ride was short and they led Daquin down a hall to the interrogation rooms. He was placed in the small room with a table and three chairs. Bradley sat Daquin in the seat closest to the wall. Nicks sat down on the other side and folded his hands neatly on the steel surface. Bradley came around the table and sat next to him. With a quick yank, Clayton removed the hood from the Frenchman and departed the room without a word to stand on the other side of the mirrored one way window with Pyke and MacTavish. Daquin looked around the room and focused on the Marshals in front of him. He chuckled.

"You're laughing?" Nicks asked.

"Yes, I am. You are not who I was expecting."

"And who would that be?"

"No one."

"Of course..." Nicks tapped his fingers on the table. "What's your business in the States?"

"I have a series of meetings this week– For business."

"And what business would that be for?"

"I work for an international investment company, surely you must already know this."

Nicks lean forward planting his elbows on the table. "I also know that your clientele are not the most upstanding of citizens."

"I suppose that depends on your definition of *upstanding*." Daquin looked around the room. "I do not inquire how my clients obtain their wealth, I just manage it."

"Yes– Along with other services."

Daquin shifted his weight and directed his attention to Bradley. "You are quiet. Does he not trust you with an interview, or– would this be an interrogation? I guess I never asked if I was free to leave, I just assumed that if I was attacked on the street, bound, and a hood thrown over my face that I was not free to leave. Are you not supposed to read me something and give me the option to have a lawyer present? That's how it works in this country right?"

"When it's concerning our national security, you have no rights," Bradley stated.

"And what have I done that is threatening your nation's security?" Daquin challenged

Bradley and Daquin stared each other down.

"This interview has nothing to do with you. We are after Shaun Garrick," Nicks said, breaking the tension.

Daquin shifted his gaze." Shaun Garrick you say."

"We know you have done business with him in the past. Are you currently working with him?" Nicks asked.

Daquin shook his head. "I haven't spoken to Garrick for months."

"You're not involved in any business arrangements with him currently?"

"No, I can assure you of that."' Nicks studied Daquin intently looking for any sign that he was lying but saw none.

"What about Makar Rosakov?"

Daquin paused and pursed his lips.

"I will take that as a yes," Nicks said.

Daquin folded his arms.

"Does your current business with Rosakov involve him working with Garrick?"

Daquin was thoroughly confused. "My last understanding was that those two loathe each other. That is no secret."

"Are they working together?" Nicks pushed.

"I can't answer that for certain but I would assume no."

Nicks stood and stepped to the door. "Have him locked up. I'm sure Interpol will want him."

Daquin sat back in the chair and rested his bound hands on the table. Bradley followed Nicks and motioned for a pair of Marshals to escort Daquin away.

Jude swiveled in the chair passing the time. Seth looked up from his computer every once and awhile making sure Jude was still there. The Marshals walked in.

"He could have been feeding us a line of shit," MacTavish said.

"And he could very well be telling the truth. Either way Interpol has a new guest," Pyke said.

Nicks glanced at Jude. "I don't think Daquin was being truthful. Nothing about this feels right."

Jude's stomach twisted. "What now?"

"We stay vigilant. We have plans in place if a situation arises. We are prepared," Pyke said.

Seth's phone rang disrupting the meeting. He saw the number and held up his phone. "Sorry, I really need to take this."

Seth stepped out of the room and walked down the hall away from any unwanted ears.

"Connor."

"I hope your time in the States is going well," Connor's supervisor, Tennent, said.

"It is."

"Good– by chance has Agent Bennet spoken to you recently?"

"Not for several days, why?"

"She had failed to report to duty."

Seth's stomach dropped. "Did you send someone to her flat?"

"Yes, she wasn't there."

"Was–"

"There were no signs of a struggle."

"I should come back and help find her–"

"We are working on it Connor. Your duty is to stay where you are."

"Sir–"

"Connor, we will find her. If you hear anything–"

"Of course."

Seth stared at his phone for a moment and went back inside the briefing room.

"You okay?" Clayton asked.

Seth picked his head up. "Yes, sorry, just a tad distracted is all."

"We were just discussing adding more cameras near the school," Pyke said.

"I will be able to arrange that," Seth said, trying to shake off the feeling of dread.

—

Hard footfalls echoed on the planked floor as Garrick walked down a hallway with artifacts and art displayed on the walls, a personal museum. Dressed in an expertly tailored suit, Garrick stopped in front of a door at the end of the hall. There was no hesitation when he opened it. A large office sprawled before him. There was a wall dedicated to a library of books. A fireplace with fine leather clawfoot chairs near them. He walked to the antique bar and poured himself a scotch from the crystal decanter and lit a cigar. He ran his hand over his shaved peppered hair and picked up his scotch before approaching a room to the left of his own desk. The room was filled with computer monitors.

"Hughes, have you found him yet?" Garrick asked and took a drag on his cigar.

A thin man with thick rimmed glasses peered through a gap in his monitors. "Sir, we have found a location, but I have not yet pinpointed an exact–"

"So, do you know where he is or not?" Garrick touched his grizzled chin.

"Bennent was not the most forthcoming with information–"

"Obviously, she is a skilled MI6 agent."

"Well… Kertch was not kind to her."

Garrick took a long breath, knowing that Kertch had killed Bennent. "Did we get anything useful?"

"James is in Chicago, but I have not been able to track down where yet."

Garrick swirled his scotch. "She sent him to the States, smart. I guess his mother being an American has paid off… for now." He took a long drink of the finely aged liquid. "Keep working, and in the meantime make arrangements for my departure. It is time we pay James a visit. Cancel my trip to Turkistan and notify Paul that I wish him to join me. He should be returning from Mosul shortly."

"Ah– Sir, we have not discussed what our plan is with Preece."

"His capture in Beirut was unfortunate– He is aware of what needs to be done."

"I am also still working on damage control from the Zagros incident."

"Just do what you have to…"

Garrick took a long drag from his cigar and exited the small room back to his luxurious office. He stood in front of the towering window gazing out of the beautiful rolling highlands of Scotland.

CHAPTER SIXTEEN

Exhaustion gripped Jude from the early morning wake up. The late night party at the Marshals office was not being kind.

"You look like shit," Nicks said, sipping his coffee.

"Can I not go to school today?"

"That's a negative ghost rider."

Jude wiped his face and picked up his backpack. "And to top it off, it's d-day for my relationship."

Nicks blinked slowly. "You'll survive…"

"Would it be inappropriate to tell you to bugger off?"

"Do you like your kneecaps?"

"Noted…" Jude saluted Nicks.

"See you at school."

Jude rolled his eyes and walked out the door. A

bike ride to wake up and settle his mind was just what Jude needed. He pulled into Bradley's driveway halfway expecting him to be standing outside with disapproval or a baseball bat. The front door opened and Kari walked out. The morning sun illuminating her hazel eyes.

He took a helmet off of the hook on the back. "Here, I brought you your very own helmet."

The helmet was the same sport style as Jude's, but hers was dark maroon. It saddened him to be giving it to her as he had bought it prior to Nicks forbidding him to see her. Like Nicks said, it won't be forever. Jude was determined to still see Kari at school. What Nicks didn't know, wouldn't hurt him.

"Jude, I hope you didn't buy this," Kari said and accepted the helmet.

"I didn't. I just have random helmets lying around," Jude said sarcastically.

Kari tilted her head and rolled her eyes. "I don't need you buying me things."

"How else am I supposed to keep you interested?" Jude chuckled.

"You are too much at times," Kari said and smacked him in the arm.

Kari put her helmet on and climbed on the back, holding onto him tight. Kari and Jude parted ways after their first two classes. They would not see each other until lunch. Kari entered the lunch room that was filled with round tables and students. She looked around and did not notice Jude or Marley. Kari stood in line patiently, after getting her salad and tea, she walked toward the table her friends sat at when they didn't leave campus. Vanessa, the girl that had broken her phone, stopped in front of Kari.

"I must say, I'm surprised you are still here, crack whore," Vanessa said and hit the bottom of Kari's tray.

The contents of the tray fell into Kari's torso. Anger flowed through Kari and all she saw was red. She had pent up anger from her destroying her father's journal. She tried desperately not to punch Vanessa square in the face. She promised Jess and Bradley she'd stay out of trouble. Kari let her food fall to the ground. Vanessa pushed Kari and she stumbled back against a cooler. Vanessa chuckled and picked up her cup of jello.

"You should just go back to where you came from." Vanessa threw the bright red jello at Kari.

Vanessa pushed Kari to the ground and poured her milk on her head. Kari planted her hand on the tile and started to stand. Vanessa placed her foot firmly on Kari's shoulder and pushed her back down. Vanessa bent down and slapped Kari across the face.

"I didn't say you could stand."

Kari's eyes narrowed and she gripped the plastic tray tightly. She couldn't tolerate it anymore. Without warning Kari swung the tray and struck Vanessa in her porcelain face.

"You're dead," Vanessa yelled through the hand clasped over her bloody nose.

"Picture me, frightened of you," Kari threw the tray at Vanessa.

"Crack whore!" Vanessa shouted and lunged at Kari grabbing her hair.

"Bitch! Get off of me!" Kari growled.

Kari grabbed Vanessa's chin and shoved her head back. Vanessa loosened her grip and Kari spun away, squaring up to continue the fight.

Jude grasped Kari by the wrist and pulled her away from Vanessa before she made matters worse. *Bloody hell you are making it difficult.*

"Miss Evans," The headmaster called.

Kari stopped and turned around. The headmaster stood with his arms folded across his chest. Behind him was Miss Taylor helping Vanessa. Kari shook her head at the dramatics Vanessa was putting on.

"My office, now— The both of you," The headmaster pointed to Kari and Vanessa.

Kari walked silently a few paces ahead of Vanessa. She sat in the chair across from his desk, her arms folded across her chest, tea stained her shirt.

"Miss Evans, your behavior of late is unacceptable…"

"Are you even going to listen to my side of the story? Vanessa–"

"You do not need to explain. I am aware of the situation. But your acts of violence will not be tolerated."

"So… You're going to expel me then? Go ahead,"

Kari said.

"Not yet, Miss Evans. I suspect that adjusting to a new life has not been the easiest. Is there anything you want to talk about or talk to someone about?" Headmaster Black asked.

"No."

"Are you sure? We have services—"

"I said no, but thank you."

"All right, my door is always open if you change your mind. But in the meantime, you will be placed on an in-school suspension for the next three weeks along with detention everyday for an hour."

"Yes, sir…"

"Now, I will have Mr. Loriti escort you to your locker to get the remainder of your course work for the afternoon. I will also be contacting your guardian about the incident."

Headmaster Black stood and showed Kari to the door. He spoke with the security guard, Mr. Loriti. The young man walked over to Kari, his hair was slicked back and his uniform pristine. Vanessa was ushered into Black's office and the door closed behind him. It was a short walk to and from her locker. She spent the remainder of the day in a small room off of the main office. She wasted the majority of the afternoon staring at a painting of a cliffed landscape. Her mind was lost while she studied the paint strokes of blues and greys.

The bell rang signalling for the end of the day.

Kari glanced out the window into the hallway, watching the students bustle through the halls. Kari huffed and pushed her textbook away from her. She continued to fume over Vanessa. The time passed slowly and the halls emptied. The plump secretary poked her head into Kari's room.

"Miss Evans, you are free to go. I will see you tomorrow."

"Yes, Mrs. Chappell."

Kari gathered her belongings and exited the office. She turned on her phone and saw a message from Jessica that she was waiting for her in the parking lot. She had just promised Jessica that she would stay out of trouble. She felt like a failure. Her footfalls echoed on the tile. Her mind raced with the thought of how Bradley was going to react. Kari turned the corner of the hall where her locker was. She stopped short when she nearly collided with another.

"Ope, Sorry–" she said and realized who it was. "Clayton? What are you doing here?"

"I, uh–"

"Who are those for?" Kari pointed to the small bouquet of wildflowers in his hand.

"Well…"

Miss Taylor walked out of her empty classroom and shut the door behind her. She turned to leave down the hallway and stopped mid stride. A smile appeared on her face.

"Clayton, hello," she said and brushed a strand of golden hair behind her ear.

"These are for you, Andi– Thought I would surprise you." Clayton handed her the wildflowers.

Kari looked from her teacher to Clayton. A logical person would come to the conclusion that they fancied each other.

"Miss Evans," Andi acknowledged.

"I was– On my way to my locker... S'cuse me," Kari said and stepped past Andi.

Kari turned around. Andi's back to her. She gave Clayton a thumbs up. She thought she saw Clayton blush, but it was difficult to tell with his beard. Kari dumped her books into her locker and left the empty school. Jessica waited patiently in the white Buick Regal. Kari opened the door and settled in.

"So– What happened to staying out of trouble?"

"I– It wasn't on purpose–"

"You attacked another student, Kari."

"She attacked me first, I was just protecting myself–"

"Kari– It was more than that."

"I–"

"Your brother is going to be furious. You were already walking a thin line with him as it was."

"Don't you think I already know that."

"A suspension, Kari–"

"So you don't even care that this girl was bullying

me?"

"There are many good ways to handle situations like that. Hitting her in the face with a tray is not one of them."

"But breaking my phone, burning my journal, spilling food on me and calling me names is all right?" Kari argued.

"That's not what I said," Jessica stated and pulled into the garage.

Kari opened the door and hopped out. "You know, I thought you were on my side."

Kari walked into the house and beelined for the steps. She paused a moment staring at Bradley's office door which sat ajar and slowly opened. Kari's stomach sank waiting for Bradley to yell. She feared that he was not going to allow her to go up north. She had been doing well with homework and staying out of trouble.

"Headmaster Black called—"

"You're not going to let me go to Joan's are you—"

"No, you can still go. I just wanted to say I'm proud of you for standing up for yourself. Never let anyone attack you. You showed better restraint than I would have in that situation. Truth be told."

Kari was shocked that she wasn't being yelled at or getting punished. A wave of affection for her hardlined brother rolled over her.

"Now, go do your homework."

"Love you." Kari smiled and walked up the steps.

Bradley smirked out the corner of his mouth and stepped back into his office closing the door.

Bradley sat down at his desk and drummed his fingers on the surface. He opened his laptop to review the latest after-action report. It referenced a raid of one of Garrick's locations, a compound off the grid in a remote region near Turkistan. He clicked on the file and chuckled. The squad leader for the fire teams was an old friend, Adam "Hatch" Karn. He served alongside Bradley for many years in Delta Force. Ironically Marcus was a part of Hatch's team.

"What are the odds–?" Bradley said.

He scrolled through the report.

"Compound is 70 meters north of us, right at the crossroads," Hatch reported to his men. They were divided into two strike teams of five men. "Viper 6-4, move up."

"Copy, moving up," Bonnet, the squad leader of the second team, acknowledged. His team came to a halt and radioed. "Covering."

"Viper 6-5 moving up."

The teams bound and overwatched through the tree lined river valley of the Syr Darya. Shrubs and grass sparsely covered the barren desert. Marcus removed his night vision, unable to see clearly from the brightly lit compound. A main building and three outbuildings were close by. Hatch raised a hand in a fist and halted his team, covering Viper 6-4 that moved to the next position of cover.

"Thermals show five hostiles outside the main building, two near the entrance of the building to the north and three outside the building to the southeast," Hatch reported over the coms. "Viper 6-4, cover west, 6-5 cover east. Execute."

Marcus crept through the shrubs towards the southeast building. Hatch to his right. Marcus flanked east and posted behind a container resting south of the building. A tango turned around the south side of the building. Marcus slung his rifle and pulled his knife. He sprang from his concealment, engaging the enemy from behind. He drove the serrated blade deep into the man's armpit piercing his lung and heart. Blood pooled from the wound as Marcus laid the body to the ground.

Gunfire erupted to the west. Viper 6-4 engaged the enemy. Marcus and Hatch fired upon a tango running to the west. Marcus posted on the corner of the southeast building.

"Badger! Shooters, second story of central target. Take 'em out!" Hatch shouted to Marcus.

Marcus stepped from cover, seeing his first target in the second story window, pinning Viper 6-4 down. Marcus pulled the trigger and the man collapsed with two rounds to the chest and one to the head. The second shooter directed his fire at Marcus. The ting of bullets pelted the side of the steel building and Marcus ducked. Friendly muzzle flashes came from behind a vehicle towards the central building. Plank's aim was true and the target from the second story fell out the window. The body plummeted to the ground, a pool of blood grew from beneath him.

"6-4, hold. Viper 6-5, shift east. We will breach the central location."

Hatch led the team along the backside of the southeast building. Marcus metered the corner, moving methodically from one side to the other and killed an enemy posted at the side door of the east side of the central building. Hatch turned to the rest of Viper 6-4 stacked behind him and signaled to his team to breach the door.

Yeti placed the breaching charge on the door and in seconds the door was blown inward. Plank entered first covering left. He encountered and eliminated two hostiles. Marcus filed in behind him and covered long while Hatch covered right. There was an open balcony to the right. A tango popped out of a room and shot at the team. Hatch returned fire, striking the enemy down. A spray of blood hit Marcus in the face. He turned to see Plank go down.

"Eagle down!" Marcus shouted.

Marcus bent down to move Plank and was propelled sideways through the air and into the wall from the force of an explosion. His ears rang as he tried to find his bearings. Hatch stood over Marcus and Plank, firing down the hall. The safehouse filled with smoke and the north side was heavily damaged. Marcus crawled to Plank and assessed him for major bleeding. Blood seeped through the fabric of his pants and ran down his arm. Marcus took two of Plank's tourniquets and applied them to his leg. He let out a cry of pain through clenched teeth.

"One more, I gotta stop the bleed," Marcus said, using one of his own tourniquets on Plank's arm.

"Badger, I need you with me," Hatch yelled over the raining bullets.

Phantom hit Marcus on the shoulder. "I got him."

Marcus stood and patched up with Hatch and Yeti. They executed their clearing by proceeding shoulder to shoulder in a single line. Marcus covering right, Yeti covering left, and Hatch covering long.

"Two hostiles down the hall," Hatch said.

Hatch threw a smoke grenade down the hall and they bound to the first room, Yeti providing suppression fire long. Marcus did a quick peek from the door and saw the muzzle of a rifle. Marcus fired into the wall. The thin, poorly made drywall disintegrated and the man fell dead. Hatch filed out of the room and they crushed the end of the hall. The other tango had been killed by Yeti's suppression fire.

"Perimeter secured," Bonnet radioed.

"Copy, 6-5. Clearing central," Hatch responded.

The team finished clearing the house and did not find any sleeper tangos. Marcus lowered his rifle in a tactical ready position and took deep breaths.

"Sierra Leader to Nest. Location secured," Hatch

radioed. "There's a negative on HVT Anchorage."

"Nest copies, location secured, negative HVT Anchorage."

"Also requesting medical EVAC, we have an eagle down."

"Copy that Sierra Leader. ETA for Romeo ten mikes. Nest out."

Bonnet entered from the west side of the building. "Hatch, we located a weapons cache in a spider hole in the west building."

"See if we can get a track on where they came from." Hatch turned to Marcus. "Badger, Yeti, go through the wreckage and see if you can salvage anything."

Marcus nodded and followed Yeti to the explosion site. It was evident that a small IED was used to destroy any evidence. Marcus sifted through debris and located a hard drive. It was in rough shape but there was a possibility it could be salvaged.

The fresh cool air felt nice against Marcus's face as he exited the building. The adrenaline dissipated and his body started to normalize. Marcus took an extended inhale and exhale moving his head from side to side. He enjoyed his brief moment of peace after the high stress of combat.

"I found this." He handed the hard drive to Hatch.

"Hopefully we'll be able to pull something from that scrap metal."

The chopper set down and the Viper Team loaded

up. They lifted from the ground their feet dangling over the open side of the chopper.

"Hit it, Bonnet," Hatch said.

"With pleasure." Bonnet hit the detonator to the charges planted.

The compound exploded, the flames reaching high into the sky.

Bradley wiped his eyes and focused on the screen, fatigued. He was frustrated that there were no new leads on locating Garrick. Bradley's phone rang.

"Evans."

"Hey, I just sent you a report," Nicks stated.

"The after action report in Turkistan? I'm reading it now."

"No– The MI6 report."

Bradley sat up and opened the file and skimmed it quickly. "Shit–"

"MI6 reports Bennent has been dark for twenty four hours."

"We have no intel on where Garrick is. We should move Jude immediately," Bradley said.

"I agree, but Pyke wants to wait on MI6's investigation. "

"If she compromised our location, Garrick could be here in hours."

"Evans, I'm aware. For now, we restrict Jude's movements. School and home, that's it. Eyes on him at all times."

"Have you notified Bradshaw?"

"I will– Is your sister going to be a problem in this?"

"No– I will deal with her–"

———

Kari sprawled out on her bed and pulled out her phone seeing a text from Jude.

Jude (16:32)
Hey, just checking in to
see how you are.

Kari (17:04)
I got an in-school suspension
Kari (17:05)
This is bullshit, this whole
thing wasn't even my fault.
Plus side, Bradley was cool

Jude (17:05)
I'm sorry, I wish there was
something I could do.
Jude (17:06)
Hey.... I have some bad news,
my uncle won't let me go this weekend.
I'm actually grounded
Because of the incident with the police.

Kari (17:06)
I'm sorry, that's my fault.

Just come anyway. What's the
Worse that can happen?
Get Grounded again?

Jude (17:07)
I don't know if that's
a good idea.

Kari (17:07)
Please... I don't want to
go by myself.
Kari (17:08)
Besides... who's going to keep
me out of trouble?

Jude (17:10)

...

Kari (17:10)
Oh come on! It'll be fun ;)

Jude (17:12)
You are going to get
me in trouble

Kari (17:12)
It'll be worth it. I promise

There was a knock on Jude's door.

"Come in," Jude said and put his phone down.

Nicks entered the room with a glom face.

"I have some bad news, kid."

Jude sat up straight, his blood running cold. "What?"

"Agent Bennent... She's gone dark."

Jude shuttered. "Garrick has her doesn't he?"

"We don't know, but we suspect so."

"Now what?" Jude asked.

"Pyke is waiting for the MI6 investigation, so for now– School and home, Jude. No exceptions. This is important– She could have given up your location."

"Does she even know exactly where I am? I mean Chicago is huge."

"No, but we can't take any chances."

"Rauri..." Jude's voice shook.

"Don't worry– We got this, you're safe."

"But for how long? He won't stop–"

"Let us worry about Garrick. I won't let anything happen to you."

"I just want my life back, I am sick of hiding."

Nicks placed a hand on Jude's shoulder. "This will all be over soon. Then you know what? We'll go to Boston and catch a Sox's game."

Jude smirked. "It would be better if we went to a Chelsea match."

"Who's Chelsea?– Why are you shaking your head? It was a valid question. Do they just put a bunch of Chelsea's together in a ring and see who wins?"

Jude stared blankly at Nicks. "Oh!– You mean like a soccer game?"

"A football match."

"Isn't that what I said? Hey, is Chelsea hot?"

"I'm going to finish my work now... So if you wouldn't mind–"

Nicks stepped to the door and put his hand on the frame looking back at Jude. "We will get through this... And when we do, you can pick where we live. I don't care where we go. You will get the fresh start you deserve."

"Even back to England?"

"If that's where you want to go."

"You'd have to quit your career... You'd do that for me?"

"I'd give my life for you kid."

Jude was speechless.

"Now, get that homework done. I have high hopes for you to go to a good college and not turn out like me."

Nicks stepped into the hall. "Rauri–" He popped his head back into the room. "Thank you, for everything. It means more to me than you'll ever know."

Nicks smiled and disappeared down the hall. Jude stared at his text book for a moment. His emotions and mind were being tugged in every which way. The thought of Garrick coming to Chicago terrified him yet, he almost wanted him to come so it could just end. Jude was ready to move on with life, a life that seemed to have a purpose and best of all someone who actually gave a damn about him. He glanced at his phone. He went back and forth trying to decide what he was going to do. He wanted to go with Kari, but at the same time he didn't want to experience the wrath of Nicks.

Jude (17:18)
I don't know if I should go,
I don't want to make anything
worse with my uncle.

Kari (17:19)
Being grounded longer
won't make things worse.
Please, you have to go.
You mean a great deal to me
And I want my friends to meet you.

The desire to be a normal teen was overwhelming. He stared at the text. He had feelings for Kari and being with her made him happy. Jude thought about the ramifications of Garrick having intel on his location. *It's not like he'll find me in Marinette, bloody hell I don't even know where that is.*

Jude (17:20)
Why am I allowing you to
Get me into trouble?

Kari (17:20)
Because you love me :)

Jude (17:20)
I won't acknowledge that
Via text :P

Kari (17:21)
You are so old fashioned, but
I love you too <3

Jude (17:21)
I will see you tomorrow :)

CHAPTER SEVENTEEN

"Breaching north door," Jedi said over the com.

With a sharp pop Hawkeye detonated the charge and the door swung open. The operators funneled into the open utility building. The beams of their lasers and mounted lights bounced as they quickly swept the neglected building. There were no rooms to clear just the open space of a crumbling structure. Loch's light fixated on a silhouette seated in a chair. With each step it became clearer. He slung his rifle and took a knee in front of Agent Bennet. Her once golden hair was matted in blood. Her once beautiful face, swollen and black.

"What did they do to you Maisie?" Loch whispered and took out a knife.

"Christ–" Jedi said and Loch cut the tethers that bound her to the chair.

—

The news of Agent Bennet's disappearance brought angst and anxiety that gripped Jude. He closed his eyes tilting his head back letting the warm rays of the sun hit his face. He took a deep breath pushing his fears from his mind. The one thing that seemed to ground him was Kari.

"It's good to see you smiling," Jude said.

"It's only because I get to spend the weekend with you away from this hell hole."

"Come on now, it's not so bad here."

Kari raised a brow. "Anyway, we can leave right after my detention, Jessica is letting me borrow her regal for the weekend."

"Actually– Can you meet me at Fairfield and 110th? I have an errand to run."

"Jude, I can drive you."

"Don't worry about it. By the time you're done serving your time, I'll be ready."

"I can't believe they're making me have detention on a Friday."

Jude kissed Kari on the forehead. "Don't hit people with trays." Kari furrowed her brow and Jude said, "I will see you after school. Enjoy your day with Mrs. Chappell."

The day dragged on and the bell rang signalling for the end of the day. Jude removed a hooded zip-up sweatshirt from his locker and threw it on over his collared shirt. He drew the hood over his head obscuring his features. The halls were crowded as he maneuvered through them looking for his target. A boy similar in stature and same hair color walked with friends down the hall a few paces in front of Jude. The unsuspecting kid wore a baseball cap that shadowed his face. Jude approached behind him and slipped his cell phone into his open side pocket of his backpack.

Jude walked out of a side entrance. The sun was high overhead and he placed his sunglasses on. He glanced around, looking for any sign of the Marshals. He walked over to the bike rack and took one that was not locked. He needed a quick escape before the Marshals realized he was making a run for it.

Nicks sat in his sedan watching the GPS on Jude's phone. He saw the signal moving from the front entrance. Nicks picked his head up from his device.

Nicks radioed. "Jude's headed towards the student pick up location. Do you have eyes? He should be going to the student parking."

"Negative, I will head that way," Clayton stated from his position on a bench at the bus stop.

Nicks looked at the signal to the area that Jude should be and spotted him.

"I have eyes," Nicks said. "He's wearing a Cubs hat… When did he get that hat? How dare he wear such trash. We will have to have a chat on his choice in teams."

Clayton quickened his pace seeing Jude. "He's getting into the black Escalade."

"What is he doing?" Nicks growled.

The Escalade pulled away from the curb and down the road. Clayton raised his hand and made a circle motion for Bradley and Nicks to follow. Bradley queried the registration information on his laptop through the DOT, department of transportation, database.

"The plate comes back to a— Beverly and Mitchell Champlain; of Burr Ridge," Nicks reported.

"Why the hell is he with them? This isn't adding up," Bradley replied.

"I'm calling him now," Nicks said and listened to the phone go to voicemail. "He's not answering."

Nicks followed at a distance down the city streets. The car stopped outside an old cathedral and campus. Jude exited the vehicle and waved goodbye. An older nun approached Jude and gave him a hug. Nicks raised a brow.

"Unless Jude has suddenly become enlightened, this is not him," Nicks said.

The boy removed his hat showing his neat hair, solidifying the fact that he was not Jude.

"His bike is still here," Clayton radioed. "I will check the school."

Clayton walked up the steps to the main entrance. Kari looked up from her studies to see Clayton walking past. He waved casually and continued on his way. Few students lingered on the sunny Friday afternoon. He wandered the halls, glancing into classrooms. He rounded the corner and ran into Andi. She dropped her purse and a stack of essays. She let out a small squeak of surprise from the encounter.

"I am so sorry," Clayton apologized and picked up Andi's scattered papers for her.

"Clayton... Hi, I– Uh, what are you doing here?"

"I was looking for a student actually," Clayton said, handing Andi her stack of papers. Confusion spread across her features. "My friend's nephew hasn't been coming home... I saw his bike in the parking lot, but he doesn't appear to be here."

"I see... What's his name? Maybe I can help."

"Jude Hendricks."

"Huh, that surprises me. Jude is very polite. Doesn't seem like something he would do."

"That's why my friend is concerned. I'm going to see if I can review the security footage."

"I can show you to the security office," Andi offered.

Clayton smiled. "I know where it is– The overzealous officer may have yelled at me a time or two for just waltzing in."

Andi laughed. "I suppose you're right."

"I would enjoy your company though."

Clayton followed Andi across the school to an office near the main entrance. She opened the door and a security guard lounged back in a chair at a desk behind a wall of monitors. He peered around the monitors to see who his visitors were.

"Larry, this is Marshal Bradshaw... He needs your assistance with locating a student."

The round security guard straightened up. "Of course, Marshal, my command center is at your disposal."

Clayton walked around the desk and looked over the system. Clayton had memorized the layout of the school and Jude's schedule. It would not be difficult to track him through the halls. Clayton scanned the footage and saw Jude leave his last class. He watched the cell phone drop. *Sneaky shithead.* Clayton watched Jude leave the school out a side entrance. Clayton walked back around to the door.

"Thank you, Larry," Clayton said.

Larry stood. "Anytime Marshal."

Andi followed Clayton out of the office. "He left through the east entrance," Clayton said over the radio.

Clayton touched his forehead and unzipped his sweatshirt to let some cool air hit him. His tactical vest was clearly visible. "Son of a bitch," Clayton said frustrated.

"I mean, he's probably just hanging out with friends that his uncle doesn't approve of. You know, normal teenager stuff," Andi said not understanding Clayton's reaction.

Clayton smiled and kissed Andi on the cheek. "You are probably right... I'll see you later."

"Jude is a good kid. Hopefully his uncle won't be too hard on him."

"Hopefully," Clayton said and left the school.

He walked across the street and down the block to where Nicks and Bradley were parked.

"What do we do now?" Bradley asked. "With Bennent missing and no intel on where Garrick is, do we assume the worst?"

"There has to be more to this... He wouldn't be so reckless– not now," Nicks said.

Bradley turned his head, seeing Kari leave the school and walk to the Regal.

"Do you think she knows where he is?" Clayton asked.

Kari pulled out of the parking lot. Bradley dialed her number and waited for her to answer.

"Hey," Kari answered.

Bradley treaded lightly on his pursuit for answers. "Just checking in."

"Of course you are."

"Jude's not with you is he?"

"No Bradley, Jude is not with me. I'm being a good girl and listened to you."

"Oh?"

Kari rolled her eyes. "Don't sound so surprised."

"I just figured that since you two are attached at the hip, that you'd sneak him with you anyway." He shook his head at Nicks and Clayton.

"Thank you for your confidence. I'm trying not to piss you off any more than I have."

"Okay, okay. I hear you. Have fun this weekend. And don't talk on the phone and drive."

"Then hang up."

"I'm gonna."

"Bye, Bradley."

"Bye."

Bradley put his phone back in his pocket. "She says he's not with her..."

"Well obviously... We saw her walk to the car, I doubt he's just magically going to appear, like a goddamn jack in a box," Clayton said.

"Damn this kid, where the hell is he?" Nicks seethed.

"We are going to have to enter him as a runaway..." Bradley said.

Jude waited at the corner a bouquet of lilies in hand. Kari pulled over and smiled seeing the flowers. Jude got in and kissed Kari.

"You are too sweet," she said admiring the flowers.

"I try."

"My brother is already suspicious that I have a stowaway."

Jude laughed. "Naturally."

Jude secured the seatbelt feeling remorse for the turmoil he has no doubt created for the Marshals.

Kari and Jude started their long journey to Marinette.

"I texted my aunt to let her know I was going to go to the party before checking in, since we won't be getting there until eight anyway. We'll at least get one night in for sure. Bradley will probably find out one way or another I disobeyed him," Kari smirked.

"If that's the case, I'm sure we will be ordered home immediately."

"Probably, he's a bit dramatic that way."

"He's trying to protect you is all. I mean– after all I am a criminal."

"That is not even the point– but he can still be a tyrant at times."

Jude chuckled. "He's doing his best."

They talked the entire way. Kari told Jude all about her friends that he would be meeting and her family. Jude loved to hear Kari talk about her friends and family, it gave her a glow he hadn't really seen before. They stopped for a break outside of Milwaukee at a gas station in a rural small town off of the interstate. The sun dipped into the horizon painting the sky in oranges and reds. After Kari purchased some candy for the remainder of the ride they strolled to the car. Jude gently grabbed her hand. It could possibly be the last time Jude would get to spend with Kari. He knew for certain after the stunt he pulled there would be zero probability that one of them would be still enrolled at Cambridge. Kari stopped and turned to Jude before opening the car door.

Jude kissed Kari. "You are beautiful."

CHAPTER EIGHTEEN

Cars lined the street and Kari found a spot a few houses away from Diego's. Jude was surprised to see so many cars.

Kari turned to Jude. "This is it. Time to feed you to the wolves."

"I think I can manage," Jude chuckled.

The bass pumped on the usually quaint small town street. Jude followed Kari up the path to the side of the giant red-bricked home and to the gate that led to the backyard. Laughter and music filled the air. People swam in the pool, danced and played yard games. Every hand had the iconic red solo cup.

"I assume that's Beth?" Jude nodded towards the blonde dancing on a table.

"Yes–"

Diego was prompt with his greeting. He walked to Jude and Kari with extra cups in hand. His hair was perfectly styled and his flowered linen shirt accented his tan skin. "Welcome, Kari. It is good to see you."

Diego handed Kari and Jude their drinks. Diego hugged Kari, kissing her on both cheeks and shook Jude's hand. "You must be Jude. I am Diego, naturally. I have only heard about how beautiful you are, and I see Kari was not wrong in her description."

Kari's cheeks flushed and Jude chuckled. "Thank you– I suppose."

"And an Englishman–" Diego turned to Kari. "My dear, you had failed to mention that little detail."

"Did she now? I would say it is one of my better attributes," Jude said.

"I bet you have many–" Diego winked. "Some of which I am sure Kari will enjoy."

Kari nervously chugged her drink. It was strong and had a faint lemon taste.

"Oh honey, these are not for the faint of heart. Slow down." Diego touched Kari's arm.

"What's in these?" Kari asked.

"A lot of vodka," Diego laughed.

Jude spotted Beth bouncing towards them with a wide smile on her face. Kari tensed from the sight of a guy behind Beth. Jude assumed it was Ryan.

"You didn't tell me Ryan was going to be here," Kari said through gritted teeth.

"I invited the team. It would be rude to exclude anyone," Diego said.

Kari took Jude's drink and put his cup in her empty one. "I'm going to need another one."

"Uh–" Jude was going to stop her but she was too quick.

Diego's attention was drawn away. "You two cats have fun now." Diego waved. "Daniel! That's my mother's china. Si respeto por las cosas buenas!"

"Hey, Kar!" Beth hugged Kari. "I am so glad you could make it."

"Us too. This is quite the party," Kari said marveled by the decor and amount of people in attendance.

"You know how Diego is. All the frills and whistles."

"He made it sound like it was going to just be a few people."

"And… you believed him?"

Kari chuckled.

"Let's get a game of flip cup started." Beth pulled her away. "You play? Right, Jude?"

"I haven't the faintest idea what game that is." Jude was astonished by the amount of alcohol consumption and assumed flip cup would only naturally involve liquid courage.

A group gathered around a table ready to play the drinking game. Jude stood behind Kari and placed his hands on her hips. His assumptions were corrected.

"Do you yanks have to do everything with alcohol? You're nearly as bad as the Irish," Jude whispered in Kari's ear.

"This is Wisconsin, Jude, we live off of beer and cheese."

"That is odd."

"So is haggis and mead."

Jude kissed Kari's cheek. "That's the Scottish love."

"Same island," Kari laughed.

"Either way– I'm just going to watch. One of us will have to drive," Jude said.

Kari kissed Jude on the cheek. "Thank you."

Beth set the game up and divided the group into teams.

A skinny boy in swim trunks and duck floaties on his arms walked up to the table. He flung his shaggy blond bangs out of his face.

"Oh! Fip cup! I wove fis game." He set his beer on the table across from Kari.

"It's nice to see you too, Billy," Kari said, getting her little cousin's attention.

"Fwhen did you ge fere?"

"Just now–"

"Weren you a fisnor of home? Fid you go– missing ferson from Chicago?"

Jude cocked an eyebrow at Billy as he stammered having great difficulty with words.

Kari laughed. "Uh– no, turns out Bradley was a fan of me using trays as self defense. Not grounded."

"Foes my motter know your fere?"

"Yes. How drunk are you?"

"Fery–"

"Although…" Kari examined her cup and took a big gulp. "I am not sure she would approve if she really knew…"

Billy waved. "Psh, she threw up in the 70s–"

"Alright! Enough chit chat! Let's get er done!" Beth shouted.

Kari was atrocious at flip cup and resulted in many drinks of Diego's special vodka lemonade. The alcohol made the world move beneath her feet. She had never been drunk before. Jude wondered if he should cut her off but she appeared to be having a good time.

Kari turned to Jude. "Do you mind?" She motioned for Jude to take her place. "I really need to use the… What do you call it? The loo?"

"Yes, yes the loo will do, or even simply a toilet."

Kari laughed. "Loo– What a silly name– I'll be right back." Kari kissed Jude and staggered away.

Kari navigated around the people standing near the pool and patio. She stepped behind the corner of the pool house and was relieved to see there was no line.

Billy nodded to Jude. "So, you and my fousin huh?"

"Ye–"

"Fat's cool, Fat's cool. You feem a lot better than the d-bag she dated fere. And by d-bag I mean ma friend Fyan."

"Isn't it premature to make a statement as such? I mean you've only just met me."

Billy pointed to his temple. "I know fings." Billy burped and swayed, clearly intoxicated.

Kari exited the bathroom and stumbled to the side. Ryan grabbed her arm and tried to stabilize her, but being drunk also he lost his balance and fell into her. Kari's back hit the wall of the pool house. Ryan placed a hand on each side of Kari blocking her from going anywhere.

"Lari— Kari, I wannated to talk to to you," Ryan said, alcohol emanating from his breath.

"I have nothing to say to you."

"You and I are s'posed to be together... We were sooooo good together, Kari. We had a furniture— future– And you threw that all away! And for what? To get laid by some lo-loaded Brimmish— Blimpish— Brittis— English prick?"

"Please move. You're drunk."

"I love you," Ryan said. He leaned close and kissed Kari sloppily.

Kari pushed Ryan away and yelled, "Get off!"

Kari took a step away from Ryan and he grabbed her arm. "Wait."

Kari slapped Ryan across the face, a red hand print forming in its wake. Ryan grasped both of Kari's biceps and turned her.

"Why'd you do that!"

Kari narrowed her eyes and kneed Ryan in the groin. He dropped his hands with a muffled groan. Kari pushed him again and with unstable feet herself, fell on top of him. She swung at Ryan but seeing two of him made it difficult to land a strike.

"I hate you!" Kari spat.

"Would you stop!" Ryan attempted to control her wild hands but proved impossible with lack of coordination.

Jude heard the yelling and rounded the corner of the pool house with Billy close on his heels.

"Kari– What are you doing?" Jude asked and grabbed her.

Billy stepped between Jude as he tried to control Kari and Ryan.

"Better keep your- your slut on a leash," Ryan warned, pointing a limp finger around Billy.

"Keep your mouf fut," Billy said.

The sight of Jude holding Kari enraged Ryan more.

"So what...? Your parents didn't leave you enough money and now you're fucking this rich ARSEhole?"

Kari froze. She did not think Ryan would say such hurtful words. Drunk Ryan on the other hand, she never had the pleasure.

"That was out of line," Jude said.

Ryan stepped forward and Billy touched his chest to keep him back. "And what are you going to do about it?"

"There are several things I would enjoy. None of which are suitable for a party."

"You're just a coward with no b-balls," Ryan taunted.

Jude placed his hand behind Kari's back. "Perhaps we should leave."

Kari nodded, choking back her tears and they walked away.

"Wow, I guess I shouldn't be surprised she picked such a pushover," Ryan said and followed them.

Billy turned around. "You fould stop while you're ahead. You're a ferson I choose to like but that won't stop me from frowing you in the pool."

Kari didn't say goodbye to anyone as she attempted to hold it together. Her mind was in a whirlwind of emotions. The alcohol amplified her feelings. Jude waved at Diego who had a sympathetic look upon his features. Billy, after pointing Ryan in the direction of the beer, ran and took flight, tucking into a half ball before splashing into the pool. Jude opened the gate for Kari and escorted her out.

They made it to the street when the gate slammed behind them.

"I wasn't finished!" Ryan yelled.

Kari turned around. "Insulting my family wasn't enough?"

"Your brother sure is doing a great job with you– Oh yeah– I heard about your pill popping trip– I can only imagine how disappointed your parents would be," Ryan said as he walked and stopped in front of Kari.

Jude glared at Ryan and struck him in the face with a forceful punch. He would not tolerate Ryan speaking to Kari in such a manner. Ryan fell into the nearest car which happened to be his own late model Ford Ranger. Ryan massaged his cheek and righted himself. He narrowed his eyes and stepped up to Jude.

"You hit like a little bitch," Ryan said and shoved Jude, who just glared at Ryan. "Kari, your dead mom would be so proud you picked such a pussy. Hopefully your brother Marcus gets blown up so he doesn't have to meet this piece of shit."

Ryan threw a beer bottle at Jude. But he did not waver from his position and batted the bottle down. Kari quickly knelt near the mailbox and picked up a landscaping rock. Kari took the rock and threw it. The glass of Ryan's passenger window shattered when the rock crashed through it.

"You fucking bitch!" Ryan seethed and dashed around Jude to get to Kari.

Jude wrapped his arm around Ryan's chest and pivoted his weight to the side. Jude fell on top of Ryan and pinned him to the ground. Jude landed a hit on Ryan's brow. Ryan grasped Jude's collar and rolled on top of him.

"Hey! Knock it off!" an authoritative voice commanded.

Ryan immediately released Jude and backed away with his hands raised high in the air. Four police officers approached them. Jude rose and pinched his temples with a heavy sigh. Kari stumbled around the car to join them.

"I am so glad you are here," Ryan blubbered. "This guy attacked me– For no reason– And her! She broke my truck face- window- thing."

"Have a seat on the curb, all of you," the older blond officer said.

They took a seat on the curb. Jude bounced his knee nervously.

"You good then, Poet?" The tall dark haired officer asked.

"Yeah, you and Sanderson are good to make contact at the house. Richter and I will be fine here," Poet said.

Poet stepped to the teens and the other two continued to the house.

"So, what exactly happened here?" Poet asked.

"I already told you," Ryan snipped.

Poet looked to Jude and Kari. "Why don't you two tell me what happened?"

Kari crossed her arms loosely and stared beyond the officers. Jude glanced at Kari and back at Poet. Jude wrapped his arm around her and kissed the side of her head. Kari leaned into Jude her emotions reeling.

"Ryan was giving her a hard time and said a few tasteless things... Seems it may have gotten out of hand," Jude answered for her.

"Where are you from?"

"Chicago—"

"No, where are you really from?"

Jude rolled his eyes. "England, obviously."

"What are you doing here?" Poet questioned.

"He's with me," Kari said. Seeing the confusion from Poet she continued with, "I'm from here and moved to Chicago."

"Right... So what exactly did he say that you believed warranted being physical with him?"

"Um... Well..." Jude looked to Kari.

Tears formed in her eyes. "We used to date." She motioned to Ryan. "He was calling me a slut and grabbed me."

Poet turned on his flashlight and pointed it at Kari seeing the red marks on her arms.

Jude looked at Poet. "No one should grab or speak to women in such a manner."

Poet dropped his gaze for a moment. "How did his window get smashed?"

Kari waved her hand. "I threw a rock through it after Ryan insulted my family. Mocking my mother who passed and then told me he hoped my brother would get blown up over seas."

"He started the whole thing when he grab—" Jude was silenced by a stern look from Officer Poet.

"That may be, but she can't just go around breaking things because she can't handle some words," Ryan argued.

"Stop talking–" Poet said with a sigh. "Can I see your IDs?"

"We're not going to jail are we?" Jude asked, putting his hands on the outside of his pockets.

"Not at the moment."

Jude was the last to hesitantly hand over his ID to Poet. "How old are all of you?"

"We're both 17," Kari answered for her and Jude.

Poet stared at Ryan. "18," he answered.

Poet handed the IDs to his partner who queried them through dispatch. "Check to see if there are any municipal priors."

Richter pulled out a PBT, preliminary breath test.

"Blow," he ordered Ryan.

Ryan took a deep breath until the small yellow machine beeped. The interface lit up 0.230.

"You're going to have a rough morning tomorrow," Richter said and changed straws pointing the machine at Kari.

Kari took a deep breath and blew, feeling lightheaded as she did it. The small machine clicked, 0.170.

"Looks like you were having a good time too."

Kari dropped her gaze and Richter moved onto Jude. 0.00. "Hmm."

"What surprised?" Jude asked.

"A bit."

After a couple minutes dispatch got back to Richter and he handed Poet the IDs.

"Those two are clear... Hendricks however, looks like he's listed as a runaway out of Chicago."

"Any repeat offenders?"

"Looks like Sleeter is in our system for a muni possession of THC."

"All right..." Poet pointed to Ryan. "Do you still live on Hockridge?"

"Yes."

"Mkay, you'll be receiving two citations in the mail. One for underage drinking and the other for disorderly conduct."

"But–"

"You are free to leave Mr. Sleeter."

Ryan rose and glared at Jude. "Commie bastard."

"What?" Jude furrowed his brow.

"Keep moving, Sleeter," Poet ordered.

Ryan stumbled back towards the house, glancing back every few paces.

"Now, because you two are not in our system, you'll need to be processed at the station. And for you, Jude... We will be contacting Chicago to see what their wishes are for you."

"What does 'processed' mean?" Jude asked.

"We take your photograph and fingerprints."

"But Ryan was the one that started all of this—"

"Yet I found you brawling in the street. It's really not that big of a deal, more of an in house record keeping than anything."

Poet motioned for them to stand.

"Can I call my uncle?" Jude asked.

"When we're finished with everything."

Jude glanced down the street and back at Poet who was thin and fit. A hiccup forced its way up from Kari. He couldn't leave her by herself. He wasn't entirely confident he could out run Poet either and if he did make a break for it, if caught, would certainly land himself in jail. The ride to the police department was short. Jude was nervous about getting his prints taken. It would jeopardize not only his safety but possibly anyone with whom he associated. His mind raced fearing that Garrick would find him if his prints hit the database. Kari and Jude sat in the processing room of the police department. He stared at the paneling of the ceiling trying to remain calm.

"Why are you so nervous?" Kari whispered.

"I can't be in trouble," Jude said.

"It's just a citation, it'll be okay."

Jude stared at Kari, wishing she was right. Jude bounced his knee as his stomach turned in knots. His vision blurred and he tried to take deep breaths.

"Miss Evans, if you would," Poet said motioning to the camera.

The camera clicked and flashed capturing the drunken state she was in. Kari sat next to Jude after her prints were acquired.

"Alright Hendricks, you're next," Poet said and waved Jude over to the fingerprinting station.

Poet rolled Jude's fingers in the ink and transferred the print onto a stock card. Jude felt lightheaded as he breathed shallowly. He stood in front of the height poster on the wall. The flash of the camera made him see orbs of light. He sat next to Kari and placed his head into his hands and bent forward between his legs. He was trying desperately not to panic.

Back at the Marshal's office, Nicks's phone rang and saw the number come up as private on his phone. Pyke pounded his fist on the door frame.

"Three former Special Operations fucksticks can't keep eyes on one fucking kid!" Pyke yelled and stormed out.

"Join the special ops division, it'll be fun, they said..." Clayton said. "It'll give you a sense of purpose they said..."

Rauri allowed the phone to buzz in his hand until Pyke had departed. "Hello?"

"Is this Rauri Nicks?" the man asked.

"It is, who is this?"

"Sgt. Ramirez, Chicago PD."

"Ah, what can I do for you Sargeant?"

"We have located your nephew. It appears he is in Marinette, Wisconsin."

"Is he now...?"

"I can give you the number of the officer on the call so you can arrange for his return."

"Thank you." Nicks hung up after getting the phone number.

Poet's phone rang. "Poet."

"Hi, this is Rauri Nicks, I was given your number from Chicago PD. You have my nephew?"

"Yes, I do. He was involved in a disturbance at an underaged party. He will be receiving a citation tonight for disorderly conduct."

"Lovely– "

"He will need to be released to an adult. He is with a– Kari Evans, whose aunt is picking her up."

Jude raised his head knowing the officer was talking to one of the Marshals.

"You can release him to Kari's aunt. Would you mind if I spoke to him?" Nicks asked.

"Sure, hold on–" Poet walked to Jude and handed him the phone.

"Hello," Jude said.

"I cannot even begin to express the stupidity you have displayed. You are careless Jude–"

"If I could–"

"Stop talking– I will have to speak with Bradshaw and Evans about how you're getting home. But for now– you will go with Kari's aunt. At least I know you're safe."

"Yes, sir–" Jude handed the phone back to Officer Poet.

Nicks sat back in his chair around a conference table at the Marshals office. Nicks looked up at Bradley who attempted to contain his anger. He forcefully shut his laptop he spent hours staring at sifting through footage of the city's camera system.

"Before you say anything," Clayton said, setting his coffee down. "He's safe, that's all that really matters at this point."

"I cannot believe them–" Bradley picked up his phone and tapped it on the table. "Should we go pick him up?"

"I would say have their dumbasses drive home– But! Obviously they are probably drunk." Nicks seethed.

"I think they will be fine for the night and can drive back in the morning. Plus, this way it'll give you two some time to cool off," Clayton said.

"I need some air before I lose my shit." Nicks stood and walked out the door.

Bradley tapped his phone a couple more times on the table and stared at the screen.

"I would advise against that... Remember you're not a psychic. It would be really odd to call your sister about a situation you 'shouldn't' know about yet."

Bradley set his phone on the table facedown. "I am going to strangle both of them."

Joan entered the lobby of the police department. She was happy to see her niece but also disappointed in the manner in which their reunion was occuring.

"Kari– I am–" Joan embraced Kari. "We will be discussing this later."

"Hi, Aunt Joan."

Joan turned to Jude. "And you must be Jude... I wish we were meeting under better circumstances."

Joan glanced at Kari. "I will be speaking to your brother about this."

"I wouldn't expect anything less–"

"Hello ma'am," Poet greeted and shook Joan's hand.

"I apologize for the trouble my niece and her friend have caused. I am embarrassed to have to be here."

"They're kids," Poet shrugged. "However, Jude was listed as a runaway. I spoke with his legal guardian who gave permission for him to be released to you, if that's all right."

"Um…" Paula looked at Kari and Jude. "Well, of course."

"Good, I just need you to sign this form." Poet handed Joan a clipboard and she signed the form. "Well then, they have their citations and are free to leave."

"Thank you, Officer."

They walked out of the police department. Poet returned to the processing room to finish his report. He picked up Jude's prints and ran them through the system to be entered. The computer chirped notifying him there was a match. Poet raised a brow, surprised that the nice boy he released had an out of state record. He clicked on the file and Jude's picture appeared. The names did not match. He looked back and forth from Jude's processing photo to the mugshot on the screen. He scrolled down to see substantial charges from the New York Police Department. The department phone next to Poet rang.

"Poet," he answered.

"Hey, Poet, there's a call for you on line one, a detective from NYPD," the secretary said.

"Uh– thanks, Sandra." Poet pressed the line button. "Officer Poet."

"Good evening, Officer Poet. I am detective Hall with NYPD," Garrick introduced.

"Hello detective, what can I do for you?"

"I received a notification that you ran a *James Garrick*'s prints. Is he still in your custody? He is a person of interest in a homicide I am investigating."

Poet froze, his blood ran cold. "Uh– No I had released him."

"Would you happen to have a current address for him?"

Poet shuffled the papers on the desk to find the copy of Jude's Illinois driver's license. "Yeah, it's 9807 S. Prospect Av. Chicago. Also, it's weird but he had a valid driver's license out of Illinois with the name Jude Hendricks."

"Huh, an alias– Thank you for the information, Officer, enjoy your evening," Garrick said and hung up.

Poet looked at the phone, the dial tone buzzing in his ear. He hung up and stared at his computer in disbelief.

Garrick set the phone down. "Hughes, is 9807 S. Prospect Av. a valid address?"

Hughes stared at the computers. "No."

"I didn't think it would be…"

"What's his alias?"

"Jude Hendricks."

"I will search school records and anything else I find. I'll get you an address as soon as I can."

"Delightful." Garrick turned to his son, Paul. "Shall we get a drink? I've been told there's an exquisite new cocktail lounge that is quite the experience."

"Or a local pub would suffice," Paul shrugged.

"Normally I would agree with you, however, I believe we are in need of a celebratory drink."

Paul chuckled. "So be it, but I will need to change my attire. I don't think trainers, a jumper and jeans are acceptable for such an establishment."

"You would be quite correct." Garrick buttoned his suit coat.

"I will be right back..." Paul exited the suit to his own.

"To be on the safe side, Hughes I do not wish to come back here. Find us a new location. I'd hate to be woken by a team of tactically inclined individuals pointing rifles at me."

"Yes, sir I will arrange for new lodging."

"I hear the Waldorf is nice."

"Yes, sir."

"Don't check us out though, I am going to leave a nice gift for the American's when they come knocking."

CHAPTER NINETEEN

Clayton drummed his fingers on the table and read an intelligence brief from MI6's recent Op. Bradley sat next to him viewing near hits on facial recognition of Garrick at airports. His attention was drawn to his ringing phone, the caller ID showed it was his aunt. He was furious that he was just now being told about the incident from last night.

"Hello, Joan," Bradley answered, trying to remain calm, after all he wasn't mad at her.

"Good morning, Bradley. I hope it isn't too early."

"Not at all– What's up?"

"Well… Kari had a bit of an incident last night."

"Excuse me? Is she okay?" Bradley tried to sound worried and hoped it passed.

"Yes she's fine. Turns out Diego's party got a little out of hand. Ryan grabbed her and said some awful things. It was really a good thing Jude was here to protect her. Poor boy got himself in trouble too."

"Jude's there?"

"Isn't he supposed to be?"

"No... His uncle grounded him. He was entered as a runaway last night..."

"Oh... Yeah the Officer did mention that last night..."

"The officer?"

"Well, because of the fight they got a couple citations is all."

"A couple citations?"

"It's really no big deal. A misunderstanding."

"Joan, when they wake up they need to come home."

"Come now, Bradley, they're kids. No one got hurt. And if I'd say so myself, that Ryan deserved everything he got."

Bradley dropped his head in his hand with a long sigh.

"Just let them stay one more night. Please, I haven't seen Kari since the funeral. This trip wasn't just for her you know. Not only have I lost your mother but I lost Kari, too."

Bradley closed his eyes. He hadn't thought about it at all. "I hadn't realized how this has affected you."

Clayton shook his head and wrote on a pad of paper in big letters **HE NEEDS TO GET BACK HERE** and showed Bradley.

"I'm sorry, Joan, they need to come home. Jude's uncle is very upset."

Joan was silent for a moment. "I understand– But Bradley, please let her visit again soon. Kari's not the only one that needs it. And Jude is a nice boy, he's welcome here anytime as well."

"She will be back. Thank you, Joan."

"You know you can be less of a stranger too, young man."

"Yes, Aunt Joan."

"Take care of yourself, and be safe out there."

"Always, I'll talk to you later."

Bradley hung up and dropped his phone on the table. He ran both his hands through his hair. "This is a fucking mess!"

Seth popped in the doorway hitting the frame with his knuckles. "Knock, knock," he said not his usual cheeky self.

"Hey, Riley," Bradley said exhausted.

"How is the new software working for you?" Seth asked.

"Much better than the old program."

"Glad to hear. Let me know if there's anything else you need."

"Thanks," Braldey said. "Hey, you okay?"

"I feel I should be asking you the same thing. This mess with Jude and your sister is certainly something." His thoughts lingered on the news he received about Maisie. "But I'm okay, just tired."

"Seems like we all are."

"I would classify myself as a permanently exhausted pigeon," Clayton piped up in a serious tone.

"Right..." Seth nodded and left the room.

Nicks walked into the small conference room passing Seth and stood silent for a moment. Bradley and Clayton stared at him.

"Bennent was found dead–"

Seth wiped his face hearing the words again. He walked away still in shock that his long time partner was dead.

"Well, great... I hope that MI6 interrogation training paid off, if not Garrick will be at our doorstep soon enough," Clayton said, setting down the file he was reading.

"We need Jude back and moved to the secondary safe house," Nicks said and pulled out his cellphone. "What's your sister's number?"

"I already spoke to my aunt and they'll be on their way today."

"Jude needs to hear it... To let the severity of the situation sink in. Perhaps that will get him to stop doing dumb shit that will get himself killed."

Bradley gave Nicks the number and he waited while the phone rang. Kari reached for her ringing phone on the end table. It was a Chicago number and it was five in the morning.

"Hello?" Kari answered, her eyes closed, already losing the battle to sleep.

"Hello, Kari. It's Jude's uncle. Is he close by?"

"Stop shouting at me." Kari's head throbbed from the hangover. "Wh—what?"

"I said, 'I need to speak with him,'" Nicks said.

Kari rolled over and shook Jude awake. "It's your uncle. He's yelling."

She held the phone out for Jude. Nicks could be heard from the small phone speaker, "I'm not yelling."

Jude took the phone and sat up. Kari rolled back over and threw the covers over her head. Jude wiped the sleep from his eyes.

"Hello?" He yawned.

"Jude– You need to get back here immediately. Bennent was murdered– We believe your location has been compromised—"

Jude's head spun and he thought he was going to be sick from the extreme anxiety that coursed through his body.

"Jude? Did you hear me? You need to leave–"

Jude shook his head. "I heard you."

"For the love of God, Jude, you will do as you are told."

"Uh– Sir, I have to tell you something," Jude paused feeling sick.

"What?"

"The police took my fingerprints last night..."

Nicks took a long breath trying not to let the rage consume him. "Of course they fucking did! Did you sing kumbaya with them too? Jesus christ! Can you just stay out of trouble!"

"I didn't plan–"

"Shut your mouth– Just get back here, now. And so help me God, don't do anything stupid." Nicks said and hung up.

Jude looked at the phone for a moment. He stood leaning against the window sill of the large bay window in the basement, the light from the sky a soft red from the rising sun. He gazed at the green grass dancing in the cool gentle morning breeze. Although the scenery of the field was pleasant, his thoughts were not. His stomach twisted and turned to the point he thought he was going to vomit. The thought of Shaun Garrick finding him swelled a devastating fear into Jude. He glanced at Kari who had fallen back to sleep. He knew Garrick, he destroyed his enemies by getting to the ones they loved. Jude knew from experience what he was capable of. Anxiety coursed through his body and he blocked the thoughts of Garrick from his mind the best he could.

—

"Get Marinette PD on the phone now!" Nicks shouted and planted his palms on the table. "Fuck! Jesus Christ!"

Bradley leaned over their table and dialed the number on the conference phone looking at his computer making sure he got the digits right.

"Why are you so goddamn mad?" Clayton asked.

Nicks took a long breath, his eyes glued to the wood grain surface.

"They took Jude's prints..."

Clayton tilted his head back shaking his head staring at the ceiling. "Garrick's going to be here in a matter of hours— if he isn't already here."

The phone rang. "Marinette Police Department this is Sandra."

"Hello, Sandra, this is Marshal Nicks. I was hoping I could speak with someone in regards to an incident that occurred last night with a couple juveniles." Nicks was enraged, he didn't care if Poet was smart enough to recognize his voice and last name from their previous phone call.

"Do you have their names?"

"The party involved is Jude Hendricks, and you know what, I believe Officer Poet may have been out with him."

"Ah, yes, it was Officer Poet. He's actually still in. I'll transfer you."

"Thank you."

"Hold please."

Smooth music played over the speaker as the Marshals waited.

"Officer Poet," he fidgeted, wondering what deep trouble one kid could be in that NYPD called and now the Marshals.

"Officer Poet, good morning. Marshal Nicks here with the US Marshals."

"Good morning, what can I help you with? Wait– Did I talk to you earlier? You're that kid's uncle right?"

"Uh– I think you're mistaken," Nicks pressed his hand to his forehead.

"Oh, you just sounded familiar," Poet said and yawned.

"You had contact with a juvenile last night, Jude Hendricks, did you happen to run his prints through any databases?"

"Um– yeah, I did…"

Bradley massaged his temples, the frustration was boiling.

"Fuck!" Clayton exclaimed and stood quickly from his chair and left the room to get Pyke.

Poet was not expecting the shout from Clayton. "Uh– also Marshal, I'm not sure what you want with this kid or what you know, but his prints came back as James Garrick. Also an investigator from NYPD had called saying the kid is a person of interest in a homicide case."

"NYPD? What was the investigator's name?"

"I don't remember–"

"Christ, he's fucking here isn't he?" Bradley asked Nicks.

Nicks stared at Bradley worried. "Thank you, Officer. I hope you have a good rest of your day."

"You as we–" Nicks hung up before Poet could finish.

"This is bad–" Nicks said.

"Ya think…" Bradley growled

Pyke stormed into the room, Clayton and Seth behind him. He was already five shades of red from the news provided by Clayton.

"You're kid is a fucking walking wrecking ball! God fucking damn it! Why doesn't he just dress up as a God damn Christmas present and mail himself to Garrick!" Pyke yelled and took a couple deep breaths before speaking again. "All right, we need to get a team on standby and assume Garrick already may be well on his way here. Fairfax–"

"It's Halifax," Riley corrected.

"That's what I said… Start running the near hits through the database again. Or do you need to find your crayons first!"

"We are on it, sir," Bradley said.

———

Jude had not moved when Kari groggily awoke an hour later. She stretched her arms and yawned. She turned over and caught a glimpse of Jude standing by the window in some sort of daze. An expression of worry painted his face. Kari slid out of bed and joined him by the window. She gently kissed Jude on the cheek and wrapped her arms around his body. She was chilled from being out of the warm bedding and his body heat helped warm her. She could feel the tension in his body as he stared out the window.

"Good morning, my lovely British lad," Kari greeted cheerfully hoping that he'd snap out of his apparent foul mood.

"Good morning," Jude replied. He gently touched Kari's warm cheek and kissed her on the forehead. "I'm going to get some breakfast. Then we need to talk."

"Jude–"

He stopped at the landing of the steps. "It's nothing– But my uncle needs me to go back to Chicago."

Disappointment spread across her face. "But we just got here."

"I know, I'm sorry. But I'm going to have to go." Jude ascended the steps leaving Kari alone.

Kari slid her moccasins on and followed Jude up the steps from the basement. Kari approached the small kitchen and pulled a stool from the counter and took a seat in the middle. Jude was to her left stirring his cup of tea. To Kari's right sat Billy, his shaggy blond hair stood up oddly from his rough night of sleep. He dropped his head in his hand and groaned. His hangover was not being kind. Joan was busy fixing her cereal for herself and she cleaned the already spotless counter.

"I spoke with Bradley this morning. He is not happy with you," Joan said to Kari. "He was very adamant that you head home this morning."

Kari looked disappointed and Jude spoke. "I unfortunately have to get home anyway... My uncle is not happy about what happened. I apologize."

"If it wasn't for Ryan none of this would have happened–" Kari fumed.

"I'm disappointed that I missed you fighting Ryan– You sure did give him a nice shiner." Billy said to Jude.

"It was probably best you weren't there. I would have hated you getting in trouble."

"Meh." Billy waved off Jude.

"Either way, I am just glad you didn't end up staying with Ryan. I never did like him," Joan said.

"Joan–"

"What? I'm just speaking the truth. You have found a nice young man here. It would be safe to say that your mother would approve too."

"Your words are too kind– I seem to be a magnet for trouble though," Jude laughed.

Kari nudged him. "That would be me– I keep dragging you down with me."

Kari ate slowly, not wanting to leave for Chicago, returning to the wrath that awaited her. Jude on the other hand, wanted nothing more than to fly anywhere and not go back to Chicago at all. He wasn't sure if he was more scared of the Marshals or of Garrick.

After they were packed and ready to go, they stood outside loading Jess's regal. Kari did not know the next time she would be up there to see Joan and Billy. It saddened her greatly knowing she was going to be grounded until the end of time. Jude saw the disappointment flood Kari. He felt awful for being the reason her weekend was ruined. It was the last thing he wanted and knew how important it was for her to spend time with her family. He regretted coming in the first place, because of his poorly calculated decisions, he may not be alive much longer regardless. Anxiety gripped him making it difficult to appear normal.

"Kari, just remember, you're welcome to stay here any time you want. You don't even have to call. You can just show up," Joan informed and embraced Kari in a big hug.

"I know, Joan. You've been telling me that since I was born," Kari replied.

"And make sure you stay in touch," Joan stated and let her niece go.

"Don't worry. I will," Kari assured.

"Perhaps I can come visit this summer," Billy said and hugged Kari.

"I would enjoy that."

"Okay, you guys have a safe trip. And I'll see you both soon," Joan said.

Kari was exhausted and not feeling the best from her night of drinking. Jude offered to drive, it gave him a distraction. The ride was long and they stopped a couple times on the way down. Jude and Kari made it to the north side of Chicago. They didn't speak much on the way home. Kari had slept a majority of the way leaving Jude to a disarray of thoughts and emotions.

—

The day ticked by and the Marshals worked diligently to find any leads on Garrick suggesting Jude's location had been compromised. Seth's computer flashed red and beeped. He clicked on the file from an O'Hare security camera. It was a partial match as the quality of the photo was not the best. The man was the right age but it was difficult to tell with a full beard, glasses, and the flat cap.

"Gents, I have a partial match," Seth announced. "It's from a couple days ago already though."

The team gathered around as Seth worked on height and build of the man matching it with the last known physicals of Garrick. He took the still image of the two men standing next to Garrick as well, their partials coming back as Paul Garrick, Shaun's son, and Henry Wallace, one of Garrick's men.

"That's him," Nicks said.

"How the eff did he get through customs?" Pyke asked.

"Good question..." Bradley muttered.

"Christ..." Nicks rubbed his face. He picked up his phone. "Jude needs to get to the nanny house. Then I'm going to head back to the inn and destroy whatever I have left there just to be on the safe side."

He dialed Kari's number and listened to it ring impatiently. Kari picked up the phone seeing the Chicago number and handed the phone to Jude. "I think it's your uncle. Where is your phone anyway?"

Jude took the phone. "I– lost it." Jude answered the phone. "Hello?"

"Where are you?" Nicks asked frantically.

"We just got to the north side. I'm on my way to drop off Kari," Jude answered.

"Don't." Nicks commanded.

Jude was confused by this. "What? Why?"

"We received a hit on facial recognition at the airport. Garrick is in Chicago. You are to go to the secondary safe house. I will meet you there," Nicks explained.

"What about Kari?" Jude asked.

"She is to stay with you. I can't risk you being unprotected any longer. Keep this phone on you."

"Yes, sir." Jude hung up.

He gripped the steering wheel and looked around nervously.

"Jude– What is going on?"

"I– I can't take you home– Kari you're going to have to trust me, and do as I say."

"You are starting to scare me."

Jude took her hand. "Everything is going to be alright and when we're safe, I will explain everything."

"Safe? What?"

"Just trust me."

CHAPTER TWENTY

A small billow of smoke rose from the kitchen sink. Nicks collected any files he could muster and lit them a blaze in the sink. The pages charred and shriveled into ash. Nicks turned the water on to extinguish the smolder and wash the evidence down the drain. Nicks didn't want to take any chances of having confidential information lying around in the event that Garrick would acquire the address. He turned the faucet on and the water washed away the once paper only leaving black ash sticking to the sides of the stainless sink.

Two sleek black Land Rovers crawled to a stop alongside the curb. The neighborhood was older with nice homes and cars. The yards were well landscaped. The tree covered street was quaint and quiet. The afternoon sun peeked through the foliage of the canopied trees. Garrick emerged from the backseat of the first car. Paul exited the opposite side. Garrick showed no emotion and eyes hid behind dark sunglasses that reflected his surroundings. He waited in front of a nice brick ranch, staring at it. Two men got out of the second car, Rozier and Wallace. They walked up to the house through the trimmed lawn, ignoring the sidewalk. They stood two and two on each side of the door. They pulled out their handguns and twisted the silencers to the barrel of the guns, except for Garrick. He nodded, giving the signal to the others. The stocky man to his left, Rozier, took a step back and with immense force he plowed his leg into the door causing the lock to snap and swing open like a loose gate. The group entered the house and fanned out to clear the home.

Nicks drew his attention to the front of the house and drew his sidearm. The men surrounded Nicks in the dining room. Nicks was not about to go down without a fight and pointed his pistol at Wallace and a muffled pop rang out. Nicks staggered back, hitting the wall and fell to a seated position. Garrick took a step forward and removed his sunglasses and stared into Nicks's stern blue eyes. Blood ran down his shoulder. He grimaced in pain trying to grip his pistol. Wallace kicked it away from Nicks.

"Now that we got that out of the way– Tell me where James is," Garrick demanded.

"I don't take orders from assholes."

"I am far from an areshole."

"You are responsible for the death of thousands. I've had friends killed thanks to your arms dealing. There is a special place in Hell for men like you."

"I am not here to discuss morality. Where is James?"

"You are delusional if you think I'll tell you," Nicks said and quickly drew his secondary weapon with his reactionary hand from his ankle.

Nicks pulled the trigger hitting Garrick center mass. He stumbled backwards. Nicks adjusted his aim and shot Rozier. Blood splattered from the entry wound on his forehead. Paul shot twice and lowered his pistol. Nicks dropped his gun and covered his abdomen with his hand. He pulled his hand away, slick with blood. Garrick righted himself, running a hand over his suit. Behind the fine pressed shirt Nicks saw the glint of concealed body armour. Nicks fell to his side and coughed blood.

"Are the lights beginning to dim?" Garrick asked. He took a step closer.

"Go to Hell!" Nicks spat.

"Americans–" Garrick turned to Paul. "Find his phone."

Paul stepped over Rozier and approached Nicks. He patted his pockets and found the phone. Nicks tried to stop Paul from taking his phone but he was too weak. Paul chuckled and stood. The phone could only be unlocked by facial recognition or passcode. Paul faced the phone at Nicks

"Smile."

Nicks turned his head away. Paul grabbed him by the hair and forcefully turned his face and the phone unlocked.

"Pathetic git," Paul said.

"I've been called worse by better," Nicks coughed and smiled showing his blood covered teeth.

Paul stood with a huff, while Garrick chuckled. Paul went through the phone. He found no saved contacts. He looked at the phone log to see who he last called. He pushed send on the most recent number and waited.

Pulled over to the side of the road, Jude typed the address he was told to memorize into the GPS. Kari's phone rang. She looked at the caller ID.

"It's your uncle–"

"Answer it."

"Hello?"

Paul raised a brow hearing a female voice. "Hi, is Jude there?"

"Hold on–"

Kari held the phone to Jude. "I told you it was your uncle. He wants to speak with you."

"Kari, I'm driving."

"Just take it."

Jude took the phone but the call ended.

"That was easier than I anticipated– And he's with a girl, Kari," Paul said and texted the number for Jude to return home. Paul secured the phone in his pocket.

"Unfortunate for her," Garrick said, staring at Nicks. Nicks drew his brow together. "Sweep the house for anything useful and let's leave this place," Garrick ordered and walked out the front door, leaving Nicks to bleed out.

Nicks applied pressure to his wound, trying to hold on. Paul and Wallace tossed the house as ordered. Paul discovered an external hard drive and tapped on it, gaining Nicks's attention. Nicks's eyes rolled into the back of his head and he went limp. Paul smirked and he and Wallace left.

A chubby short man wobbled over to Garrick outside. "Boss, where is Rozier?" the jolly looking man asked.

"Jelly, I'm afraid he won't be joining us any longer," Garrick replied plainly. "Get in the car."

"The house is clean. I did find this though," Paul said as he handed Garrick the hard drive.

"Nicely done." Garrick opened the door to the SUV. "Wallace, stay here and bring James to me, alive."

"Yes, sir." Wallace said and disappeared around the corner of the house.

Nicks coughed and his eyes fluttered open. He turned onto his stomach and scanned the house. It did not appear that anyone was there. *Idiots should have made sure I was dead.* Nicks dragged himself across the tiled floor towards the living room. "Fuck me– A career as a

Delta sniper and this is how I die? Bleeding to death in a fucking dainty decorated house."

Nicks made it to a secondary go bag. He dug inside and pulled out a second cell phone. He tried to turn it on but the blood made it difficult. He texted his team, *compromised, nighthawk.* The exertion from his movement was too much. Darkness encroached his field of vision and he collapsed.

Paul plugged Nicks's phone into a device while they were driving in the Land Rover.

"Hughes, Paul is sending you data from a phone we recovered," Garrick said over the phone.

"I have it. I'm cross matching the numbers now. I will have a list of names in two minutes."

Bradley's phone vibrated on the table along with Clayton's. Bradley picked it up and his stomach dropped. A snap sounded and Clayton broked his phone in half. Bradley did the same tossing the pieces on the table and rose.

Clayton was already to the door. "I'll get to the secondary location."

"I'll deploy a team to the inn."

They left the room and Seth looked out from his work station. "Don't worry, I'll hold down the castle."

The parking ramp was dark making it difficult finding a phone in a black bag. Clayton's hand maneuvered over ammo, firearms, and various other supplies. He dialed a number and closed the trunk of his SUV.

"Hello?" Andi answered.

"Hey, it's Clayton."

Andi heard the stress in Clayton's voice. "Is everything okay?"

"Not really, it's hectic at work right now."

"I'm sorry to hear that."

"I was hoping you could pick Amelia up from daycare this evening? I'm not really sure when I'll be home."

"Not a problem. We will have a princess tea party and a slumber party if need be."

"I love you."

"I love you, too."

"Gotta go," Clayton hung up.

———

Jude read the text message from Nicks over again. Something was not right. Jude tried to call but it went straight to voicemail. Jude's hands were shaking as he turned down his street. The house was in sight. Nothing looked out of the ordinary but his anxiety was overwhelming.

Jude turned to Kari. "If anything should happen to me. You will leave and call your brother," Jude demanded. "Do not come after me."

"Jude, what's going on?"

"Just promise me," Jude repeated staring into her eyes.

"I promise–"

Jude opened his door and walked down the street. When he got closer he saw that the front door was open and the frame was splintered. Dread swept through Jude and he bolted into the house. Jude immediately saw Rozier dead in the dining room. He saw a streak of blood leading to the living room. He cautiously stepped further into the house and turned the corner to the living room. Nicks was motionless, surrounded by blood. Jude hurried over to him and knelt down.

"Rauri!" Jude shook him.

Nicks's eyes fluttered open. "Ah– Fuck, why are you here?"

"You texted me–"

Nicks shook his head no. "Garrick is here– They have my phone– Don't call the others– They will trace it from your phone– Go to the safe house. MacTavish will be there."

Nicks's eyes closed and he fought to keep them open. His breaths were shallow. He pushed his go bag to Jude. "Take this..."

Jude took the bag and saw the grip of a Glock inside along with magazines and various other items.

"I can't just leave you here," Jude pleaded.

"I was really looking forward to taking you to a Sox's game– I'm sorry," Nicks siad touching Jude's face.

"You just need to hang on..." Jude dug through the bag looking for gauze. "Please! I can't do this on my own."

"Can't? Are you serious? Have I not taught you anything? *Can't* is an excuse. You *can* do this Jude. You're strong and you will overcome this. You will fight and you will win."

"Stop! I just need to get you out of here, you'll be fine."

Nicks coughed up blood and touched Jude's arm, his gaze going blank. "It's a lie... There's no light at the end... I can't see shit."

Jude pressed his hands on the side of Nicks's face. "No! Hold on! You can't die—"

Nicks's body went limp and a peace crossed his features.

Jude stared at the man who gave his life to protect him. Tears fell from Jude's eyes. "No..."

"Hello, James." A man said, emerging into the living room from the kitchen.

Jude's head flew up and he stared wide-eyed at Wallace. He quickly wiped the tears leaving blood in their wake.

"I figured I'd give you a minute to say goodbye..."

"You've been here the whole time?"

"It would have been rude to interrupt your last moment..."

"Let me go, Wallace, you know he's going to kill me."

"I can't do that James... I let you go once and that was a mistake... I can't do it again. You have a lot to answer for. And really– how many people are going to die for you before you realize you can't hide forever," Wallace said.

Anger engulfed Jude. He thought about shooting him.

"I won't go with you." Jude stood and gripped the pistol in the bag.

"Don't make this harder than it needs to be."

"It's already complicated." Jude pulled the gun and shot at Wallace. Jude did not watch to see where or if he hit Wallace. He bolted past him to get to the back door.

Wallace winced in pain from the bullet grazing his arm. He took off after Jude with his gun drawn. Jude dashed out the back door and rounded the corner of the house. Wallace was close behind him. A man in light tactical gear was walking away from the black Land Rover parked on the street. Wallace pointed at Jude and yelled something in a northern accent. Jude glanced back at the other man. He recognized him as Collin, his once ally. Jude ran into the neighbor's front yard and gunfire erupted behind him.

"Stop shooting at him!" Wallace yelled as Jude sprinted to the car and Wallace hit Collin's arm.

"Kari, start the car!" Jude shouted.

Kari slipped into the driver's seat shaking from hearing the gun shots. She turned the key. The car roared alive. Kari had never been so scared in her life. Kari put the car in drive and waited for Jude to get in. Jude tossed the bag on the floor.

"GO!" Jude screamed, clenching the gun tight. "Go, go!"

Kari floored it as Jude situated himself in the seat.

"Jude!" Kari was frantic and sped away.

"Just go," Jude said as calmly as he could. He looked out the back window after they turned the corner and saw the black Land Rover following not too far behind. "I don't know why I would have thought any different."

Wallace leaned out of the passenger's side window with his gun in hand. Bullets pinged off of the back of the car as Wallace aimed for the tires. Kari screamed and accelerated to get to a main road. Jude wiped Nicks's blood on his pants, not bearing to stand the sight.

"Jude! I don't know where I'm going. I don't know Chicago!" Kari shouted nearly in tears.

"Uh…put the cruise control on and we'll switch spots."

"Are you crazy?"

"Right now!"

Kari and Jude maneuvered around each other. Jude kept his hand on the steering wheel for control and watched the road. "Keep your head down."

Kari did as she was told and sank in the seat. Her heart beat rapidly from the adrenaline flowing through her veins. Kari glanced over at Jude. The traffic seemed to stand still as they maneuvered through the cars in their attempt to lose the men behind them.

Kari pulled out her phone. "We should call my brother."

Jude grabbed the phone from Kari and threw it out the window. "No!"

"Look in the go bag for a phone," Jude said.

Kari pawed through the bag not finding a phone. "There isn't one in here."

"Damn it!"

Jude turned sharply down a narrow two-lane street drifting into the other lane. He corrected the turn and swerved back into his lane, avoiding a head-on collision with oncoming traffic. There was a parking ramp ahead and Garrick's men were close behind. Jude zoomed into the parking ramp smashing the small tube-like barrier with the front of the car. They continued to the lowest possible level of the parking ramp. Jude stopped the car for a moment hoping he lost them. He heard the screeching tires. An old iron gate blocked the way to a small tunnel. It was big enough to fit the small car through.

"Jude, don't even think about it. We won't fit," Kari stated in a frantic tone.

"It's the only way," Jude muttered.

The tires squealed on the cement as Jude pushed the accelerator to the floor. The car lurched forward. Kari sunk in her seat further and covered her eyes. The front of the car hit the thin iron gate. The gate split into two, bounced over the hood of the car and clattered to the ground. Water splashed up the sides of the car as they drove through the dark tunnel. Light was soon within sight at the end. The pursuers' large Land Rover squealed to a halt at the entryway of the tunnel. The men hurried out of the car and opened fire in a last ditch effort to stop Jude.

Jude pushed the accelerator to the floor increasing their speed. The engine roared as they traveled through the last few yards of the tunnel to freedom.

"JUDE!" Kari screamed bracing herself.

The small Regal flew out of the end of the tunnel into the brightness of a sunny day. They found themselves in a wide culvert. Jude slowed his speed dramatically and drove up the sloped side making his way back on to paved roads.

"Are you okay?" Jude asked.

"Well, besides us being shot at, yeah. Peachy."

"I'm sorry," Jude said and hit the navigate function on the screen to route the address to the safe house.

"What's going on Jude? Christ! Why are those men chasing you? What happened to your uncle?" Kari asked.

Jude looked back to make sure they were not being followed. "Uh–" Jude didn't know where to begin. "My name isn't Jude, it's James. I don't have an uncle. My "uncle" was Marshal Nicks."

"Wait, what?"

"Those men behind us– They work for a powerful arms dealer. The same man I once worked for."

"I don't understand. How could you be involved with a man like that?"

Jude paused. "Because he's my father... He was grooming me to take over the business. He found out my mother had been funneling millions of dollars into an offshore bank account in my name and killed her for it. I betrayed him, by trying to help my mother flee. After he killed her I went to MI6 and told them everything I knew. The information I provided them has linked him to several terrorist groups."

"Jude–" Kari was speechless. "So my brother..."

"He and Marshal Bradshaw..."

"Wait but– Marshal Nicks!"

Jude choked back the tears. "Is dead... My father got to him."

"Is Bradley?" Kari choked.

Jude glanced at Kari. "I hope not."

Kari turned to look out the window, watching the buildings pass. She noticed they were in an old part of the city. The neighborhood was not run down or a slum by any means. Jude kept checking his rear view mirror to make sure they weren't being followed. A few minutes later Jude slowed the car to a stop and parked the car in front of a small two-story white house. He killed the engine removing the keys from the ignition and shoved them into his pocket. Jude grabbed the gun on the floor by Kari's feet that he had dropped when they switched places. Jude looked at it for a moment, reflecting on past events and placed it back in it's holster.

"Where are we?" Kari asked and unbuckled her seat belt.

"The safe house," Jude answered and opened the door.

"Jude– I am terrified."

"Me too. We'll get through this." Jude hugged Kari.

Jude rang the doorbell and within seconds there was scuffling on the other side of the door. The door opened abruptly. MacTavish grabbed Jude and pulled him inside.

"Were you followed?" MacTavish asked.

MacTavish shut the door. Kari looked around the bare house.

"Nicks is dead," Jude announced. "My father is here. The other Marshals?"

"I haven't heard anything. If Nicks is dead, I'm sure everyone went dark."

MacTavish glared at Kari. "Who are you?"

"I'm–"

"That's Marshal Evans's sister."

"Sister. Great, just what we need…"

MacTavish leaned up against the wall in thought.

"Where do we go from here?" Jude asked.

"We wait–"

CHAPTER TWENTY ONE

The tires of the MRAP hummed on the pavement. Bradley sat shotgun doned in his tactical gear. His rifle hung from him, the barrel resting on the seat between his legs. He looked back at his men as they made final adjustments to their gear and weapons. Traffic moved out of the way from the lights and siren of the armored vehicle. Bradley killed the siren and lights when they turned down the quaint street. Anderson, the driver, hopped the curb and drove the MRAP onto the lawn parking right in front of the main entrance of the inn. Bradley swallowed hard, seeing the forced entry. The back doors of the MRAP swung open and the team stacked up on each side of the MRAP using the ballistic doors as cover.

"This is the US Marshals, come out with your hands up," Bradley ordered over the loud PA.

Bradley waited a few seconds and gave commands. "This is the US Marshal, come out with your hands up. This is your final warning."

There was no movement inside the house. Bradley crawled from his seat into the back and out the door.

"Let's go," Bradley ordered.

Bradley fell in line with his team as rear guard. His team approached the short distance to the front door rifles pointed at windows scanning for threats. They dynamically entered the threshold and fanned out covering unknown areas.

"Man down, DOA," the point, Karcz, said and stepped over Rozier's body.

Bradley's eyes focused on the thick trail of blood that led around the corner to the living room. He followed behind Karcz as he metered the corner.

"Eagle down!" Karcz announced and stepped past Nicks to finish his job, clearing the house.

The team continued to clear the house as Bradley stood frozen for a moment. Nicks's lifeless eyes were fixed and glassy. Blood saturated his shirt and pooled around him. Bradley took a knee and slung his rifle. He slid Nicks's eyes closed and he looked at peace. Staring at his mentor and friend, Bradley choked back tears. They had been through countless firefights in war ridden shitholess. He never expected to lose a brother outside the war, not there, not like that.

"House is clear," Karcz reported to Bradley.

Bradley cleared his throat and rose. "Call it in."

—

Hughes opened the front passenger door of Garrick's vehicle and got in. Hughes turned in his seat and handed Garrick the file.

"All the information you need about the Marshals on James's case are here."

Garrick opened the file to see Nicks's military photo.

"For being decorated Special Forces he did not fare too well." Garrick flipped the page to Bradley. "Marshal Bradley Evans– impressive, Army as well– He saved countless lives and was awarded a Bronze Star– Who do we have next? Marshal Clayton Bradshaw. Not army, but a Navy SEAL… and not just any Navy SEAL but DEVGRU. We will see what kind of fight they put up–"

Garrick flipped to the page containing the personal information of each Marshal; phone numbers, addresses, family members.

"Excellent work, Hughes. Why don't you put together a couple of teams and pay a visit to Evans's wife Jessica and Bradshaw's daughter. Find the sister too."

"I suspect that Evan's sister was the one I spoke to on the phone since the number is the same," Paul said

"Well that's convenient. Once you have them, the Americans will need motivation to contact me… A photo perhaps with the gift I already left at the Langham. Hughes, you're free to leave."

Hughes nodded. "Yes, sir."

Garrick handed Hughes the hard drive. "Oh– and see if there is anything useful on here."

———

Bradley walked towards Pyke's office. He could see through the window that he was animatedly using the phone. Bradley cautiously approached the door.

"How the fuck did he get in the country! CIA my ass– Hellen Keller could have seen him– No! Figure it out! You're the CIA, not the Mickey Mouse club!" Pyke yelled and threw his phone at his desk.

Pyke fumed and placed his hands on his hips and adjusted his tac vest. Bradley knocked on the door worried his wrath would be directed at him.

"Evans– What's the status on Nicks?"

Bradley took a moment. "He's dead..."

"Fuck! God damn it! Jesus Christ!" Pyke spewed and leaned over his desk wiping his face with his hands.

A long time friend and colleague gone in an instant. There was always the risk of giving your life to the job. But you never expect it to be you, or someone you're close with. Pyke took the news hard and took a moment to collect himself.

"Where do we go from here?" Bradley asked.

"Well... I will notify Bradshaw and MacTavish about Nicks after this– But we may have a lead...

Halifax was able to use traffic cams and tracked Garrick to The Langham. I need you to head your team and hit that location."

Pyke handed Bradley a file. "Here is the layout and room he will be in."

"Yes, sir."

"Catch that bastard."

—

The afternoon sun was high in the bright sky. Thin wispy clouds scattered in the never ending blue. Children's laughter filled the air. Amelia ran around the playground with little care in the world. She heard a whistle and she stopped mid stride and turned to the sound. A well groomed man stood at the fence.

"Hey," he beckoned her over.

Amelia looked around and trotted over to him.

"Hi, I'm Ben. What's your name?"

Amelia looked the man over for a moment. "Amelia."

"Say, Amelia, you haven't seen a black puppy running around here have you?"

"No–"

"Do you maybe think you could help me look for him? It won't take very long."

Amelia shrugged and shook her head yes. Ben motioned for Amelia to follow him to the gate. He opened it for her scanning the daycare playground to make sure there were no adults watching; they were oblivious, chatting with each other.

"Let's search down this street first," Ben said, leading Amelia away from the daycare.

A Land Rover pulled to the curb. Ben placed his hand over Amelia's mouth, picking her up and handing her to a man in the back. The door closed and they drove away.

Recess was over and the teachers counted the students as they entered the building. Kristen was missing one. She scanned the playground realizing she hadn't seen Amelia.

"Amelia?" Kristen called taking a step towards the play equipment.

She walked inside to look in the classroom, she wasn't there.

"Amanda, have you seen Amelia?"

"No, I haven't. Is she in the bathroom?"

Kristen and Amanda checked the rest of the daycare calling Amelia's name and did not locate her. Kristen began to tremble, a teacher's worst fear.

"We have to call the police."

—

Four men walked into the lobby of the US Bank building. The security guard was shot immediately and his body crumpled to the ground. The lead man aimed at the horrified receptionist and pulled the trigger.

"We have five minutes."

They entered the elevator and rode to the fourth floor. The lift dinged and the doors opened. The receptionist of the law office had no time to react before a bullet pierced into her body and she fell forward on the desk. The men entered the main office. Cubicles mazed the open space. A man with a subcompact automatic rifle sprayed rounds into the ceiling. People screamed in fear and ducked under desks.

"We are here for one person. No one else will be harmed," Wallace said in his thick northern accent next to the gunman.

A young man rushed the gunman. He wrapped his arms around the intruder. The gunman hit the young man in the side of the head to loosen his grip followed by a swift boot to the chest. The man pointed his pistol at the young man and shot him in the head. A pool of blood oozed around him and screams of horror filled the air from the office.

"We don't need any heroes– Now where is Jessica Evans?"

Jessica peaked around from an office and her heart raced. A woman looked back at her giving away her location. One of the men walked over pointing his gun at Jessica and took her by the arm. Jessica was too frightened to fight. She was escorted out of the building into the alley where a Land Rover was waiting. The car sped away as sirens filled the busy city streets.

—

Bradley stood in front of his strike team blood soaked in the knees of his tactical pants. He laid out the ops plan for the team.

"Our analyst Halifax located Garrik checking into The Langham a few days ago."

Pyke walked into the room. Worry spread across his features.

"We suspect– Sir?"

"There was a shooting at the US Bank building–"

Bradley did not wait for Pyke to finish and bolted past him.

"Evans!" Pyke called after him.

Bradley sprinted out of the building. Jessica's firm was three blocks away. People on the sidewalk gave Braldey skeptical looks as he dashed past them in a frantic state. Police had a perimeter established around the block. Adrenaline pumped as he neared. Bradley ran between squad cars. An officer held his hands up and prevented Bradley from passing.

Bradley motioned to uniform. "Marshal, move!"

The officer was confused but let Bradley through. He looked over his shoulder at Bradley and radioed. "Sarge, did we call the Marshals?"

"Negative, why?"

"Uh... Cuz one just ran through our perimeter."

Bradley moved past the elevators which were stuck on higher floors. He took the stairs and ran them two at a time. He reached the fourth floor and flung the door open. An officer photographing the receptionist stared at the out of breath Marshal. His worst fear was confirmed.

The officer raised a brow. "I wasn't aware this was a Marshal's case."

"It is now." Bradley walked into the office.

He could barely stand straight, fearing that he was going to see his wife's body. Stephanie, Jessica's coworker and friend, hurried to Bradley before the officers noticed him.

"They took her," Stephanie said. "Those– Men!"

"Can you describe them?"

"Uh, when they spoke– I think they were British."

Bradley stared straight ahead in a daze.

"Excuse me," a sergeant said, stepping to Bradley. "What are you doing here? This is an active scene."

"My wife, she's the one that was taken." Bradley's mind whirled terrified of what torture Garrick was going to inflict upon her.

"Oh–"

Bradley paced. "I have to go."

"Wait!" The sergeant called after him.

Bradley exited the building, barely holding himself together. Pyke approached with a team of Marshals behind him. Bradley's eyes were wide and darted in every direction. He felt sick to his stomach and the world around him spun.

"Take a breath, Evans." Pyke placed a hand on his shoulder.

"He took her— He fucking took her!"

Pyke turned to one of his men. "Reagen, head the investigation here. Tell that puke stain Lieutenant George, that the Marshals will handle it."

"Yes, sir."

Bradley was spiralling out of control. He placed his hands on his knees and bent forward. He had been on numerous top secret ops and never waivered. He'd been shot at, blown up, and fallen out of the sky in a couple ton bird. He even killed and apprehended high value targets while with Delta without a blink of an eye. His stomach turned and he vomited on the concrete. Out of everything he had been through, the uncertainty of his wife's life brought him to a place he had never experienced.

Pyke patted Bradley on the back. He took a calming breath and slowly straightened. "We will find her... I cannot even begin to understand what you are going through but this is not the time to lose it. You're Delat Force for fuck sakes. This asshole is one punk, and we will get him. Now get your head straight son, you have a team to lead. I am counting on you. Your country is counting on you."

"Yes, sir."

"Karcz," Pyke beckoned. "Accompany Evans back to the office."

Pyke's phone rang and he held up a finger for them to wait. His eyes slowly drifted to Bradley. "Send a team there."

Pyke ended the call. "Clayton's daughter is missing from daycare."

Bradley's blood turned to ice and he stared at the ground, shaking his head.

———

Clayton sped down the street. The ringing of his phone drew his attention and he picked it up.

"Bradshaw."

"It's Pyke– Bradshaw, I need you to listen carefully and not do anything rash– What I'm about to say is not going to be easy, Your daughter is missing, we believe Garrick has her."

Clayton slammed on his breaks. A car blared its horn behind him as he abruptly pulled over.

"Evans's wife has been taken as well."

Clayton could not think straight. "I– I–"

"You will continue your duty and get to the secondary safehouse. Protect your asset. I will handle this. Bradshaw, we will find your daughter."

Clayton sat for a moment after the phone call with Pyke. His hands were shaking uncontrollably. He took a deep breath trying to calm himself to focus on the job at hand. He merged back into his lane of traffic. Clayton parked his vehicle several blocks away and approached the safehouse on foot. He stepped to the door and it swung open. MacTavish ushered Clayton inside.

"Is he here?"

MacTavish nodded. Kari heard the familiar voice from the other room and hurried to the living room. Jude followed behind. Clayton laid eyes on them and he let out a sigh of relief.

"Clayton," Kari said, glad to see he was in one piece and hugged him.

Kari stepped back, worry flooded her voice. "Bradley– Is he okay? Marshal Nicks–"

"He's at the office."

"I don't mean to interrupt your little reunion, but... where are we at? Are there any leads?" MacTavish interrupted.

"Halifax was able to trace Garrick to a hotel downtown. Evans is leading a hit there. Then–" Clayton tried to keep himself together. "We– Uh–" Clayton couldn't finish. He placed his head in his hands.

"What is it?" MacTavish asked.

Clayton looked him in the eye. "Garrick has my daughter and Evans's wife."

MacTavish's mouth was agape. Kari let out a soft cry and Clayton's eyes darted to her. Jude wrapped his arms around her. His blood ran cold. He could not bear the thought of anyone else getting hurt because of him.

CHAPTER TWENTY TWO

The stairwell was small and hot. Bradley stacked up behind his men. His team ascended the steps to the eleventh floor.

"Going dark–" an operator radioed and the lights flickered before being extinguished. "Power cut."

"Arvin, I don't know why the power is out– I'm taking the stairs," an elderly woman yelled down the hall and opened the door to the stairwell. "We're only on the fifth floor Arvin, you can walk–"

She turned to see the team of men. Her eyes opened wide.

"Oh my–" she ducked back into the hallway. "Arvin, I think you were right about the Russians, perhaps we should check out early."

Bradley waved and walked past the door. "Red Leader to Blue Leader, the eleventh floor has been evacuated correct?"

"That's affirmative, Red Leader. Staged in lobby."

"Copy."

The team climbed the stairs, metering corners and quick-peaking to the above floors.

"Perimeter is secure. Eye on target room from exterior. No movement," another operator said.

"Eleventh floor reached."

The team stacked up on the door. Karcz was opposite of the handle and pulled the door open. On the other side, Anderson crouched down and slid a smoke grenade down the hall. It rolled near the target door. Thick smoke billowed filling the hall. The Marshals got into a line formation and proceeded down the hall. Bradley gave a signal and halted his team.

"Breaching," Bradley said and Karcz rammed the door.

The jam popped with ease as the metal door swung inward with a hard clank hitting the wall. Bradley tossed in a flash bang. The piercing sound caused his ears to ring. They entered the room quickly and fanned out into the large suit. Bradley entered the bedroom, the last room to be cleared. No one was inside. He lowered his rifle.

"Target is clear. Garrick isn't here."

"Copy that, Red Leader."

Bradley walked to the main living area of the suite and stared out at the cityscape of downtown Chicago. The room was clean. There was nothing left to suggest Garrick was staying there.

"Evans– You may want to see this," Karcz said, pointing to the dining room table.

Bradley approached the table and his heart sank. His eyes lingered on the photo of his wife and Clayton's daughter bound. Terror gripped their faces and tears streamed down their cheeks. A piece of paper accompanied the photo, a phone number. A bottle of Macallan single malt scotch and two glasses sat next to the photo. Bradley could not contain his anger and grasped the bottle and threw it at the wall. The glass shattered and the couple grand worth of liquid gold trickled down the wall. Bradley picked up the photo and number and exited the suite.

Once at ground level Bradley crossed the street to the command bus. He pulled open the van door. Pyke removed his headset and Seth looked over his shoulder. Bradley handed Pyke the photo and number.

"I need to call him– Pyke, my wife."

"Evans, you would be playing into what he wants. You are in no condition to make such a phone call."

"If I may, sir," Seth pointed to the phone number. "I can try and ping the number."

Bradley folded his arms over his chest. Seth turned and worked his magic.

"Well– Good news or bad news?" Seth said, staring at his computer screen.

"Riley–" Pyke said.

"Right, I was able to ping the phone… However, it's plotting to the west coast of Africa, more specifically in the Pacific Ocean."

Pyke put his head in his hand. "I'm not surprised."

"Pyke we have to call him," Bradley insisted.

Pyke stared at Bradley and placed his hands on his hips with a long sigh.

"I may have better luck tracking the call directly," Seth added.

Seth handed Pyke the phone. "Ready when you are."

"Dial it–" Pyke pushed the speaker phone.

"I was beginning to think you weren't going to call me," Garrick answered.

"Sorry we're a little late to the party."

"It's simple really, you deliver James to me or Mrs. Evans and poor Amelia will die… You have twelve hours."

"You know we can't do that," Pyke replied.

"I feel you are not grasping the severity of the situation– Let this be some motivation."

A loud pop sounded and Jessica let out a horrific scream. The phone line went dead. Bradley's back thudded against the wall of the van and he slid to the floor. The world spun around him as he stared blankly in front of him. It felt as if the floor had been pulled out beneath him. A crushing weight came down upon him not knowing if his wife was going to die, that the last thing he would hear would be her blood curdling scream. He was supposed to protect his wife and there was nothing he could do. A thought of giving up Jude crossed his mind to save the person he loved most in the world. But the betrayal to his country would destroy him.

Pyke crouched in front of Bradley. "Evans, the fight isn't over. He wouldn't kill her, there's still time. We need to continue the fight. We cannot falter now."

Pyke's words fell onto deaf ears and Bradley stared blankly in front of him. Pyke snapped his fingers in Bradley's face and it did not phase him. A loud crack of a slap sounded. Pyke shook out his hand and Bradley's eyes darted to him. He massaged his jaw from the sudden assault.

"Fucking Christ, son. Focus," Pyke shouted.

The initial shock of hopelessness and despair passed being replaced with an intense rage. "I'm going to kill him."

"Rein it in, but that's the attitude I need."

———

Clayton paced in the living room checking the windows with each step. Kari leaned her head on Jude's shoulder and intertwined her hand with his.

"I'm sorry I've gotten you into this mess," Jude said and planted a kiss on her forehead.

"We're safe now. That's all that matters," Kari replied. "But– I feel like I don't even know you."

Jude swallowed. "I'm still the same person, Kari."

"I don't know anything about you... I don't even know if I should call you Jude or James."

Jude bowed his head. "I didn't want to lie to you–"

"But you did– How much of us is a lie?"

"You mean more to me than anything."

Clayton's phone rang. "Bradshaw."

His eyes darted to Jude and he stepped into the other room where MacTavish was waiting. "Calm down."

Jude patted Kari's hand and stood.

"Jude..."

Jude held his finger to his lips and crept to the door that was a crack open. Clayton held the phone and looked to MacTavish.

"Garrick shot Jessica. He wants Jude in twelve hours or he's going to kill them both. But for all I know they could have killed them already."

"What's the plan?" MacTavish asked.

"I don't know–"

Jude stepped away not wanting to hear anymore. His stomach dropped knowing that people were going to die because of him. In the grand scheme of things, the U.S. Government would risk two civilian lives to get Garrick, and Jude was part of getting Garrick. Jude sat next to Kari.

"What's wrong?" she asked.

"People are going to die because of me... I can't let that happen."

Clayton stormed out of the room to resume his post on the windows.

"What are you planning on doing?" Kari whispered.

Jude squeezed her hand. "I can't stay here."

"Jude, no–"

"It's the only way. I can't stand idle and allow my father to kill innocent people. Your family, Bradshaw's daughter. I just can't–"

"But he'll kill you."

"No, he won't... Not right away at least."

"How are you going to find him anyway?"

Jude nodded to the backpack Clayton set down in the spare bedroom. "I'm sure Bradshaw has another phone in there. Steal it and sneak out when they think we're sleeping."

"So you're just going to drive right to him then?"

"That's the plan."

"Jude, please don't do this."

Jude leaned in and kissed Kari. "I am going to miss you."

Kari pulled back and stood quickly. She wiped the tears from her eyes and bolted to the bathroom. She slammed the door and locked it behind her.

"Is this how it's going to be? Teenage drama?" MacTavish asked.

Clayton looked to Jude. "What was that all about?"

"She's mad at me. Is it not obvious?" Jude said and walked to the bathroom.

"Well I can tell ya we certainly don't need anything to draw attention here. Do you think that is obvious?" MacTavish said and threw the closest thing to him, a roll of paper towel. "Ya damn fool."

Jude narrowed his eyes at MacTavish and knocked on the door. "Kari–"

"Go away, Jude!" Kari looked at the small window.

"Kari, you don't need to yell– Just come back out."

"No! I don't want to be near you right now."

Jude sighed heavily and sat down in the living room with a clear view of the bathroom door. Kari walked to the window and opened it. The screen popped off easily and it slipped from her hands tumbling down the side of the house. She stared at the door hoping no one heard it. A few moments passed with no banging on the door. Heart racing, she hoisted herself up onto the sill and slid out of the window. The sky was dark and the crickets sounded. She looked both ways around the house and sprinted towards the car. Adrenaline coursed with the fear of being caught. Jude was going to sneak out and she was not about to let him give himself up.

The magnetic hidden key box was harder to find than Kari had anticipated. The gravel scraped her as she crawled under the passenger side and was able to discover it. She opened the door and climbed into the backseat throwing a blanket over her. A shine caught her attention and she found a handle of a knife under the seat. The handle was a sleek shiny black. She clicked the button and a blade popped out of the end. With another hit of the button and the blade retracted into the handle. She tucked it into her brown ankle boot.

"It's getting late, perhaps you should get some rest," Clayton suggested. "She'll come out when she's good and ready."

Jude stood not wanting his last interaction with Kari to be them arguing. "I didn't want her to get involved."

"I know," Clayton placed a hand on his shoulder.

"I didn't want anyone to get involved– For anyone to get hurt because of me…"

"Jude–"

"Thank you for everything you've done for me Marshal Bradshaw." Jude stepped into the bedroom and closed the door.

Clayton started at the door for a moment.

MacTavish chomped down on a Snickers bar. "Poor kid, can't imagine what he's going through."

"He hasn't had an easy life."

"Nicks really cared about him didn't he?"

"He did..."

MacTavish moved the window curtain and gazed down the dimly lit street. "Think Pyke is going to plan a fake swap?"

"Garrick would assume we would try that. I don't know if Pyke is willing to risk losing Jude."

MacTavish studied Clayton closely looking for turmoil but all he saw was calm and collective. "How are you so calm?"

"And what would falling apart do for us?" Clayton removed his SEAL knife examining the edges. "I can assure you of this though– If given the opportunity I will drive this knife through Garrick's heart for laying his hands on my daughter."

"There's the Bradshaw I've come to know and love."

"Don't push it, MacTavish," Clayton pointed the knife at him.

"Well my friend, I will do everything in my power to make sure you get to the honors."

Jude stepped away from the door hearing the Marshals distracted in conversation. Clayton's go bag was sitting up against the wall. There was one item he wanted as he rummaged through it. In the front pocket Jude found the burner phone. Securing it in his pocket he stood and glanced one last time at the door, hoping Kari would be there so he could say goodbye. With a heavy sigh he walked to the window and opened it. Small chunks of dirt and dry grass crunched under his feet and he jogged to the Regal. The car roared alive and sped down the road. Jude turned the phone on and dialed the number his father made him memorize for emergencies. Listening to the phone ring made Jude's anxiety soar causing his hands to shake.

Garrick pulled out the phone from his suit pocket. He looked around to his men seeing them all there and hoped the U.S. Military didn't raid another one of his locations. The screen read restricted and he knew it was not any of his men.

"Who is this?" Garrick answered.

"It's me, dad... James."

"James– This is an unexpected surprise."

"I don't want anyone else to get hurt because of me... I want to trade myself for Jessica and Amelia."

"Do the Marshals know you're calling?"

"No–"

"Where are you now, James?" Garrick asked and motioned to Hughes to track the call.

"I'm in the car. Where can I meet you?"

Kari could not stay silent any longer. She was angered by the lack of self preservation Jude had. She threw the blanket off and grabbed the phone.

"I can't believe you!" She hung up the phone.

Jude swerved from the sudden shock.

"Kari!" Jude yelled.

She climbed over the seat and buckled herself into the passenger seat.

"Give me the phone," Jude ordered and held out his hand.

"I won't let you give yourself up."

"Kari... He has more than likely tracked this phone."

"Then I'll toss it out the window."

"You do that, then you're condemning Jessica and Amelia to a death sentence."

Kari set the phone down in his hand.

"I can't believe you right now." Jude pulled the car over. "You can't be here, you need to leave."

"I'm not going anywhere!"

"Kari– Please!"

The phone rang and he answered it. "Hello?"

"James... Who was that?"

"No one." Jude looked at Kari.

"You are not instilling confidence by lying. Let me rephrase that question. Is that the Marshal's sister?"

Jude went silent.

"That's what I suspected. You will bring her with. I don't need her running back to her brother."

"Please, she has nothing to do with any of this–"

"Do not argue. It's simple, if you don't bring her... Marshal Bradshaw will be burying his daughter."

"Please–"

"This should go without saying, but, don't do anything foolish. I would hate to have to take more lives. I will text you the coordinates... I look forward to seeing you, son." The phone line went dead.

CHAPTER TWENTY THREE

MacTavish was perched on the counter watching the door. Clayton sat on the floor across from him, his thoughts lingering on Amelia. He hated waiting and feeling useless.

"She's been in there for a long time…"

Clayton glanced down the hall. He grumbled and stood. He knocked on the bathroom door.

"Kari…"

There was no answer. Clayton leaned close to the door and listened for movement and heard none. He sighed heavily and stepped down the hall. He was in no mood to deal with teenage girl drama. Clayton opened the bedroom door.

"Jude, tell–" The room was empty and the window was open. "Fuck! Son of a bitch!"

Clayton marched down the hall and did not hesitate to boot the bathroom door. He was not surprised to see Kari gone. "Fuck!– Fuck!– God Dammit!– Son of a bitch!"

MacTavish hopped down from his perch to investigate Clayton's spewing of profanities.

"They're fucking gone!" Clayton yelled.

MacTavish went to the bedroom and picked up Clayton's go bag. He dug through it. "Burn phone is gone."

Clayton inhaled, trying not to lose it. He hammer fisted the wall with frustration. "Do they have a death wish! I'm gonna lose my shit!"

"This is why I don't have kids..." MacTavish said.

Clayton glared at him and pulled out his other phone. He dialed Bradley's number.

"Evans."

"They're gone and they took a phone."

"Wait– What did you just say? Gone? Gone where?" Bradley questioned getting Pyke and Seth's attention.

"I don't know. They snuck out of the goddam window."

"Why weren't you watching them!" Bradley nearly shouted.

"Lower your voice– I didn't think I had to watch them sleep."

Seth turned back around and started typing on his computer. Pyke stared at Bradley turning a deeper shade of crimson.

"I have them," Seth interrupted. Bradley turned, lowering the phone from his ear relieved. "They're headed towards the lake." Seth craned his neck and shouted. "I–" Bradley put the phone next to Seth. "Oh, sorry… I will send you the coordinates."

Clayton said to MacTavish. "Halifax was able to track the phone."

"Get your team ready. We're moving out," Pyke ordered.

"Did you get that?" Bradley asked Clayton.

"Yeah, I heard. MacTavish and I will meet you there."

—

Gravel crunched beneath the Regal tires as Jude slowed the car to a stop. Wallace tapped Jude's window with the barrel of his gun. Jude killed the engine and Wallace opened the door.

"Get out," Wallace ordered and pulled Jude by the arm.

Jude did not fight Wallace as he pushed him against the car. The cold barrel of the gun pressed against Jude's head. Wallace searched him and removed the gun from Jude.

"What's this, eh?"

"Can never be too careful these days."

"Et's a good way for ya tae get killed…" Wallace nodded towards Kari. "Or ya lass killed."

Collin pulled Kari from the car, her heart racing. Her eyes were glued to the small machine gun slung around Collin. Wallace continued his search and removed the cellphone from Jude's pocket. He tossed it on the ground and stomped his heel into the glass.

"Can't bea hav'n that either."

"Got yourself a pretty one didn't you, James?" Collin said and frisked Kari for weapons, neglecting to check her boots.

"Don't touch me!" Kari growled.

"And a mouth too." Collin backhanded Kari across the face.

"Touch her again and it will be the last thing you do," Jude warned.

Collin laughed. "Look at this, itty bitty Jamie is all grown up."

"If given the opportunity, Collin, I will kill you."

"We'll just have to see about that. Little Jamie and his threats."

"Enough! Let's get them inside," Wallace ordered, impatiently. He ushered Jude into the abandoned warehouse on the shores of Lake Michigan.

Jessica and Amelia were tied to chairs with pieces of cloth tied around their mouths. Blood saturated Jessica's jeans from the gunshot wound. She tried to scream when she laid eyes on Kari. Jude took a sharp inhale when his father turned around. Their eyes locked.

"James... Son, it is good to see you," Garrick said and hugged Jude.

Jude did not move and Jessica's eyes widened in disbelief. Paul crossed his arms annoyed by the pleasantries. Garrick turned his attention to Kari.

"And you are..."

"None of your concern," Jude said with a bite.

"There is no need to talk back, James... Marshal Evans's sister, Kari. My dear you are beautiful."

Garrick grasped Kari's hand and kissed the top of her hand. Her pulse quickened and she tried to pull away, fear flowing through her veins,but he held on tight.

"Don't touch her!" Jude seethed and pushed his father.

Garrick released his grip on Kari and laughed, taking a couple steps back. Collin did not find the situation comical. He hit Jude with the butt of his handgun in the side of the head. The blow disoriented Jude and he dropped to his knees. Collin pressed the cold barrel against his head. Kari's heart sank and she feared he was going to kill Jude. It felt like she was in slow motion. She bent down wrapping her fingers around the handle of the knife and withdrew it from her boot. The handle pressed into her hand from how tightly she gripped the blade. She didn't think about the repercussions of her actions. She hit the button, the blade popped from the handle and she drove the blade deep into Collin's neck. Blood sprayed from the wound. Collin dropped the gun and turned to face Kari. His eyes were wide with confusion as his skin turned white. Jude stared up at Kari, horrified. Collin collapsed to the ground. Kari felt cold, her eyes glued on the blood dripping blade in her hands.

"Well... this was certainly a change of events... Would someone please take that knife from her?" Garrick said, not phased by the violence.

Paul drew down on Kari. "Give me the knife."

Kari was dazed and held out her hand. Paul grabbed the knife and tossed it to Wallace. Paul grabbed a hold of Kari by her jacket, tucking her into his body, and pressed the gun to her head. A cry escaped her lips and she trembled. Garrick stepped towards Kari.

"Please, don't do something like that again. You seem to have a promising future, I would really hate for anything to happen to you."

"Just let them all go... I'm the one you want," Jude pleaded not wanting Kari anywhere near his father.

"You certainly are... I have gone to great lengths to find you. Imagine my disappointment when I learned you went to MI6. This could have all been avoided if you would have just come to me with the information your blasted mother told you... I had high hopes for you, James. You had a promising future– power, wealth, whatever your heart desired. And why? You threw that all away..."

"I don't want to be like you."

Garrick grabbed Jude by the jaw, narrowing his eyes.

"I am only going to ask this once... What is the account information?"

"Kill me... I won't tell you."

Garrick laughed. "My dear boy, I will not be killing you– But." He pointed to Kari. "Her– I can kill her."

Kari wasn't prepared to die. Fear overtook her and tears streamed down her hot cheeks. Jude swallowed hard seeing the terror in Kari.

"I don't know it..."

"I have a hard time believing that... I won't ask again– Paul."

Paul moved his finger to the trigger of the gun. Kari screamed. "Please!"

"Fine! Fine! Just don't hurt her!" Jude shouted. "I don't know it, but I know where it is."

"Do not lie to me again." Garrick struck Jude across the face. Jude wiped the blood with the back of his hand and stared at his father.

"Are you going to say anything or just stand there and bleed?"

"If I tell you, you'll let them go?" Jude motioned to Jessica and Amelia.

"If I feel you are being truthful."

"The information is in a locker at Paddington Station," Jude said.

Garrick patted Jude on the arm. "See that wasn't so difficult, now was it? What locker?"

"284..." Jude mumbled.

"Pardon? You need to speak up. When did you become so meek?"

"I said, 284–"

Garrick tapped the side of Jude's face. "Good boy." He nodded to Paul. "We have a flight to catch."

Paul pushed Kari forward, keeping the gun pointed at her. "Walk."

Wallace grasped Jude's arm tight. "No funny business now."

"Wait! I thought you were going to let her go?" Jude asked, frantic, knowing if Kari stepped foot on a plane she would never see her family again.

Garrick raised a brow. "You said them..." He pointed to Jessica and Amelia. "Nothing about her... No, she may be useful later."

Jessica screamed through the cloth in her mouth. Kari looked back with tears streaming down her face. Wallace pushed Jude into the backseat of the Land Rover.

"Torch it," Garrick ordered and walked to the second SUV.

"NO! You said you'd let them go!" Jude yelled and fought against Wallace's strong arms.

Garrick paused. "I said if I felt you were being truthful... Frankly my son, I have little trust in you."

Wallace pushed Jude into the SUV and shut the door.

"Jude– We have to do something," Kari cried.

Jude looked deep into Kari's eyes. "I– I'm sorry, Kari... There's nothing we can do."

Kari covered her mouth with her blood stained hand. She shook as the tears continued. Her mind in disarray. The thought of losing Jessica and Amelia was too much. She looked down at her hands and gasped for air. Terror and panic washed over Kari. Jude held her in an attempt to ground her.

"Kari– I'm so sorry... Please..."

The SUVs pulled away from the building. There was an explosion and violent flames billowed out of the windows. Kari turned around in the seat and screamed. Jude wrapped his arms around Kari and held her as she wept. *What have I done?*

———

MacTavish sped down the road the black smoke visible in the sky. The car came to a halt in front of the warehouse. They had beaten the TAC team there. Clayton prayed Amelia was not in there. They ran towards the building, the flames violently engulfing the structure. MacTavish booted the side door and they entered. Clayton could hear the faint screams over the roar of the fire. The heat bit at their skin as they pushed into the belly of the building. The flames clung to the walls, black smoke veiling the empty space.

"Amelia! Jessica!" Clayton called out.

The screams became louder. MacTavish hit Clayton on the arm and pointed to the left. Clayton coughed and the smoke stung his eyes. He hurried over to Jessica and Amelia. Tears cascaded down Amelia's soot covered cheeks. Clayton cut her binds and her small arms reached out to her father. MacTavish lifted Jessica into his arms. A large flaming support beam crashed to the ground in front of them, blocking their path to the exit. Clayton dropped to the ground shielding Amelia from falling debris. She buried her face into Clayton's chest. He rose and followed MacTavish. Every turn was blocked by more falling debris and walls of flames. Clayton tried to remain calm but panic set in. Amelia clung tight to him.

"Over here!" MacTavish yelled over the roaring flames.

The fresh air was welcoming when they passed the threshold of the door. Fire engine sirens sounded in the background. Clayton's vision blurred from the smoke and his lungs heaved. He collapsed to all fours and set Amelia beneath him. He coughed violently. Bradley ran to the building. Relief washed over him when he saw Jessica in MacTavish's arms. He embraced his wife as she coughed and wept. MacTavish bent over and hacked.

"Jessica... I love you," Bradley said and kissed her.

"They have Kari... They took her, Bradley," Jessica cried.

She put her weight on her leg and winced in pain. Bradley scooped her into his arms.

"Did they say where they were going?"

Jessica's mind was whirling. "Jude... Jude, said something about Paddington Station– Bradley, you knew about all of this didn't you?"

Bradley grimaced. "Jude is my asset."

"I–"

"Jess..."

"She's not breathing!" Clayton screamed and started giving Amelia rescue breaths, tears streaming down his face.

She was unresponsive and he began chest compressions. "Come on, sweetheart."

MacTavish pushed Clayton out of the way and took over life saving measures. Clayton crawled to Amelia's head, still coughing. Jessica gasped, clapping her hand over her mouth. Bradley filled with sorrow watching his friend fall apart. Paramedics rushed past Bradley and Jessica to get to Amelia. Fire crews battled the blaze in the background.

"God, no," Clayton cried.

MacTavish knelt next to Clayton and placed a strong arm on his shoulder. The paramedics placed Amelia on oxygen and continued to work. Clayton gasped between his coughing fits and tears. His hands shook uncontrollably as he watched the paramedics work. There was nothing he could do.

"We got her back," one of the medics said looking at the steady rhythm on the monitor.

One medic pushed drugs through an IV line while the other continued to breathe for her. They lifted her onto a board and placed her onto the cot.

One of the medics crouched in front of Clayton. "She has a strong pulse... We intubated her in case of smoke inhalation. We will take good care of her. Kids bounce back strong, she should be okay."

Clayton gasped sitting back on his heels. Wiping the tears away. "Thank you."

Pyke was yelling at his men to check the surrounding area even though he knew Garrick was long gone. He marched over to Bradley and the others. Jessica was being assisted onto a cot by paramedics. Bradley kissed Jessica one more time.

"I love you," he said again and the medics wheeled her away.

Pyke pointed to Clayton and MacTavish who were still hacking. "Jesus, get yourselves looked at."

Pyke ushered his men to an ambulance. "What do we know so far?"

"Jess said Jude mentioned Paddington Station... It's safe to assume they are headed back to the UK," Bradley informed.

Clayton and MacTavish sat on the bumper of an ambulance, the paramedics handing them O2 masks.

"Then let's mount up," MacTavish said, putting his mask down.

Clayton bowed his head, thinking about Amelia. It tore at his heart to not be with her but he had a duty to fulfill.

Pyke put his hands on his hips. "Do you forget who you work for? You're a U.S. Marshal– Your jurisdiction is Stateside."

"Garrick has my sister– If–"

"You're not going anywhere, this is now out of our hands," Pyke said. "It's the CIA and MI6's turn to play."

"Sir–"

"Evans, that is an order– You're grounded. I have a flight to catch in the morning, so help me god!– If you fucksticks do something stupid!" Pyke turned to leave.

Bradley paced. "He can't expect us to sit around and do nothing."

"We don't have a choice," Clayton said.

Seth walked over hanging up his phone and tapping it against his hand.

"Please, tell me you have something," Bradley said.

"How would you gents like to cross the pond?" Seth asked in a British accent.

They stared at Seth perplexed. "Wait– What?" Bradley asked.

"I suppose I have some explaining to do. Right, well then... I'm Agent Seth Connor... With MI6," Seth explained. "I can see you're confused... "

"Why would MI6 send an agent here?" MacTavish asked.

"Ah– Yes well, you see MI6 wanted accurate intel on the progress Stateside. There are times you yanks don't play well."

Clayton laughed. "That's funny– This, this is funny."

Bradley raised a brow. "What are you proposing?"

"I heard your conversation with Pyke, lovely man. Really– But I'd like to invite you to assist in our investigation."

"I've always wanted to see Big Ben," MacTavish said.

"Looks like we're going rogue," Bradley added.

CHAPTER TWENTY FOUR

The sun was beginning to peek through the blanket of clouds. Kari leaned against Jude, staring out the small window of the private jet. The numbness reminded her of what she had done. Jude had since washed the blood from her hands but she could not stop thinking about it. She could still feel the blade dig into the man's neck. She killed someone. She watched the life leave his eyes. Her mind shifted to Jessica and Amelia. She closed her eyes tight trying to block out the sound of the explosion.

"I'm not going to see Bradley again am I?" Kari asked.

Jude's stomach dropped but Kari spoke the truth. The likelihood that either of them would make it out alive seemed slim. The guilt of the innocent lives lost was weighing on him heavily. His throat tightened thinking about Nicks. He glanced at Kari knowing her fate was going to be the same as his. He would do everything in his power to assure she would walk away from all of it but he was uncertain it would be good enough. "I am going to do my best to get you out of this."

"I wish I was able to say goodbye to my brothers…"

"You'll see them again." He wanted to believe his own words, but he knew his father, and even more so, he knew his brother.

"I hope you're right."

Jude kissed her cheek and she closed her eyes, eventually drifting to sleep. She was tired and could not physically fight off her exhaustion any longer. Jude glanced up to see his father staring at him from the other side of the jet cabin. Paul sat beside him studying paperwork. He set it down and followed his gaze. Wallace emerged from the door behind Garrick.

"Hughes didn't find anything on the drive, but he wants to speak with you." He handed Garrick the phone.

Garrick glanced at Jude again and disappeared behind the door of the main cabin. Paul settled himself in the seat across from Jude. The last thing Jude wanted was to speak to his brother.

"What have you gotten yourself into little brother?"

"The fact that you can remain loyal to him baffles me." Jude glared.

"You were always the weakest one... Especially after Jon's death. That really fucked with your head didn't it?"

"He killed our mother, Paul."

"She betrayed us. Why can't you see that?"

"She wanted a better life for us after Jon was killed. But you made sure that wouldn't happen... How did our father find out about the account I wonder–"

"How long do you think it would have taken him to notice a couple million missing?"

"Long enough for her to have fled–"

"And how unfortunate her timing was..."

"You're just as bad as he is," Jude said.

"There's one difference between father and I– I won't hesitate to kill you." Paul stood. "I was the one that killed your Marshal by the way. He seemed to actually care about you, pity."

"I cannot wait for the time to come where you draw your last breath." Jude seethed.

Paul chuckled. "Unfortunately, you will never see that day."

Jude did everything to restrain himself when his brother turned his back and returned to his seat.

"Your brother is a prick," Kari whispered her eyes closed.

"I thought you were sleeping..."

"I was trying." Kari sat up. "I feel silly for the drama I've subjected you to when you've been dealing with all of this."

"Don't... Your problems are important to you. Never feel bad."

"How have you done this on your own?"

"I had Nicks–" His throat tightened.

"Jude–"

Jude's eyes moistened and he took a long breath.

"—Hey..." Kari intertwined her hand with his.

"Nicks... He was talking about adopting me after all of this– To have a chance at a normal life. Not that it matters– I'm as good as dead now."

"Don't talk like that. My brother will find us."

"Kari, your brother is a Marshal. He has no jurisdiction in the UK."

———

Bradley sat next to MacTavish on a jet that MI6 had graciously provided.

"Jessica mad at you?" MacTavish asked.

"Oh– furious... Rightfully so, I mean she did get kidnapped, shot, and nearly died in a fire because of me... But I saved her... That should get me something."

"I mean I technically saved her–" Bradley cocked a brow. MacTavish waved a hand. "She knew what she signed up for with marrying you."

"No–"

"Eh– That's why I won't settle down."

"That and, well… you're ugly and kind of an asshole," Bradley said.

MacTavish motioned to Clayton. "Now… He's making a mistake getting involved with someone."

Clayton sat at the other end of the cabin talking to Andi on the phone. "I know this is a lot to ask."

"No– I am heading there right now. You have nothing to worry about. I'm just glad she's safe, honestly, I don't know what I would have done if I got to the daycare and all of this was still happening," Andi said.

Clayton pinched his forehead. "You are too good to me. I will be home as soon as I can."

"Stay safe."

"In case I don't come back… Know that I love you wholeheartedly and if given the chance I'd bring you to the lush rolling hills of Virginia and ask you to marry me."

"Clayton… I— Just come home in one piece. Then we can go to Virginia. I love you."

"It's a date then."

"I will see you soon."

"I hope so…" Clayon hung up and stared at his phone.

MacTavish rolled his eyes. "Are you trying to make us vomit? Christ man, you are soft."

"It is not my fault you do not know how to speak to a woman properly."

"Right– Now then… Can we get back to it?" Seth asked.

"My apologies Agent Connor." Clayton emphasized Agent.

Seth took a long breath. "I spoke to my supervisor and we will be bringing on SAS due to the nature of this op. There will be two strike teams, one going to Paddington Station and then, ours going to the Tilbury Docks where Jude had stated was their main location of business. We've had MI6 surveillance on the location for sometime now, but it will not be easy. Garrick has a heavily armed presence patrolling the site."

"This'll be fun," MacTavish said with a grin.

Seth handed each of the Marshals a file containing satellite photos along with the list of operators and designated teams. Clayton's eyes focused on two names from the SAS list, Finlay Reid and Ty Grayson, but he knew them as Jedi and Loch.

"Well butter my butt and call me a biscuit," Clayton said and looked up to see the confused expression on his comrades' faces. "What?"

"I will not go anywhere near your ass nor call you a biscuit," MacTavish replied.

"Was that English?" Seth asked.

Clayton cocked a brow and pointed to the file. "I know two of the SAS guys."

"How? Ya know what, never mind– I forgot you were... Just, of course you would know some of SAS," Seth said.

"Yeah, we had a few joint ops in Kunar... and other places–"

"I hate that goat trail infested hell hole," MacTavish piped in.

"I have seven pieces of shrapnel in a jar above my desk. A gift from them, signed and delivered direct to my ass... fond memories," Bradley said.

"Perhaps we should butter *your* buns and call you biscuit," MaTavish laughed.

"It's butt, not buns," Clayton corrected.

"Shall we get back to the ops plan?" Seth suggested.

They went over the plan in great detail. Afterwards they threw their ops gear onto the small tables. Seth stared at the Americans in disbelief at the amount of gear they packed. Bradley laid out his M4 with a suppressed fourteen inch barrel. He turned on and adjusted the EOTech optical red dot sight to make sure it was functioning. Clayton removed his rifle from its case.

"Ooo what do you have there?" MacTavish asked.

Clayton lifted his rifle, proud of its splendor. "This my friend, an H&K 416 with a ten inch supressed barrel and... and my favorite infrared laser and sight."

"She's exactly your type. Impressive–" MacTavish held up his submachine gun. "Say hello to *my* prom date."

Bradley rolled his eyes. "I knew you never went to prom."

"Can it."

"The MP7 was my go to gun for tight quarter ops," Clayton said.

"With the suppressor, it's the quietest killing machine I have ever had the pleasure to hold in my hands."

"Wouldn't even wake the others in the next room."

"Exactly..." MacTavish kissed his rifle. "Ain't that right Silent Beauty?"

Bradley elbowed Seth. "This is why you can't have two SEALs together, they get all hot and bothered... I'm not really sure what the requirements are in the Navy, but I've heard stories..."

"Well regardless your gents are making me feel inadequate about my firepower. Here I am with an AR... That's it, just an AR," Seth said.

"Are you two squids finished?" Bradley asked.

Clayton smirked. "What?"

"We should probably try and get some rest before we land," Bradley said.

MacTavish set his rifle down. "Filling those team leader shoes quickly I see."

Clayton turned his optic off. "Too soon, MacTavish..."

Bradley scowled at MacTavish before slumping in a seat and stretched out his legs. Clyaton rummaged in his bag and pulled out a French press.

"Coffee anyone?"

Bradley shook his head. "I can't believe you brought that along..."

"I have brought this on every deployment, it would be bad juju if I left it behind."

"I'll have some!" MacTavish raised his hand.

Bradley looked at Seth and rolled his eyes. "Don't ask."

CHAPTER TWENTY FIVE

The small jet landed and came to a halt.

"Stand up," Wallace ordered.

Jude stared at Wallace defiantly.

"Are ya deaf now?" Wallace grabbed Jude and pulled him to his feet.

Wallace secured Jude's hands behind his back.

"Yer next princess," Wallace said motioning for Kari to stand.

She did as she was told, too scared to oppose the frightening man. They followed Wallace down to the tarmac. Paul ushered Kari and Jude into the backseat of the waiting SUV.

Paul pointed his gun at Jude. "Remember, I won't hesitate to kill you."

Paul shut the door and approached the SUV in front of theirs.

"Where are we going?" Kari asked Jude.

"I don't know..."

Garrick rolled the window down. "Now– remember, if something comes up you are to go to the secondary location. Do your best to keep your brother alive..."

"I do not see why you insist on letting him live–"

"He's our blood."

"Right..."

Paul walked back to the SUV where Jude and Kari were and hopped into the passenger seat. Kari was trembling from fright and it tore at Jude. He leaned over and kissed her cheek. Jude had grown up in this lifestyle; he was not afraid of what would happen to him. He feared for Kari's wellbeing. A tear trickled down Kari's cheek. She was trying to keep it together the best she could. Her mind jumped from the blood soaked knife she removed from that man's neck to the fire she could still smell from the warehouse. Kari looked down at her trembling leg.

"Have you ever killed anyone before?" Kari asked with nearly a whisper.

"I have..."

"Does this feeling ever go away?"

"Not exactly, but it does get easier– I shouldn't have put you in that position."

"I thought he was going to kill you–"

Paul snickered. "Nothing was going to happen to little Jamie, not yet anyway... But you– I can guarantee you will not be around much longer."

Kari recoiled and anxiety flared. "Don't talk to her," Jude warned.

"I'm just speaking the truth... Perhaps you should start saying your goodbyes to each other."

Kari shook and tears fell. "Jude–"

He wanted to wrap his arms around her. "Shhh... It's going to be okay."

"But it won't..." Paul said.

"Stop!" Jude shouted.

"Look, Wallace, I upset Jamie."

Jude leaned back and kicked at Paul but only struck the seat.

"Are you finished?"

"You're dead! I will kill you!"

"So much anger–"

Kari reached her hands around the best she could angling her arms and grabbed Jude's jacket.

"It's going to be okay– Jude– Look at me," Kari pleaded.

Jude reluctantly looked at Kari. He was ashamed and scared that he would not be able to protect her.

"Hey... Just remember whatever happens, it's not your fault."

Jude rested his forehead on Kari's shoulder. "I won't lose you."

The SUV came to a halt and Paul opened the back door. The fresh air filled Kari's senses. The waterfront smell reminded her of her home in Marinette. Paul pushed Jude forward towards the tin warehouse. He knew exactly where they were, it was one of many of his father's supply warehouses, but this was a main one. He had given MI6 the location months ago. Water bordered two sides of the portion of the pier they were on. Stacked shipping crates lined the property. There was a fleeting moment of hope that Kari could be rescued until Jude saw heavily armed men patrolling the property. They were escorted to the tin building that butted up against the water. The inside was open and had many crates lining the floor nearly to the ceiling. Wallace escorted them to the far side of the building. They were secured to steel chairs near the open water of the dock.

Paul's phone rang. He stepped away and answered it. "Hello?"

"We are just getting to Paddington station. How is James?" Garrick asked.

"Oh, he's lovely."

"May I speak with him?"

Paul pushed the phone to Jude's ear. "What?"

"We will need to work on you manners. I did not raise you to be rude. Now, before I waste my time searching this station. I'm going to ask you one time– Are you certain the information is here and it's in locker 284?"

"I wouldn't lie to you."

"That is delightful to hear. Remember if you are untruthful, I may not kill you but your girlfriend... I won't hesitate–"

"I haven't lied!"

"Don't raise your voice to me, son," Garrick said sternly. "Let me speak with your brother."

Jude glared at Paul. "Pops wants to talk to you."

Paul took the phone away from Jude. "Yes?"

"When I arrive I will send in a team to retrieve the documents and proceed to your location. If anything goes awry... Go to the secondary location."

"Understood."

———

The wheels hit the tarmac and the Marshals trekked across the vast concrete to awaiting MI6 vehicles.

"We have confirmed surveillance on the docks stating that Paul is there with James and Kari," Agent Graham said. He looked the Marshals over. "Sorry no time for introductions, we need to rendezvous with the other teams."

Usually Bradley would thrive in the high stress environment, but not with the op involving his sister. During the ride they threw on their gear and readied their weapons. Bradley felt like he was suiting up for a mission when he was still Delta Force. The vehicle came to a halt and they unloaded in the town west of the docks.

"Es tha' you, Indy?" Finlay 'Jedi' Reid said in a thick Scottish accent.

"Can't be, he looks too proper–" Ty 'Loch' Grayson said, getting close to Clayton staring at his face. "Where's your viking beard and long hair?"

"It's nice to see you guys, too," Clayton said.

Jedi hugged Clayton and picked him up. "Ay thin' ya gained some weight tae?"

Jedi set Clayton down and Loch shook his hand and gave him a hug. "It has been too long, my friend."

"All right, Outlaw teams are getting into position to hit target Alpha," SAS team leader, Griffin said. "Gents, it's time."

The SAS operators, Bandit 1, climbed into the two small zodiac boats. The SAS snipers, Bucket and Storm, took one while the remaining land siege team took the other. The remaining teams made up of the Marshals and MI6 piled into paneled vans. MacTavish was assigned to Bandit 3, who would be responsible for perimeter security from the northwest. Bradley and Clayton were assigned to Bandit 2, with Seth. They were responsible for perimeter security from the northeast. Bandit 1's main objective was to secure the assets in the main building from the south.

Bradley tapped his finger on the side of his rifle and bounced his leg.

"I don't have to worry about you do I?" Clayton asked.

Bradley swallowed. "I can't lose her…"

"So I should worry– We will get them home safe. Please… Just don't do anything rash."

The vans killed their lights and jerked off of the road into a gravel lot two miles north from the location. Seth opened the back door and the team jumped out. The air was brisk and the sun was barely visible over the horizon. The Tilbury Docks was a large area with the port in the shape of an 'L.' There was only one narrow channel into the dock from the River Thames into the southwest end of the docks.

"Bandit 2 and 3 at the Y approaching the X, ETA twenty minutes." Graham said over the radio.

"Copy, Bandit 1 in position, standing by for seige," Griffin said.

"Falcon 1 boarding ship now," Bucket said and slung his sniper rifle behind him.

Bucket removed a rope from his gear with a hook and tossed it up the towering wall of the ship. The hook clattered and he made his ascent to take his position south of the compound to provide cover and eyes. Storm beached his small DVP, diver propulsion vehicle, and removed his diving gear. He and Bucket had disembarked their zodiac at the southernmost point of the docks where a large ship was docked on the inside of the port. Storm continued through the thousand feet of water to his position on the opposing dock from where Bucket was to face west having eyes on the entire eastern side of the property.

"Falcon two, I just reached shore. Climbing to my post shortly," Storm said and looked at the massive crane used to lift shipping crates.

Bandit 2 and 3 proceeded with their approach around the large docks. They stuck to the cover of buildings, vehicles, and shipping crates, avoiding the road. Bandit 2 hugged the eastern side while Bandit 3 handled the western side. They made good time considering the two mile trek with sixty pounds worth of gear on.

"We are approaching the compound now. Bandit 1, you are clear to engage," Graham radioed.

"Weapons free, gents," Griffin said to his team in the zodiac.

Bandit 3 set up to breach the fence to the northwest while Bandit 2 readied to breach the southeast. McKidd knelt next to the chain link fence and cut a slit in the metal links. He climbed inside holding the fence back for the rest to enter. Clayton posted in front of the group keeping watch for any hostels. Heavy gunfire erupted from the far south.

"Wae're tak'n fire!" Jedi yelled over the radio.

Griffin turned the zodiac sharply away from the shoreline trying to avoid the hidden machine gun nest. They ducked trying to take the little cover they could from the powerful spray of bullets.

"Falcon 1 has the target." Bucket squeezed the trigger and blood sprayed in a plume from the large caliber round striking the enemy in the chest.

The zodiac whizzed behind the small watergate and ran ashore. The zodiac was riddled with bullet holes and rendered inoperable. It was a miracle they made it to shore at all. Bucket adjusted his aim and took out the second fighter in the nest.

"Targets neutralized. You're clear to engage." Bucket radioed.

Loch hopped out of the zodiac his weapon pointed to the unknown covering his teammates. There was a groan behind him.

"I'm hit," Hawkeye grimaced in pain and applied pressure to his shoulder.

"Fuck, mate," Jedi said and pulled a tourniquet from Hawkeye's gear.

"Hawkeye is down," Loch radioed.

Clayton glanced at Bradley. "This isn't going well."

"Well, now that they know we're here..." Seth said, stepping past everyone to take point. "Let's make some more noise."

"Stay frosty, my friend," Clayton said to Bradley.

A smoke screen billowed from the edge of the docks masking the property.

"Falcons are smoked out," Storm said. "You are on your own for now."

Paul turned his head to the security monitors. Kari's heart dropped seeing Bradley on one of the screens traversing amongst shipping containers. Paul gave his men the locations of the intruders.

"No!" Kari shouted and tears streamed from her eyes.

Kari held her breath as Bradley proceeded down an aisle. One of Paul's men stepped out from a crate to Bradley's right down a tight aisle and opened fire. Bradley dove forward and crouched near the edge of the crate. The others took cover where they could. Bradley quickly peeked around the corner and shot a burst of rounds. A hail of the bullets tinged into the steel shipping container and the others struck the assailant. His body hit the container and he fell to the ground. They regrouped and maneuvered down the aisle. Kari took a breath.

"Don't worry I have a surprise for them– If they get here that is," Paul said.

Gunshots sounded to the west as Bandit 2 encountered teams of fighters.

"Edwards is down!" Graham yelled over the radio. "We are pinned down!"

Bradley could see the building at the end of the shipping containers. They were close to getting to Kari and Jude. Seth halted his group and stared in the direction of the gunfire. He turned down a narrow row to the west.

"Bandit 1 is oscar mike to your location," Griffin radioed and led his team to the north.

Seth stopped and turned around. A muzzle flashed followed by the cracking of a gun. Seth dropped to the gravel with a bullet tearing through his calf and the thigh of his right leg. Clayton stepped in front of Seth and squeezed the trigger of his rifle having noticed the hostile crouched around the corner of a crate. The bullets sprayed hitting the crates and thudded into the shooter's body. McKidd grabbed Seth by the handle on the back of his tactical plated vest and dragged him from danger. Bullets whizzed past them from the other direction. Bradley returned fire, dropping the shooter.

"Connor is down," McKidd radioed.

McKidd knelt down and applied pressure to the wound, blood gushed between his gloved hands. Seth let his head fall back hitting the gravel, he felt woozy and weak. Bradley pulled his Quick Clot from a pouch and tore the plastic packaging with his teeth. The bandage soaked the blood as it was driven deeper into the entrance wound. A groan escaped Seth's lips as McKidd knelt on the wound. He removed a tourniquet from his pouch. Clayton stood over them keeping watch for hostiles. The blood made McKidd's hands slick as he pulled the tourniquet tight near Seth's groin. Seth clenched his teeth and groaned.

"Bandit 2 to House," McKidd radioed.

"Go ahead, Bandit 2."

"House, requesting secondary team and MEDEVAC."

"Copy. ETA fifteen."

Seth's face was drained of color and sweat beaded on his forehead. "You gents continue."

"We can't leave you," Bradley said.

"I'll get him outside the X and wait for the MEDEVAC," McKidd stated.

"You're wasting time, go—" Seth said.

Bradley touched Clayton's shoulder with his and they proceeded. Clayton halted, the leg of an assailant lighting up his thermal optic. He squeezed the trigger, blood splattered from the fighter's leg. He fell forward from behind the crate. Clayton took the shot and killed the man. The clank of a shipping crate door sounded followed by rapid fire. Bradley hit the ground with a thud and Clayton redirected his aim in a split second and sent rounds to the bright flash on his optic. He fired until the blob of light collapsed.

"Bradley!" Clayton shouted.

Bradley ran his hands over his plates. "I'm good."

Clayton grabbed his arm and lifted him to his feet. "You sure?"

"Well I'm not bleeding. Let's finish this."

They posted at the end of the row of crates that opened into a large gravel lot. There were a row of cars ahead of them near the road access. The building where they suspected Jude and Kari was to the left. Hostiles patrolled the area and waited behind cover.

"There are six roaming tangos," Clayton whispered.

"Let's take out the pair near the cars. Moving up to that position for cover. It will give us a better view of the building too."

"I'll take the one on the right."

"Roger."

Bradley aligned his optic and with two shots to make sure, he dropped his target. His partner fell next to him.

Clayton and Bradley ran to the cover of the cars while bullets flew by and hit the tin of the cars. Clayton and Bradley returned fire.

"Bandit 2, we're taking heavy fire," Clayton radioed.

"Bandit 3, oscar mike to your six," Graham radioed.

"Bandit 1, we are going to go around to flank," Jedi radioed.

Bradley crouched behind the car, lead whacking into the steel of the cars.

Paul smirked. "Are you ready for this?"

"Are you ready for them to break that door down and take you out?" Jude asked. He was confident that their rescuers were going to destroy Paul and his men. They had to, they were Jude's last hope to save Kari.

"Please–" Paul nodded to Wallace.

Anxiety pumped through Kari's body. Her heart raced as she stared at the screen watching the fire fight. Wallace pushed a small detonator. The screen lit up. Bradley and Clayton were propelled into the air. The shock wave from the explosion blasted through their bodies and the heat bit at their skin. The blast rattled the building. Jude stared at the screen, mouth agape in disbelief.

"Wallace, go make sure they're dead."

A scream escaped Kari's lips and tears flowed down her face. Kari thrashed against her binds. "You're a monster!"

Jude slowly turned his head to Kari. He tried to contain his sorrow. He just got her brother killed and yet more people were perishing because of him.

The force of the explosion rendered Bradley unconscious. His arms were splayed out and blood dripped from his nose. Clayton groaned trying to find his bearings. He turned over to his stomach and pawed at the gravel. The fire roared and crackled as he crawled to Bradley. The world was blurry from the effects of the blast and hazed plume of smoke. Fear swept through Clayton thinking his partner was dead.

Through the blanket of smoke Wallace walked towards Bradley with a handgun. Clayton staggered to his feet and fell forward. He pushed himself from the ground scrambling to his feet. He did not have time to look for his lost rifle. Wallace was focused on his intended target and stood over Bradley. He smirked seeing the blood on his face and motionless. The sights aligned on Bradley's face and Wallace applied pressure to the trigger. Clayton used every ounce of energy to propel his body forward into Wallace. A shot rang out and the bullet went wide missing Bradley.

Clayton grasped the gun with both hands and dropped his weight prying it from Wallace's grip. It clattered into the gravel and was kicked away. Wallace threw a punch, connecting with the side of Clayton's head. He stumbled and shook off the blow. He shifted his weight and struck Wallace. They both clutched each other in a grappling match. Wallace thrusted a knee into Clayton's abdomen causing him to loosen his grip. Wallace followed through with an elbow to the chin. The world spun and Clayton stepped back to regain his bearings.

Wallace gripped Clayton by the collar of his shirt and narrowed his eyes. Clayton reached out to grab him by the throat. A sharp pain erupted in his abdomen. A low rumbled chuckle escaped Wallace. Clayton's blood ran cold and he inhaled sharply. With a stumble Clayton fell to the ground backwards. A knife protruded from Clayton's stomach and blood pooled from the wound. He blinked slowly watching Wallace step over him.

Bradley dove and tackled Wallace to the ground. Clayton's eyes fixated on the scene in front of him. He was too weak to do anything but watch. Bradley parried a blow and kneed Wallace in the abdomen. Gripping tight, Bradley directed Wallace to the ground positioning himself over Wallace. With a quick hand Wallace grabbed a handful of gravel and dirt and threw into Bradley's eyes. It felt like glass cutting his eyes. Bradley squinted trying to fight through the pain. Fist after fist hit Bradley. He dropped to the ground and Wallace straddled him. The punching continued, and Bradley's head lobbed blood dripping from his nose and mouth.

Clayton lifted his shaky hand with a groan. He gripped the handle of the embedded knife. Resigning himself to the truth of his imminent death, he resolved to help Bradley win his fight. With every last ounce of might, Clayton pulled the blade from his stomach and threw it to the ground. He shifted painfully to one side and drew his handgun from the drop holster. With gritted teeth and a trembling hand, he aimed and pulled the trigger. The round embedded into Wallace's hip. Clayton missed the intended target of Wallace's face. Wallace hissed in pain nonetheless. Clayton's head lobbed to one side, his fight diminishing. His vision began to blur and darkness encroached his field of vision. He failed Bradley. Staring at Clayton, Wallace's eyes went vacant. Blood splattered out of the side of his head and he tipped over dead. Clayton's fight was over. Before he fell into the invading darkness, he saw MacTavish running toward him lowering his rifle. Bradley turned over onto his stomach and stared at Clayton's motionless body.

"Fuck!" MacTavish yelled and clapped his hand over Clayton's wound. "Hang in there, Bradshaw!"

Gunshots sounded over the hiss of the fire. Bandit 1 encountered hostiles to the south.

Paul turned to his henchman. "It's time to go, Kingston."

Kingston struck Jude in the back of the head with the butt of his rifle. There was a horrifying crack and Jude's head fell forward, unconscious.

"No!" Kari cried.

"I have had enough from you," Paul said and grasped the back of Kari's chair.

Kari screamed as she was dragged to the edge of the concret.

"Goodbye," Paul said and pushed Kari into the dark water.

The cold water clawed at Kari pulling her into its depths. She struggled against the ropes in panic.

Jedi placed a hand on MacTavish's shoulder. "Go."

Bradley and MacTavish took off at a sprint, a couple others following behind. MacTavish booted the door to the warehouse and the remaining team of operators entered, fanning out quickly. Bradley spotted Paul through the large windows running down the dock. He saw Kingston tossing Jude into a zodiac. Anxiety coursed through Bradley with Kari's absence. MacTavish bolted towards the large garage door to chase Paul.

Bradley ran towards the far end of the warehouse where it had open access to a covered dock. His eyes caught a glimpse of the fresh marks of a chair being dragged in the dirt. Bradley tossed his rifle to Loch and dove into the eeri black water.

Kari grew tired and stopped fighting. The cold and dark engulfed her. Bradley swam deeper into the water in a frantic search. The weight of his gear pulled him down. His hand hit the steel back of the chair and he grabbed it. He felt the rope that bound Kari's torso to the chair. The binds frayed and tore apart when Bradley ran his knife through them. He wrapped his arm around her and kicked hard to the surface. It was a struggle to swim with the added weight and resistance. The water splashed when Bradley surfaced. He took a deep breath and lifted Kari from the water to Loch. Bradley climbed out from the water as Loch cut the rope from Kari's wrists. She coughed violently and gasped for air.

Bradley, exhausted, crawled to Kari and embraced her. Her coughs and gasps of air turned into sobs. She turned into Bradley wrapping her arms around him. He picked her up holding her tight.

"It's going to be okay," Bradley whispered.

"They're going to kill Jude."

"They're gone! I couldn't get to them in time," MacTavish radioed out of breath from his sprint.

"I couldn't get a clear shot," Bucket said disappointed. "They made it out of the channel and went south on the river."

"Bandit 1 to House. Compound secured. Requesting helo's to the X. We have two yellows, a red, and a black." Loch radioed.

"House copies. Helo inbound ETA three mikes."

"Falcons to House, we will continue our rendezvous to drop location."

"House copies."

The loud hum of the helos sounded overhead. Jedi had since removed Clayton's armor and cut away his clothing. He did his best to stop the bleeding but the blood continued to flow. His breath was shallow, his skin was ashen and damp.

"Indy, yae stay wit mae. Gotta get yeh on the bird aye," Jedi said and the helo's landed in the middle of the open gravel lot.

Jedi helped load Clayton onto the helicopter, shielding themselves the best they could from the rotor wash. Bradley lifted Kari to the open side of the bird, MacTavish helping her on board. Loch hopped in along with the other SAS operators. Jedi and Loch did not waste time and opened up the med bags. They established IVs and hooked Clayton to a monitor. He was limp and blood seeped through the bandage flowing onto the floor of the chopper. Bradley dropped his head and stared at his friend who clung to life.

CHAPTER TWENTY SIX

The helos touched down on the tarmac and the awaiting medical crews took the injured parties. Bradley watched Clayton being unloaded onto a cot and wheeled away, IV lines and wires attached to him. Bradley ushered Kari to the hanger where the Bandit teams regrouped. Kari stood in the large door staring out over the tarmac. She was numb, her mind desperately tried to catch up to reality. It was difficult to process the events that had happened, for there was too much. The weight of grief was lifted when Bradley told her Jessica and Amelia were all right. However, she feared for Jude and her heart ached. Her thoughts were pulled from her by the abrupt outburst behind her.

"Are you fucking kiding me?" MacTavish yelled. "This is just wonderful!"

Graham stared at MacTavish, not appreciative of the hotheaded American.

"How are we going to proceed?" Bradley asked.

Kari turned around eavesdropping intently on the conversation.

"Our people are in contact with the CIA as we speak to figure that out," Graham said.

"It's going to be another wild goose chase," MacTavish added.

"Jude has provided a substantial amount of intel. Both of our governments have had surveillance on a number of locations. We are hopeful we'll find Garrick and get Jude home safely."

"That kid is as good as dead... Our only shot to save him was now, and we failed."

Kari froze. Her breath still. The ones who were supposed to save Jude were not optimistic about the outcome. Kari wanted to cry but she had no tears left. She blinked slowly in a daze. Bradley glanced in Kari's direction. He excused himself from the brief and walked to her.

"Hey..."

"He's going to die isn't he? I'm never going to see Jude again am I?"

Bradley touched the tops of her shoulders not sure what to say. "Kari– It isn't that simple. There are a lot of people working on getting Jude back safely."

For the first time Kari was able to see Bradley clearly under the bright lights in the hanger. She was too caught up in everything to really look at her brother. He had risked his life and it showed. Dried blood and dirt caked his face. His cheek and eye were slightly swollen and his lip was cracked open. There was a tear in the sleeve of his arm and the fabric was saturated in blood. Tears cascaded down her cheeks and she hugged him.

"I'm sorry for putting you through this–"

"Kari– Don't–"

"No– I nearly got you killed."

"I would have given my life for you."

Bradely's pocket vibrated and he let Kari go to dig his phone out of a cargo pocket on his pants. The caller ID came up as restricted.

"I'm sorry, I have to take this," Bradley said. "We will talk more later."

He stepped away from Kari and she wiped away the tears. A female MI6 agent approached her.

"Let's get you changed out of those wet clothes. A hot shower perhaps?" She asked and placed her hands on Kari's shoulders.

Kari nodded and Bradley mouthed, "thank you," to the MI6 agent.

"Evans," Bradley answered, peaking MacTavish's interest.

"Goddamn it, Evans! You fucking son of a bitch!" Pyke yelled. "I deliberately grounded your asses!"

Bradley held the phone away from his ear and MacTavish raised a brow. "He's mad," Bradley said and MacTavish smirked.

"I gave you an order! Christ sakes! Now I'm getting calls from the CIA because you pissed in their sand box and stole their juice boxes. Do you know how much bureaucratic shit I'm dealing with because of your fucking stupidity?!"

"Sir–"

"Don't 'Sir' me, Evans! What the fuck were you thinking? Jesus Christ! The CIA and the Brits are at each other's throats over this. And you! You had to get us involved!"

"Are you done yelling?"

"No!– Fuck!" Pyke took a breath. "I am supposed to be on vacation, Evans! With my wife! You are disrupting my vacation! My wife is furious that my phone is ringing every ten minutes! Jesus Christ!" Pyke picked up a fruity drink with an umbrella and took a sip through the straw, beach goers glaring at Pyke for the rude shouting. "What are you looking at?" Pyke asked an old couple that gawked at him. They turned around quickly. There was a long pause and Pyke asked calmly. "How is your sister?"

"She will be fine."

"And they don't know where Jude is?"

"Not as of yet."

MacTavish leaned in. "He stopped yelling... I can't hear."

Bradley pushed him away.

"Fuck..." Pyke muttered and removed his bucket hat exposing his already cherry bald head.

"Sir– We have an Eagle down..."

Pyke paused his heart sinking. "Who?"

"Bradshaw, sir. He's critical– I– I don't know if he'll make it... He's in rough shape."

MacTavish dropped his head. He was thankful he got to Bradley in time or he would be speaking to Pyke about two Eagles KIA. It could have been worse, much worse. Clayton was strong and MacTavish believed he would pull through, he had to.

"You and MacTavish are to come home immediately. I can't afford to lose any more good men."

"Sir–"

"That is an order Evans. Please, I do not want to be draping American flags over your caskets."

"Understood... We will be wheels up as soon as Bradshaw is stable to travel."

"Evans– I swear to God, if you disobey my orders I will fire you and then beat the ever living fuck out of you. Understood?"

"Yes, sir."

Pyke tossed the phone on the lounger he had been relaxing on. He placed a hand on his hip and downed his fruity drink. He looked at his wife. "I'm going to need several more of these, sweety."

Bradley hung up and tapped the phone in his hand. "So?"

"We have orders to head home as soon as Clayton is able to move."

"Okay... That could be awhile, so we're going to find this fucktard right?"

"MacTavish..."

"That's not a no."

———

Waking to a throbbing pain in the back of his head, Jude fluttered his eyes open. There was a gentle hum of jet engines and Jude sat up, his hands still bound. Panic set in when he did not see Kari.

"Where is she?" Jude asked, anger flowing.

"Pardon? Who?" Paul asked.

"What did you do?" Jude knew the answer but he did not want to believe it.

"Oh, the girl that was with you– Yes, how unfortunate it was. Seems that I pushed her into the channel."

"You son of a bitch!" Jude leapt from his seat towards Paul.

Paul waited a moment for Jude to get close and kicked him hard in the hip causing him to fall back. Paul jumped on Jude and withdrew a knife, placing the cool steel blade against his throat.

"It's like you have a death wish," Paul whispered. "Don't push me or I will kill you."

"Just do it all ready," Jude seethed and pushed against the blade. A small line of blood trickled slowly down his skin.

Paul stood. "Here? Now? How boring of a death that would be." Paul returned to his seat. "No– I have plans for you, if Father allows it."

Jude pushed himself from the floor and his handcuffs clanked against the table as he sat down. Tears formed in the corners of his eyes and he stared out the window trying desperately not to let them fall. Many people have died because of him and their deaths weighed heavily on his heart. Flashes of Kari laughing and smiling filled his mind. The tears fell, and he wiped them away. Sorrow filled every inch of his being knowing he would never see her smile, hear her laugh, feel her hand in his.

Paul's phone rang and he was not surprised to see it was coming up as a random number from Africa. After things had gone south Garrick kept his men split going to seperate safe locations.

"Hello?" Paul answered.

"Paul, I assume you made it safely in the air then?"

"We have."

"I am disheartened we lost good men, but we knew this was a possibility."

"It would not have happened in the first place if it weren't for James," Paul replied.

Jude stared at Paul, hate brewing.

"How is he?"

"Alive... If that is what you're asking. I can't say the same thing for the girl."

"Paul, was that necessary?"

"It was."

Garrick took a long breath. "You need to learn to control your anger. I am transferring the funds to the account now. I will be in touch."

Paul set the phone down and met Jude's gaze.

The flight was long and the ride into the Caucasus Mountains felt even longer. The road had long ago turned to dirt and the pot holes bounced the SUV around. Jude had little hope that anyone would be coming to his aid. He was on his own.

Paul pulled Jude from the back of the SUV and pushed him towards the one story house. The few men patrolling glanced at the arrivals and continued with their respective posts. The house had little furnishings except for old couches and folding tables. The living room had a desk setup with a wall of screens and weapon caches by every window. Paul took hold of a chair and dragged it across the bare floor.

"Sit," Paul commanded.

Jude did as he was told and stared at a TV mounted on the wall in front of him. A soccer match was on. He was thankful for a distraction. Kingston leaned against the wall staring at Jude as Paul milled about the house.

"Here." Paul tossed a blanket on the floor next to him along with a bottle. "You are not to leave this spot."

"Can I get something to eat, or are you purposely starving me?"

Paul rolled his eyes departing to the kitchen. He handed Jude a power bar and a sports drink.

"Much appreciated," Jude replied.

"Fuck off." Paul assumed his position behind the desk studying the camera locations of the property.

—

Sharp talons gripped Kari's bicep. Fear and anxiety engulfed her body. Heat erupted where Garrick clutched her. His face was distorted and dark. A groan escaped Jude's lips and he dropped to the ground. Collin stood over him with the barrel of his pistol pressed against his head. Kari felt the echo of her heartbeat and heard the sharp inhales of her own breath. Her vision pulsed as she stepped forward. The ground moved beneath her feet. Darkness surround her but Jude and Collin were lit in a dim red hue. Garrick's deep laugh was distorted and distant. Kari gripped the handle of the blade in her boot. The feel of the blade had a strange comfort. Kari thrusted the blade into Collin's neck. She could feel the slight resistance of flesh and could hear the gush of blood. Blood dripped from the blade and her hand was painted in a dark crimson oil turning black with each passing moment. The concrete split and crumbled. Kari screamed as she fell into the depths of darkness. The cold water wrapped around her dragging her deep into the unknown.

With a gasp of air Kari sat up frantic. A bead of sweat rolled down her temple and into her hair. Her breath was quick as she regained her bearings. The dim lights from above had a calming effect. Her eyes scanned the empty waiting room of the hospital until they fell upon MacTavish. He was lounging on a couch similar to the one Kari had fallen asleep on.

"Are you okay?" MacTavish asked.

Kari rubbed her face and wiped her eyes. "It was just a nightmare." It had been twenty four hours since that nightmare was a reality.

"You've been through a lot. I'm astonished by your bravery."

Kari looked down and folded her once bloody hands into each other. "I wouldn't call it bravery, survival maybe..." Kari locked eyes with MacTavish. "I was afraid, not brave."

MacTavish waved Kari over. "Being brave is overcoming fear. I would say you've done that."

"I'm afraid to sleep. Everything keeps replaying in my head and I can't get it to stop."

"You've been through a great deal of trauma, it will take time."

Kari felt the pressure behind her eyes and her throat tightened. "I thought they were going to kill Jude... I did something terrible– It didn't even matter because they're going to kill him anyway." Kari wiped the moisture from her eyes before any tears could fall.

"I'm not going to lie to you, the probability of a successful rescue op is not in our favor."

"You are just a ray of sunshine."

"I'm not about to give you false hope after what you've been through."

"I can still see the blood on my hands..." Kari pulled at her fingers.

"What happened, Kari?"

Kari kept her gaze on her fingers. Under her nails there was dirt and dried blood. "I thought he was going to kill Jude. I didn't even think about it when I did it." Kari looked at MacTavish. "I killed a man without even a second thought." Kari closed her eyes and took a breath. Her thoughts shifted to Jude. "I just wish I killed Paul too. Then Jude would be safe. Does that make me a monster?"

MacTavish did not know how to respond. He was not expecting Kari to confess to killing someone. "No, you were protecting someone you loved."

"I'm afraid this feeling will never go away. That it will haunt my dreams forever."

"It gets easier... Why don't you try and get some rest."

"I don't know if I can."

MacTavish removed his jacket and draped it over her shoulders. "I'll be right here. I'll even let you use me as a footrest."

Kari sprawled out on the couch. "Please don't tell Bradley."

"I won't."

The elevator dinged down the hall and footsteps echoed around the polished halls. They got louder and MacTavish lifted his head to the door. Jedi and Loch stood in the doorway.

"We have news. Where's Bradley?" Loch asked.

Kari propped herself up on an elbow.

"He's with Bradshaw," MacTavish answered.

"Fill him in," Loch said and departed down the hall.

Loch knocked on the doorframe of Clayton's room. "How's he doing?" Loch asked.

"Stable, for now."

"He's a strong lad."

"Yeah..." Bradley texted a message on his phone and gave Loch his undivided attention.

"I remember this one time in Fallujah we were clearing a complex and there was a sleeper fighter that had popped out of a hole in a wall on our flank. Due to the close quarters, Indy tackled him into what he thought was a wall... Turns out it was a blanket covering a shaft that fell several stories... Thought for sure we lost him.

He walked away covered in dust and a couple bumps and bruises. Saved our asrses."

"I'm sure he'll be bossing everyone around in no time."

Loch chuckled and leaned on the frame. "How's Agent Connor?"

"Uh– restless… I actually just texted him you were here."

A loud crash sounded down the hall. Loch peaked around the door frame. Wheelchair bound Seth had crashed into an equipment cart. A petit nurse tried to assist him.

"Sir, you need to rest."

"Blimey, I'm fine!"

Loch laughed.

"That's him isn't it?" Bradley asked.

Loch nodded and Bradley sighed heavily.

Seth wheeled down the hall in haste. "Don't start the meeting without me."

"I would never…"

Seth banged into the door frame and Loch abandoned his post with a hop to evade being run over.

"And here I thought you wanted to visit…" Clayton's weak voice cracked.

"Oh good! He's awake," Seth said, wheeling into the room.

"Keep your voice down," Clayton said and coughed. "So, Loch, if you're not here to visit, what's the news?"

"They think they located the asset in the Caucasus Mountains."

"Which side?" Bradley asked.

"Russia," Loch stated.

"Wonderful…" Clayton said and struggled to sit up. "What's the plan?"

"There's going to be a joint op of SAS and Delta Force. We leave in three hours." Loch turned to Bradley. "The guys and I advocated for you and MacTavish to be a part of the operation in the pit."

"Not exactly where the action is but it'll do," Clayton said and swung his leg over the bed with a groan. "Let's do this."

Bradley crossed the short distance and pushed Clayton's leg back in the bed. "Think again."

"Good luck with that, you'll probably have to handcuff him to the bed," Loch smirked.

Clayton rolled his eyes.

"I don't think I am receiving an invitation either," Seth said.

"While you're on pain meds? You are correct," Loch replied and motioned for the door. "Shall we?"

"Make sure he doesn't escape," Bradley said, patting Seth on the shoulder.

They walked down the hall. "I will drive you back to the hotel. McKidd and Stark will continue security posts and stay with Kari when you are gone," Loch explained.

Kari could not believe what she was hearing. *They found him? They're really going to do a rescue op?* The hope she lost was coming back in full force. Her eyes lit up seeing Bradley walking down the hallway.

"I can't believe they found him," Kari said. "You have to let me come with you."

"Kari, you know that is not going to happen. You'll be staying at the hotel with the MI6 agents. I promise I will let you know what happens when I can."

Kari was scared and relieved at the same time. She wrapped her arms tight around him. "I wish you were going with them."

"Me too."

CHAPTER TWENTY SEVEN

"This is your captain speaking," the pilot's voice sounded in Marcus's ear. He glanced at Hatch and chuckled. "Please make sure your seats and tray tables are in their full upright position."

Jedi was seated next to Marcus on the empty C-17 and pretended to secure a tray.

"This is your six-minute call," the pilot said. "I would say fasten your seatbelts and prepare for landing... However, get your shit and get ready to jump."

The ten joint SAS and Delta Force operators stood. Marcus checked his gear again as he did before every HAHO, High Altitude, High Opening jump. When falling from a perfectly good airplane at 30,000 feet, there was no room for error. The ramp of the C-17 lowered, exposing the dark unknown.

Bradley stood before the wall of monitors, his eyes glued on the screen with the GPS signals. More specifically the dot labeled "Evans." One by one the dots began to drift away from each other and Braldey knew they started their jump.

The icy wind howled against Marcus. He counted in his head slowly to twelve and pulled the cord to his chute. The canopy fluttered open and his plummet discontinued with a violent jerk. He jammed his wrists into the loops knowing he would be losing feeling shortly due the negative temperatures and trying to steer with numb hands never worked well. It was time to settle in for the long glide into Russia.

"I'm tangled!" Storm yelled over the team's closed net radio.

The cords wrapped around Storm sending him into a spiral.

"Sir! We have a problem," an analyst announced. He was in charge of monitoring the camera footage from the operators helmets.

"Is it one of ours?" a commander asked but knew the answer reading the name on the screen.

Bradley's head snapped to the other screens. His heart raced seeing the whirl of footage knowing that someone's parachute malfunctioned. MacTavish crossed his arms, his eyes glued to the screen.

Storm grasped his fixed blade and frantically sawed at the cords. There were too many tangled around his body and panic began to set in. Even if he would be able to free himself, his hands were numb and the chances of being able to release his reserve chute were slim.

"Anyone have eyes?" Griffin asked.

"I'm above him. He needs help," Bonnet said. "I haven't deployed, I'm going in."

Bonnet stretched his limbs behind him and dove through the sky towards Storm.

"Bonnet! We don't need two dead operators, disengage," Storm shouted over the com.

Bonnet hit Storm hard and clasped him to his harness. Bonnet pulled his knife and cut the death lines on the other side of Storm. The last of the cord snapped free and death flapped away into the darkness. Bonnet's hands were numb as he pulled his chute. His heart stopped for a moment until he heard the bustle of the canopy deploying and the comfort of the jerk of his momentum being slowed.

"I got you," Bonnet said.

"Thanks, mate, I'll owe you one," Storm said out of breath, his heart pounding against his chest.

"You guys good?" Hatch asked.

"Yeah, we're good…"

"Blimey… That was terrifying, thought one of you wank sticks would be visiting my mum."

"You were dropped on your head as a child weren't you?" Griffin said.

"Could have been the lead paint I ate."

Marcus tried to enjoy the view but the deep blanket of clouds obstructed his sight of the ground. The green light from the GPS attached to his arm was barely visible with the fog of his goggles. HAHO jumps were Marcus's least favorite thing to do. He was freezing and it would be awhile before his feet would touch ground, if he even had feeling left in them when they landed.

"Nest to House."

The commander pushed down the button to speak on the radio. "Go ahead, Nest."

"Projected LZ for Bonnet and Storm is four clicks south of the rest."

The Commander stared at the satellite image. "Looks like our gents will have a long uphill hike ahead of them."

"We will advise one of them to switch over to be monitored by your House."

"Roger that Nest. Have Storm move to BinOps 4."

"Roger House, BinOps 4."

"Nest to Vipers."

"Go for 6-4," Hatch said.

"6-5," Griffin acknowledged.

"Nest to Viper relay to your stragglers to have one of them switch over to BinOps4, House will be monitoring their traffic. Their projected landing will be several klicks south of the LZ."

"Roger that Nest," Hatch replied.

"6-5."

Hatch keyed the closed net team radio. "Listen here tandem girl scouts, good job on totally fucking up your decent. When you land, adjust your skirts and one of you switch over to BinOps4. House will be monitoring your jolly stroll in the woods. See you after your tea party."

Storm sighed. "I'm never going to hear the end of this."

Boots landed on the ground and the team took turns removing their chutes while others provided cover. The clearing was surrounded by tall pines on each side. The thick clouds obscured any light the sliver of a moon would have provided. Marcus removed his mask and turned on his night vision. They moved swiftly to the tree line to get out of the open. Once in the cover of the trees Marcus posted at the point of the group. Yeti knelt down on the cold earth and removed his pack. Yeti grinned like a child and the small Hornet Drone buzzed alive, lifting into the air.

"Are you sure you can fly that thing?" Hatch said and watched the drone fly out of sight.

"I can pilot this better than you can shoot," Yeti said, glancing at Hatch with a stern face.

"Well... That's not saying much," Marcus piped in.

"Do you want to become the pack mule?" Hatch asked.

Plank rolled his shoulders under the extra weight of equipment he was forced to carry with being the junior man. "Would be nice."

"Oh, do you mean carrying the halogen and charges? I'm already doing that."

"Drone planted," Yeti announced and pushed a control. "–and we are offline in 60 seconds."

"Viper 6-4 to Nest, Hornet deployed."

"Copy that Viper 6-4."

The team moved out without a word. The movements were swift through the dark forest towards the target location. The team split into two, Griffin leading a team due west of the target to a guard house. Hatch led the rest to the safe house. Based on intelligence there were not many men stationed around the compound.

Jude pretended to sleep as he listened in on Paul's conversation with their father.

"A new ally? Are you sure you can trust him?" Paul asked.

"Trust? No, but similar interests have aligned for both of our benefits," Garrick replied. "He will be expecting you in 48 hours, don't–" The phone line went dead.

Paul looked at the phone seeing the signal dropped and stepped to the desk.

"Kingston, would you mind going to the satellite and figure out why it's offline."

Kingston nodded grabbing a rifle before disappearing out of the door. The satellite looked perfectly fine and Kingston was far from an expert on anything technology related. He opened up the control box.

"What am I even supposed to be looking at?" he huffed and keyed his mic. "Paul, you should look at this yourself. I don't know what the fuck is wrong with it."

"I will be right there."

Paul set the radio on the desk and stepped over Jude. "Get up!" He kicked Jude in the side.

Jude groaned and rolled to his side, glaring at Paul. "It will be a nice day when a bullet goes through your head."

Paul grasped Jude by the arm and lifted him to his feet. "Sit here, you fuck."

Jude fell into the chair. "Must be hard for you, not being able to kill me."

Paul uncuffed one of Jude's hands, ratcheting it to the back of the chair while he pulled out a second set of cuffs.

"Your time will come," Paul said and secured Jude's other wrist to the back of the chair.

"I'm not afraid of death."

"We will see when the time comes." Paul slung a submachine gun over his shoulder and disappeared into the kitchen out the back door.

Bucket rolled a set of spike strips across the dirt road. The rest of Viper 6-5 concealed themselves in the tree line to wait incase fighters came from the guard house.

"Viper 6-5 to 4, spike strips deployed. You're clear to engage," Griffin radioed.

"Copy that. Engaging," Hatch acknowledged.

They descended down the wooded ridge.

Bradley crossed his arms, resting his chin in his hand. His eyes did not veer from the body cams.

"You good?" MacTavished asked.

"I don't enjoy standing around doing nothing. We should be there."

"I was all for sneaking on that plane."

"Next time."

The safe house came into view. They crouched in concealment observing the area. Hatch looked through a monocular.

"There's a guard on both corners. I can only assume there will be ones on the north side of the house as well."

"We should split into two. Take them out quietly," Loch said.

"I was just about to say that... Badger and I will take the west while you take east."

"Jedi, you will have rear security while the three of us clear the house," Loch added.

"Stay frosty, my friends," Hatch said and they separated, moving out.

Hatch and Marcus descended down the rest of the slopped weald. A guard leaned against a tree, his weapon slung in front of him and his arms crossed. Hatch dropped to his knee behind a tree and peered through the thermal optic of his suppressed rifle. The trigger pulled back to the sear. A splatter of blood flew from the guard's head and he dropped to the ground. Marcus led, swiftly stepping over the downed man. The light from the safe house flooded into the car park in front of the structure.

Marcus posted behind a tree scanning the area. The guard on the northwest corner strolled back and forth in an arch from north to south. Marcus's eyes bounced from the guard to the windows of the house. With a steady breath Marcus pulled the trigger quickly twice. The red and yellow silhouette in his optic collapsed to the ground. Marcus lowered his rifle to a tactical ready position and looked over his sights to see that indeed his target was down.

"West tangos down," Hatch radioed.

There was a pause. "East tango down," Loch said. "I'm coming to your position."

Marcus watched the windows of the house, still seeing no movement. It didn't seem right. They moved up to the front door standing off to each side and waited for Loch to approach. Jedi moved to the south east corner of the house to watch the rear entrance. Hatch tried the door knob and it was locked. He nodded to Marcus. Marcus smiled and removed the charges from his loadout placing the adhesive device near the door jam.

Paul stepped back from the satellite tower and noticed the faint blinking green light. The beacon drew his attention and he noticed it was a small drone.

"Fuck!" Paul said.

Kingston raised a brow.

"We have company," Paul announced and turned on his heel and jogged towards the house. Paul radioed to the guards. "Get to the house now."

Hatch nodded and Marcus detonated the charges. There was a sharp snap and bright flash. The door frame splintered and cracked inward. They filed into the building anticipating hostiles. Jude's head snapped to the door, his eyes wide.

"Viper 6-4 to Nest, Denali has been located," Hatch radioed.

Bradley watched the body cam footage and placed his hands on the table in front of him. Jude was alive and unharmed.

Gunfire erupted in the distance. Viper 6-5 opened fire on the guard's SUV. Bullet holes riddled the front and cracked the windshield. Blood painted the interior of the compartment.

"Viper 6-5, hostiles neutralized."

The team swiftly cleared the kitchen and bathroom. Paul pointed out Jedi to Kingston as they halted at the edge of the tree line. Kingston nodded and Paul continued to the north to flank the house. He picked up a stick and hit it against a tree as he jogged. The sights of Kingston's rifle aligned on Jedi who's attention was drawn north from the noise. Jedi raised his rifle seeing the green outlined hue of a figure running in the tree line. Two faint whizzes were barely heard and Jedi fell to all fours with a sharp expulsion of air.

He tried to raise his rifle to defend himself from the assault. Blood seeped through his pants from the gunshot wound in his thigh. Breathing was difficult as the second bullet entered near his armpit missing his armor. Jedi collapsed onto his back trying to catch his breath through the immense pain. Kingston emerged from his cover walking swiftly towards Jedi to make sure he was dead.

Bradley's eyes glanced at Jedi's cam and he focused on it as it was pointed to the sky.

"There's something wrong with Jedi," Bradley announced to the room, getting everyone's attention to the body cam monitors.

Kingston stood over Jedi, still seeing life in his eyes. The barrel of Kingston's rifle hovered over Jedi's face.

"This is your end," Kingston said.

Jedi clenched his teeth and grasped the barrel pulling it offline as Kingston pulled the trigger. The round buried itself into the ground. Jedi wrapped his reaction

arm around the gun and pinned it to his side, pulling
Kingston in who attempted to pull his rifle free. Jedi
removed his sidearm from his drop holster and pointed it
at Kingston. A hard kick sent the pistol tumbling out of
reach.

The commander hit the mic. "House to Viper, Jedi
needs immediate back up."

Loch's head turned to Hatch and Marcus as they
finished clearing the building. Without a word Loch and
Hatch disappeared through the kitchen to the back door.
Kingston fell to the side of Jedi, a knife protruding from
his neck. Gasps of air escaped Jedi's lips. The pain was
unbearable. A cool tingling sensation swept through his
body. Loch rounded the corner of the building and put a
round in Kingston's head for good measure. He and Hatch
knelt next to Jedi. A weak hand touched Loch's arm.
Blood seeped through Jedi's clothing making it difficult to
know where he was hit and how many times.

"You're going to be fine," Loch reassured and
began a quick trauma assessment checking major bleeders
starting with the major arteries first and working out.

"Viper 6-4 to Nest. We need immediate
MEDEVAC, Eagle down," Hatch radioed.

Loch desperately tore Jedi's gear off to get to the
gunshot wound in his chest. A loud groan sounded in
Hatch's ear when he tightened the tourniquet around
Jedi's thigh.

"HVT Togo is EKIA. HVT Kodiak is unaccounted for," Hatch radioed.

Marcus stood behind Jude and released one hand from the handcuff that tethered him to the chair. Jude was in disbelief that someone had come for him. He had come to terms with being on his own.

"Where is Paul?" Marcus questioned.

"He went with Kingston to the satellite," Jude answered his anxiety growing from Marcus's inflection in his voice.

"Viper 6-4 BOLO, HVT Kodiak was with Togo," Marcus radioed.

Marcus drew his attention back to uncuffing Jude's other hand. In the corner of Jude's eye he saw movement. Without a second thought he turned and drew Marcus's pistol from his drop holster. A muzzle flashed followed by a sharp bang. Paul staggered forward, his eyes widened and focused on Jude, disbelief washing over him. Jude squeezed the trigger twice more sending rounds into his brother. The rifle Paul had clattered to the ground and he collapsed. A pool of blood formed around him. Jude stared at his dead brother. His eyes still staring blankly at Jude.

Marcus held out his hand. "Give me the gun."

Jude handed the pistol to Marcus. Jude slowly looked at Marcus in relief.

"He was your brother…"

"I know who he was."

"Jude just saved Marcus's life," Bradley said to MacTavish and let out a breath.

"HVT Kodiak terminated," Marcus radioed.

Marcus finished uncuffing Jude and placed a hand on his shoulder. His life was saved by a kid, who killed his own brother. Hatch bolted into the living room, blood covering his uniform. He looked from Marcus to Paul's body. Marcus crossed the room and tossed the rifle away from Paul for good measure. Jude stood over Paul. He had come to terms that Paul was going to kill him and he had given up all hopes of being rescued. Jude bent over his hands on his knees.

"Interesting how things turned out... I'm not sorry," Jude said and straightened.

The loud thumping of the helo's blades sounded overhead. "We need to go, now," Hatch said.

Jude followed Hatch out of the building massaging his raw wrists. Bonnet and Storm appeared out of the trees at a sprint, their breath heavy. The helo landed sending dirt and debris in every direction from the rotors. A team of PJs, Air Force pararescuemen, lept from the helo and rendered aid while securing Jedi. They lifted him onto the helo in haste. Loch watched with uncertainty that he would survive.

"The second helo is ETA 5 mikes," one of the PJs yelled over the roar of the helicopter.

The helo lifted from the ground and disappeared into the night sky. The team regrouped and waited for the second helo to touch down. Marcus extended a hand to Jude and assisted him aboard. The metal of the wall was cool against Jude's back as he settled in. He tucked his knees close to his chest making room for the operators. Marcus's feet dangled out the open side as the bird lifted from the ground. He looked back at Jude grateful for saving his life.

Jude dropped his head into his knees. A rescue Jude did not expect ended in his brother's death at his own hands. But did it matter? Jude believed Kari to be dead and he knew his father would never stop looking for him. Jude was not truly safe until Garrick was dead.

"Viper 6-4 to Nest, Denali secured. Viper teams enroute back to base," Hatch radioed.

"Roger that Viper. Good work."

CHAPTER TWENTY EIGHT

Kari paced in the hotel suite waiting for news, something, anything. The anticipation of the op was causing an overwhelming amount of anxiety. A knock at the door drew Kari's attention and her heart sank. She expected the worst. The door creaked open and Agent McKidd entered. Kari froze waiting for him to speak.

"I received word, the op was a success. James is safe," McKidd said.

Kari clasped her hand over her mouth and tears flowed from her eyes.

"When will he be back?"

"I do not have that answer. The Marshals will be back momentarily, I would assume."

Kari wiped the tears from her cheeks. "Thank you."

Agent McKidd nodded and left the room. Kari walked to the window and stared at Big Ben. A weight of relief washed over her. All of it would be behind them and they could return to Chicago. Life would never be normal but it didn't matter as long as she could be with Jude.

———

The sun was hot as it beat intense noon rays down upon the tropical paradise. There was nothing better than the taste of a strong strawberry margarita sitting on a white sandy beach. The umbrella over head provided much needed shade as the harsh Bermuda sun had turned Pyke's tender pale skin a hue of red. He wiggled his toes brushing the sand from them and listened to the calming sound of the waves lapping onto the shore. His wife, Meredith was nose deep in a book.

Pyke watched as people walked by on the beach enjoying paradise. He adjusted his reflective shades. A bucket hat covered his sunburnt bald head. He glanced up at two men down the beach strolling towards the tropical bar on the other side of Pyke's camp. He casted his gaze back to the ocean and his stomach lurched. His eyes darted back to the pair and he spilled his margarita down the front of his bright flowered linen button up shirt, some of the fruity drink getting stuck in his greying chest hair that poked through the top.

"Ah fuck!" Pyke exclaimed quickly trying to right his drink even though he wore most of the contents of the glass.

Garrick walked past with a smirk watching the comical sight and continued to the thatched beach bar.

"Oh fuck, fuck... Hun, where's my phone?"

Meradith didn't lift her eyes. "In the tote."

Margarita rolled down Pyke's floral shirt as he furiously dug through the bag.

"I don't see it!"

"Try the pocket."

"It's not there!"

"What is wrong with you?"

"Nothing! Christ, okay I found it... It was in the pocket–"

"I told you."

Pyke scrolled through his contacts, the text slightly blurry from the amount of oddly delightful fruity alcoholic consumption. He held the phone to his ear impatiently waiting for an answer.

Bradley watched as the body cam screens went dark. A buzz and flash from his phone caught his attention. He picked it up from the table and answered.

"Evans."

"Bradley, Bradley," Pyke whispered covering his mouth with his hand.

"Why are you whispering? Are you drunk?"

MacTavish raised a brow.

"Maybe. Definitely. Those Triple Berry Passion Fruity Margaritas really sneak up on you. It's like black ops. Not the point," Pyke slurred. "Bradley, Bradley, he's here…" Pyke whispered barely audible. "Garrick is here."

"In Bermuda? How much did you drink?"

"A lot. But I can still see."

Bradley rolled his eyes to MacTavish and covered the mic. "Pyke is hammered and thinks he sees Garrick."

MacTavish burst out laughing. "Ask him if Garrick is wearing a ducky floaty and water wings."

"Okay… take a picture of the guy you think is Garrick," Bradley said, playing into Pyke's hallucination.

"Fucking Christ! Is my word not good enough? It's him, you fucker."

Meredith glanced to Pyke cross. "Language, darling."

"Listen to your wife," said Bradley, bemused.

"Sorry, dear." Pyke turned his attention back to Bradley. "If that will get you to believe me then fine… Stand by."

Bradley covered the mic again. "This will be good, I can't wait to see this guy."

MacTavish giggled. "Twenty bucks he sends a selfie."

"I'll take that."

"It's probably not even a man… I picture a rather rotund lady with a 'stache."

Pyke struggled finding the camera on his phone while remaining on the line with Bradley. He swiped his shades off and set them on the lounger.

"This damn thing..." Pyke pushed his thumb on the screen. "Ah, here we go."

Pyke sat up and swung his feet to the side of his lounger in the direction of the bar. Garrick was on the opposite side of the bar facing him. Pyke angled his phone and pretended to be occupied with it. He snapped the photo and sent it to Bradley.

"You should have it now."

Bradley pulled the phone from his ear, putting Pyke on speaker and opened the message. An image of Pyke filled his screen. His beard was grizzled and bushy from not grooming adding to the stylish bucket hat and beach attire. His skin was bright cherry. One eyelid drooping lower than the other. MacTavish burst out laughing from Pyke's mug filling Bradley's screen.

"I hear laughter... What's so goddamn funny?"

"I owe MacTavish a twenty. And my screen just melted from the heat coursing off your sunburn. Can you flip your camera around and not take a photo of yourself?"

Pyke looked at his phone. "Ahh damn it all to Hell! Christ, hold on."

Pyke switched the view of his phone and took another photo. "There, you asshole. I sent it."

"Ethan–" Meradith said.

"Yes, yes, sorry honey."

Bradley brought up the picture and went silent. His eyes widened, staring at the photo in shock. Garrick was standing next to his right hand man, Jelly.

"Holy fuck," MacTavish said.

"Garrick is in Bermuda." Bradley replied.

"No shit, you fuckstick. If you would have listened," Pyke said.

Meredith touched Pyke's arm. "Love. Language."

"Yes, dear, I'm sorry." Pyke leaned over and kissed her on the cheek. "You fucking asshole bitches need to get here now."

"Sir, what about the CIA?"

"We're going to piss all over their goddamn sandbox."

"Roger that, sir," Bradley said with a smirk.

Bradley held his phone in his hand for a moment, letting the gravity of the situation sink in. He picked up his head to see the SAS commander staring at him.

"Let me see it," the commander said and Bradley handed him his phone. The commander stared at Garrick. "I don't believe it."

The commander handed Bradley his phone back and said, "You won't have to worry about the CIA. I'm giving your team privileges. You're going into our territory now. I'll have some friends meet you there. You'll need the help."

"Good luck telling Bradshaw," MacTavish said and walked away.

Bradley shrugged his shoulders. "Why would I tell him?"

—

A crash sounded down the hall from Seth running into the door frame of his room with a wheelchair.

"Sir– You need to stay in bed," an angry nurse scolded him and took a closer look seeing he was dressed in his tattered blood stained pants. "Sir!"

Seth waved at her and continued down the hall in a mad dash. The chair crashed into Clayton's door announcing Seth's arrival. Clayton threw a pillow over his face with a frustrated groan.

"They're leaving without us!" Seth shouted.

Clayton withdrew the pillow. "What?"

"Right, I see you're confused... Evans and MacTavish are leaving. I just received news from my supervisor that Garrick was located and they're loading up."

Clayton slowly sat up holding his abdomen. "What are we still sitting around here for?" Clayton ripped the IV out and pulled the leads of the cardiac monitor off of his chest.

Seth grinned. "I'll call the taxi."

The monitor beeped and whistled. Clayton ignored it as he hobbled over to his clothing sealed in a bag. He held up his shirt that had been cut and saturated in blood.

"I can't wear that." Clayton tossed it behind him.

Two nurses hurried into the room, slightly out of breath, thinking Clayton had gone into cardiac arrest. Clayton had removed his gown and held onto nothing but his pants. The younger nurse clapped her hand over her mouth with a muted gasp. Clayton turned and immediately held his bloodied pants over himself.

"Uh–"

The older nurse placed her hands on her hips. "What do you think you're doing?"

"Leaving." Clayton slowly bent down putting his pants on, clenching his teeth from the sharp pain. "We have a flight to catch."

"You are not fit to leave, Mr. Bradshaw, or you Mr. Connor," she barked.

"See, but I already phoned us a taxi," Seth said pointing to his phone.

"Get back to bed! The both of you," she ordered.

Clayton gathered his boots, the laces tied together. He glanced at Seth who positioned himself to face the door.

"You guys were fantastic, but we need to leave," Clayton said and quickly stepped to Seth.

He cringed in pain, tossed his boots in Seth's lap and clutched the handles of the wheelchair. Each bounding step sent a shockwave of pain through his body. A man was entering the elevator.

"Hold the lift!" Seth called out.

The man, shocked at the scene in front of him, did as he was told. The nurses stood outside the room, arms crossed irritated. The door clanked shut. Clayton bent over and groaned.

"I don't know why you felt the need to run... They can't force you to stay," Seth said.

"I didn't know that."

"Uh– Sir? You're bleeding?" The kind older man said.

Blood rolled down his abdomen and collected on the already blood stained waist of his tactical pants.

"See and now you're bleeding everywhere."

"Give me a sock."

Seth pinched the dirty black sock with his thumb and forefinger. "I would strongly advise against this."

"Oh, son..." The old man held out his handkerchief. "Use this, freshly washed."

"Thank you." Clayton pressed the cloth to his wound tilting his head to the ceiling fighting the pain.

The elevator chimed and Clayton pushed Seth to the front doors to their awaiting cab.

———

Bradley got Kari situated in her seat for the flight. She swatted his hand away.

"I know you're trying to help, but I can manage to tighten my own seatbelt," Kari said.

"Right..."

"Bradley, what about Jude? Where are they going to take him and when will I be able to see him?"

"I'm sorry, Kari, I don't have those answers for you. Just know that he's safe."

"Lads, we have two on the tarmac," a member of the crew shouted and Bradley turned around.

Kari craned her neck and looked past Braldey down the ramp.

"What the–" Bradley said, walking past MacTavish who strapped down their gear.

"What are you doing?" Bradley called out as he walked down the ramp to meet Clayton and Seth.

"Did you think I would miss this?"

"How did you even find out–"

Seth raised his hand. "Me."

"Speaking of which, you can wheel his ass up the ramp." Clayton walked past holding the soiled cloth on his wound. "I hope you packed my gear," he said to MacTavish.

MacTavish secured the last strap. "Most of it anyway."

"I can't believe you a-holes were just going to leave me here."

MacTavish shrugged and threw a shirt at Clayton. "Quit your bitching, you're here now."

Clayton pulled the shirt over his head and noticed Kari. "Kiss my go-to-hell! All y'all were going to leave me in a gown with my butt in the breeze and you let the kid come along?"

Bradley shoved a trauma kit into Clayton's hands. "Sit down and fix yourself."

Kari giggled and Clayton sat next to her. "Just for that, I will not share my gummy worms with you."

"You wouldn't be that cruel."

Bradley strapped himself on the other side of Kari and the ramp of the C-17 closed.

—

Jude felt a tap on his arm and he was pulled from his sleep. He opened his eyes to see Marcus crouched in front of him. His eyes scanned the chopper as operators unloaded quickly. Marcus waved Jude to follow. The operators swiftly walked towards another plane that was being readied for flight.

The thump of the helo faded and Marcus was able to speak without trying to yell over the noise. "There's been a change in plans. Your father has been located in Bermuda. We're headed there now."

"So... What are you going to do with me?"

Marcus stopped. "Until we can escort you back to the Marshals, you stay with us."

Jude crossed his arms and bit his lip. "If he finds me, he's going to kill me for what I did to Paul."

"How would he know about that already?"

"He doesn't, not yet. But when Paul doesn't answer his phone at the next check in–"

"When is that?"

"It changes everyday, but I would assume there isn't a whole lot of time."

"We won't let anything happen to you."

Jude smirked. "I've heard that before."

"I bet you have," Marcus continued his walk.

Jude didn't move. "Do you actually think you're going to catch him? My father, he won't come easily."

"One way or another he's leaving that island with us."

"I hope you're right."

———

The warm sun cast its rays down upon Kari. She closed her eyes and took in the moment. The gentle breeze danced through her hair and the scent of salt water was calming. The waves lapped against the shore and she sent her gaze out to the never ending sprawling blue.

"We're on vacation! Are you kidding me?" Meredith scolded Pyke.

Kari turned around as Meredith stormed past her on the deck and onto the beach. Pyke took a calming breath and directed his new visitors on where to put the gear and equipment.

"I guess, just put it wherever," Pyke said. "Oh and look, you brought a gimpy Tory."

Bradley threw his rifle case on the coffee table.

Seth wheeled himself into the dinning room. "Still sour I see."

Pyke huffed and turned to Clayton. "Good to see you in one piece, Bradshaw."

Clayton nodded slowly setting down a duffle bag, his abdomen in immense pain. Pyke stepped to the kitchen table and donned on a tactical vest over his bright linen floral shirt.

"Are those flip flops?" Bradley asked.

Pyke looked down at his bright red foam flip flops that he attached to the front of his vest. "I'm on vacation, Evans, I *would* like to enjoy the beach when this is finished."

Pyke swiped his bucket hat from the back of the couch and put it on his bald head. There was a knock on the door.

"It's open!" Pyke shouted and walked into the kitchen. He picked up a kiddie cocktail and sucked down the fruit contents accompanied by an umbrella.

Kari turned her head already knowing it would be the SAS operators she heard Bradley talking about. Time slowed down as the first soldier entered. It wasn't a SAS operator at all but Marcus.

"Marcus!" Kari ran the length of the beach house and embraced her brother before he knew what hit him.

He wrapped his arms around her. "This is certainly something I wasn't expecting. What are you doing here?" He looked to Bradley for answers.

"It's a long story…" Bradley said, setting his rifle down.

Jude walked into the beach house after Hatch. He cocked a brow wondering who Badger was hugging. Dark hair cascaded down slender shoulders. His heart stopped and couldn't believe his eyes.

"Kari?"

She lifted her head. She pulled away from Marcus and was immediately embraced by Jude.

"I thought– I can't believe you're here," Jude said holding her tight.

Jude placed both his hands on the sides of her head and kissed her. Marcus looked from the pair to Bradley.

"I missed something…" Marcus said pointing to the teens.

Bradley nodded and Clayton chuckled. Kari and Jude walked past everyone to the deck.

"Indy, it's good to see you again," Loch said with a handshake.

Clayton looked past him. "Where's Jedi?"

Loch dropped his head. "Germany."

Clayton's heart sank. "How bad?"

"We haven't had word since our op. It didn't look good. Took a round to the thigh and axillary."

"Fuck–"

"Yes, yes, welcome to the shit show. I see Delta Force has also graced us with their presence. But enough of the chitter chatter, we have work to do," Pyke said and opened a laptop. "We don't have much time to find this fuckstick."

"No we don't, Jude said that Anchorage checked in with Kodiak at set times. He may already know that location had been compromised."

"Great... Then we really have to get going." Pyke displayed the image of his laptop on the dining room wall. "Tax records indicate that this is Garrick's estate..."

Jude intertwined his hand with Kari's, letting Pyke's words fade into the background. The sun was setting over the ocean, the warm rays casting an auburn hue to Kari's hair. Jude admired her beauty.

"I'm not staying–"

Kari furrowed her brow. "What?"

Jude looked out over the landscape. "This place has brought me much joy. It was my mother's favorite place to vacation." His eyes met Kari's. "I have to finish this— My father, he needs to pay for what he's done."

"Jude... Don't– Let them take care of it." Kari motioned to the room full of soldiers. "I thought I lost you once, please– don't do this."

"This is the only way..." Jude kissed Kari.

"Jude, please, don't–"

"I have to, for my mother... for Nicks..."

"Jude–"

Jude touched Kari's cheek. "I love you."

"If you go, I will tell them."

"I know." Jude hugged Kari tightly and left the deck at a run.

Kari watched for a moment as he disappeared around the corner of the beach house. She let out a sharp muted cry fearful she may never see him again. She wiped away the forming tears.

"Bradley?" She tried to stay strong but her throat tightened.

Bradley turned with immediate concern flooding him, watching Kari's attempt to keep herself together.

"He's gone..." she said motioning to the open patio door.

Pyke dropped his head into his hands. "Fuck that kid. I'm going to shoot him myself."

"I knew we should have used duct tape," MacTavish muttered.

"I have a feeling this has happened before?" Hatch asked.

Pyke lifted his head and glared at Hatch.

"Time is of the essence, shall we?" Griffin piped in. "Agent Connor, are the coms ready?"

"Yes, sir."

"All right girl scouts, let's get after it," Hatch said and slung his rifle over his body armor.

Clayton seated his magazine in the well of his rifle. Bradley nudged him with his elbow. "Can you not die this time."

Clayton chuckled. "Always a personal goal of mine."

A golden glow emanated from the windows of the three story vacation estate. Memories of a past life flowed through Jude's mind. His family, smiling, laughing, enjoying life without a care pained him. How events had drastically changed. This was his mother's sanctuary, a space to escape her husband's work, where they could just be a family. Memories of Jude's childhood filled his mind. He and his father playing in the shallows of the ocean, building sand castles, and playing tag on the beach. He had thought the world of his father.

Garrick walked past the front window of the study and picked up a cigar, scotch in hand. He receded back into the home to enjoy the evening on the covered lanai. Jude snapped back to reality and walked to the side of the house. He gripped the vine covered trestle that he had so often used to sneak out of his second story bedroom. The window opened with ease and Jude stepped inside the cool room. He glanced at a bookshelf seeing a photo of his family from a couple years ago posing on the beach.

The chair from Jude's desk scraped on the floor as he pulled it away and knelt on the planked hardwood floor. The board popped easily from the floor and he set it aside. Jude reached into the floorboards and withdrew a pistol. It was heavy in his hand as he stared at it. Jude proceeded out of his bedroom and down the stairs. Family photos lined the walls. Jude paused his eyes lingering on a photo of him and his brothers laughing. A pang of guilt hit Jude but he proceeded down the steps.

The stairs led to the open main floor. The lights from the lanai glowed in through the glass wall. The patio door was open wide, the breeze from the warm evening air tussled through Jude's hair. Garrick lounged in a wicker chair, a cigar in one hand and a book in the other. Jude stepped from the shadows and pointed the gun at his father. Hughes, who sat on the wicker sofa, rose quickly drawing his sidearm. Garrick lifted his cigar hand signaling for Hughes to hold his fire. Garrick set his book down in his lap and removed his thick rimmed reading glasses.

"This is an unexpected surprise, James." Garrick motioned to the pistol. "Are you here to kill me?"

"Well I certainly wasn't planning on tea," Jude snapped.

"Why don't you put the gun down and we will have a conversation like adults."

"A conversation? You've taken everything from me," Jude said gritting his teeth

"What do you mean? I've *given* you everything. Look at this empire I've built for you."

"You murdered my mother and killed Nicks." Uncontrollable anger flowed through Jude. Images of his mother and Nicks's lifeless bodies flooded his mind.

"Your mother betrayed us," Garrick said calmly.

"She was trying to get away from you!" The gun shook in Jude's hand.

"No, James, she was leaving all of us," Garrick corrected.

"It doesn't matter, you murdered her!"

"It had to be done. To protect the business, to protect you," Garrick said sharpley.

"Do you still want to protect me? After everything I've done?"

"Yes, James, you are my son. We can fix all of this. You just need to put the gun down."

"You're going to kill me if I do," Jude shook his head.

"No, son, we will work through this," Garrick said, trying to calm Jude.

Jude attempted to keep his emotions in check. "Paul's dead…"

Garrick was filled with sorrow from the news.

"I shot him–" Jude was unraveling, the pistol shook in his outstretched hand.

"James… Put the gun down."

"I can't–" Jude pushed the pistol forward and moved his finger to the trigger.

There was a loud pop. Pain erupted in Jude's chest and he collapsed to the ground with a thud. Numb, Garrick stared at Jude in disbelief. Garrick rose quickly, gripping the pistol he had tucked between his leg and the cushion of the chair. With one quick shot, a bullet entered

Hughes's forehead dropping him where he stood. Garrick tossed the gun and fell to his knees beside his son.

Blood saturated Jude's clothing as Garrick applied pressure to the wound. Tears fell from Jude's eyes.

"Dad... I'm... Sorry..." It was difficult for Jude to speak from the crushing weight he felt in his chest.

"Shhh, don't speak... You're going to be alright," Garrick lied as his heart broke.

Garrick retrieved his phone from his pocket, the blood making it slick and difficult to grip. Blood trickled from Jude's mouth as he coughed weakly. His breath was becoming quick and shallow. Blood smeared across the screen of the phone making it impossible to call for help. Jude stared at his father, fear consuming him as darkness encroached in his field of vision.

Garrick touched Jude's face, his other palm still pressed firmly over his wound. "James, son, please... please hold on."

—

The street was silent as the team converged upon Garrick's estate. Bradley led point through the first level of the house. The eerie silence and darkness made Bradley's blood run cold. The glow of the lights on the lanai grew brighter with each step. In the corner of Garrick's eye he saw movement. His head snapped up seeing the operators at the patio door. Garrick immediately shot his hand into the air but did not dare release pressure from the wound with the other. Bradley's finger moved to the trigger, his sights aligning on Garrick. Jude's eyes closed and his head fell to one side as he slipped away.

Dynamically Bradley crushed his target and kicked Garrick in the chest sending him flat on his back. "You son of a bitch!"

Bradley stood over him his barrel inches from Garrick's head. Clayton kicked the handgun that rested next to Jude away. Clayton removed a pair of flex cuffs from his vest and secured Garrick's wrists.

"HVT Anchorage, secured," Bradley said over the com. His eyes fell upon Hughes, brain matter splattered in a pool of blood surrounding him. "HVT Sitka DOA." The scene in front of Bradley pieced itself together and he understood what had happened.

Kari sat next to Seth. "What does that mean?" She asked.

"Garrick has been caught and one of his men is dead."

Kari let out a breath of relief.

"Denali is down," Pyke said on the air and knelt next to Jude seeing the seriousness of his condition. "Someone get the fucking van!"

"I'm on it," Griffin said and sprinted through the house.

A crushing weight descended upon Kari. Seth turned to her. She stared straight ahead frozen.

"Kari…"

Her throat tightened, her breath shallow. "Please don't–" Tears poured as she feared the worse.

Yeti and Bonnet grasped each one of Garrick's arms and lifted him to his feet. Bradley knelt next to Jude as Pyke ran a knife through Jude's saturated shirt.

"He has a pulse, faint, but it's there," Marcus said and handed Pyke the combat gauze. Marcus looked to Bradley seeing the anguish over his brother's features.

Pyke pushed the gauze, lined with a hemostatic agent, into the bullet hole. Jude let out a gurgled groan. Garrick craned his neck to watch them desperately save his son's life. Bonnet pushed Garrick forward.

"Don't you let him die," said Garrick, wrought with emotion.

"Let's go," Bonnet said and Plank fell in behind the trio.

A rustle in the shrubs sounded as Jelly rounded the corner of the garden, his wide frame brushed against the hedge.

"They didn't have the green sauce you like, but I got–" Jelly froze, tacos in hand, his eyes wide at the scene before him. "Blimey…"

Jelly turned and waddled as fast as he could. Bucket and Storm glanced at each other and took off at a trot towards the far end of the garden. Jelly's toe caught on an uneven stepping stone sending him face first to the ground. The numerous taco's crushed beneath his hefty body. He was quickly apprehended and secured into flex cuffs. Bucket and Storm assisted Jelly to his feet. The remnants of what could have been a good dinner had stained his white button-up shirt.

"HVT Unalaska detained," Bucket radioed.

"We're losing him," Pyke said. "I need to get this bleed under control."

"His trachea is deviating," Bradley said as he squeezed the IV bag for the line that had been established. "Come on Jude, FIGHT!"

"Here!" Loch said, pulling the seal off of the thoracostomy kit and handed it to Pyke.

Bradley rolled Jude to his side and placed his limp arm over his head. Pyke took the scalpel and cut deep into Jude's flesh and inch down the midaxillary line. He gripped the clamp and bluntly dissected the tissue until he was in the chest cavity. A muffled groan escaped Jude's lips as Pyke inserted the tube. Blood spurted from the tube drenching Pyke. Bradley held the tube in place as Pyke quickly secured the tube with sutures.

"His pulse is getting stronger," Bradley said.

"How's his airway?" Pyke asked.

"Good," Lock said, squeezing the bag valve mask that was attached to the end of the endotracheal tube.

"We need to move him," Pyke said and looked around trying to find something to use. "Just grab that towel, we need to go."

Hatch pulled a towel from the shelf and tossed it to Bradley. He and Clayton stuffed the towel under Jude the blood soaking it red. Together the team lifted Jude's limp body and navigated the house. Sorrow engulfed Garrick as he peered down the block seeing his son being carried out of the house.

"Get in," Plank ordered.

Jelly stepped into the van followed, reluctantly by Garrick. Storm and Bucket rounded to the front of the van while the three Delta operators climbed into the back.

Jude was loaded onto the floor of the van, Pyke and Bradley climbed in behind. Loch continued bagging Jude as he gripped onto life. The back doors closed and Griffin stepped on the gas.

"Sierra leader to House. HVTs enroute to the airport for prisoner transport. Asset Denali critical, enroute to trauma center," Hatch radioed.

"Roger, that Sierra leader. We will have a team waiting at the airport. Good work lads."

Marcus placed a hand on Clayton's shoulder. He didn't move as he watched the van speed down the dimly lit quaint road. Blood ran down the floorboards of the van from the draining tube in Jude's chest. Bradley stared at Jude's limp body praying for him to hold on. The van came to a screeching halt under the Emergency overhang. The operators unloaded Jude from the back of the van.

"We need some help!" Griffin yelled into the emergency department.

Staff ran to their aid. Jude was laid onto a gurney and rolled into a trauma room where they worked on him.

The operators slowly followed into the emergency department. Bradley leaned against the wall outside the trauma room and slid to the ground. He removed his helmet and let it clank to the ground between his legs. Thoughts in disarray Bradley placed his blood soaked hands in his hair propping his elbows on his knees and stared at the scene in front of him.

CHAPTER TWENTY NINE

The spring sun casted much welcomed warm rays. The green grass was lush and gently danced in the breeze. Kari sipped her warm tea from a local coffee shop. She sat in the vast green space of Millennium Park. She gazed at the grand skyline of Chicago. It had been months since she had flown home from Bermuda. What happened, what she did, was nothing but a memory. She plucked a blade of grass and twirled it between her fingers.

Bradley sat in the grass next to Kari. "Pretzel? It's from your favorite stand."

"No, thank you. Not in the mood for food."

He pointed to the envelope in her lap. "You've been carrying that around for weeks. Are you finally going to open it?"

"I wanted to wait…"

"I know this has been hard for you," Bradley said.

Kari stared at the blade of grass in her hands. "I keep waiting for it to get better."

"In time–"

"I know…" Kari took a deep breath.

Bradley stood, his attention drawn to an approaching party. "It gets easier. You just need to be patient."

"Yeah, yeah."

"If you need anything, I'll be at the office," Bradley said and took a step.

"Marshal Evans," James greeted.

"James," Bradley nodded. "I'll see you tomorrow."

"Yes, sir."

James sat beside Kari, wrapped his arm around her and kissed her cheek.

Kari twirled the envelope in her hand. "I'm still not used to calling you 'James'."

He smirked. "I'm just glad you can call me something."

Kari leaned her head on James's shoulder and moved the collar of his shirt down to look at his scar. A wound that nearly took his life.

"I wish you weren't going," Kari said.

"It's time."

"You could wait until after graduation."

James looked at Kari sideways.

Kari giggled. "Okay, yeah. I suppose."

"Plus it doesn't matter if I'm leaving because you will be too." James motioned to the envelope. "Would you just open it already."

Kari took a breath and slid her finger under the flap breaking the seal. James stared at Kari impatiently waiting for the verdict. Her jaw dropped in disbelief.

"I got in. I can't believe it. I actually got in."

"I knew you would." James saluted Kari. "Lieutenant."

"Stop it!" Kari laughed and shoved James.

"See, you'll be off to West Point. With how busy you'll be, you'll forget who I am in the first year."

"James–"

"It'll be a good thing." James wrapped his arms around her and squeezed.

Kari wiped the forming tears away. "I'm not ready for goodbye."

"We will see each other again."

"I don't know why you can't just stay."

"You know why. It's time. I need to go."

"It feels like just yesterday that I bumped your desk and you gave me that death glare," Kari giggled.

"It was all downhill from there." James smirked and tilted Kari's chin. He memorized her smile and gently kissed her. "I love you."

"I love you, too."

Kari intertwined her hand with James's and leaned against his chest. He didn't want the moment to end. But it had to, he needed to close the door on this chapter of his life and move forward.

—

The morning came quick. Sun filtered through the patio door of Nicks's condo. MacTavish and Clayton grabbed a few lingering boxes.

"This should make it to your humble abode in England by the time you get there," Clayton said.

James glanced around the condo that Nicks had left him. In a perfect world James would have been moving in, adjusting to a new life with Nicks, but his brother made sure that would never be a possibility. James had spent a couple months going through his belongings sorting what to keep. Nicks had no family and the only people close to him were the four men standing in the living room with him. James was grateful for the Marshals as they had collected everything from the inn and brought it to the condo so he would not have to relive that nightmare again.

"Are you ready?" Pyke asked.

James looked down at a printed photo from six flags. A tear splashed onto the corner of the photo. James nodded and said. "Yes, sir."

Pyke took Nicks's Sox hat, that he wore religiously, from the counter and placed it on James's head. "He would have wanted you to have this."

James smiled, trying to contain his grief. Bradley held the door open for MacTavish and Clayton carrying the boxes. James filed in behind them. They loaded the boxes into the already crowded bed of MacTavish's Jeep Gladiator. James tucked the photo into his backpack and set it down next to Pyke's vehicle.

"Well that's everything," MacTavish said and clapped his hands.

"Thank you, for everything," James said and stepped towards MacTavish and Clayton.

"Don't mention it. Good luck, you'll need it," MacTavish said and grasped James's hand and hugged him from the side.

James smiled and pulled away. "I mean how hard can it be?"

MacTavish chuckled with a grin.

"Nicks would be proud, or would have tried to talk you out of it," Clayton said and hugged James.

"Honestly, he probably would have taken joy in torturing me to make sure I'd be somewhat prepared... Like driving next to me while I run, yelling at me."

Clayton laughed. "This is true."

"Enough chatter. We have a flight to catch," Pyke announced.

James picked up his bag and loaded into the trunk and gave Clayton and MacTavish one last wave. Watching the skyline of Chicago pass by was bitter sweet, but James was ready to leave, off to start his new adventure and a new challenge. Bradley pulled James's bag from the trunk and set it on the ground at the terminal doors.

Pyke placed a hand on James's shoulder and he turned and hugged him. "Good luck, kid. You're going to do well. I have no doubt in my mind. If you need anything, you know how to reach us."

"Thank you, sir."

Bradley hugged James and handed him his bag. "Make sure you write to my sister. I don't want to have to hunt you down."

"Yes, sir." James smiled.

"Enjoy your time in D.C. and safe travels home."

"Thank you." James turned and headed into the airport.

—

The feeling of standing amongst heroes who had given all to protect freedom and justice cannot be conveyed into words. The pristine lawn and immaculate headstones of the fallen on a vast landscape weighs a heavy beauty on the heart. James stood in the heart of Arlington National Cemetery. Nicks's name and rank were etched into the white marble stone. Emotion swept over him and he dropped to his knees and placed a hand on top of Nicks's stone. Tears streamed and he let a cry escape his lips.

James rocked back onto his heels and sat down. "I'm sorry for everything. This never should have happened... I wanted more than anything to have called you my family. Without you I probably wouldn't be here."

James took a breath looking up at the clear sky and wiped away his tears. "I think you're going to be mad– I enlisted into the British Army... I can hear you yelling at me already. It gets worse– the goal is SAS... Do I hear you rolling in your grave? Yeah, thought so."

The time passed by and James stood placing his hand on the top of the grave stone. "This is goodbye then."

—

Cool raindrops fell from the gloomy sky. James was filled with anxiety about being back home for the first time since the night of his mother's death. He shut the door to the taxi and stood outside his family's estate. The place that his father had killed his mother. James stared at the front door with disdain, but he was only there for one reason.

The steel of the door handle was cold when James grasped it. He opened one of the heavy doors into the grand entrance. It looked the same in reality as it did in his memory on the night he left. Cecil dressed in a well tailored suit and his white hair perfectly neat, walked out from the archway on the left.

"Master Garrick, it is nice to see you home finally," he said and approached James.

"I wish I could say it was good to be back... But it is good to see you Cecil." James set down his bag and hugged him.

Cecil had been his family's butler since James was born. He had been James's primary caregiver more times than his own father.

"I received your note. The belongings you had shipped from the States have been placed into storage, except for the motorbike and this parcel of mail." Cecil handed James the large envelope.

"Thank you, Cecil."

"I have prepared the master suite for you, sir."

"I appreciate it, but it is not necessary. I won't be staying."

"Pardon?" Cecil cocked a brow.

James opened the envelope and pulled out the stack of paper. He stepped to the small table against the wall near the staircase. He picked up a pen and signed a few highlighted pages.

"I don't own the estate anymore– You do." James held the pen up for Cecil to take.

Cecil did not move. "I do not understand, sir."

"Take the pen, Cecil. Sign the papers. You deserve this estate more than I do."

"I don't know what to say, sir."

"You don't have to say anything."

Cecil accepted the pen and signed the papers.

"Thank you, sir," Cecil said and returned the pen to it's stand.

"No, Cecil, thank you. For everything."

"Would you like to stay for a bit of celebration whiskey?"

James smiled. "Perhaps another time. I should be going."

"You are welcome back anytime, Master– well I suppose it's Mr. Garrick now."

"Actually, it's Nicks now," James corrected.

Cecil nodded. "Goodbye Mr. Nicks."

"Goodbye, Cecil." James gave Cecil a parting hug.

James slung his bag over his shoulder and headed for the garage. Nicks's bike waited for him. He slid his hand over the handlebars like he did the first time he saw the bike. He put the helmet on and mounted the bike. Cecil opened the garage door, whiskey in hand. The bike roared alive, the single headlamp illuminating the dreary night. James waved and pulled the throttle going down the driveway. Cecil smiled and closed the door and walked back inside his estate.

James maneuvered the city streets of London until hitting the open road that led to the countryside leaving behind an old life. He pulled back on the throttle letting the bike roar over the pavement. Relief and a new sense of purpose filled his being. James was finally free.

Made in the USA
Las Vegas, NV
08 December 2020

12371080R00275